SUBVERTING JUSTICE

Jack Taggart Mysteries

SUBVERTING JUSTICE

Don Easton

A Jack Taggart Mystery

DUNDURN
TORONTO

Cover image: 123RF.com/ Ying Feng Johansson
Printer: Webcom

Library and Archives Canada Cataloguing in Publication

Easton, Don, author
    Subverting justice / Don Easton.

(A Jack Taggart mystery)
Issued in print and electronic formats.
ISBN 978-1-4597-3980-2 (softcover).--ISBN 978-1-4597-3981-9 (PDF).--
ISBN 978-1-4597-3982-6 (EPUB)

    I. Title. II. Series: Easton, Don. Jack Taggart mystery.

PS8609.A78S83 2017   C813'.6   C2017-902153-2
                                             C2017-902154-0

1 2 3 4 5   21 20 19 18 17

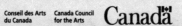

We acknowledge the support of the **Canada Council for the Arts**, which last year invested $153 million to bring the arts to Canadians throughout the country, and the **Ontario Arts Council** for our publishing program. We also acknowledge the financial support of the **Government of Ontario**, through the **Ontario Book Publishing Tax Credit** and the **Ontario Media Development Corporation**, and the **Government of Canada**.

Nous remercions le **Conseil des arts du Canada** de son soutien. L'an dernier, le Conseil a investi 153 millions de dollars pour mettre de l'art dans la vie des Canadiennes et des Canadiens de tout le pays.

Care has been taken to trace the ownership of copyright material used in this book. The author and the publisher welcome any information enabling them to rectify any references or credits in subsequent editions.

— *J. Kirk Howard, President*

The publisher is not responsible for websites or their content unless they are owned by the publisher.

Printed and bound in Canada.

VISIT US AT

 dundurn.com | @dundurnpress | dundurnpress | dundurnpress

Dundurn
3 Church Street, Suite 500
Toronto, Ontario, Canada
M5E 1M2

To the families of those on the front lines:
Few people recognize or appreciate what you have
endured and continue to endure. Thank you for the
sacrifices you've made.

Chapter One

It was early afternoon when Corporal Jack Taggart slouched back in his office chair, massaging his temples with his fingertips. Unfortunately the images he'd seen a few hours earlier remained — along with any chance of erasing the knowledge of what had taken place next.

Three people had been tortured and murdered where they lived, in a farmhouse an hour's drive away. The atrocity was horrible to see, and when he thought his brain couldn't handle any more, he learned that a fourth murder had taken place at an unknown location somewhere else within the lower mainland. That victim was Damien Zabat — a man who'd recently given Jack information in exchange for keeping his wife and son out of jail. *Damn it, Damien, I'm sorry. I never meant for this to happen.*

Staff Sergeant Rose Wood cleared her throat as she entered his office, and he sat up, hoping to hide his emotions. She was his boss and in charge of the Royal

Canadian Mounted Police Intelligence Unit in Vancouver. She was also a person he respected and liked, someone he protected by not sharing all the details of the methods he used — methods Jack referred to as the grey zone.

Rose's arrival caused him to worry about someone else — Laura. She was more than his subordinate. She was his partner and his close friend. Both worked undercover together and she was not someone he hid details from. Their survival often hinged on their ability to instinctively know what the other thought and how the other would react when the unexpected happened. He glanced at her empty desk, then looked at Rose and raised an eyebrow.

Rose's face expressed her concern. She sat down in Laura's chair. "You were right to have me check on her. When I first went into the washroom she was hiding out in a stall. I could hear her sobbing."

Pure E, you son-of-a-bitch. You'll pay for this.

"I calmed her down. She's quit crying but isn't ready to come out yet. She's still in shock … trembling."

"Not to belittle your master's in psychology, but should I go in and talk to her?"

"No. Definitely not you." Rose's tone was sharp.

"You say that like I'm to blame."

He watched as Rose paused, as if she was unsure of how to respond.

Maybe it is my fault.

"I'm not blaming you," she finally said, "but let me explain. Laura's suffering from feelings of helplessness, intense fear, revulsion —"

"She said that?"

"Not in those exact words, but we discussed what you two have been through in the last week."

In the last week? Try this morning.

"Her feelings were pretty obvious." Rose appeared to study Jack's face.

"What is it?" he asked, touching his face. "Blood on me from the crime scene?"

"No, but the dark circles and bags under your eyes say something. How much sleep have you had in the last couple of days?"

"I don't know. Maybe three hours Tuesday and another three last night. Laura likely didn't get much more."

Rose shook her head. "That's insane. Especially when you were undercover with someone who commits murder without hesitation."

"It wasn't like we had a choice. We did a UC with his associates Tuesday night in Vancouver. That set up our meeting with him in Victoria. Last night we did the arrest. By the time I did my notes, then caught the first ferry back … well, I'd hoped I'd be taking today off — until all hell broke loose."

"Exhaustion compounds how Laura's feeling, increases the stress she's under."

"Exhaustion, yes. But you said she felt helpless? She's anything but helpless. Believe me, I couldn't do what I do without her."

Rose studied Jack's face. "What you do is part of the problem. Six days ago you staged being shot — something Laura was against, despite her loyalty to you. But she felt helpless to put a stop to it because you're her boss. And then when it *did* happen, it didn't go according to plan and she thought you'd been killed."

"I know, I know," Jack muttered. "I feel bad about that. She made it clear from the beginning that she was against the idea."

"As I'd have been … if I'd known," Rose replied icily.

"You have to admit it worked. Damien thought Vicki tried to kill me. He never suspected she was my informant."

Rose's face hardened. "Don't even go there. I told you what I'd do if you ever pulled a stunt like that again."

"I know."

"Then there was last night at the marina in Victoria. Laura heard the shot and again thought you'd been killed."

"She thought the bad guy had fired. It was the cover team who let off a round."

Rose sighed in exasperation. "Put yourself in her shoes. She was watching with binoculars when he pulled his gun. When the shot rang out, you dropped from sight below the gunwale on the boat. She thought you were dead."

"I tackled the guy. I was fighting to save my life and there was —"

Rose put her hand up to silence him. "Jack, quit being defensive. I'm trying to explain to you why Laura feels helpless and why I want you to give her some space. In my opinion you're in shock yourself. Yes, Laura was crying, but at least she's able to express her emotions. You're trying to bury everything."

I'd like to bury Pure E.

"Being in denial will complicate and worsen your emotional well-being."

Jack glared at the staff sergeant. "How do I deny that without proving your point?"

"I wasn't making a point. It's an observation. We're discussing Laura. Twice within a week she thought you'd been killed." Rose stopped for a moment, as if giving him time to let her words sink in. "Of course she felt helpless. Then there's this morning. As soon as you get off the ferry you're both taken to that farmhouse. How revolting was that? A man you set up to look like your informant murdered in that manner."

Jack closed his eyes. *Burned hair and blackened flesh — the smell is all over me. Wish I could go home and get these clothes off and shower.*

"How do you feel about that?" Rose asked.

"How do I feel?" Jack was surprised by the question. "I'm angry! Three people tortured to death and later a fourth murdered because his own wife set him up. That was after he risked his life to save her. Damn right I'm angry! Aren't you?"

"It's upsetting."

"Upsetting?" Jack exclaimed. "That's an understatement. I expected Neal to be killed, but I'd no idea that Pure E would order the torture and murder of his brother and sister-in-law."

"Neither did Laura, which adds to her feelings of helplessness, not to mention revulsion."

"Her feeling of helplessness will pass once we do something about it," Jack replied.

"And if you can't do anything about it … how will she feel then?"

Jack was incensed. "Can't do anything about it? You know me better than that!"

Rose's face hardened. "I don't like your tone — but will attribute it to exhaustion." She paused, then added, "Don't let anger cloud your judgment. You're better than that."

Cloud my judgment? It'll hone it like a knife.

"Furthermore, I suggest you display a more professional attitude when we meet with Assistant Commissioner Isaac." She glanced at her watch. "Which will be shortly, so get it together."

Jack sighed. "Okay, I admit I'm tired. It's difficult to stop thinking about the farmhouse." *Who wouldn't stop thinking about it? Two grotesque figures ... blackened and twisted, tied to chairs. The third disembowelled ...* He looked at Rose. "It makes me feel nauseated just thinking about it."

"The same feeling I'm sure everyone has."

Not Pure E. He ordered it.

"It's bad enough hearing what happened in that farmhouse. You and Laura saw it. The both of you smell of ... well, you know. If we weren't meeting with Isaac, I'd send you home. I am sending her home right away — or at least as soon as she calms down."

Jack nodded in agreement.

"Then there was the message left at the crime scene," Rose added. "Seems right out of a horror movie."

Yes. The 4 U JT *painted across the wall with a broom dipped in blood.* Jack felt his rage rise to the surface again. "Pure E made it personal. That's something Damien would never have done."

"Purvis Evans," Rose said. "The new national president of Satans Wrath. After what happened, I'd say his nickname 'Pure Evil' or 'Pure E' is deserved."

"'Sick Bastard' would suit him, too," Jack replied bitterly.

Rose gestured with her hand for Jack to calm down. "Let's continue. I think I've covered Laura's feelings of helplessness and revulsion. Let's talk fear. Six days ago you took down Damien Zabat when he was national president."

"*I* took him down? His wife, Vicki, did that. She's the one who made a bogus phone call and intentionally leaked it that he'd provided me with information. I was simply stupid enough to put the nail in his coffin by trying to call and warn him. Then to have Pure E answer Damien's phone and goad me ..." Jack shook his head in self-recrimination.

"The point is," Rose said, "Damien's been replaced by a psychopath. Damien was dangerous, but Pure E is far worse. The message at the triple murder in the farmhouse was directed at you, but Laura has every right to feel threatened as well."

"Okay ... I can see why she's scared."

"Why she's scared? What about you? If you don't feel scared, then you're definitely in denial. And if that's the case, I seriously question whether you're fit for duty."

"Of course it scared me. I'm married with two kids. I worry about my family — but we can't back down. If Pure E gets away with leaving a message to taunt me at a murder scene, it'll give him the confidence to do worse things."

"Yes, and we'll talk about him when you've had time to rest and think things through. We're discussing Laura. I want you to understand why you shouldn't talk to her at the moment. It would only trigger another emotional outburst. Give her time."

I feel like shit. She's my partner. I should've —

"Are you listening to what I'm telling you? If she comes to you, fine, but don't you go waltzing into the women's washroom and —"

"I won't. I trust your judgment on that."

"Good."

"When you sum things up the way you have, I realize what an ass I was. I'm her boss. I should've done a better job of looking after her."

"You must be doing something right. I know she cares deeply about you."

"The feeling goes both ways, but I was so pigheaded about catching Damien that I trampled over anyone I thought was getting in my way. And for what? I thought he was a monster. Turns out I'd no idea what a monster was."

"Do you think that weenie-wagging informant of yours would know anything about what they did to Damien?"

"He doesn't know about it yet. I called him when you went to talk to Laura. He's already drunk and I suspect he's swallowed a handful of pills to get high. You think Laura and I had it rough seeing what happened at the farmhouse? Imagine what it was like for him. He was there and watched it happen. He was so shaken by what took place that he could hardly tell me the details."

"If he's combining drugs and alcohol, he's liable to —"

"I know. I've been trying to get him to straighten out. He's on the verge of a mental collapse, what with being an informant and then seeing three people murdered the way they were."

Rose glanced at her watch again. "We're meeting Isaac in fifteen minutes. Have you calmed down enough not to come across sounding like a cowboy in a lynch mob?"

"I'll behave. As far as a lynch mob goes, I'd love to, but I've got a family. Pure E's proven he's not averse to killing family members to spite someone. He has the backing of his club. Any action against him will have to be carefully thought out."

Rose nodded. "Sounds like you're regaining your senses. Isaac told me that his replacement, Assistant Commissioner Mortimer, will attend. First impressions and all … I want you to be on your best behaviour."

"I thought Mortimer didn't start until a week from this coming Monday."

"Yes, but today he met Isaac for lunch while waiting for the moving truck to show up from Ottawa. Isaac thought it would be good for him to sit in on the debriefing as a way to bring him up to speed. He'll be in again next week, too, before officially taking over the reins the following week."

"Great," Jack replied, scowling. "This is a guy who spent the better part of his career in an admin job in Ottawa. He's never been on the front lines. I can only imagine what he'll think."

"Jack —" Rose eyed him briefly "— are you sure you're up to the meeting? Isaac only wanted you to know that the triple murder was a consequence of his decision and not yours. I could tell him that I relayed that to you."

"He doesn't know what happened afterward … with Damien?"

"Not yet, but I know enough of the details that —"

"Thanks, but no. It's best he hear it from me. I need to face up to what I did."

"What you did was try to warn Damien. We'd all have done the same." When Jack didn't reply, Rose went on, "I'm going to check on Laura and send her home."

"Tell her she's not alone. I'm so frustrated I could put my fist through a wall."

"Maybe I should take that as a good sign," Rose said.

"How so?"

"Your frustration indicates you plan to play by the rules and aren't planning to do something foolhardy."

"You think I'm prone to acting foolhardy?"

"It's more polite than saying homicidal."

"Yes, we must remember to be polite," Jack said. "Should I apologize to Pure E before or after I put a bullet in his brain?"

Rose tossed Jack a dirty look, then left.

Chapter Two

Lance Morgan parked his blue Honda Odyssey minivan and sat for a moment to take in his surroundings. Stanley Park was situated in the heart of Vancouver, but at this time of year it was largely deserted. Being early October, the tourist rush was over. And the usual lunch crowd had gone back to work.

He reached for the glovebox and grabbed a bottle of antacids. As he munched on the tablets he reflected on the morning's activities — and his own life. As president of the Westside chapter of the Satans Wrath outlaw motorcycle gang, he'd seen more than his share of action. He glanced in the rear-view mirror at his reflection. *Christ, I look old. Mid-forties? Hell … I look mid-sixties.*

He rubbed the half moon scar on his forehead. When he was stressed, as he was now, it tended to redden. The scar was obtained in his early days with the club — someone had caught his attention with the broken end of a wine bottle. He'd viewed the scar as a badge of honour.

In those days he'd also had a beard and long hair. Coupled with the scar and his height — he stood half a head taller than most men — he was someone most people instinctively feared. And when he was younger, he took delight in intimidating others. But with age came maturity and that line of thinking was gone. These days he was clean-shaven and kept his thinning hair closely cropped.

He looked at the empty car seat in the back of his van. His first and only grandchild was a year old. *When I held him the other day he touched my scar with his little finger. What do I tell him when he learns to talk and asks about it?* He ran his tongue over his teeth to dislodge any remnants of antacid as he thought about it. *Think I'll tell him it's a badge of stupidity.*

He got out of his van and despite the presence of a few homeless people, didn't bother to lock the doors. Two prospects for the club were sitting in a nearby car, which indicated that some of the club's hit team must be around, too.

So why're they meeting twice in one day? Did the team bungle their assignment and allow Damien to escape? Or is the team being given another job?

The prospects' presence was to ensure that whatever vehicles the hit team drove would remain free of any electronic tracking devices. The hit team had been code-named the three-three team, but the code wasn't kept secret from the police for long.

The prospects cast their eyes on him, but their stature in the club meant they hadn't yet earned so much as a nod of recognition from someone in his position. He turned and took the path leading to the meeting spot.

His mind still felt numb. Four hours earlier he'd gone to the park for a meeting at the request of Pure E. That was when he learned that Damien had been the one who tipped off the police about a boatload of cocaine. The boat was on its maiden voyage and the shipment had been seized in France the day before. The club's new pipeline to Europe was severed before it started.

At first Lance refused to believe it. Damien had been a close friend for years. Then he learned what Damien had been presented with ... and *did* believe it. It was a culmination of factors. Damien's son, Buck, was a new member of the club who belonged to Lance's Westside chapter. Twelve days previously that cop Jack Taggart had videoed Buck beating a rival drug dealer to death. The death was not intended, but it happened. Rather than try to coerce Buck into becoming an informant, Taggart set his sights on Damien — offering to destroy the video in exchange for Damien supplying information. At that time Damien had refused to co-operate and alerted the club about what Taggart had done.

A week ago Taggart took part in executing a search warrant on Damien's house. He seized all of Damien's assets, including a secret bank account that Damien had in the British Virgin Islands. This morning the club heard that Damien's wife, Vicki, had overreacted to the search and tried to kill Taggart — something Damien hadn't told the club. Lance was told that Taggart had given Damien the choice of either informing or seeing both Vicki and Buck go to jail.

Lance frowned. *Obviously Damien made the wrong decision — except I'd have done the same thing if it was my family on the chopping block. Christ, I already have.*

Years earlier Lance had received a similar visit from Taggart. The cop had had evidence to put him and two other club members in jail for attempted murder. Taggart said he wouldn't if Lance became his informant.

Initially Lance had refused to co-operate, but Taggart threatened to put him in protective custody and provide the prosecutor with a report that would ensure a reduced sentence to make it *look* like he'd co-operated. Lance knew that if the club couldn't get to him, they might take it out on his wife or children. In his mind he had no choice but to co-operate. A year later Taggart set him free of his obligation, apparently feeling Lance had fulfilled his end of the bargain.

Lance's thoughts came back to the meeting he'd attended four hours earlier with Pure E. Whiskey Jake, who was the president of the Eastside chapter, had attended, along with Buck and all four of the three-three team who lived in British Columbia.

Buck had taken the news hard when Pure E told him what his father had done. Tears of disbelief stained his cheeks, followed by sorrow and then outrage.

At the time Lance wondered if Pure E was going to have Buck killed in front of Damien as added punishment. A similar thing had taken place the night before to punish another drug dealer by the name of Neal Barlow, who they believed was an informant. This time, however, Pure E had another idea. Buck agreed to wear a wire and confront Damien while the three-three team listened nearby. Buck also agreed to be the one to execute his father.

Lance grimaced. *Pure E isn't wasting any time living up to his nickname. The guy is pure evil. Getting Buck to kill his own father … fuck. Guess that's one way to prove which family his loyalty is with. Dumb kid barely got his colours and Pure E told him that if he did what he was ordered to, Pure E might assign him to the three-three.* Lance thought at the time it was a bad idea, that it would raise some eyebrows — *including Taggart's.* Lance's thoughts didn't matter. Pure E was not a man who accepted criticism.

Lance neared the meeting and saw Whiskey Jake ambling away from a concession stand while munching on a hot dog. His hair, a mix of black and grey, was pulled back in a ponytail and his beer belly hung over his belt. He usually had a beard, but following his latest divorce, he'd shaved it off. He'd told Lance he thought being clean-shaven would make him more appealing to younger women.

What they find appealing about you, Lance thought, *is when you leave.*

Behind Whiskey Jake at the concession stand were two long-time members of the three-three team — Floyd Hackman and Vic Trapp. Hackman was assigned to Lance's Westside chapter while Trapp belonged to the Eastside.

Lance looked around. The two other members of the hit team, Pasquale Bazzoli and Nick Crowe, were not present. They also belonged to Whiskey Jake's Eastside chapter, although Bazzoli was currently living in Kelowna. His current assignment was to discreetly check and see if it would suit their interests to open a chapter there.

Whiskey Jake spotted him and they met at a nearby picnic table. Once seated, Lance raised an eyebrow questioningly.

"It's done," Whiskey Jake replied abruptly.

"Buck?" Lance asked.

"Yup." Whiskey Jake used his hand to simulate shooting a pistol. "One through the head. Our lawyer called Taggart to tell 'im we knew Damien was the rat and Taggart immediately called Damien to warn him. It went down exactly like Pure E predicted." Whiskey Jake uttered a hoarse chuckle. "I bet Taggart shit himself when Pure E answered Damien's phone."

"This ain't nothin' to laugh at," Lance stated.

After a few moments, Whiskey Jake nodded. "You're right. What the fuck would everyone think if they knew Damien ratted? We'd all lose respect."

That's not what I meant. Damien was my friend. "How's Buck doing?"

"Fuck. When it came to poppin' his old man, they said he was as cold as ice. Gotta give Damien credit for that. He raised the kid right."

"Pure E took a chance being there," Lance noted.

"Not really. All four of the team were there. If Buck even *thought* of tryin' to rescue his old man, he woulda been wasted."

"I'm not talking about Buck changing his mind or try-ing to save Damien. Pure E put himself at the scene and then threw shit in Taggart's face by answering Damien's phone. Same for the farmhouse last night when Neal was offed. It was bad enough torturin' his brother and sister-in-law to death first, but to leave Taggart a fuckin' message on the wall … that's insane."

"I was there when you tried to talk Pure E out of it. All he did was get pissed off at you and say things are gonna be different."

"*Different?* Is that what you call it? He's been national prez all of five days and we've taken out four people. Two who weren't necessary. When Damien ran things, we tried to maintain the peace. We hadn't whacked anyone for a couple years."

Whiskey Jake shrugged. "Pure E won the vote. Nothing we can do. You saw how pissed off he got when you tried to offer some advice."

"I know he was voted in, but we've done too much recruitin' over the last few years. Lots of young blood in the club. They're not smart enough to think of the future. We should have a rule that they can't vote until they got ten years under their belt."

Whiskey Jake rolled his eyes. "Yeah, try and bring that in and you'll find yourself starin' up at the grass."

Lance scowled. "I'm almost afraid to ask, but why the fuck did you send word to meet again? Where's Bazzoli, Crowe, and Buck?"

"Bazzoli and Crowe are disposin' of Damien. Buck's around — he went to the shitter." Whiskey Jake gave a nod of his head. "There he is."

Lance glanced over his shoulder and saw Buck heading over to where Hackman and Trapp were waiting. The men knew to watch their club presidents from a respectful distance and wouldn't approach within earshot unless invited.

Whiskey Jake cleared his throat, then turned his head and spit before answering. "Why I called the meetin' is because of Damien's old lady."

"Vicki? Buck was supposed to tell her that Damien split the country to keep himself out of jail. What changed?"

"He told her all right — but she knows."

Lance leaned across the table. "Whaddaya mean, she knows?"

"She *knows*. It wasn't her lawyer's secretary who called our lawyer askin' about the charges being dropped against Buck because Damien ratted. It was Vicki pretendin' to be the secretary. She set Damien up."

Lance's mouth flopped open and he sat back in shock.

"Buck met with her a couple hours ago. Earlier she told him she was going out, but she lied. She stayed home and was upstairs. She heard when Buck talked to Damien and watched when the guys came in and took him away."

"She wanted us to kill him? But why?"

"She was pissed that he wouldn't save Buck from bein' charged when he beat that dealer to death. She also blamed him for Buck getting involved in the club."

"But didn't she try to kill Taggart last week when they searched the house?"

"Yup. That's what tipped the scales for Damien. He made a deal with Taggart to let Vicki and Buck off."

"So he saves her ass and she responds by setting him up? That evil fucking bitch!"

"Yeah, evil." Whiskey Jake smirked. "Maybe she should marry Pure E now that she's single."

Lance's face must have shown his anger, for Whiskey Jack said, "Hey, lighten up, I'm only jokin'. That's why I called a meeting. It's to let Pure E know and find out what he wants done."

"Maybe he'll want Buck to go back and do her," Lance suggested. "Make a clean sweep of both his parents."

"Yeah, welcome to the club Buck-o-boy."

Lance shook his head. "This new management style — I'm gettin' too old for this shit. It's makin' me think it's time to retire."

"Movin' down to the Caymans?"

"Maybe for six months of the year. My kids are established here and now that we've got a grandson, things have changed. I'd still keep a place here."

"Well … we both got the capital to do that. Gotta admit, I'm gettin' a little tired of managing whores and strippers. They're always a headache. I imagine goin' to your amusement centre every day must be a drag."

"It's okay — but you're right. I'm looking forward to enjoying the benefits of our real money."

"Thank fuck we didn't go in with Damien."

"It wasn't like he offered," Lance noted. "He was smart to recommend we keep our money apart from his. You and I probably should've kept ours separate, too."

"Ours is safe," Whiskey Jake replied. "The only connection was through the lawyer in Mexico. He got those files out of the office long before the Federales came by."

"I still question how the cops got on to Damien's secret account."

Whiskey Jake looked puzzled. "What're you talking about? Damien's lawyer had another client who got busted and ratted out the lawyer. Rather than go down for money launderin', the fuckin' lawyer then ratted out Damien."

"So it appeared, but with Taggart involved, I'm always suspicious."

"What makes you so leery of Taggart?"

Because I was once his rat and know how he operates. "He's on the RCMP Intelligence Unit. I always wonder what they're up to."

"You're paranoid." Whiskey Jake nodded suddenly. "The man's arrived."

"Hey boys, what's up?" Pure E asked as he approached. Lance slid over on the picnic bench to make room.

"Wait'll you hear this," Whiskey Jake replied. "Buck came back with some interesting shit." He then told Pure E that Buck had discovered it was Vicki who set Damien up for them to kill.

Pure E looked taken back, then grinned. "Sounds like she doesn't like rats, either."

"She manipulated us," Lance said. "What do you want done?"

Pure E glanced toward Hackman, Trapp, and Buck. He paused, then turned to Lance. "Normally I'd be pissed off, but if it wasn't for her, we wouldn't have known who ratted out our boatload of coke."

"Still, do you want the boys to take care of her?" Whiskey Jake asked.

"No. She did us a big favour. Too bad she didn't come to us direct, but either way, she did the right thing."

"She told Buck that she saw the guys take him away," Whiskey Jake said.

"So what?" Pure E scoffed. "It wasn't like he put up a fight. It even fits in with the story that we snuck him out of the country. It's not like the cops will ever find his body."

"But she knows we killed him," Lance stated.

"Fuck, who cares?" Pure E replied. "She's part of it. She's not gonna say anything. If word ever leaks out he was killed, we could say it's a rumour we started to keep the cops from trying to find him."

"Guess that'd work, too," Whiskey Jake said.

Pure E snickered. "Wish I could've seen Taggart's face today when he called to warn Damien."

"I still think that was a big mistake," Lance said. "Pokin' the bear with a sharp stick is never a good idea."

Pure E stared at Lance. "I looked in that fuckin' mini-van of yours as I walked past. You've got a baby seat in the back."

"Yeah … so what? It's for my grandson."

"Yeah, grandpa, great fuckin' image for a chapter president. What's even worse is sitting here and listening to you talk like an old man."

"An old man with a lot of experience," Lance said evenly.

"I can't believe you'd worry about Taggart. Sure he knows we killed Damien. I wanted him to know. But knowing and proving are two different things."

"But what you did to him … twice in one day. First the message on the wall and then answering Damien's phone when he called to warn Damien."

Pure E sneered. "So what?"

"You've just moved from Winnipeg, so you don't know Taggart. We've dealt with him before. He'll go crazy and he isn't beyond stepping outside the law. All you did was paint a big target on your back."

"You want to speak to me about targets? Think about your buddy Damien. This shit wouldn't have happened if Taggart hadn't messed with his family. Threatening to put Buck in jail — that's what drove Vicki to take a shot at him."

"Yeah, and so?"

"If Taggart's gonna make me a target, then maybe it's time to put him in his place." Pure E paused to flick an ant off the table. "I heard he's married with a couple kids?"

"His wife's a doctor," Whiskey Jake offered. "They got two young sons."

"Perfect."

Oh, shit. "What're you thinking?" Lance asked.

Pure glanced at his watch. "I'm thinking if we light a fire under Hackman and Trapp's asses, they can be at Taggart's house when his kids come home from school."

Shock registered on Lance's face. "You're not —"

Pure E shut Lance up with a look of contempt, then said, "I'm gonna give Taggart a present he'll never forget. That fucker cost us a tonne of coke. It's payback time!"

Lance swallowed. *Oh, fuck.*

Chapter Three

Jack fidgeted with a pen as he spoke on the phone. Exhaustion and stress had put him in a daze and he had to make a conscious effort to focus on his conversation with his wife. "I should be home about four-thirty," he mumbled.

"Perfect timing. I'll probably have the fall cleanup in the yard finished by then," Natasha said brusquely.

"I'm sorry."

"Come on, I'm teasing. I need something to keep me busy for the next week before I go back to work."

"Looking forward to working at a new clinic?"

"I think so. It's a safer neighbourhood. The doctor I'm replacing told me she loves it there, but she's too ill to work and is scheduled for more chemo."

Jack looked at a streak of soot on the cuff of his shirt. *Christ, what they must have gone through. What would it be like, being tied to a chair and watching your wife being burned to death?*

"The other two doctors seem really nice. I think I'll fit in well." Natasha paused for a response. When none came she asked, "Are you okay?"

Jack sighed. "It's been a hell of a day."

"When you called earlier you said it went well in Victoria. I expected you home by noon. It's almost three."

"Things did go well in Victoria. It's *here* that everything went to shit." Rose gestured to him from the doorway. "I gotta go. Meeting with the brass."

"Okay, I love you."

"Love you, too, babe."

Floyd Hackman slowly drove past Taggart's house. The white van he and Vic Trapp were in was in need of a wash, and the magnetic signs stuck to the doors read *Abe's Furnace Repair*, along with a phone number. They saw a woman who fit Taggart's wife's description crouched with her back to the street working in a flower bed.

"Fuckin' perfect," Trapp said. He glanced at his watch. "Bet their kids'll be home from school soon. Park up ahead. It'll be easy to shoot out the back," he added, gesturing with his thumb toward the curtained-off portion of the van.

Chapter Four

"Assistant Commissioners Isaac and Mortimer are expecting you."

Jack nodded cordially to the secretary, then followed Rose in. Isaac and Mortimer sat in upholstered chairs, part of a cluster around a coffee table. Jack took in Mortimer's appearance. Double chins coupled with an egg-shaped bald head. His skin was a pasty white and his hands, wrists, and fingers were pudgy. *Looks like somebody put Humpty Dumpty back together again.*

Isaac looked up and his face became grim.

Yes, sir, I feel sickened by what happened, too. Then Jack's eyes met Mortimer's and he saw the look of disapproval. *Okay, so my beard is down to my chest and the bags under my eyes make me look like a raccoon. You try doing what I do.*

Isaac's voice was grave. "Assistant Commissioner Mortimer, this is Staff Sergeant Rose Wood. She heads our intelligence unit. Corporal Jack Taggart is one of her investigators."

Mortimer acknowledged the introduction with a grunt.

Isaac gestured for them to sit and then focused on Jack. "We'll talk about the main reason you're here in a moment, but first, I received a call from Inspector Dyck about your undercover operation in Victoria. Please explain the circumstances to my colleague here. I was told the suspect pulled a gun and that a weapon was discharged during the arrest."

At the mention of a gun, Mortimer stared bug-eyed at Jack.

"Yes, sir. Basically, I was involved in an undercover operation to gather evidence on a murder. The suspect lived on a boat and I wanted to have a look at the tender —"

"Tender?" Mortimer questioned.

"The small boat, often a dingy, that larger boats use to get to shore." Jack saw Mortimer nod, so he continued. "The motor on the tender may have been damaged by the victim seconds before he was murdered. The suspect invited me on board, but caught me looking at the tender and pulled a gun."

Mortimer glowered at Jack. "What were you doing working on cases where guns were involved?"

Jack was aghast. "Sir?"

"That sort of thing should've been turned over to the police! You shouldn't have been involved in something like that!"

Turned over to the police? What the hell? Jack's tone displayed his contempt. "Sir, I don't know about you, but I *am* a police officer. I've got a badge and everything, including a gun. Many of the people I investigate carry guns or have access to them."

Mortimer opened and closed his mouth, seemingly at a loss for words.

Jack glanced at Rose. *Come on Rose! Don't be giving me the hairy eyeball! This guy's so far removed from reality he doesn't even think of us as police officers! What the hell?*

"It's okay," Isaac assured Mortimer. "Nobody was hurt and the suspect was apprehended. I'd like to hear about the weapon being discharged, though."

"Yes, sir," Jack replied. "Corporal Connie Crane —"

"A member from the Integrated Homicide Investigation team I assigned to be part of the cover team," Isaac noted for Mortimer's benefit.

"Yes," Jack said. "I-HIT had a cover team hidden in a nearby boat. When the suspect pulled the gun, Corporal Crane ordered him to drop it. He didn't. She fired a shot, which distracted him, and I was then able to disarm him. I believe Corporal Crane saved my life."

"Similar to how Inspector Dyck reported the incident," Isaac added. He faced Jack but his eyes momentarily shifted toward Mortimer. "Except I was told how your jacket was damaged."

Right. Connie tried to shoot the asshole as I tackled him. The bullet went through my collar. He glanced at Mortimer. *You'd probably want her fired.* Jack tried for nonchalance as he said, "It was an old jacket. I threw it out and won't be claiming any expenses for it."

Isaac nodded. "Enough said. Congratulations on a job well done." He paused for a moment. "Let's move on to why I called you in. That delicate matter you brought to my attention ten days ago became an indelicate matter. By your odour, I presume you were at the farmhouse?"

"Yes, sir. When we got off the ferry from Victoria, Corporal Crane was with me. She received a call and we went to the scene. After that I spoke to my informant."

Isaac looked at Mortimer. "Corporal Taggart was investigating Satans Wrath Motorcycle Club. They were exporting shipments of marijuana to Dallas, Texas, in a semi being driven by a Robert and Roxanne Barlow. After the marijuana was unloaded and the Barlows left, we had the DEA seize the shipment."

"How much marijuana was seized?" Mortimer asked.

"About 250 kilos," Isaac replied, "but that's incidental to what took place later. Neal Barlow, who's Robert's brother, is a member of the Gypsy Devils motorcycle gang. They're a puppet club controlled by Satans Wrath and were responsible for looking after the delivery. During the investigation, seventy-five kilos of marijuana were surreptitiously taken from Neal."

"So 325 kilos were actually seized," Mortimer said.

What part of "incidental" don't you understand?

"It caused the bikers to suspect that Neal had cut a deal with the police in exchange for Robert and Roxanne's freedom. We expected that Neal would be murdered, but we didn't expect Robert and Roxanne to also be murdered, let alone in the heinous fashion that they were."

Mortimer just gaped.

"We could've had Robert and Roxanne arrested in the States," Isaac went on, "but Satans Wrath believed the Gypsy Devils were responsible for the shipment being seized and had given them two weeks to plug the leak. If they didn't, the clubs would be at war and most of the Gypsy Devils would've been murdered."

"Good God," Mortimer spluttered, then glared at Jack. "Your actions are reprehensible!"

"It was my decision," Isaac said forcefully. "The ones who are reprehensible are the criminals he's working on."

Mortimer frowned, then sat back in his seat and folded his arms across his chest.

Isaac cleared his throat. "So, to continue … I was left with the choice of either agreeing with Corporal Taggart's plan to set Neal up as a sacrificial lamb, or have Robert and Roxanne arrested — which may or may not have prevented Neal's murder in the resulting gang war. That war would've also jeopardized the lives of innocent people."

"This is unbelievable." Mortimer's jaw quivered. "What a thing to ask Ottawa."

"There wasn't time to sit around while Ottawa procrastinated," Isaac declared. He looked at Jack. "Did your informant have any information about what happened?"

"Yes, sir. My informant was present when the murders took place and he —"

Mortimer interjected. "You're telling me that you allowed an informant to take part in a triple murder?" He leaned forward and gripped the arms of the chair as if prepared to run away.

"Yes, sir, I did," Jack replied. "As it turns out he was basically a spectator."

"You don't catch sewer rats with church mice," Isaac stated. "The murders would have taken place regardless." He glanced at Jack. "Please proceed, Corporal."

"Yes, sir. Two members of Satans Wrath and eight of the Gypsy Devils took part in the murders. Under orders from Satans Wrath, the Gypsy Devils bound, gagged, and tied their three victims to kitchen chairs. Cans of lighter fluid were given to the Gypsy Devils." Jack had to steel himself to continue without emotion. "They burned Roxanne first, then Robert. After that, Neal was disembowelled and a Satans Wrath member dipped a broom into his blood and painted a message on the wall. It read the number four, the letter *U*, and the initials *JT*."

"For you, JT," Isaac said, looking at Jack.

"Yes, sir. I was told that Purvis Evans ordered the message be left for me."

Isaac glanced at Mortimer's stunned face. "Purvis Evans is the new national president of Satans Wrath," he explained.

"He also goes by the nickname of Pure E, which is short for Pure Evil," Rose added.

"A title that he obviously deserves," Isaac said.

Jack nodded. "Sir, I'm sickened by what transpired. When I approached you with the question of whether or not to arrest Robert and Roxanne, Damien Zabat was still national president. He never would've done what Pure E, I mean, Purvis Evans, did."

"Pure E seems more appropriate than Purvis," Isaac said dryly. He paused, then added, "They say hindsight is twenty-twenty, but given the situation, were it to occur again, I'm not certain I'd do anything different."

"Your informant witnessed these murders," Mortimer stated.

"Yes, sir."

"Then he can testify!" Mortimer sat forward again, looking pleased with himself.

Gee, why didn't we think of that? "No, sir. I promised the informant I'd never put him in that position. He's not a paid agent, but was caught doing a crime and agreed to supply information in lieu of being charged."

"What kind of crime?" Mortimer asked.

"He's a weenie wagger."

"A what?"

"He was caught exposing himself in public. Satans Wrath would likely murder him if they found out because of the embarrassment it'd cause if it became public. Initially he provided me with information about a marijuana grow-op."

Isaac turned to Mortimer. "Corporal Taggart then worked his way up the ladder. His work was instrumental in discovering how Damien Zabat, the previous national president of Satans Wrath, had been laundering money. Last week we raided Damien's home and also conducted searches of lawyers' offices in Vancouver, the British Virgin Islands, and Chihuahua, Mexico. We seized somewhere in the neighbourhood of twenty million dollars, along with another five or six million in assets. Further to that, to prevent his son from going to jail, Damien provided Corporal Taggart with information about a boatload of cocaine being delivered to France. That shipment was seized last night."

"I heard about it on the news," Mortimer said. "Four Satans Wrath members were arrested, along with several Europeans. A tonne of cocaine was seized." He paused. "There was no mention of involvement from us. The news made it sound like the investigation originated in Europe."

"That was to protect the informant," Jack explained.

Mortimer frowned. "That was dumb. The press coverage would have benefited us all."

"Not the informant," Jack said sharply.

Isaac glanced at Mortimer. "I think it best to let Corporal Taggart call the shots on informant safety."

Mortimer stared silently at Jack.

Isaac said, "I won't keep you any longer, Corporal. I'm sure you'd like to go home and get some much needed rest."

Rose cleared her throat. "Sir, there's been a further development you need to know about. I think it best to let Corporal Taggart explain."

Jack felt the dryness in his throat and swallowed. *Talk about a bad day at the office.* "It was Damien's wife, Vicki, who provided me with the financial information allowing us to seize his money and assets."

"His own wife was your informant?" Mortimer asked in astonishment.

"Yes, sir. Her son, Buck, is a member of Satans Wrath. I recently videoed him beating a drug dealer to death."

"You what?" Mortimer's gaze swung from Jack to Isaac.

"I was aware of it," Isaac said.

"In exchange for keeping her son out of jail, Vicki gave me the information on her husband. When we seized Damien's assets, I staged a phony situation where it looked like Vicki tried to attack me as we were searching his house." Jack paused. *Firing a bullet into my Kevlar vest ... I think that qualifies as an attack.* "Damien then told me about the cocaine shipment, believing he was saving his wife and son from going to jail."

Isaac stared at Jack. "What you described as an attack — it's the first I've heard about it. Was it something you'd planned all along?"

"Yes, sir," Jack admitted.

"You arranged this so Damien wouldn't suspect his wife had informed?"

"Yes, sir."

"The attack must have appeared realistic, perhaps even deadly, for Damien to think she'd receive a serious jail sentence," Isaac noted. "So serious that he gave us a tonne of cocaine."

Please don't go there. Rose already gave me shit. Mortimer would probably have me committed. "I'd already shown Damien the video of his son beating the drug dealer to death. I believe his reason to co-operate was a combination of factors."

"I'm sure it was," Isaac said. "Continue."

Good. You see through the layers. You know there was more to it. Jack cleared his throat. "Unfortunately Damien didn't tell me about the cocaine until after he'd obtained a lawyer for Vicki."

"Basil Westmount?" Isaac asked. Before Jack could reply, Isaac glanced at Mortimer and said, "He's the lawyer Satans Wrath keeps on retainer."

"No, sir, it wasn't Westmount, although he was representing Buck. For Vicki, Damien picked a respected lawyer by the name of Edward Gosling. Gosling met with her first and it was subsequent to that that Damien decided to bargain with me."

"A worthwhile bargain for us, considering what was seized last night in France." Isaac stared at Mortimer until he eventually gave a nod of agreement.

"The problem is, sir, at noon today I received a phone call from Basil Westmount. He said he'd received a call from Gosling's office telling him they were representing Vicki and said they wanted to confirm if the charges against Buck had been dropped now that Damien had given us the boatload of cocaine."

"Oh, Lord, no," Isaac muttered. He glanced at Mortimer. "Westmount is as crooked as they come and no doubt will tell Satans Wrath." He turned to Jack. "I take it you've warned Damien?"

"I called Damien's number immediately, but ..." Jack swallowed.

"But?" Isaac prodded.

"Pure E answered. He said he was expecting my call and told me that Damien wasn't available ... but he'd let Damien know I called."

"Oh, Lord," Isaac repeated.

"There's no doubt Damien's dead," Jack said. "I then called the number I had for Vicki, but it wasn't in service. Following that I called Edward Gosling's office and discovered no one in his office made any calls to Basil Westmount."

Isaac's eyebrows knitted together. "I'm not sure I understand."

"I couldn't prove it in court, but it had to be Vicki who called Westmount. She was furious with Damien for not informing when I first showed them the video of Buck beating up the dealer. Damien wouldn't have told anyone that Vicki attacked me or have made any mention of Gosling."

"A modern-day Judas," Isaac said. "Have you called I-HIT?"

"Yes, they're trying to trace Damien's cellphone — but Pure E wouldn't have risked talking to me if there was any chance of us finding evidence."

"Any idea at all what they might've done with his body?"

"No, sir. The three-three squad turn their phones off when they're doing a hit ... so their movements can't be traced."

"Three-three squad?" Mortimer questioned.

"Satans Wrath's professional hit team," Jack replied. "Individual members belong to various chapters, as do those assigned to the three-three. The area they are from, such as Vancouver, Calgary, Montreal, and so on, is written across the bottom of their jackets. In their lingo it is referred to as the bottom rocker. The difference is the three-three are utilized by various chapter presidents across the country. Although their bottom rockers don't say Canada, unofficially they're thought of as the Canada Chapter. The third letter of the alphabet is 'C,' which is where the term three-three originated from."

"And you think Damien's been murdered?" Mortimer again.

"Yes, sir."

Mortimer gave Jack a look of disgust. "Didn't it occur to you, Corporal, that last week you obtained evidence to charge him with money laundering? Not only weren't you thinking clearly when you tried to warn him, I suspect it highly probable that he fled the country and is hoping you'll think he's dead."

"Sir, he's definitely dead. Pure E wouldn't have allowed Damien to get away with giving us the cocaine pipeline to Europe. Particularly with a seizure that large."

"You're only guessing." Mortimer scoffed. "I find it difficult to accept that they would kill their top man. In my opinion, you've been led down the garden path."

Jack's face darkened. "I'm not a medical doctor, so I'm only guessing that Neal, Robert, and Roxanne Barlow are dead. I'd be pleased to take you to them so you could form your own opinion. That being said, I'm positive that Damien is dead."

Mortimer looked first at Jack, then Isaac. His jowls quivered and he spluttered in an apparent attempt to form a reply.

Crap. That was a dumb thing to say to my future boss.

Isaac's face revealed his ire. "Corporal Taggart, your emotions have obviously affected your professionalism and the respect you normally hold for your superiors."

"Sir, he's only had six hours sleep in the last two days," Rose said. "With what he witnessed this morning and —"

Isaac silenced Rose with a wave of his hand and focused on Jack. "Your outburst gives me cause to wonder if you're suffering from post-traumatic stress. If that's the case, you should be removed from active duty and put on stress leave. If that's not the case, then your behaviour to Assistant Commissioner Mortimer is nothing short of insubordination."

Son-of-a-bitch. Apologize or else.... Jack swallowed, then looked at Mortimer. "Sir, I'm sorry. The events this morning were disturbing, but that's no excuse for me to be discourteous and unprofessional. Please accept my apology."

Mortimer stared long enough for everyone to feel uncomfortable. "I accept your apology ... this once."

"Thank you, sir."

"We're done for now," Isaac said. "I'll contact I-HIT and we'll adjourn until 10:00 a.m. tomorrow to decide what action to take." He looked at Jack. "I suggest you get some sleep."

I feel like I've let you down.... "Sir, I'm extremely embarrassed," Jack replied sincerely. He then gave a conciliatory nod to Mortimer. *As far as you go, Humpty Dumpty, I'm in the mood for an omelette.*

Chapter Five

Rose scowled at Jack as they walked back to their offices. "I can't believe you spoke to Mortimer that way!"

"The man's an idiot! You heard what he said. If someone has a gun, I should turn the investigation over to the police. What the hell's he thinking?"

"He's about to be our new boss. Didn't it occur to you that he could seriously hinder your chances to go after Satans Wrath? Maybe even have you transferred?"

Jack took a couple of steps, then admitted, "Yes ... I screwed up."

"Isaac may have saved your bacon by getting you to apologize."

"I don't know if Mortimer's that dumb."

"You don't think he bought it? At least you sounded sincere."

"Even if he accepted my apology, he's so incompetent it'll be a nightmare trying to get things approved."

"He'll be the top dog. Not much we can do about it."

"Damien was top dog, too."

"What're you saying?"

"Damien's dead," Jack said coldly, "and he was twice as intelligent as Mortimer."

"Meaning? What are you planning?" Rose asked sharply.

"The man is such a buffoon I don't think he'll be able to handle the job. Either the stress will get to him or Ottawa will clue into the fact he's not the right person for the job."

"Oh … I see," Rose murmured.

Then again, a little nudge to knock Humpty off the wall wouldn't hurt. His thought was interrupted when he saw Laura at her desk. She glanced at him, then looked away.

Don't be embarrassed. Who wouldn't be stressed?

"What're you doing here?" Rose demanded of Laura. "I told you to go home."

"I'm okay, I just —"

"You're not okay," Rose said firmly. "Neither of you are. Both of you go home."

"I won't be able to rest," Laura said, then focused on Jack. "Not until I find out what you intend to do about Pure E."

What I intend to do?

Rose waited a beat, then gave in. "Okay, we'll talk about that, but then you're both going home."

"How did it go with Isaac?" Laura asked as Rose wheeled a chair over.

"Isaac and *Mortimer*, as it turned out," Jack said. He waited until he sat down, then continued, "Not well. Mortimer thinks Damien isn't dead and that we've been tricked."

"Tricked after we seized a boatload of coke?" Laura exclaimed. "He obviously doesn't know anything about bikers. Did you enlighten him?"

"Oh, Jack enlightened him," Rose interjected. "So much so that Isaac made him apologize."

"Oh, Jack." Laura looked askance. "What did you say?"

Jack shook his head in amazement. "Mortimer's so far removed from police work that he doesn't consider us to be police officers. He reprimanded me for investigating people who carry guns. He said those types of cases should be turned over to the police."

"No, really … tell me what happened," Laura said.

"I'm not making it up," Jack replied. "Ask Rose."

The staff sergeant nodded. "He's telling you the truth."

Astonishment registered on Laura's face. "That's absurd!"

"I'm still in shock," Jack said. "I think Isaac was, too."

"But you had to apologize?" Laura asked. "I bet you gave him that tone you use when you're being sarcastic."

"I was sarcastic," Jack replied. "I suspect Isaac had me apologize to save my career." *I'll deal with the idiot somehow.* He saw Laura staring at him and knew she was reading his thoughts. *She's under enough stress. She doesn't need this.* "Guys like Mortimer won't be around long," he offered. "I bet he does a stint here for a couple of years on the pretence of gaining experience, then scurries back to Ottawa where his credentials justify another promotion."

"So you're saying you'll simply bide your time for a couple of years until he leaves." Laura's tone was dry. Before Jack could respond, she said, "I'm sorry. That was a dumb thing to say."

You'll simply bide your time. She didn't say we'll *bide our time. Crap! She's thinking of leaving — and why shouldn't she? What sane person would put up with this bullshit?*

"We're meeting Isaac again tomorrow at 10:00 a.m.," Rose noted. "I-HIT will be there, as well, and we'll formulate a plan." She stared at Jack. "That being said, do you have some suggestions? I don't want you spouting off tomorrow about how you'd like to … I don't know, steal a snowplow and take out a bunch of Satans Wraths next time they're on a ride."

"Actually I wondered if on some rainy night a phony detour could send them over a cliff." At Rose's horrified look, Jack said, "Relax. I'm only joking." *Sort of.*

Rose's only response was a glare.

"There'll always be groups like Satans Wrath around no matter what we do," Jack said. "Even if they all died, someone else would take their spot. The real menace is the guy in charge. We've never had to deal with the likes of Pure E before. He sent us a message and we need to send one back. He needs to be stopped."

"Yes, but how?" Rose asked. "After seeing his message, I'm sure you'd like to put a bullet in his brain."

"I wouldn't want to even if it was justified," Jack replied. "He has the backing of the club. If he pulled a gun on me some night and I killed him, the club would accuse me of murder. There'd be repercussions. I'm not going to jeopardize my family by knocking off some criminal who'd only be replaced." His bitterness was almost palpable. "I never thought I'd say this, but I wish Damien was still in power."

"So how will you handle it?" Rose asked.

"Legally and professionally … but perhaps not ethically. If we're to catch Pure E we may need to sit back and watch a few murders take place first."

"Murders?" Rose frowned.

"Satans Wrath use their three-three team for hits. We need to concentrate on them. In the past the national president wouldn't be involved if the three-three was simply knocking off local dealers. Club presidents could okay that. The national president would only be involved if the club was making an incursion into the territory of someone who had the clout to go to war with them. Either that, or someone connected with law enforcement or the judiciary."

"So you're thinking we target the three-three and hope to catch Pure E giving them their orders," Rose continued.

"Exactly. Wiretap … informants … surveillance. All of that. The odds are we'll end up watching a few local dealers get murdered before something happens to involve Pure E, but if we made any busts on the small fry, it would tip our hand."

"It's been years since anyone has gone to war with Satans Wrath in this part of the world," Rose stated. "What you're suggesting might never take place."

"I disagree. Pure E is far more ambitious and prone to violence than Damien was. I think he thrives on it. My guess is we won't have to wait long. He's trying to make a name for himself. Using violence, torture, and intimidation is how he plans on doing it. We need to catch him on wire ordering the hits."

Rose pursed her lips. "Okay, you've convinced me and I'll push for that tomorrow morning. Now I want the both of you to go home."

Laura glanced at Jack. "Mind giving me a ride home?"

Jack nodded. *Here it comes….*

***

Neither Jack nor Laura spoke until they got in the car, then Jack turned to her and placed a hand on her shoulder. "It's okay," he said softly. I don't blame you in the least."

Laura pulled back. "Blame me for what?"

"For wanting a transfer."

Laura's eyes welled with tears. "Is that what Rose told you? She's mistaken. I was upset — but I never said that."

"She didn't tell me — *you* did."

Laura took a couple of deep breaths, and then it came out. "Oh, God … you know me so well." She wiped away a tear. "I really don't know if I can handle it any longer. I'm so bloody tired and upset I can't think straight."

Jack slid over and wrapped his arm around her shoulders. "It's okay to go," he whispered. "We've been through more crap over the years than I care to think about. The enemies we've made, the things we've seen …"

"That's just it!" Laura cried. "I never get a break. I can't stop thinking about it. At night, if a car slows down driving past our house I wake up. I'd feel safer sleeping under the bed and probably would if I wasn't married. Instead, I sleep with my gun on the bedside table."

"I understand exactly," Jack said. "If Natasha wasn't beside me, I'd put the pillows under my sheets and sleep in my closet with my gun in my lap."

"Because your mattress wouldn't stop the bullets. Yes, I've thought of that, too."

"I wake up with nightmares or fighting in my sleep four or five times a week."

"Likewise," Laura admitted.

"Once I kicked so hard that I knocked Natasha out of bed. Another time I delivered a punch that just missed her face. I wake up immediately, but that's no way to live."

Laura pulled away to look at Jack. "It's not only the fear of someone trying to kill me. It's things you and I've done in the past I worry about."

Jack shifted uncomfortably in his seat.

"You know what I mean." She stared at him a moment, then added, "I won't even speak about it for fear the car is bugged. Now with Pure E doing what he did, I'm afraid. Afraid for you ... and for what you might do."

"Weren't you listening to what I said to Rose a moment ago?"

Laura's face darkened. "Hey — I'm not Rose. Maybe I don't read you as well as you read me, but I'm not stupid. I know you pretty well."

Jack swallowed. *Time to change tack.* "The point is, I'm not blaming you for wanting out. I was thinking the same thing myself until Pure E left that message on the wall. He threw down the gauntlet for me. I can't back down ... but you can."

"How can I run out on you at a time like this? I ... I'd feel so guilty." She looked dismayed. "I need time to think it over. Maybe a good night's sleep will —"

"When have we worked together that there wasn't a time like this? The jails are releasing them faster than we can catch them. We'll never see the end."

Laura looked sad, then reached for her seat belt. Neither spoke for the next half-hour as Jack drove. When he pulled up to her house she turned to him. "Promise me you're going straight home."

"What else would I do?"

She made a face.

Jack frowned. "What I told Rose about not jeopardizing my family is true. I won't do anything stupid. As for going home, I'm exhausted … so yes, that's where I'm going. I'll make a couple of phone calls on the way, but that's all."

"A couple of calls?"

"One to John Adams."

"Your special agent friend with U.S. Customs in El Paso," she noted. "What do you want him to do?"

"It's what he's already done," Jack replied. "He's getting his wife to transcribe the files on Damien he obtained from the Mexican lawyer."

"Obtained?" Laura scoffed.

It's better than saying Adams stole them from where they were hidden after the lawyer was tipped off that a search warrant for his office was being obtained. "The lawyer would've been warned if another warrant was issued," Jack replied.

"You'll never be able to use the files in court."

"Not in Canada, but the U.S. is a different story. There are two boxes of files. John's wife is Spanish, but that's still a lot of translation. There's no hurry on Damien, but maybe other names will pop up."

"And your other call?"

"I want to know if I-HIT had any luck determining where Damien's phone was when Pure E answered. I think Damien was there. Pure E's the type who'd want to see the look on Damien's face when I called."

"It's not your fault you called. I would've done the same thing."

Stress and exhaustion caused Jack's voice to sound monotone. "Tomorrow's Friday. As soon as the morning meeting's over, I think we should go home and take the rest of the weekend off."

"No argument there."

"I'll pick you up on the way in. Right now all I want to do is get home, shower, hug my family, and go straight to bed."

Chapter Six

As Jack drove home he called John Adams. After exchanging niceties, Adams said, "Yolanda is about halfway through the first box of records. So far they pertain to Damien Zabat's money-laundering scheme through the phony real-estate sales."

"Well ... there's no rush on Damien," Jack said blandly. He then told Adams that Damien must have been murdered and that Pure E had answered Damien's phone when Jack called to warn him.

"Those whoremongers!" Adams said.

"There's more. I laid heat on a biker to protect an informant. It worked, but the bastards made him watch as they burned his brother and wife to death before gutting him. Then they dipped a broom in his blood and left a message on the wall for me."

"For you? Jesus fuck!"

"So Pure E's become my number-one target."

"I don't believe it," Adams said.

Jack was confused. "What I told you is true."

"No, not that part. I don't believe Pure E is still alive."

"I'm trying to do things by the book. If he dies and the club suspects I played a role in it, they're liable to come after my family."

After a few moments of silence Adams said, "Yeah, I hear ya."

"So, back to the files. Did Yolanda look in the other box? I'm hoping Damien isn't the only Canadian mentioned."

"You're in luck there. There are two other Canucks."

Bingo.

"The lawyer dealing with Damien was Francesco Lopez. Yolanda skimmed through the file folders in the second box. They actually belong to another lawyer by the name of Miguel Herrero. His office is in the same building as Lopez."

Oh, please, let it be, let it be....

"She hasn't had time to read those files yet," Adams continued. "I told her that Damien was the priority. She said, though, from what she *did* see, the second box pertained to a Lance Morgan —"

Yes!

"— and a Jake Yadamenko, or some name like that. I'm just going by memory, but it —"

"Yes! Yes! Yes!"

"You havin' an orgasm, Jack?"

"Lance Morgan is president of the Westside chapter of Satans Wrath in Vancouver." Jack couldn't keep the excitement out of his voice. "Jake Yevdokymenko is president of the Eastside chapter and goes by the nickname of Whiskey Jake. Getting something on either of those two would be fantastic."

"Whiskey Jake," Adams repeated. "Good. Helluva lot easier to remember."

"He's left-handed, so occasionally they call him Lefty or South Paw, but Whiskey Jake is his most common moniker. John, you did great! Past informant info said that Lopez had introduced them to another lawyer, but we didn't know who."

"Guess Lopez thought he was being extra cautious by hiding those files, as well."

"Peaks and valleys. Today we hit a peak. Please ask Yolanda to concentrate on Morgan and Yevdokymenko."

"You got it. Might be a week or so. I'll let you know."

Jack glanced at the white van with *Abe's Furnace Repair* on the door as he slowed to turn into his driveway. He was too tired to pay it much thought. As he jabbed the automatic garage-door opener, Natasha appeared from around the side of the house carrying a bucket of weeds and plant clippings. He parked and then walked out through the open garage door to give her a hug and a kiss.

Natasha stepped back. "You look and smell awful. Want to talk about it?"

"I hardly know where to begin. This morning I went to a triple homicide. It was gruesome. I think I should spare you the details."

"I'm a doctor. I've seen gruesome. If something is affecting you, I want you to talk to me about it."

Jack took a breath and slowly exhaled. "A man and wife were tied to chairs in their kitchen. The husband was made to watch as his wife was burned to death, then it was his turn. The third victim was the man's brother. After being made to watch the other two, he was disembowelled."

Natasha winced and briefly closed her eyes.

"It gets worse. One of the killers used a broom to leave a message in blood on the wall for me."

Natasha gasped. "For you!"

"It said, 'For you JT' with the number 4 and letter *U* used instead of the words."

"Why? Why would someone do that?"

"I'd set it up to make the brother look like my informant. I expected him to be killed, but not like that. Satans Wrath has a new national president by the name of Purvis Evans. Turns out he's more vindictive and evil than I knew."

"So you're feeling responsible," Natasha said.

"There's more. At noon I received a call from Basil Westmount. He's the club lawyer and told me he discovered it was Damien who gave me the info about a boatload of cocaine that ended up being seized in France last night. I called Damien to try to warn him and … and …" In exasperation he made a fist.

"And what?"

"Purvis Evans answered. He was waiting for my call. There's no doubt Damien is dead." Jack paused as he reflected on the situation. "Damn it, I meant to call I-HIT to see if they could trace Damien's phone … but I guess that can wait."

"How did they find out Damien was working for you?"

"His wife, Vicki. She did it."

Natasha shook her head in disgust. As a doctor, she'd seen more than her share of people seeking treatment over domestic fights.

"And I fell for it," Jack said bitterly. "It was me who put the final nail in his coffin."

Natasha hugged him. "You always do what you feel is morally justified." Her voice was soft and loving. "You're a good person."

"That's another thing," Jack said dismally. "Speaking of good people … Laura is thinking about asking for a transfer."

Natasha maintained her hug, but looked up at him. Her face was grim. "But not you?"

"I can't. I've got unfinished business."

"That message on the wall?"

"Yes. There needs to be a reply."

Jack saw the strain on Natasha's face, then she released her grip and walked away. *She's worried about what I'll do and the possible repercussions.* He stared after her. *I can't let him get away with this. Natasha, I'm sorry.*

Chapter Seven

An hour out of Vancouver, Corporal George Hobbs turned off the Trans-Canada Highway onto a road lead-ing to a cellphone tower near the top of Sumas Mountain. Constable Dan Philips, a new arrival to I-HIT, sat beside him. Following in another vehicle was an officer with the canine unit.

The location they were headed to was where Damien's cellphone had been answered by Pure E earlier in the day. Since then, the phone had been shut off and its current location was unknown.

As they approached the summit, Philips pointed to a road sign. "Isn't that the name of the member who called you?"

Hobbs glanced at the sign. *Taggart Road. Is this another message for Jack?* "Yeah, same name."

"What do you make of it?"

"I don't know. Maybe it's a coincidence … or maybe it isn't."

"Hope this isn't a wild goose chase," Philips said, sounding disgruntled.

"You heard about the message someone left for Taggart at that triple murder this morning?"

Philips wrinkled his nose. "Yeah, I heard."

"Then I think we should take it seriously."

"How well do you know this Taggart fellow? If it's as serious as he said, you'd think he'd tag along."

"He was called in to meet with the brass. From what I've heard, the guy has a good rep for clearing cases. Connie Crane has worked with him on and off."

"But you've never worked with him?"

"No." Hobbs was quiet for a moment. "Rumours are that a lot of the suspects he identifies never live long enough to go to court."

Philips looked sharply at Hobbs. "What're you saying?"

Hobbs shrugged. "I don't know. Probably shouldn't have said that. Taggart works undercover. A lot of real badasses have tried to kill him over the years. Most of 'em end up dead. It's always justified, though." *At least on paper.*

"I heard he and Connie arrested a murder suspect in Victoria last night. The scoop is the suspect pulled a gun and was going to shoot Taggart. Connie was hiding behind the guy and yelled for him to drop it. I guess he didn't and she was about to double-tap two in his back when Taggart tackled him and saved the guy's life."

"Yeah, I heard that, too," Hobbs said.

"Goes to show you shouldn't listen to rumours."

"You're right." Hobbs gestured ahead. "End of the road. We're here," he said, coming to a stop.

For a moment, both men gazed up at the cellphone tower, which loomed above the trees. "So now what?" Philips asked.

Hobbs glanced at his watch. "It's twenty to five. Gonna be dark soon. Especially in the woods. We'll let the dog handler do his thing."

"If there's a body in there the mutt should find it," Philips said.

"Taggart says we got a body ... and I tend to believe him. The big question is where."

Two hours passed and it was dark when the dog handler called off his search. "No bodies today, gentlemen," he reported. "Picked up some scent — people have been up here recently, but we didn't find anything."

"I appreciate the effort." Hobbs glanced at the German shepherd and added, "From both of you."

His phone rang and he answered it. Seconds later, he gave Philips a thumbs-up sign before jotting down an address in his notebook. Upon ending the call, he turned to Philips and said, "Damien's phone has been reactivated. We've got an address."

"Meaning Damien is still alive?" Philips asked.

"Or someone found it ... or some other biker's got it." Hobbs punched a number into his phone. "I'm calling Taggart. I'm told he knows these guys inside out."

Jack was about to push himself away from the supper table when his phone vibrated. "I-HIT," he said by way of explanation to Natasha, before answering.

"Jack, it's George Hobbs. I'm calling about that cellphone you sent us out on."

"Any luck?"

"Maybe. The call you made at noon to Damien took us to up Sumas Mountain to a cellphone tower."

"Did you find anything? Being that close to a cellphone tower makes it hard to triangulate and pinpoint the exact spot."

"We had the canine unit take a look, but came up negative. Incidentally the road leading into the tower is called Taggart Road … if that means anything."

Pure E, you bastard! Enough already. "It wouldn't be the first message I received today," he said tersely.

"I've some interesting news, though," Hobbs said. "A couple of minutes ago the phone was turned on."

"Bet they tossed it and someone found it," Jack replied.

"Sort of what I was thinking, but I've got an address and I'm wondering if you know who lives there. If it's Damien who's got the phone, all this is for nothing. If he's dead, then I want to know who has his phone and how they got it."

"I've got a list of addresses in my notebook — hang on a sec." Jack pulled his notebook from his hip pocket. As he did, he glanced at his two sons. Ten-year-old Mike was clearing dishes from the table. His brother, Steve, a year younger, rudely shoved his empty plate toward Mike for him to take away. Jack smiled to himself. Next month it was Steve's turn to do dishes, and he knew Mike would get even. "Okay, what's the address?"

When Hobbs spoke, Jack didn't need to check his notebook. The terror he felt was intense.

"Any idea who lives there?" Hobbs asked.

Jack turned to Natasha. "Take the boys and go down to the basement!" he yelled. "Don't turn the lights on and keep away from the windows!"

Natasha's face was white with fear, but she knew this was not the time for questions. "Mike, Steve, let's go!" she commanded.

Both Mike and Steve hurried down the basement steps. Natasha gave one quick look at Jack over her shoulder, then followed them down.

"What's going on?" Hobbs asked.

"The address you gave is mine," Jack said.

"What? How'd you end up with the cellphone?"

"Good question."

"Maybe you should call the number and listen for it to ring."

"Cellphones can be used to detonate bombs," Jack said abruptly while running to his bedroom to retrieve his Smith & Wesson 9mm pistol.

"Oh, Christ!"

"Stay on the line. I'm going to take a look around. There was a van on the street when I came home. Hadn't seen it before."

"Can you describe it?"

"It was white with a sign on the door saying *Abe's Furnace Repair*." Jack grabbed his pistol and peered out a window. "It's gone. I'm going to take a look outside."

"Maybe you should call the bomb squad," Hobbs suggested.

"Got my family in the basement. I want to make sure there isn't a package in a window well or something. If you hear a blast, call 9-1-1 for me."

"Christ," Hobbs said again.

Jack grabbed a flashlight, went into his garage, and slipped out the side door. A quick search around the basement foundation didn't turn up anything. It was when he circled the house and arrived at the front door that he noticed the lid on the mailbox was up. He cautiously approached and looked inside. The cellphone was there. At first he felt relief that it wasn't attached to a bomb — then anger set in and he grabbed it. "You fucking bastard!"

"Me?" Hobbs said.

"No, Purvis Evans. I've got the phone. It was left in my mailbox. There's no bomb."

"What a relief. I was shitting bricks here. Do you … want us to come over?" Hobbs asked.

"No, I'm sure whoever left it is gone — so's the van. I'll bring it in tomorrow. I better get back to my family. They'll be scared."

"Can't blame them. So was I."

On ending the call, Jack entered his house. "False alarm!" he yelled. "Everything's okay. You can come up."

As his family headed back up the stairs, Jack examined Damien's phone. *Hey … it's not even password encrypted.* Then he saw three pictures: Natasha gardening, Mike and Steve arriving home from school, and him embracing Natasha. *Pure E, you've just made the biggest mistake of your life.*

"What's going on?" Natasha's face was sombre as she returned to the kitchen, followed by Mike and Steve.

Jack took Natasha into the living room, leaving the boys in the kitchen, and told her what had transpired and showed her the pictures. He expected her to be scared. She wasn't. "I'm fed up with this bullshit," she said, jabbing a finger in his chest. "You deal with it and you deal with it now!"

Jack's voice was deadly serious. "You know I will. Pure E is only doing this to scare us, but believe me, I'll take care of it." He glanced toward the kitchen and then his gaze met Natasha's. "I think I should let them know what happened."

Natasha, her demeanor calm now, nodded.

"We need to talk," Jack said as he and Natasha returned to the kitchen and sat down.

"Do you and Mom need privacy?" Mike asked.

His question sounded so mature. Normally Jack might've smiled to himself, but the situation was too serious. "No, it's better if you and Steve know what happened so you don't start imagining things or worrying."

"So we don't need to be afraid?" Steve asked, sitting down.

"No. What happened was that I asked people I work with to help look for a phone that belonged to an informant of mine."

"How did he lose it?" Mike asked.

"I believe my informant was murdered this morning," Jack replied. "He was also a bad guy."

"Did other bad guys find out he was your informant?" Steve asked.

Jack nodded. "His wife was angry with him and told the other bad guys."

"So she's a bad guy, too," Steve said.

"Yes, she certainly is," Jack replied.

"And the phone showed up here," Natasha said matter-of-factly.

"Yes." Jack nodded. "Someone left it in our mailbox."

"You think it was bad guys who put it there?" Mike asked.

"Bad guys did put it there."

"Because they were too afraid to knock on the door and give it to you?" Steve questioned.

"Partly," Jack replied. "They also took pictures of us all."

"Can we see?" both boys said at once.

Jack showed them the photos and saw the concerned looks on their faces. Natasha stared back at him and her face was very still. He looked at her. "I promise, I'll deal with it," he said quietly.

"There was a van on the street when we came home," Mike offered. "I never saw it before."

"I saw it, too," Jack replied.

"Why'd they take our pictures?" Steve asked.

"They want to scare Dad so he won't try to put them in jail," Mike stated.

"Exactly," Jack replied.

"Are you scared, Dad?" Steve asked.

"If they really wanted to hurt us, they wouldn't have done what they did."

"So you're not scared?" Steve persisted.

"No, I'm not scared. I'm angry."

Mike looked at his brother. "They're in a lot of trouble," he said seriously.

You got that right.

Chapter Eight

It was 7:30 a.m. when Jack picked Laura up in front of her house. As she fastened her seat belt she said, "Amazing what twelve hours of sleep can do for a person."

"Glad you're feeling better." Jack pulled away from the curb. "Have you given more thought about asking for a transfer?"

"Wow, you don't waste any time."

"Sorry ... good morning. Are you putting in for a transfer?"

Laura hesitated, then said, "Jack, I'm sorry."

Shit. I'm going to miss you something awful. "Don't be sorry. You have to do what's right for you. Besides, we'll always be friends." He tried to give her a reassuring smile but realized she knew how he felt.

"'Friends' isn't the right word. You're like family to me, but this thing with Pure E leaving that message on the wall ... I think I should stay until —"

"Don't worry about it," Jack said, trying to sound casual. "Like I said yesterday, there's always something."

"I know, but how about I stay until January? That's three months away. By then I'll have a pretty good idea about how you plan on getting Pure E."

Jack gave her a sideways glance. "You thinking you'll be able to keep me out of trouble?"

"Someone has to."

"You sure? I don't mind if you want to leave before then."

"I'm sure. Besides, I'm really embarrassed about the meltdown yesterday. It's not how I want you to remember me. Three months might give me time to redeem myself."

"You don't need to redeem yourself. Not after all you and I've been through. There'd be something wrong with us if we didn't have the occasional meltdown." He paused, then went on, "In our line of work there comes a time when you need to extricate yourself from the stress and be smart enough to realize it. It takes more than hiding out in the women's washroom and a night's sleep to fix that. I think a transfer is the right decision."

"And you?"

"Actually, hiding out in the women's washroom seems to work for me."

"Funny man." Laura paused, then said, "Look at me a sec." Jack glanced at her. "What?"

"You look worse than you did when you dropped me off yesterday."

"It was a long night," Jack replied. "I doubt I got more than a few hours' sleep."

"You upset because of me?"

"No, that wasn't it."

"Oh ... you told Natasha about the farmhouse. I bet she was upset."

Jack shook his head. "I better update you on what happened after I dropped you off yesterday. It's one of those good news, bad news things. The good news is I spoke with John Adams. One of the file boxes he took pertains to Lance Morgan and Whiskey Jake. I'll know more details within a week or so."

"Fantastic! That's great news. You turned Lance once before — think you can do it again?"

"Hope so. If there are enough details to link him with money laundering, we could threaten him with extradition. He'd serve big time in the States."

Laura's voice became grave. "What's the bad news?"

"Pure E thinks he has a sense of humour ... other than what he showed at the farmhouse."

Laura's voice became edgy. "How? What's going on?"

"I-HIT called me at suppertime, telling me that Damien's phone had been turned back on. They got an address to where it was."

"Where? Did you go out? You should've called me."

"No, I stayed home. It was my address. Someone dropped the phone in my mailbox."

"Jack!" Laura was obviously shocked.

"There were photos on it. You can see for yourself." He dug the phone out of his pocket and passed it to her.

Laura flipped through the photos. "Oh, man. Jack ... your kids ... you and Natasha."

"Like I said, Pure E has a real sense of humour. Natasha isn't amused, though."

"She must be terrified," Laura replied.

"Not terrified — angry. Told me she was fed up with the bullshit." Jack paused, then added, "I said I'd deal with it."

Laura was quiet for a moment. When she spoke, her voice sounded grave. "How, exactly, do you plan to on doing that?"

"Don't worry. I can't step outside the law and make it personal. There'd be retaliation. That being said, we need to send a message. What I want to do is submit a plan to have Drug Section, Combined Forces Special Enforcement Unit, Integrated Proceeds of Crime, and any other relevant section to focus their attention on Satans Wrath. Traffic Enforcement, as well. I don't want these guys to be able to move without being hassled. Show the assholes what their new leader has brought down on them. Given what happened, I'm sure the brass will approve it."

Laura looked at the pictures again.

"They weren't emailed to anyone," Jack noted. "Bet they used their own phones and sent copies to Pure E, though."

Laura scowled. "We can't let him get away with this."

"I won't."

"*We* won't," Laura said forcefully. "I told you, I'm with you on this. Forget the three months. If it takes longer, so be it."

Jack felt the lump in his throat. "We'll see. If you change your mind and want to go, I'll be okay. To be honest, I don't know how you held on this long."

Laura chuckled. "Maybe because I'm as pigheaded as you are."

"I've no idea how long it'll take."

Laura cast him a sideways glance. "With the home visit you got yesterday, I don't see you letting Pure E get away with it for long."

***

As soon as Jack and Laura arrived at work, they met with Rose in her office and Jack told her about finding Damien's cellphone in his mailbox.

Rose's jaw slackened, then concern crossed her face.

She's worried for my safety. "Don't worry. As my ten-year-old-son figured out, Pure E was just trying to scare us."

"*Scare* you!" Rose exclaimed. Her face hardened. "Pure E doesn't know you, but I do. What are you intending to —"

Christ! She's concerned for his *safety!* The rage Jack felt was instant. "What the hell?"

Rose stared at him.

"You're worried about his safety?" he said.

"And —"

"My family is the victim here! Yes, I'm pissed off, but I don't plan on running off half-cocked."

"I am worried about you and your family. That worry includes how you'll respond."

Jack forced himself to calm down. "If anything," he said, "my anger makes me more focused on the best way to handle it."

"Which is?"

"We're meeting Isaac and Mortimer this morning. I want your support, Rose, to submit an operational plan to make Satans Wrath a priority in this province. Drug Section, CFSEU, Integrated Proceeds of Crime ... everyone needs to get involved. Right down to the members handing out traffic tickets. We have to send the bikers our own message."

"Of course you'll have my support for that," Rose said. "There are what, about 115 Satans Wrath members in the province?"

Laura spoke up. "I think 127, if you include prospects."

"Okay … and as a rule of thumb, for every member, there are about ten hard-core criminals affiliated with them," Rose noted. "So altogether you're talking about 1,270 professional criminals."

"Yes. I realize we are badly outnumbered, but —"

"'Outnumbered' is an understatement," Rose said. "Then there's the puppet clubs who work for them, such as the Gypsy Devils. Also we're only talking about the army they have in this province. These guys cross borders and intermingle on a daily basis."

"I know, but we can't give up. Something needs to be done."

"I totally agree, but if extra manpower is allotted, they'll be looking to you to provide them with specific targets. Have you given any thought to that?"

"Only briefly," Jack admitted. "I've got one source who might come around."

"Weenie Wagger."

"Yes."

"Who you told me is stressed out, drinking, and using drugs."

"I've tried the drinking," Laura said dryly. "Doesn't work." She must have seen the sour look on Jack's face, because she elbowed him in the ribs. "Hey, only teasing. I'd never turn down one of your famous olive soups."

Jack eyed Laura briefly. Her humour seemed forced. *She's trying to show me that she's not stressed out and that it's game on as usual.* He gave her a smile, then turned back to Rose. "He's more than paid his debt, but I might be able to turn him around."

"Money?"

"No, I think he'll be looking for a friend. Offering money would negate that. The problem is, even if he does cooperate, he's only a peon. He's not even allowed to speak to Pure E or chapter presidents unless they expressly okay it."

"Are there any other avenues of investigation available?"

"Possibly. I'm expecting to receive some intel from down south that might help."

"You're talking about the connection Satans Wrath has with the West 12th Street Gang in Texas and the money-laundering scheme Damien had going in Mexico?"

"Yes."

"I read a preliminary report that International Proceeds of Crime did from their raids last week. Except for Damien, none of the other bad guys in the files they seized were Canadian. I don't think there's anything there that could help us."

"I-POC doesn't know everything," Jack replied quietly.

"Oh?" Rose raised an eyebrow. "You holding something back from me?"

Jack waited a beat. "I had the distinct impression when Mortimer spoke to us yesterday that protecting informants wasn't his priority. He'd rather get his name in the newspaper."

Rose frowned. "That's Mortimer. You're talking to me."

"I know, but someone stuck their neck out to get some information for me. The info is in Spanish and needs to be translated. It might take a week or two. Once we get it, I'm optimistic it'll give us the leverage we need to turn a high-valued source."

"This person who stuck their neck out — how far out?"

"Far enough to be fired if found out."

"I see. How much time do you need to get an operational plan together in the meantime to get the ball rolling in the event this new source doesn't pan out?"

Thank you for not digging deeper. "Two or three weeks."

"Two or three weeks?" Rose sounded dismayed.

"We definitely need to target the prospects and the three-three."

"The three-three is obvious. I presume you said 'the prospects' because they're responsible for taking most of the risks?"

"Yes. We'll need to verify where everyone lives before submitting any operational plan. These guys move around a lot. Two or three weeks isn't long to do all that."

"It's said that vengeance is a dish best served cold," Laura added.

Rose peered at Laura over the top of her glasses. "Not you, too," she muttered. She looked at Jack. "I was actually questioning if two or three weeks is long enough to put an op plan together. I don't want you to rush into this. We need to be thorough."

"We'll have to work night and day, but it'll be thorough," Jack said adamantly. "After that, if we do get a new informant, we'll have to adjust the op plan depending on what we learn. Money laundering, drug dealing, prostitution, credit card rip-offs … it's all handled by different factions within the club."

Rose nodded. "Even if you get this new source, it could still take a long time to nail Pure E."

Jack glanced at Laura. "We know, but we're optimistic.

The potential source is a chapter president and is able to consult with Pure E directly."

"Chapter president?" Rose pursed her lips. "Sounds good."

"That being said, we may not be able to act on a lot of things he'll tell us for fear of putting him in jeopardy," Jack cautioned.

Rose looked reflective, then said, "I came away from yesterday's meeting with the same sense of foreboding over Mortimer's lack of concern about informant safety. I understand your worry."

"If we get this new source, and I think we will, protecting him will be my top priority."

"I'm sure you'll come up with some way to protect him," Rose said.

Like pointing a finger at someone else? Another sacrificial lamb like Neal Barlow? That makes me sick.

"Sorry, I didn't mean what you thought I meant," Rose hastened to say, apparently reading Jack's expression. "I'm sure you'll think of other ways."

Jack decided to change the subject. "So we're set for the meeting? We have your backing?"

"Not quite. You never mentioned I-HIT in the equation," Rose said.

"They're already involved, what with the four murders yesterday."

"I realize that … so I think they have enough work. Don't you agree?"

"We're dealing with Pure E. I'm sure more bodies will surface sooner or later."

"Bodies attributed to Pure E aren't what I meant," she said, staring at Jack.

Chapter Nine

When Jack and Laura returned to their office, Jack took out a laptop to watch a video.

"What is it?" Laura asked, coming around to look over his shoulder.

"A copy of the video they took when they caught Weenie Wagger exposing himself that day in the parkade in Surrey."

Laura spun on her heel and returned to her desk. "I know his face. I don't need to see the rest of his anatomy."

Jack stared silently at the video, then shut it off.

"Didn't know some guy exposing himself would be your type of show," she commented.

Jack grimaced. "Initially I got a copy of the video thinking I might need it to prod Weenie Wagger along. Considering everything he's done for us, I think he's repaid society for his crime."

"You cutting him loose?"

"Yes, but I think there's a good chance he'll return. At the moment he may still think of Satans Wrath as family, but it'll bother him that he informed."

"So you'll provide a sympathetic shoulder?"

"Maybe. He's kind of pathetic, when you think about it. I'll give him a call next week and cut him loose. That'll give a few more days to see if he hears anything about the visit to my house."

Laura nodded in agreement.

"Okay, let's find out everything we can about the three-three first," Jack said. "Where they live, where they eat … everything. They act on Pure E's orders. It could be his Achilles heel."

Laura glanced at her watch. "We meet the brass in half an hour."

For the first time he noticed tiny worry lines on Laura's face. *Christ, I'm an asshole for what I've put her through.*

"We've got a little time," Laura said. "Shall we start pulling files and selecting targets?"

"Naw, plenty of time for that later. Let's grab a coffee instead."

Jack, Laura, and Rose arrived at the conference room and saw that I-HIT was represented by Inspector Dyck, Staff Sergeant Randy Hundt, and Corporal George Hobbs. Isaac and Mortimer weren't there yet.

While waiting for them, Jack made eye contact with Randy, who was Connie Crane's boss. "Where's Connie?" he asked.

"She called me to request the day off," Randy said. "She's, uh, a little shaken from yesterday. I told her to book off sick." He paused, then added, "I'll check in with her on the weekend."

Jack nodded. *You take care of your people, something I should've been doing, too.*

Upon Isaac and Mortimer's arrival, Hobbs related how he'd traced Damien's cellphone to the top of Sumas Mountain and once there, discovered it had been turned back on. "I obtained an address for its new location and called Corporal Taggart to see if he could associate the address with any Satans Wrath members." Hobbs turned to Jack. "Maybe you should take it from here."

"The address obtained was mine," Jack said. "Someone dropped it in my mailbox. There were pictures on it of my children coming home from school, my wife doing yard-work, then both my wife and I when I arrived home."

"You allowed yourself to be followed home?" Mortimer asked in apparent disbelief.

"My children arrived home from school an hour before I did. The bikers were already there, as is evident by the pictures that were taken. I spotted a van I didn't recognize near my house when I came home and I think it was involved. These guys have sources. They don't need to tail us to find out where we live."

"And you didn't think to phone the police about the van?" Mortimer asked.

The police? Here we go again. Jack felt Rose tap his leg with her shoe. *Don't worry, I won't remind him who we are.* He cleared his throat. "At the time I didn't pay it much attention — not until I found the phone. By then, the van was gone."

The concern was evident on Isaac's face. "This is a threat against you and your family," he stated. "What can I do to help?"

"Obviously it was only meant to scare me," Jack said. "Pure E is holding me accountable for the boatload of cocaine seized in France. Perhaps he thinks intimidation will stop us from working on him. What I'd like is to target Satans Wrath in a joint operation with all the relevant units."

"So that's Drug Section, Integrated Proceeds of Crime, Combined Forces Special Enforcement Unit ..." Isaac paused. "You also should have Special O to conduct surveillance."

Special O was a unit that did surveillance to assist with high-profile cases and were experts in their field. Jack was more than pleased. "Yes, sir. They'd be a huge help."

"You're looking at tying up about thirty members," Mortimer noted.

"If we're going to catch Pure E, that would be the minimum it'd take to get things going," Jack said.

"How long would this take?" Mortimer asked.

"I don't know, sir," Jack replied. "I'm thinking about a year, but with investigations like this, it's hard to predict."

"A year!" Mortimer exclaimed.

Jack sighed. "Perhaps we'll get lucky. Maybe turn a high-level informant or something to speed things up. Even then, it will take time to get enough solid evidence to convict Pure E. He's well-insulated."

Isaac looked at Mortimer. "Satans Wrath and their cronies add up to well over a thousand criminals in this province alone. If we can cause them serious damage and bring their top man to justice with only thirty officers, I'd say it was a bargain." He turned to Jack. "Purvis Evans — or Pure E, as I think I'll refer to him — came into his position as a result of a national election by the club, did he not?"

"Yes, sir," Jack replied.

"Then I think our response should be nationwide, as well. They threatened not only you and your family, but our whole justice system. Once your operational plan is submitted, I think Ottawa should be pressed to unite task forces across the country."

Yes! Jack exchanged a broad smile with Laura. *Peaks and valleys. We're on the mountaintop.*

Isaac continued emphatically, "With manpower redirected to terrorism and street gangs shooting each other up, entrenched organized crime families have been given free rein. It has to stop. We need to send a clear message to Satans Wrath that we will not tolerate acts of intimidation."

"There isn't the manpower," Mortimer objected. "The news media has been focusing on the shootings from the street gangs. Obviously that's who we need to go after."

"You're right, those investigations are important, but I don't think we should take our cues from the news media," Isaac said icily. "As far as a shortage of manpower goes, once we start submitting large claims for overtime, Ottawa will realize it'll be more cost-effective to send us more people. If they don't, we'll pull in people from around the province to form a task force."

Mortimer frowned. "I've a serious concern. There's no real evidence that Damien Zabat is dead. His phone showing up in Corporal Taggart's mailbox may simply be a ploy to have us believe that. This whole thing may not be intended to intimidate at all. It's only conjecture." He paused, then added, "We'd look pretty silly in the eyes of Ottawa submitting an operational plan based on a supposition that Satans Wrath murdered Damien. How'd we look if it turned out he was still alive?"

"To start with, the phone placed in the corporal's mailbox last night is not conjecture," Isaac stated. "It's —"

Mortimer interrupted him. "I understand that Corporal Taggart and perhaps his family may feel uncomfortable about what happened, but there's no proof that it was an act of intimidation." Mortimer looked at Jack. "Taking pictures of your family may simply have been a joke, albeit not a good one."

You asshole. Jack felt Rose's tap on his shin again. *It's okay, Rose, I won't take the bait.* "That's an interesting theory," he responded. "I must admit, I hadn't thought of it as a joke."

"I don't consider it a joke." Isaac's words were harsh and he glared at Mortimer. "I also don't consider the triple murder in the farmhouse yesterday a joke. Or the message left on the wall there for Corporal Taggart."

"Well, of course … that," Mortimer conceded. "Yes, something should be done."

"I'd suggest we get things going in this province first," Isaac said, "but with the international aspects of this organization, I'm sure the investigation will spread quickly to other provinces and other countries." He looked at Jack. "How long will it take you to prepare an operational plan to get things started?"

"Two to three weeks," Jack replied. "Specific targets will need to be identified and located."

"Two to three weeks," Isaac repeated. "I'll be retired by then." He cast a wary glance at Mortimer.

Mortimer hesitated, then nodded. "I agree they need to be looked at. Once I receive the plan, I'll give it the urgency it deserves."

"Okay, then," Isaac said, refocusing on Jack. "How concerned are you? I see no problem with the force paying for you to have a home security system installed."

"Do you really think that's necessary?" Mortimer interjected. "I'd hate to set a precedent that every time a member feels uncomfortable he receives a free alarm system."

"I already have an alarm system," Jack said, looking at Isaac, "but thank you for the thought."

Isaac stared quietly at Mortimer for a moment, then looked at Inspector Dyck. "Let's discuss Damien Zabat's disappearance and Corporal Taggart's … qualified opinion that he's been murdered."

"Unless proven otherwise," Dyck responded, "our office is treating it as a homicide investigation."

"Good," Isaac replied. "For a variety of reasons, including that Corporal Taggart's informant was present during the murder of Neal, Robert, and Roxanne Barlow, he should not be directly involved in the investigation. That being said, I see no reason why Corporal Taggart couldn't assist you with your investigation into Damien Zabat."

"I agree," Dyck replied. "As it would appear that Vicki Zabat is the one who set her husband up, I'm considering asking Corporal Taggart and Constable Secord to talk to her and see if they can get her to make an admission. Something we can get on wire."

Isaac looked at Jack and Laura. "You know her. What do you think?"

"We can try," Jack said, "but I'm not optimistic. She's been around a long time and knows the game."

"Give it your best shot." Isaac glanced at Dyck. "I think we can adjourn this meeting as far as Assistant

Commissioner Mortimer and I are concerned, but feel free to use this room to discuss strategy with everyone else in regards to how or when Vicki Zabat should be approached."

"Yes, sir," Dyck replied.

Isaac and Mortimer got up to leave the room, but at the doorway, Isaac looked back. "Corporal Taggart, please step out for a moment. I'd like to have a word with you concerning your attitude at yesterday's meeting."

Shit. I was hoping he'd forget about that. I already apologized.

When Jack met Isaac and Mortimer in the hallway, Isaac looked at Jack and said, "Your outburst yesterday was uncharacteristic. I appreciate that you were under extreme stress and had gone days with little sleep."

"Sir, I'm still embarrassed by my conduct yesterday."

"Today you appear to be completely in control of your emotions. Considering the threat made on you and your family last night, I'm sure that's not easy."

Crap, hope you're not thinking of hiding me out among a herd of reindeer. "I believe it was simply an ill-conceived attempt at intimidation," Jack replied. He glanced at Mortimer who looked at him stone-faced. "At this time I see no reason for any extreme measures to be taken."

"Extreme measures?" Isaac gave Jack a hard look.

"Such as a transfer. I believe the best response is to go after the club from all angles."

"I see. Good … I agree." Isaac paused. "You've had a remarkable career so far and have overcome much adversity. I want you to know that you've earned my respect over the years."

"Thank you, sir."

"I leave feeling confident that you're completely capable of handling any obstacles or problems you will no doubt encounter in the future."

Jack saw Isaac's glance flick toward Mortimer as he spoke. *Did you give me permission to "handle" this asshole, or are you warning me to be careful?*

Isaac extended his hand and Jack shook it. Looking into Isaac's eyes, Jack thought he discovered the answer. *Both.*

Chapter Ten

Jack caught Rose's curious look as he returned to the boardroom. "Assistant Commissioner Isaac appreciates the stress I feel as a result of the threat made on my family," he said, "and has forgiven me for the insolent remark I made to Assistant Commissioner Mortimer yesterday."

"Insolent?" Dyck questioned.

"Our new assistant commissioner said we shouldn't work on people who carry guns and told me the police should be called to handle those individuals. He also suggested Damien's disappearance was a ruse to stay out of jail. I became sarcastic."

Dyck looked stunned, then said, "I can assure you that there's no doubt in my mind that Damien's been murdered. They'd never allow him to get away with squealing about a tonne of cocaine."

"I agree," Hobbs said, "but murdered by who? And where's the body?"

"It was likely done by their hit team, which they call the three-three," Jack replied. "I'll give you file copies so you don't need to write it down, but in a nutshell, in this province the three-three comprises four men. One by the name of Pasquale Bazzoli, who is a butcher by trade, but recently moved to Kelowna and isn't working at anything legit. He has a history from when he was a kid for torturing and killing neighbourhood cats and dogs. He's long since graduated from people's pets."

"I often go to Kelowna to visit friends," Randy noted. "Remind me not to buy any meat from him if he opens a shop there," he added dryly.

Jack grinned. "The other three live in the lower mainland. Floyd Hackman works in construction and operates heavy machinery — like diggers. He has numerous convictions for assault, including bodily harm. Criminal psych reports from before he joined the club note he talked about what a thrill it would be to kill someone. When Desert Storm came along, he spent five years with the U.S. Marines. Following that, he spent two years as a prospect with Satans Wrath, then got his full patch about four years ago."

"Join the U.S. Marine Corps," Laura said. "Travel the world, meet interesting people ... and kill them."

Laura, that doesn't sound like you, putting on a facade to hide your stress. You really do need a break. Jack cleared his throat. "Then there's Victor Trapp. He's into martial arts and has worked off and on as a bouncer at various bars. The fourth is Nick Crowe, who drives a tow truck."

"Drives a tow truck," Hobbs noted. "At least that doesn't seem bad."

"I should mention that Crowe has a brother who works for a demolition company," Jack added. "I'm certain that Nick knows his way around explosives, too."

Hobbs grimaced. "You got addresses for them all?"

"I do on Bazzoli and Crowe. The other two are always moving. Half the time living with strippers or hookers. Hackman belongs to the Westside chapter and the other three belong to the Eastside. The third Thursday of every month is church night for Satans Wrath. If you do surveillance of their clubhouses then, you might be able to follow these guys to their addresses, providing you're lucky enough to see what vehicles they're in."

"Church night?" Hobbs looked bemused.

"Party night. Nothing illegal is discussed inside the clubhouse. They're too bug-conscious. Mostly they'd discuss upcoming rides, paying club dues, and other general stuff that a legitimate club might talk about. These guys are always surveillance-conscious. The three-three won't even say hi to you unless it's approved by their lawyer."

"Which is the criminal lawyer by the name of Basil Westmount," Dyck said.

"'Criminal' being the operative word," Rose said.

"What about Abe's Furnace Repair?" Hobbs asked. "Isn't that what you said was on the door of the van outside your house yesterday?"

"Likely a magnetic stick-on that's easy to take off," Jack said. "To my knowledge, that business doesn't exist." He glanced at Hobbs. "Did you pull phone tolls off Damien's number?"

"I did, but the phone was only put in service last Friday."

"When we raided his house and turned him," Jack said. "That figures. He wouldn't want to risk me pulling intel off any other phone he used. It's not uncommon for guys in his position to have more than one phone. One for idle talk and then disposable ones that few people would know the number to."

"There were only three numbers that he called in the week on that phone. One was yours, one was to Vicki's old number — which was terminated three days ago — and then there was a third number we haven't identified. Vicki's old phone also indicated calls to that same third number."

"Likely Buck's regular phone," Jack said.

"Sort of what I figured," Hobbs replied. "There were two calls placed yesterday morning from it. Both were tri-angulated to Damien's house. The first one, at 10:00 a.m., was to a new number. The second call was right after to Damien's number. Both calls were brief."

"I bet the first call was to Vicki's new number," Jack said.

"That's my guess. I was hoping I'd see her calling Basil Westmount's number, but she didn't make any calls after that."

"Vicki's too smart for that," Jack said. "She would've used another disposable phone that nobody knew she had."

"What's interesting is that *Buck* called Damien right after," Hobbs said. "Why make two calls? Couldn't he have had Vicki pass her phone to Damien? Seems odd to me."

"Maybe Buck was checking to see if they were both home," Jack suggested. "Vicki might've said she was out when she wasn't. She told me she visited her dad for lunch every day at his hospice. Maybe that's what Buck expected.

Then for him to call Damien right after …" He stopped talking as he pondered the possibilities.

"You think Buck helped them grab Damien when he thought the coast was clear?" Dyck questioned.

"I don't know," Jack replied. "Maybe he didn't know what was going on. He might still not."

"The thing is, if they took Damien and had him at the top of Sumas Mountain by noon, he'd have had to be out of the house soon after the calls were made," Hobbs pointed out.

"You need to consider that Buck has been brainwashed, told all his life that the club comes first," Jack said. "With Damien being national president, I'm sure the kid idolized him. If he found out that his father was an informant … I don't know what he'd have done."

"Damien only became your informant to save Buck and Vicki from going to jail," Randy inserted. "You'd think Buck would realize that."

Jack nodded. "I'm also curious that the phone wasn't password-protected when it was put in my mailbox. I'm inclined to think Damien would've done so and I'm thinking that only Buck or Vicki might've known what his password was."

A silence fell over the room for several moments as everyone doubtless pondered whether Buck could have set up his own father. At last Randy cleared his throat and said, "You know these guys better than we do, Jack. What do you propose we do first?"

"Well, I believe the three-three is the weakest link," he replied. "They take their orders either from Pure E or through chapter presidents who have spoken with Pure E.

Either way, the investigation will be long, require lots of investigators, and probably some luck. It may take a few times to find out where they dispose of their bodies."

"Times?" Dyck repeated. "Are you proposing we let them get away with murdering someone simply to find out how they dispose of the bodies?"

"Sometimes it's difficult to predict a murder," Jack said. "There may not be time to save someone. If you do save them, it may mean there's no evidence to charge anyone. If we get Pure E on a wire giving the order first, we could charge them with conspiracy, but I'm not optimistic that we'll be able to do that immediately. I think the odds are more likely that some murders will take place during our investigation before we catch Pure E giving any orders."

Dyck's face darkened. "In other words, it'll lead into what you on the intelligence unit refer to as 'a delicate matter.'"

"Yes, or as Isaac later referred to it, 'an *in*delicate matter,'" Jack said.

Dyck sighed. "No doubt tough decisions will have to be made. We'll deal with them when they arise." He looked at Jack. "I know you're not optimistic about approaching Vicki, but I still think it's worth a shot. We need solid evidence to link her. Without that we're screwed."

"Laura and I will try," Jack said, "but if she knows we're coming, she'll be calling a lawyer. We need to catch her by surprise. Maybe when she leaves the house or goes shopping. She'll be expecting us, so let's give her time to relax, then approach her when she's not expecting it."

"Makes sense," Dyck replied. "I'd also like to see if she reports Damien missing. If she does, fine, but if she doesn't, how about approaching her a week from Monday?"

"Works for me." Jack nodded. "Come to think of it, Laura and I'll find out which hospice her father is in and approach her there."

As everyone stood to leave, Hobbs said, "This is going to be one tough case to solve."

"I think it's already solved," Laura stated. Her eyes met Jack's. "It's bringing the culprits to justice that's the tricky part."

Taking pictures of my family. Believe me, justice will be served.

Chapter Eleven

Jack sat down at the dining-room table and Natasha raised a glass of Pinot Noir toward him. *"Budem zdorovy."*

Jack hadn't learned much Russian from his wife, but that was one phrase he knew. *Yes, let's stay healthy.* Their wineglasses chimed and he saw the candlelight glimmer in her eyes as she took a sip. *I'm so lucky to have married you. I love you so much.*

Years earlier it had been Natasha's idea to try to set Friday night aside as "date night." It was a shared moment each week that gave them time to unwind, reconnect with each other … and value their lives together.

Jack shared Natasha's smile when Mike and Steve quietly passed by on their way to the family room to watch television. Friday nights, both boys knew, was time for Mom and Dad to be alone.

"It's been quite a week," Natasha noted. "Did you happen to check for mail when you came home? I decided that should be your job from here on in."

Jack nodded. "That little surprise might turn out to be the biggest mistake Satans Wrath ever made."

"You think the task force will harm them that much?"

"If it goes right across country, it could. At least it might set them back a few years, which would cost them a lot of money when others stepped in to replace them."

"And the guy you call Pure E?"

"He's the number-one target."

Natasha looked silently at Jack.

"It's okay," Jack assured her. "Once it goes national ... and likely international, they'll be hit from all sides by dozens of investigators from numerous jurisdictions. Pure E will have a lot more on his mind than thinking about me."

"Good. So no worries?"

"No worries. I promised you I'd deal with it."

Jack grinned and looked at his plate. "This lasagna is delicious."

"You haven't tasted it yet."

"Nothing beats your lasagna. It's always delicious."

"Thanks, but you're still picking up the mail from now on."

Early Saturday afternoon Jack received his third work-related call of the day. The first call had been from two undercover operators in the Drug Section by the names of Sammy and Benny; they called together. The second was from a retired operative by the name of Bobby. Word of the threat against Jack's family was spreading and all three volunteered to do whatever Jack wanted in regard to Pure E.

Jack thanked them, but said that an operational plan was being prepared and he was optimistic that they would soon have a task force fully dedicated to the matter. The third call was different. It was from his informant Weenie Wagger, a.k.a. Mack Cockerill.

"There's somethin' I'm gonna tell you," Cockerill said, "then we're done. You and I are finished." His voice had a whine to it, revealing his stress.

"As far as I'm concerned, you fulfilled your end of the deal," Jack replied. "A deal is a deal. We're done."

Cockerill's sigh of relief was audible. "Good. Glad you agree."

"You still popping pills and drinking heavy?" Jack asked.

"I did after Thursday — but who wouldn't after seein' people get lit up like that?"

"I warned you before about poppin' pills. It'll attract suspicion from the club, let alone the obvious health risk."

"Health risk? Fuck, that's a good one. The health risk was workin' for you." He paused. "Don't worry, I won't be messin' my head up with that shit now that you and I are done."

"What were you going to tell me?" Jack asked. "Although now that we're done, don't feel obligated to tell me anything."

"I'll tell you. It ain't nothin' you won't find out about soon enough. Damien's split the country. Gonzo. Don't know where, but word is you guys'll never find him."

"Who told you?" Jack asked.

"Got it from the prez."

"Lance Morgan."

"Yeah, my prez. Westside. He popped in to see me unannounced yesterday. Think he wanted to see how I was doin' after … you know, the farmhouse."

"How *were* you doing?"

"I was sober. Too hungover from drinking all night Thursday."

"Drinking doesn't make it go away. You have to start thinking outside the bottle. Alcohol is a depressant."

"I'll be a lot happier now that you and I are done."

"Did you know someone dropped Damien's phone in my mailbox Friday? Had pictures of me and my wife and kids on it."

"What? Fuck, I didn't know. You shittin' me?"

"No."

"Well, I got nothin' to do with it."

"I'm surprised Lance didn't mention it," Jack said.

Cockerill paused a moment, then said, "Yeah, me, too. Guess he forgot."

Or knew it was a mistake and was embarrassed. "You and I need to meet face to face."

"What the fuck for? You said we're done!"

"Yes, but there's something I need to tell you. It won't take long. All you have to do is listen, then you can go on your merry way and never call me again."

"Can't you tell me over the phone?"

"No. Never trust phones."

Cockerill snickered. "Fuck … you sound like one of us. Yeah, okay. Where and when?"

Jack parked in an underground parkade and soon saw Cockerill plodding toward his car. Their eyes met and Cockerill got in beside him.

"Glad you're not waving your pecker around," Jack said glibly.

"You better destroy that video," Cockerill snarled, glaring at Jack.

"No worries," Jack replied.

"So what do you wanna say to me?"

"Two things. The first has to do with your future well-being."

"My future well-being? What the fuck? I thought you and I was finished!"

"We are," Jack assured him, "but there's something you need to know."

"Okay, what?"

"You're having trouble handling the stress. Mixing drugs and alcohol. I'm not trying to be your mother, but I've dealt with a lot of people in your position. You need to be careful."

"You had me come here for this?" Cockerill glowered. "Fuck, you already told me that."

"You're thinking because you and I are done the stress will go away."

"Yeah, it already has. Finally feel like I can breathe again."

"Only because you haven't had time to think."

"About what?"

"It was your info that pointed me to the grow-ops and to busting the weed shipment the Gypsy Devils delivered to Dallas."

"I know. So?"

"And it was your info that led me to video Buck beating that dealer to death."

"Yeah, yeah. What's your point?"

"My point is that you're not going to be looking at Satans Wrath the same anymore. You turned on them and it's going to eat away at you. I think you're going to continue drinking and popping pills."

Cockerill brooded for a moment as he stared out the windshield, then turned back to Jack. "So what the fuck do you care?"

"Yeah, I know. I'm a cop and you're some guy who gets his jollies by jumping out from between parked cars and waving his dick at people." Jack yawned as if Cockerill's indecent acts bored him and meant nothing, then said, "I probably shouldn't give a shit about what happens to you."

"Exactly. So why're you talkin' like this?"

Jack made a face. "The thing is, I don't think you're that bad a guy. You don't have any record for assault or violent crimes. By how you reacted after seeing the people murdered in the farmhouse, I knew you were upset."

"Upset? Fuck … it made me puke," Cockerill admitted.

"So all I'm sayin' is it would be better for you, as a person, to get out of the club. With Pure E running things, it won't only be the eyes of three victims you'll be remembering. Pure E is barely getting started. Are those the kind of memories you really want to collect?"

Cockerill turned away, possibly to hide his face.

"Start making friends with different people. Put all this behind you."

Cockerill folded his arms across his chest and kept silent.

"You've been straight with me," Jack said, "so I thought I'd be straight with you. The one thing about advice is it's free. What you do with it is entirely up to you."

"You said there were two things you wanted to say to me. What's the other? Gonna remind me to brush my teeth before bed?"

"It's about Damien. He didn't flee the country. He's dead."

"Dead?"

"He became my informant to keep Vicki and Buck from going to jail. It was Damien who told me about the boatload of coke in France."

"No way," Cockerill said in disbelief. "Vicki? What did you catch her with?"

"Last Friday when we searched Damien's house she shot me. If I hadn't been wearing my vest I'd be dead."

"Are you shittin' me?"

"No." Jack pulled up his shirt to expose a bruise directly over his heart.

Cockerill's jaw slackened. "I never heard nothin' about that. The search and takin' all his money, yeah, but Vicki tried to kill ya?"

"Damien made the deal shortly after," Jack said.

Cockerill appeared to digest this new information, then said, "And the club found out and is spreadin' the word that Damien took off, so nobody will know the top man ratted?"

Jack nodded. "Vicki let them know. She was pissed off that Damien wouldn't become an informant to save Buck at the beginning. She pretended to be a secretary for her own lawyer and called Basil Westmount and leaked what Damien did."

"Holy fuck … which means me givin' you information to catch Buck ended up in Damien gettin' whacked."

"Yup. So don't blame yourself for talking. Others have, as well, including Damien."

Cockerill stared out the passenger-side window for a moment, then turned back to Jack. "Are we done?"

"Yeah, take care of yourself, Mackie boy. I mean that."

Cockerill grunted, then got out.

Jack watched him walk away, then saw him pass a woman carrying shopping bags and give her the once-over, so he tapped his horn. When Cockerill looked his way, Jack gestured to his own eyes with two fingers, then pointed them at Cockerill. *I'll be watching you, asshole.*

Cockerill gave Jack the finger, then smiled.

Chapter Twelve

On Monday morning Laura gulped the last of her coffee and left the mug on a table in her foyer when Jack arrived to pick her up for work. She wasn't surprised when he told her about his meeting with Cockerill, but did feel a slight pang of disappointment. *Cutting him loose right when we're tasked with coming up with a viable operational plan that's time sensitive.*

Jack glanced at her. "Fair is fair. He's more than repaid his debt to us."

"Could you at least let me say what I'm thinking, rather than reading my mind?"

Jack gestured with his hand as if to ask, *What's the difference?*

She decided to let it go. "I'm not saying you shouldn't have cut him loose. All I'm saying is the timing stinks. It would've been nice to have his help tracking down addresses for the op plan."

"The guy is on the edge of losing it completely. If I'd told him he needed to give us more, he'd have refused. It also wouldn't be right. Besides, I doubt he knows where most of these guys live. You and I will have to find that out on our own."

"Still, it must be hard for Cockerill to look at the guys he was so close to, knowing he's responsible for a lot of what happened."

Jack braked for a red light. "Exactly. I did try to make him feel better."

"Hoping he might come back to you," Laura said.

"It would be nice, but in the meantime he needs a break." He turned in his seat to face her. "So do you."

Laura was pissed off. *You jerk. Quit sounding like this isn't bothering you, too.* "And you don't?" she retorted. "Bet Natasha and your boys wish you'd take a break, too."

Jack frowned. "I'm sorry. That didn't come out right. I'm just worried about you."

Probably not as much as I worry about you. And what troubles you'll get into.

"You're right, though," Jack continued. "My whole family could use a break, including me. Stevie had a nightmare Saturday night that bad guys were coming in through his bedroom window."

"Poor little guy." *This job is tough enough on me, but to have children … oh, man.*

"It hurts to know that your nine-year-old son is suffering because of what you do." The light changed to green and Jack accelerated. "I told both my boys that these particular bad guys would never hurt them, because of what I or some other operator would do to them."

"They believe you?"

"Yes, they should." His tone was deadly.

"You and I might know that," Laura said quietly, "but your kids are little."

"My kids have grown up with what I do. I've had a few contracts on my life over the years. Mostly by dope dealers. As one of them said, it wasn't personal, it was only to stop me from testifying." His tone turned sad. "I've always made sure my sons know that if they get up in the night, they're to call out to me so I don't shoot them by mistake."

"Oh, man," Laura lamented, this time aloud.

"Yeah, makes me sick when I think about it. They shouldn't have to go through that. Anyway, I assured them that these guys are different. They're more professional — at least I used to think they were. Mike asked what I'd do to them. I gave them a hint of how the torture would go. I think he felt sorry for them after that."

"Jack, they're little kids! What did you say to them?"

"They're smart. They know the game. What I said is too gross to repeat, but they both slept well last night."

Laura shook her head. "If I ever have kids, I don't want you telling them any bedtime stories."

Jack chuckled. "Enough of that talk. We'll push it hard for the next few weeks. Once the op plan is completed, it'll take time to get the task force together. We'll take a break then."

"It won't be any too soon. I'm looking at the task force coming in like the cavalry in an old western. I feel like the two of us are barely hanging on."

"I know." He glanced at her. "There's something else troubling you. What is it?"

Laura grimaced. "I'm worried about going up against Pure E. We could never do it alone."

"We won't be alone."

"I know, but with how Mortimer is, I hope he doesn't try to scale down the task force after a couple months. This is going to take time."

"We nailed Damien on our own," Jack reminded her.

"Yes, but it took ten years. Then we only got him for money laundering — his wife killed him. You want to leave Pure E out there that long?"

Jack stared straight ahead, but Laura saw his nostrils flare, like a wild animal checking the air. It was something that happened when he was particularly enraged — either when he was about to attack or formulating a plan. A lethal plan.

"What're you thinking?" she asked, fearing what his response might be.

Jack's words sent a chill up her spine. "Pure E isn't going to be out there for long. We'll get him one way or the other."

Jack parked in the stall at work, then stole another peek at Laura as they entered the building. *She hasn't spoken in twenty minutes. Bet she's upset. She's stressed out as it is and then I go and say a dumb —*

"What is it?" she asked. "Have I got something stuck in my teeth? You keep looking at me."

So much for being sneaky. "No, I was thinking what I said to you — one way or the other — was stupid. No wonder you get stressed out around me."

"Was it stupid?" Laura shrugged. "Made sense to me. I know you're not going to roll over and play dead for the likes of Mortimer." She turned to face him. "I won't, either."

Jack felt relief. *I'm really, really going to miss you when you go.*

"Darn right you'll miss me."

Did I say that out loud?

Laura smiled. "See, hotshot? You're not the only one who knows what people are thinking."

Jack gave a lopsided smile.

"So where do we begin?" she asked as they entered their office.

"Start by pulling out the files on the three-three, along with all the files on the 'prospects.' The Gypsy Devils, too. I want the most recent photos and addresses."

"Why the GDs?"

"They're not any better than the prospects. They still do a lot of the dirty work."

"Gotcha."

"While you're doing that, I'm going to phone CFSEU and give them a heads-up as to what's coming down the track." He then tapped the number into his phone and waited.

"Combined Forces Special Enforcement Unit, Sergeant Morris," Roger answered briskly.

"Hey, Rog. It's Jack Taggart."

Roger groaned. "How many bodies do you have and where are they?"

"You're joking, right?"

"You tell me," Roger replied.

"Sorry to disappoint, but dead gangsters isn't the kind of good news I'm calling about. How busy are you over there?"

"Busier than a one-armed wallpaper hanger with a case of the shits, why?"

Jack told Roger what had transpired during the past week and the meeting with the brass, who had directed him to submit an operational plan.

After Roger expressed his displeasure about the phone left in Jack's mailbox, he said, "You're talking about putting a big task force together. We don't have the manpower."

"Isaac suggested pulling members in from around the province," Jack said. "Your office already has a mix of different police forces. It would be the most likely place for them to work out of. If it gets too crowded, we'll find a place to rent."

"Then that'd be great. It's about time is all I can say. We've been so busy with the punks shooting each other that we haven't looked at the really bad boys for years. You running an informant or two to give direction once it starts?"

"I had one I cut loose a couple of days ago. I'm hoping he'll come back in time, but I'm not using him at the moment. That being said, I'm optimistic that I'll be able to turn a better one within a week or so."

"So money isn't your informants' motivation," Roger said.

"No, their motivation is more like a get-out-of-jail-free card."

"Then be careful. All our informants in here have to be turned over to CAST."

"What the hell is CAST?"

"It's a new thing. The Covert Asset Support Team. They handle all the informants and everything is done on legally signed contracts."

"The kind of people I turn need more of a personal touch and their reasons for talking don't usually jibe with writing it down on paper," Jack said.

"That's what I figured. Like I said, be careful and try to hang on to them yourself. I'm hearing rumours about new policy coming from Ottawa."

"What've you heard?"

"I don't know the details yet, but few cops know how to turn informants and even fewer know how to handle them — and that's people I know in the field. Ottawa bureaucrats are ... well, what can I say. I doubt it'll be good. Their priorities are to ensure we don't get sued. It would probably make them happy if we didn't have any informants. My fear is that anyone with informants will be ordered to turn them over completely."

"Lovely," Jack replied.

"Yeah," Roger agreed. "So how soon can we expect the task force to be up and running?"

"I'll have my op plan submitted in about three weeks," Jack said.

"At the end of October, then."

"Right. So by the time it's approved, then sent to Ottawa and they decide who to pull from what sections, I'd say we're —"

"Looking at January at the earliest."

"Exactly," Jack replied. "No worries. As my partner reminded me, vengeance is a dish best served cold."

The next few days passed with Jack and Laura trying to locate where their targets were living and taking new photographs of them. It meant long hours of surveillance; they were seldom home before midnight and usually back at work by 7:00 a.m. Some addresses turned out to be one-night stands and the real residences weren't always easy to establish.

By 4:00 p.m. Friday they both decided they needed a break. They were about to leave the office when Jack received a call from Special Agent John Adams in Texas.

"Well, you hillbilly cop," drawled Adams, "it looks like I've come through for you again. Though this time I guess the credit should go to my wife."

"Yolanda found something on Lance and Whiskey Jake?"

"Yup, did enough translation to get a clear picture. They're both tied to the same realty company in Chihuahua that Damien was."

"Realty Rápido?"

"That's the one, except their money goes from the real-estate office to a lawyer by the name of Miguel Herrero, who transfers the money to a company owned by Lance and Whiskey Jake. It's called Nighthawk Development and is registered in the Cayman Islands."

"Where the money ends up," Jack stated, while writing the details in his notebook.

"Yup. I've got the name of the bank and account numbers that I'll email you. Both Lance and Whiskey Jake have been getting equal shares of the money and have their own accounts."

"You've no idea how happy this makes me," Jack said. "Do you have a rough tally of how much money's been transferred over the years?"

"Yup. In U.S. dollars each one has in the neighbour-hood of about five mil."

"I love it!"

"More than that, I've been able to connect some of the names on the documentation from the real-estate company as belonging to members of the West 12th Street gang out of Dallas. I'm pretty sure if I send these files to the right people, they'd request extradition on your two."

"I might ask you not to do that," Jack replied.

"You're hopin' to roll one of these guys to give you Pure E," Adams guessed.

"You got it."

"No problem. I'll scan and send what Yolanda translated from Spanish, as well as copies of the transfers to the Caymans."

"You okay with not using it against the West 12th Street boys? I know they're badasses you'd like to put in jail, as well."

"Their day'll come. After what Pure E did to you, I'd say your need to get that asshole outweighs our needs down here."

"Thanks," Jack said. "Since I talked to you, he also had his guys drop Damien's phone off in my mailbox. There were pictures of my wife and kids on it."

"Christ, Jack! You can't let him get away with that. If you do, it'll give them the confidence to start murdering police officers and their families. You'll end up like Mexico."

"I won't let him get away with it. We're putting together a task force. His days are numbered."

"Good. *Adios, amigo.*"

Jack told Laura what Adams had discovered.

"That's absolutely perfect," she said. "What now?"

"What now is we aren't going home yet. Time to pay someone a visit."

Chapter Thirteen

Lance Morgan answered his office phone on the second ring. "Good Times Amusement Centre."

"You alone?" Jack's voice was terse.

"Yeah, heading out in fifteen minutes. Who's this? One of the guys?"

"Open your door to the alley."

Jack hung up, and as he and Laura waited at the bottom of the two steps leading into Lance's office, he could hear Lance moving around inside. Seconds later the door partially opened and Lance peeked out. "We need to talk," Jack stated.

Lance opened the door halfway. Jack could see his scowling face.

Jack raised his voice. "Remember when you used to talk to us about the club?"

Lance's scowl changed to alarm. He leaned out of the doorway, nervously checking to ensure nobody was within earshot. "That was years ago," he hissed. "We're even on that."

"Let me refresh your memory," Jack said more quietly. "Last time I caught you for attempted murder you agreed to wear a recorder and tip me off about other club members, remember?"

Lance's voice was resentful. "How could I forget?"

"Then when I said we were even and shook hands, I warned you to keep an eye in your rear-view mirror because I'd be watching you."

"I remember." Now he sounded worried.

"We need to talk again."

Lance looked silently at Jack, then at Laura. He was met with an unflinching gaze. "Yeah, okay. Can't say I'm surprised you came by for a chat." He stood aside. "Come in."

On doing so, Jack saw Lance lean a baseball bat against the wall. Their eyes met.

"No gun?" Jack asked as he and Laura sat on folding chairs while Lance sat behind his desk.

"Ditched that years ago when you first met me in here. I was afraid you'd use it as an excuse to come back with a warrant — not that you'd find anything," he added.

"To do that would risk burning you. You know I don't operate that way."

"I learned that after I met you. I wasn't so sure the first time we talked. Plus, I'm a granddad." Lance pointed to a photo on his desk of him and his wife holding their grandson. "He visits me here. I'd never leave something like that lying around."

"Glad to hear it," Jack replied.

"I take it this social call is about the message?"

Jack's face darkened. "Which message you referring to? The one addressed to me in blood at the Barlow farmhouse or the one left in my mailbox with the pictures of my wife and kids?"

"None of that was my idea." Lance scowled again. "We're under new management." He paused, then added, "I tried to talk him out of it."

"You've got four kids, don't you?" Jack asked. "Two of each?"

"Yeah, still got a son and daughter at home. They're both going to university. My other boy is working in Alberta and my other daughter is married and lives close to us in Surrey."

Jack nodded grimly.

"If you're here to give me a message that I got family," Lance said, "it isn't necessary. I know what Pure E did was stupid and —"

"We're here because we'd like your help again."

Lance looked surprised. "No way. I may not agree with how things are being run, but they're still my brothers. My days of ratting are gone."

"You want to talk about Nighthawk Development instead?" Jack asked politely.

Lance gaped, then his face reddened. He hammered his desk with the bottom of his fist. "Shit!"

"Yes … shit. You're in it up to your neck. So deep that Texas will ask for your extradition. They're digging up evidence as we speak of the dope deals your club's been doing with the West 12th Street gang. That includes how you've been laundering money through phony real-estate deals in Mexico and transferring the money to the Cayman Islands." Jack leaned across the desk and showed him part of a text message on his cellphone. "Recognize your account number?"

Lance remained silent.

"Imagine the sentence you'll get in Texas when they see you've got at least five million stashed away. You'd die of old age, if you were lucky, before you'd ever walk out of prison and be with your family again."

Lance leaned back in his chair and opened his mouth to speak but then closed it. Using his thumb, he unconsciously twirled his club ring around on his finger. The image of the horned skull on the ring would disappear only to reappear with each twist. He then swallowed as he looked at Jack and Laura.

Jack leaned forward and picked up the picture from the desk. "Nice-looking grandson."

"Fuck, no need to smash it," Lance said. "You got me. I take it we can make a deal? Is it too late to stop Texas from goin' after me, or am I gonna have to serve some time?"

Jack and Laura exchanged glances. Neither displayed any emotion. *Man, we're getting good at hiding our excitement,* Jack thought.

"Come on, you guys!" Lance pleaded. "Don't leave me hangin'. Can I deal it off completely or not?"

"You'll need to deal it off completely. I won't risk going for a reduced sentence, because it might burn you. Letting you off also means we have to let Whiskey Jake off. We can't bust him without burning you. Same goes for seizing your money. We couldn't do that without burning you, as well. That's a better deal than Damien got."

Lance nodded. "So in other words, I'd owe you big time."

"Definitely," Jack replied. "The only reason you're not broke and on your way to Texas is I want Pure E more than I want you and Whiskey Jake combined. It'd be the same as before. You'd work for us until I feel you've repaid your debt. If you hold back on something or lie about anything … well, you know what'd happen."

Lance seemed indifferent. "You treated me fair last time. I'll be straight with you, so what you said doesn't worry me."

"And if you treat us fair, we'll never burn you," Laura stated.

"Yeah. I know that from before, too." Lance looked at Jack. "Mind if I ask you a question?"

"Go ahead, but I may not answer."

"The farmhouse … Neal, was he working for you?"

Jack set the photo back on the desk, then waited a beat. "What do you think?"

"I know you protect your sources better than that. I figure either it wasn't him or he did something to piss you off."

"You figure right," Jack replied. "Which it was, I won't say."

Lance nodded. "One more thing — how the hell did you get the files on Nighthawk?"

"You didn't know they were missing?" Jack said.

"No." Lance paused. "Herrero — that fuckin' Mexican lawyer — he musta been too scared to tell us they were gone. He told Jake and me they were stashed someplace safe."

"Not safe enough," Jack replied. "An anonymous person found them and passed them on to a friend of mine."

"Anonymous person … yeah, right." Lance stared at Jack. "So what do you want?"

"I want Pure E taken down hard. Real hard."

Lance cleared his throat. "What he did — having the boys leave you a message at the farmhouse, pokin' you by answering Damien's phone, takin' pictures of your family, all that shit — I tried to convince him not to."

"He should've listened to you." Jack paused. "Just curious — how did your guys find out where I lived?"

"Property tax records," Lance replied.

"That figures." Jack nodded.

"Pure E," Lance said. "That fucker's got no respect for anyone. He likes to rub it in that I'm getting old. Even calls me grandpa."

"You are a grandpa," Laura said.

Lance looked at the picture on his desk and gave a half smile. "Yeah … and I'm glad to be one." His face hardened. "Pure E won't be easy to get. He was recently voted in and it's like the fuckin' honeymoon phase. The majority think he's great."

"Then the majority need to be educated," Jack asserted.

"I know. Whiskey Jake and I were talking about it the other day. Lots of the younger guys will think what he did is cool. Gives them the impression that we're invincible and can do what we want." Lance paused, seeming to contemplate something, then his eyes met Jack's. "In the long run, getting rid of Pure E will be doing the club a favour. I'm fine with however you wanna do him."

Jack nodded. He wanted the revenge he was about to exact upon Pure E to be brutal. Getting Lance on board was a plus.

Chapter Fourteen

Jack dug out his notebook, then glanced at Lance. "To start with, what can you tell me about Pure E in general?"

"He's never been married and spends most of his time whoring around with Whiskey Jake."

"Who's married," Jack noted.

"Not anymore," Lance replied. "He's divorced again."

"Any particular place that Pure E and Whiskey Jake like to go?"

"A lot of nights they go to a nightclub called Pleasure Me on Burrard Street."

"I've heard of it," Laura said. "Mostly the under-thirty crowd from what I hear."

Lance snorted. "That'd be Pure E. He likes the ones who have daddy issues."

"Is Whiskey Jake still managing Satan's Girls Entertainment Agency for the club?" Jack asked.

"Yup. It's not a lot of work. He's got a secretary. He told me he usually shows up at noon for a couple hours and that's it. For him, going clubbing and partying all night with Pure E isn't a problem."

"With what Whiskey Jake runs, I thought he'd be supplying Pure E with women."

"Yeah, Pure E dips into the coke sluts on occasion, but he prefers to go for the ones who aren't into dope. Probably trusts them more."

"I would've thought Whiskey Jake far too old for the crowd at Pleasure Me," Laura said.

Lance shrugged. "Pure E likes him because the fat bastard makes him look good. That and he uses him to drive him everywhere. Whiskey Jake isn't afraid to brown-nose, so the two of them get along well."

"Okay, let's move on to Damien," Jack said. "What do you know about his murder?"

"I know Buck was the one to put a bullet in his brain."

"Buck?" Jack glanced at Laura. He knew he wasn't the only one shocked.

"Yeah, I feel the same way," Lance said. "Havin' a kid kill his old man as a test of loyalty doesn't seem right." He paused, then added, "Guess he passed with flying colours, though."

"Were you there?" Jack asked.

"Nope, but I was there for the planning. "Last week, Thursday, I got a call at about 9:00 a.m. from Whiskey Jake. All he said was we should meet the next day and grab a smokie. Then —"

"The next day?" Jack interjected. "Thursday was when I called to warn Damien and Pure E answered. I presumed that was when he was murdered."

"We always say one day later than a meeting really is in case we're being listened to. Grabbing a smokie means it's urgent and we're to meet where we usually do at Stanley Park for a face-to-face. If it wasn't urgent, he'd say grab a burger."

"Where in Stanley Park?" Laura asked.

"Near the children's play area beside Burrard Inlet. There's a small parking lot north of it on the ring road. From there you walk down an incline to the play area, go under an overpass where the washrooms are, then out the other side. That's where we meet. There's a concession stand and picnic tables there."

"And who was at the meeting?" Jack asked.

"Whiskey Jake, Pure E, Buck, the three-three, and myself." Lance looked at Jack. "I'm presumin' you know about the three-three and who's in it."

"I know about it, but refresh my memory about who's in it," Jack said.

"Floyd Hackman. He's in my chapter. Then there's Vic Trapp, Nick Crowe, who goes by Black Bird, and Pasquale Bazzoli. They're in Whiskey Jake's chapter, although Bazzoli lives in Kelowna these days."

"Good. Continue."

"Pure E said he got a call early that morning from Basil Westmount explaining how someone who worked for Vicki's lawyer called his office and let it slip that Damien gave up that boatload of cocaine in exchange for keeping Buck and Vicki from going to jail." Lance waited a beat. "Later Buck talked to Vicki and she told him she'd pretended to make the call from the lawyer's office."

"I discovered that when I called her lawyer's office myself," Jack said.

"She's an evil bitch," Lance said bitterly. "Damien was my friend. All he was doin' was trying to save her and Buck from goin' to jail."

"Her day will come," Jack told him.

"Hope so. Buck was pissed off at her when he found out. Said he hasn't spoken to her since."

Jack nodded. "So tell me about the meeting."

"Right, so Pure E decided to have Buck confront his old man while wearing a wire so the three-three could listen. At first Buck didn't believe his old man would do such a thing, but then he met him and he admitted it." Lance stopped for a breath. "Not that the admission was necessary. There was no doubt in Pure E's mind that Damien had blabbed, so he was dead either way. Buck would have been, too, if he hadn't gone along with it."

"So Buck was forced to shoot him," Laura said.

"No, Buck said if Damien admitted it, then he wanted to kill 'im himself. It makes me wonder if Damien knew the position Buck was in. He might've been saving the kid's life by telling him to his face and prompting him to do what he did."

"And the body?" Jack asked. "Is it buried up on Sumas Mountain someplace?"

"The hit took place there, but the body would've been moved."

"What makes you say that?"

"The last road leading up to Sumas Mountain is called Taggart Road."

"So I heard," Jack replied, irritated.

"Pure E laughed about it when he saw it. He said the cops would be tearing up the whole countryside along that road looking for his corpse, so I know it's not there."

"Homicide told me they did conduct a thorough search," Jack admitted.

"The three-three suggested the area up there to wait while you were suckered into calling Damien to warn him. Right after your call, Buck shot him. Bazzoli and Crowe then disposed of the body, but how and where I don't know. It isn't something I could ask about, either."

"Pure E must know," Jack said.

"Nope. There's no reason for him to know, let alone risk having his DNA tied into wherever it's hidden. All Pure E said was he didn't want the body found or word of Damien ratting to ever get out."

"It would be bad for morale," Laura commented.

"No shit. We're letting it leak that Damien skipped town to avoid his money-laundering charges."

"And you have no idea at all where his body could be?" Jack said. "Damien isn't the first guy to disappear."

"No, that's for sure." After a moment Lance suggested, "It could be somewhere else on Sumas Mountain. There are other roads up there. I doubt it'd be too far from there because the less time the three-three are packing a body around the better."

"I'm surprised Pure E was involved as much as he was," Jack said.

"Me, too. Maybe because Damien was special. In the past, if hits could have serious ramifications for the club, Damien would be involved at the exec level. Once a hit was approved, either Whiskey Jake or me would call Trapp and meet him to pass the order on. Trapp would then contact the other three and they'd come to the park to discuss strategy, like whether or not recon is needed. At that point anyone at the exec level would've already left. Pure E seems to be more hands-on, but I don't see him changing the way things work when it comes to ordering hits."

"Trapp works nights as a bouncer, doesn't he?" Jack asked.

Lance nodded.

"Do the three-three ever meet him where he works? Perhaps in a back office?"

Lance shook his head. "If you're thinking of a bug, forget it. They never talk business inside any building. Same for vehicles. Any talk is done outside."

Jack sighed.

Lance eyed him. "Yup, Pure E is going to be hard to get."

"Does the three-three get paid extra money for what they do?" Laura asked.

"No, it's more for the prestige. Sometimes they get money for food, car rentals, and hotels. Basically only whatever they need to get the job done. Their expenses generally aren't questioned." Lance smiled. "They're a bit like our politicians. Receipts aren't necessary. It's a matter of trust."

"Right ... so what do you know about the Barlow murders?" Jack asked.

Lance gave the details, describing how he'd used Mack Cockerill, the go-between for Satans Wrath and the Gypsy Devils, to gather them together. He then described how the murders took place.

Jack and Laura already knew the details from Cockerill, but feigned surprise at the appropriate moments. The revulsion they felt when Lance described what took place in the farmhouse was genuine.

"You hear much from the Gypsy Devils since then?" Jack asked.

"Dropping like flies," Lance replied. "It's only been a week and I understand they're down to six guys. Any less and they won't qualify as a club."

"Who are the six left?" Laura asked. "Also, do any of them have legit jobs?"

"Carl Shepherd is still president. He's a mechanic and works out of his garage at home. Their sergeant-at-arms I only know as Thor. He's the one who gutted Neal."

"Norman Thorsen," Jack said.

"Yeah, he's built like Godzilla but doesn't have the brains that God gave a goat. He used to be a bouncer but got canned for putting some university student into a coma."

"And the other four?" Jack asked.

"One guy goes by Mouse and runs a stretch-limo service."

"Mickey O'Bryan," Jack said.

"Okay, then there's Banjo. Don't know if he works or not."

"Banjo is an alias for Frederick Smith. He's only a prospect."

"Until two days ago," Lance said. "They gave him his full patch when the others quit so they'd still have enough to form a club."

"I see."

"Another guy goes by the name of Smiley. He's missing his upper two front teeth and has never bothered to get false ones. I got no idea what he does."

"David Greene," Jack said. "He works part-time as a drywaller."

"The last guy is Bad Boy — sometimes called Bad Boy Brent or Triple B."

"That'd be Brent Jones," Jack said. "I don't know much about him."

"I don't think he works. His guys tease him about spending all day blogging on his computer. Originally he's from Toronto, but has a brother out here he's living with."

"Do you think anyone in the Gypsy Devils would ever make the cut to patch over to your colours?" Jack asked.

"I doubt it," Lance replied. "Bad Boy has smarts, but he hasn't lived here long enough for us to really know him. As far as the Gypsy Devils go as a club, I doubt they'll be around much longer."

"Your club planning any hits?" Jack asked.

"Not that I'm aware of. Some Chinese gangs are giving us a headache. I thought we'd settle things peacefully, but with Pure E, it's anybody's guess."

"Tell us who in your club is up to what," Jack said.

Over the next half-hour, Lance gave the names of a dozen club members involved with prostitution, credit-card thefts, drug trafficking, and other assorted criminal ventures.

"Any significant dope deals on the horizon?" Jack asked.

"Got two taking place around the end of the month," Lance replied. "One for three hundred keys of weed and another for one hundred and twenty of coke."

"Wow, one hundred and twenty kilos of cocaine sounds nice," Jack said. "Very nice."

"Yeah, I thought that'd grab your attention. It's coming in from Montreal."

"Montreal?" Jack was surprised. "I'd have thought you'd be dealing direct with the Mexicans or bringing it into Vancouver through the port."

"We were, until we found out Damien talked. We know he told you about the boatload you took down in France, but we don't know what else he told you. Pure E wants to let our regular connections cool for a while."

"Do you know how it's being delivered from Montreal?"

"A guy from here by the name of Shane McRooney is driving it back."

"I don't know him."

"That's the idea. He's not a club member and doesn't have a record. He's rented a storage locker to stash it in once it's here."

"Under a fake name?"

"Nope. He runs a small moving company. It'll be locked in some trunks and stored in among some household furniture. He'll have a fictitious invoice to make it look like he was paid to haul household goods back from Montreal."

"With the idea of being able to deny knowing about it if the police got onto it."

"Yup. I don't know where the storage locker is, but his truck won't be hard for you to spot on the highway 'cause it has his name on the door. I'll know more details about both transactions next week."

"Does McRooney then deal the coke out himself?"

"No, his part is only to get it here. After that, we use a prospect from my chapter — Buster Linquist. He sometimes does legit work for McRooney, so the storage company is used to seeing him come and go. It's one of those places where you supply your own padlock. Both McRooney and Buster have keys to the outside lock, but only Buster has keys to the trunks."

"Buster Linquist," Jack repeated.

"Yeah, I don't know where he lives, but if you like, I'll have one of the guys call him and a couple other prospects to the clubhouse and give them some shit job to do. Then you can follow him after."

"Don't bother, I know where he lives," Jack said, feeling pleased that the hours he and Laura had spent on surveillance of the prospects earlier had already paid off.

"Figures that you'd know and I don't," Lance said dryly.

"You've done good," Jack said. "We'll give you our numbers. Anything happening, day or night, I want —"

"Yeah, I know. I'll call."

"There's one more thing." Jack pulled a tape recorder out of his jacket pocket. "I've recorded our chat. Still am."

Lance's mouth fell open in both shock and rage. He leaned forward, placing his hands on his desk like he was about to leap over it. "What the fuck?"

"Settle down. This is our insurance policy. Don't try to move your money out of your Cayman account or do anything else to piss us off until we're even."

Lance sat back in his chair. "Christ, Jack, where's the trust?" he grumbled.

"Five million is a lot of trust."

Lance appeared to think about it. "Yeah ... I guess. Make damned certain you take care of that recorder."

"No worries." Jack waited a beat. "In the end, the consequences for Pure E need to be serious."

Lance raised an eyebrow. "Serious or fatal?"

Jack didn't answer him, just turned off the recorder and stared hard at Lance.

***

Jack saw the smile on Laura's face when they returned to their car. "Happy?" he said.

"Happy? That's an understatement! That was fantastic!"

Jack grinned. "Pure E isn't going to be popular for long. We'll have to protect our friend, but we'll still be able to create havoc — and tell the investigators to thank Pure E for every bust that's made."

"Our friend is going to be a gold mine of information. In fact, he already is."

"You're right about that. Better enjoy the weekend. Once the task force is up and running we're going to be busy."

"Can't be any busier than we've been all week." Laura yawned. "Getting home tonight before midnight will seem like a treat."

Jack's thoughts were elsewhere. "They'll never know what hit them. Might even get the one hundred and twenty keys of coke seized in Montreal. That'd let them know that Pure E's tactics will affect them nationwide."

"When you picked up the picture from Lance's desk, he said there was no need to smash it. What did he mean?"

"The first time I turned him, he had a family photo on his desk. Things got a little heated when it came to convincing him to talk. I smashed the picture and told him if he didn't co-operate he'd never see them again."

"Bet that caught his attention."

"It did."

"One more thing. You never answered when he asked if the consequences for Pure E needed to be serious or fatal. All you did was shut off the recorder and stare at him."

"I wanted to let him wonder what lengths we'd go to if our families were threatened. If Pure E brings the idea up again, maybe he'll try harder to talk him out of it."

"I see," Laura said thoughtfully. "It's kind of funny he brought it up. He's had such a violent life that he automatically made a presumption that you wanted Pure E dead."

Perhaps he knows me better than you realize.

Chapter Fifteen

On Sunday afternoon Jack's game of pool with his son Steve was interrupted by a phone call. He answered and a man said, "It's me."

Jack recognized Cockerill's voice. "Are you okay?"

"Yeah, yeah."

"Didn't expect to hear from you."

"What, you thought I meant it when I gave you the finger last time? I was only fuckin' with ya."

"You're okay, though?"

"Yeah, I'm fine. Thought I'd pass somethin' on to ya."

"You don't need to. As far as I'm concerned, we're even."

"I know, but you treated me good, so I thought I'd give you a little heads-up. I was at the clubhouse last night and your picture's on the wall. I was told to get a prospect to deliver a copy to the Gypsy Devils."

"My wife and kids, too?"

"Nope, only yours. A good face shot of you walking out of your garage." Cockerill paused. "With your hair and beard you look like one of us, but they got the word 'cop' written underneath. There'll be a copy in the Eastside clubhouse, too."

"Thanks for letting me know."

"Yeah, yeah, no sweat," Cockerill mumbled. After a moment, he said, "There's somethin' else you might want to know."

"Oh?"

"Buck's struttin' around with '3-3' tattooed on his arm."

"Already?" Jack pretended surprise. "Isn't it unusual for someone to go into the three-three without some kind of special training or connections? Especially considering he only got his full patch a couple of weeks ago."

"I talked to Floyd Hackman about Buck joining his team so soon. He told me that there ain't nothin' Buck wouldn't do. 'Ice cold' is how he described him. Said he was born to be a killer. Everyone outside the three-three thinks Damien fled the country, but from talkin' to you, I knew better."

"No, you're not telling me that —"

"Yup." Cockerill paused. "Buck whacked his old man. I'm sure of it."

I'm sure of it, too.

On Monday Jack picked up Laura on his way to work and told her about Cockerill's call and Buck's new three-three tattoo.

"The bloody psychopath is proud of what he did!" Laura was aghast.

"So it would seem. I was also told they've got my picture up in the clubhouses and gave a copy to the Gypsy Devils. Only mine, though, not Natasha or the boys."

"Those assholes," Laura muttered.

"Don't worry about it. I was already thinking about changing my appearance. Natasha doesn't like beards. Especially bushy ones. She says mine has gone to seed."

Laura glanced sideways at Jack. "I'd have to agree with her." She paused, then said, "Guess the good news is Weenie Wagger is coming back to us. It's always nice to have two informants to verify what each of them tells us."

"I don't think Weenie looks at the club as his family anymore."

"Great, so we adopt him," Laura said, feigning disapproval. Then she pointed out the window. "Hey, you missed the turnoff."

"I'm going straight to I-HIT. Today is when we're supposed to take a run at Vicki. They'll want us wired up."

"Oh, man, I forgot all about that."

"It'd be nice if we could get her to admit something."

"Good luck with that," Laura replied. "She's one wicked woman."

Jack and Laura sat in their SUV in the hospice parking lot near Vicki's vehicle, a white Cadillac Escalade. George Hobbs and Dan Philips from I-HIT were parked a block away, listening through Jack's hidden transmitter.

"I've got a visual on T-1," Jack said. "Approaching her car now. It's showtime."

"Not even 1:00 p.m. yet," Laura noted as they walked toward Vicki.

"The dutiful daughter," Jack said. "Probably shoved a spoonful of porridge down his throat and left."

"Maybe he should consider himself lucky she hasn't killed him," Laura replied.

Vicki was pulling her keys from her purse when Jack and Laura caught up with her. "You set Damien up to be killed," Jack said, sounding matter-of-fact. "We'd like to know why."

"What on earth are you talking about?" Vicki gave a tiny gasp and put her hand over her heart. "Are you telling me my husband is dead?"

"Knock it off, Vicki," Laura said. "We know. We're trying to help you out. Get your story out before I-HIT takes you down."

"My *story?*"

"Come on, Vicki," Laura persisted. "We know it must have been hell living with him. Was he … physical with you? We know he had a temper."

"Never! I love my husband. I can't believe what you're saying. I'm horrified." Then with a sneer, she took her hand off her heart and said, "If he's really dead, I'd like to see the body. I'm sure you're mistaken. If you're not, what a cruel way to tell a loving wife that her husband is dead … and then to accuse her of having something to do with it! I'm tempted to go to the media."

"How do you feel about being charged with conspiracy to commit murder?" Jack said sharply.

"I'm innocent. You've got nothing on me — unless of course you're thinking of framing me for something. I certainly wouldn't put it past you."

"You don't think we have something on you?" Jack shook his head. "Three weeks ago you met us in a hotel room and gave us the information on Damien's money-laundering scheme, complete with bank accounts. I told you then that if you weren't being straight with us, I'd feed you to the wolves."

"Are you threatening me? First you tell me my husband is dead. Then you accuse me of killing him. Now you're saying I squealed on him? My God! I came to you that day to beg you to drop charges against my son, as any loving mother would. Bank accounts? Money laundering? From what I heard, it was one of Damien's lawyers who ratted." Vicki actually looked amused.

You bitch! That does it. You won't be laughing when I'm done with you.

"This meeting you allege we had," Vicki said smugly, "I'm sure you would've recorded it, wouldn't you?"

"You know we didn't," Laura said. "Our concern was to protect you and keep your identity secret."

"Unlike today, I suppose." She looked at each of them and then smiled.

Jack looked at her, stone-faced. "I'm guessing you watched when Buck and the three-three took Damien away."

"So what if I did? I don't know where they took him or what they did when they left."

Good. I've established that you at least were a witness to that. "You must be proud of Buck."

His comment appeared to affect Vicki. "Buck's family is the club," she said sullenly. "I don't have anything to do with him anymore. If you think you've got something on me, go ahead and arrest me. I'd like to call a lawyer. If not, then fuck off."

Jack and Laura glanced at each other, then returned to their SUV. Once inside, Jack said, "Sorry, guys. We tried. I did get her to admit that she saw them take Damien away.

Might come in handy later. I'm shutting the wire off," he added, then flicked a switch on the transmitter hidden under his shirt. He turned to Laura. "I'm not going to let Vicki get away with what she did. Someday ... somehow ... justice will be served."

"I think she thought that exposing Damien as an informant would bring Buck back to her," Laura said. "Instead, the opposite happened."

Jack felt his phone vibrate and answered.

It was Rose. "You still waiting to talk to Vicki?" she asked.

"No, we tried a few minutes ago and she told us to fuck off."

"Which you expected," Rose noted.

"Do have some good news, though. Friday night Laura and I reconnected with that new source we'd talked about. I'll fill you in when we get back."

"Good, but I've something to tell you. It's a little disconcerting. You need to get in here pronto. Mortimer wants to see you."

"His first official day in the office and we're granted an audience? Must think we're important people," Jack joked.

"There's no 'we,'" Rose said gravely. "I told him we'd be there as soon as you returned and he curtly informed me that if he wanted me to attend, he would've said so. He only wants to see you."

"That's weird. Did he say why?"

"I told him you were about to have a talk with Vicki and that if he wanted an update on the operational plan, I could give it to him."

"And?"

"He practically bit my head off."

Jack felt his stomach knot.

Chapter Sixteen

"Close the door and sit down," Assistant Commissioner Mortimer said bluntly, indicating a chair across from his desk.

Jack obeyed and then returned Mortimer's stare. A clock mounted on the wall slowly ticked off twenty seconds. *What is this? Junior High? Are we supposed to see who blinks first?* At forty seconds Jack thought, *Okay, this is stupid. Acting defiant won't help.* He faked a cough and looked away.

Mortimer's face registered his sense of accomplishment. "Let me make this perfectly clear," he began menacingly.

Guess you're not interested in whether or not Vicki said anything.

"You will never, and I repeat never, put me in a spot like you did with Assistant Commissioner Isaac."

"Sir?"

"Don't play stupid with me, Corporal! You know full well what I mean."

Well, no, I really don't, but I get why you didn't want Rose here. You don't want anyone to witness this.

"In the future, if you ever submit a report that even hints at being — what did Isaac call it, a delicate matter? — I'll see to it that your career is over and that you spend the rest of your time on administrative duties. Do I make myself clear?"

Okay, stay calm. The important thing is to get the task force up and running. "Yes, sir. Perfectly clear," Jack said submissively. "It was apparent to me when we first met that you disagreed with the type of investigations performed by the intelligence unit. May I ask what direction you'd like us to go?"

"Are you being impertinent?"

"No, sir. Not at all."

Mortimer appeared taken back. "Well … perhaps you should liaise with other agencies, such as U.S. Customs or something to identify potential drug or money-laundering routes. Then turn that information over to the appropriate sections."

"I see. More of a systemic approach."

"Exactly. You're in the intelligence unit. You shouldn't be doing anything hands-on. Particularly with a group like Satans Wrath. They're grubby, dangerous, and not worthy of the kind of criminal you should be focusing on."

You're right. Some of them even carry guns.

"It presents a far better image to go after white-collar criminals. Leave the bikers to CFSEU. There are city police officers in there who can deal with them."

"The problem is, sir, that Satans Wrath are international. They go well beyond the jurisdiction of municipal police forces."

"Have you not been listening to me?"

"Yes, sir, but I've an informant in the club who —"

"Yes, a Mack Cockerill — I made inquiries," Mortimer said, tapping a piece of paper on his desk. "When was the last time you spoke to him?"

Jack saw his informant's name scrawled on the paper and his anger rose further. Informants were identified in reports by a number to protect their identity. Someone of Mortimer's rank would have clearance to identify who they were, but to do so would be highly unusual.

"I asked you a question, Corporal."

"Yesterday afternoon," Jack responded. "He called me at home and I met him shortly after. Would you like me to shred that piece of paper when I go?" he added, gesturing to his informant's name.

"You let him call you at home?"

"My informants don't work Monday-to-Friday jobs. Often what they tell me is urgent in nature."

"That's absurd!" Mortimer looked stunned. "That clearly explains to me how you came to be threatened. You practically invited them to your house."

Bite your tongue, Jack, bite your tongue. At least he thinks of it as a threat now and not a joke.

"It also tells me you've no idea how to handle informants. As such, Cockerill will be turned over to CFSEU immediately."

"Sir, this informant is extremely stressed out at the moment. He's not paid and became an informant to keep himself from being charged."

"Yes, you told me you took it upon yourself not to charge him for indecent exposure."

"Yes, sir, and since then he has more than repaid his debt."

"How long have you been subverting justice?"

What the hell? "Subverting justice, sir?"

"Deciding on your own who should face criminal prosecution and who shouldn't." Mortimer pushed himself back in his chair. "My God, you really are clueless." He looked at Jack with disdain. "People like you don't have the experience or intelligence to make such decisions, which is why Ottawa's been forced to formulate new policy to stop that practice." He appeared to run out of steam, but then added, "Perhaps certain instances may be allowed with approval of the attorney general, but basically such methods are terminated immediately."

"Sir, that is our most valuable tool for catching criminals. We need informants. For many, their impulse to talk is fleeting. Having to wait for approval from someone like the attorney general would greatly hinder the opportunity and expose the informant to further risk."

"Is that a fact?" Mortimer's words were sarcastic.

"Sir, a few years ago we discovered that a sister of a Satans Wrath member was carrying on an affair with the attorney general." Jack paused to let that sink in. "So going to him for permission is … well, not only potentially dangerous, but many officers wouldn't take the time to fill out the amount of paperwork required. Our eyes and ears on the street would virtually disappear."

Mortimer's tone remained sarcastic. "I'm sure, Corporal, that with all your vast knowledge and experience you feel qualified to question Ottawa's decisions."

"Sir, members in Ottawa who are caught up in the administrative and bureaucratic processes have different goals and agendas. Their goal may be to prevent some future lawsuit without any sense of what is needed to do effective policing. Most members have never developed or worked with informants. Sir, this new policy needs input from people who are knowledgeable about —"

"Enough, Corporal!" Mortimer snarled. "Let me assure you that you are not qualified to speak on the subject. Your lack of knowledge about informants is shameful. I'll be calling the chief superintendent in charge of CFSEU to have someone there take over the informant. You may speak to Cockerill once more to let him know. After that you're not to have any further contact with him ... or any other informants, for that matter, until such time as I believe you have learned to act responsibly."

Jack struggled to keep his rage in check. *Does he want me to punch him in the face? No, he's just a sanctimonious bureaucrat. Violence is as foreign to him as actual policing is.*

"Did you hear me, Corporal?"

Jack's nostrils flared slightly, before he answered politely. "Yes, sir."

Chapter Seventeen

Jack walked past his office and motioned for Laura to follow. Seconds later they each took a seat across from Rose's desk and waited as she spoke on the phone. Jack noticed her face turn a ruddy red as she listened to the caller, then a moment later she said, "Yes, sir, you've made yourself perfectly clear." Upon ending the call, she stared at Jack.

"Mortimer?" Jack asked.

Rose nodded. "I've been accused of allowing you to act like a cowboy."

"I like cowboys," Jack replied. "Honest and hardworking people."

Rose glared at him. "This is serious!" she snapped. "He made it clear that it's not only your career that's in jeopardy."

"I know it's serious. Did he also mention I'm not qualified to handle informants and I'm to turn Weenie Wagger over to CFSEU? In fact, he had Weenie Wagger's name written on a piece of paper on his desk and said he was going to call CFSEU himself."

"No, he didn't tell me that." Rose leaned forward, putting her elbows on her desk, and covered her face with her hands. "Oh, God," she mumbled.

"He told you to turn your informant over to CFSEU," Laura repeated in disbelief.

"I told him Weenie wasn't ready for that, but he wouldn't listen. What's even worse is he told me that policy is being written in Ottawa. We'll no longer be allowed to turn informants in lieu of having them charged, except in exceptional circumstances."

"You gotta be kidding," Laura said.

"Wish I was. Mortimer refers to it as 'subverting justice.'" Jack shook his head in frustration. "It's that *policy* that'll be subverting justice."

Rose sat back in her chair. "Without informants, how does he expect us to do our job?"

"He doesn't want us to do our job," Jack stated. "He's afraid it might force him to make a decision on something he could be criticized for. That's why he didn't want you there when he told me. He didn't want anyone to witness what he said to me."

"I don't know what to do!" Rose exclaimed, gesturing with her hands in the air. "He's too far up the totem pole to try and go above him."

"We'll work around it," Jack said quietly. "Crime Stoppers are always getting anonymous tips. Maybe I'll change my name to Mr. Anonymous. Intelligence reports won't be going out, but we could still do a number on the bad guys."

Rose bit her lower lip as she appeared to ponder the situation. Then she gave a slight nod. "Glad you're keeping the promise you made to me last month to keep me informed."

Yeah, well … that was before they threatened my family and Mortimer took over.

"This is disastrous," Laura said. "How can Mortimer sleep at night?"

"His priority is political," Jack stated. "Climb the corporate ladder to the top. He sees people who actually do police work as dumb."

Laura looked confused. "How'd he get to be where he is? It's crazy."

"Bureaucrats have different agendas," Rose said, "and it has little to do with police work. I refer to it as the enemy from within."

"The enemy from within," Jack echoed. "I agree. Now it's a matter of eliminating that enemy."

"Eliminating?" Rose's brow furrowed. "You can't kill him … much as I'd like to."

"Well, it's like you said, bureaucratic interference goes with the job. This isn't the first time, but I'm optimistic we'll get past it."

"How?" Laura asked. "You figure out a way to give him a coronary?"

"We're not allowed to submit any reports that'd cause Mortimer any stress, let alone a coronary," Rose said. She looked at Jack. "I'm almost afraid to ask. Why are you optimistic?"

"To start with, Laura and I turned a high-level source within the club Friday night."

"The one at executive level?" Rose asked.

"Yes. He's co-operating fully. Once the op plan takes effect, there'll be so much going on that Mortimer won't be able to ignore it. Hell, it'll probably end up making him look good in the eyes of Ottawa. As long as I use Crime Stoppers, he won't know the info is coming from us. I don't care who gets the credit as long as the job gets done."

Rose pursed her lips. "This source … what stick are you holding? Murder?"

"No … money laundering and five million in savings."

"Five mil!" Rose exclaimed.

"Kind of gives a person incentive," Laura noted.

Rose chewed her lip for a moment, then said, "Few people would have the inside information he'd have."

"I know," Jack replied. "We may have to let a few crimes go by to protect him. Obviously we won't be submitting any reports. I'll use Crime Stoppers entirely. There are a couple of drug shipments scheduled to arrive at the end of the month. One of my objectives is to make busts and attribute the extra attention Satans Wrath is receiving to Pure E. If we ever find Damien's body it'd put further heat on him. The club would know he lied to them."

"That and they'd know Damien informed," Laura said. "It would damage morale. Plus, if someone of his stature informed, it might encourage others."

"Any ideas what they might've done with his body?" Rose asked. "Doesn't your new source know?"

"I asked. The three-three keep that info to themselves."

"I see." Rose was silent for a few moments. At last she said, "So what do you plan on doing now?"

"Work on the op plan. The report will need to reflect what we learned Friday night. Not easy to do when I'm not supposed to have an informant. I'll make it sound like it's old information but that the targets are still active. With luck, I'll have the report on your desk by Friday."

"Good." Rose studied Jack's face. "Is there something else? You look worried."

Jack took a deep breath and slowly exhaled. "I was thinking about Weenie Wagger. I need to give him a heads-up."

On returning to his own desk, Jack called Roger Morris at CFSEU and told him about his conversation with Mortimer.

"Christ, Jack. That's … I don't know what to say. I'm sorry."

"We're not dead in the water yet," Jack replied. "As far as any, uh, other sources go, there's always Crime Stoppers."

"I guess, but with Weenie Wagger, the Covert Asset Support Team will have to follow orders. There's some good guys in there, but they'll still need to approach him."

"I know. I'll do my best to prepare him, but I don't think he'll co-operate."

"Then there's not much to worry about. He either does or he doesn't."

"I know, but it's wrong. He'll think I'm treating him like a piece of property you can sell or give away."

"I hear you. I'll find out who is detailed to approach him and give them a heads-up. Tell them not to push too hard. Maybe make an initial offer of money and then leave him to decide on his own."

Jack's next call was to Cockerill, who responded sleepily. "You free to meet?" Jack asked.

"What the fuck. You woke me up. Why're you calling? You said we was even."

"We are. Some shit came down from above here. I'd like to meet with you."

"Some shit is happening and you wanna meet?" Cockerill sounded incredulous. "In other words you're hopin' to weasel something more out of me! You promised we was done! I'm not seein' ya!"

"You and I are done, which is why I'm calling. We've got a new boss. He's going to send a couple of people from CFSEU over to talk to you and —"

"What the fuck! You told the gang unit about me?"

"It wasn't my idea, but they're going to offer you money and —"

"I ain't rattin' out my guys for money! What the fuck! You think I'm a low-life piece of shit you can use and pass around? Fuck you!"

"Mackie, please, let's meet and talk a bit about —"

Cockerill hung up.

"Didn't go well, I take it?" Laura looked at Jack as he put his phone down.

"No, it sure didn't." Jack sighed. "Guess he knows he doesn't have any friends."

Chapter Eighteen

Wednesday, October 15, was Natasha's birthday and Jack made it home from work at 6:00 p.m. Half an hour later he sat in the living room, smiling from behind the camera as he watched Mike and Steve give their mother a present. At only nine and ten, the boys didn't have big allowances, but the gift of two small porcelain geese came with a lot of heart.

Natasha oohed and aahed over the gift, but Jack could tell she took more delight in receiving the homemade birthday cards. Treasures, he knew, that she'd tuck away with the other cards she'd received over the years.

Jack handed her his gift.

"Beautifully wrapped," Natasha noted. She smiled as she held the small box to her ear and shook it.

"Open it, Mom!" Steve pleaded.

Natasha smiled. "I don't know … the box is so pretty, but okay."

She opened it, then held up the pendant it contained. "Oh, Jack, it's beautiful!"

"It's called a mother pendant," he said. "The two stones on it are Mike's and Steve's birthstones — a bright blue tanzanite for Mike and a diamond for Steve."

Before Natasha could say more, an unexpected noise from outside their front door erased everyone's smiles. It was the metallic sound of the mailbox lid. Jack saw the boys look sombrely at each other while Natasha looked sharply at him.

Damn it … probably nothing. My gun is in the bedroom — no, leave it. How can I expect my family to relax if I show fear?

"Jack?" Natasha's voice was wavery.

"Probably advertising," he said. "I'll check."

Moments later Jack returned with a pizza flyer. There'd been no need for alarm, but the happy mood was gone for the night.

Thursday afternoon Jack and Laura were at their desks working on the operational plan when Corporal Connie Crane from I-HIT strode in. She stood with her hands on her hips, glowering at Jack.

The last time he'd seen or spoken to her was two weeks previous at the scene of the triple murder. At that time she was furious and had held him accountable. *What can I say? She was right. Isaac made the final decision, but it was my doing.* "Connie," he acknowledged her.

"Why didn't you call me after we left the farmhouse?" Her tone was accusatory.

"I couldn't," Jack replied. "I've got an informant to protect. There was nothing more I could say about the matter."

Connie grimaced. "Inspector Dyck called me in. He made it clear that what happened wasn't your decision. He told me he was there when Isaac spoke to you about it."

"So you're not angry at me any longer?"

"I wouldn't go that far. I'm so pissed off over the whole situation that I'd like to kick somebody."

"Don't you own a cat or a dog?" Jack asked.

Connie let out a snort. "God, you're a piece of work. I never know how to take you."

"What do you mean?"

Connie grabbed a chair and sat down. "A few years ago I watched you put a badly injured cat down in an alley. You looked like you were going to get sick after you shot it, so don't give me that shit about kicking a cat."

I remember, too. Someone had broken its spine with a bat.

"Too bad your soft spot doesn't apply to humans," Connie said.

"Some animals only look human," Jack replied, "but in reality they're sick animals and should be put down. So why're you here?"

"Several hours ago we ran a name of a Satans Wrath member and got the automatic response to notify you of the reason for the check. We didn't, but I know you'd still get a computer printout saying we ran his name. I could see you not bothering to call if it was Highway Patrol, but I-HIT? How come you weren't curious?"

"I've got all of them entered in the system," Jack said. "I didn't call because I didn't know about it. The paperwork is probably still in Telecoms or the mailroom. That being said, have we got a murder? Who was —"

"You tell me if it's murder," Connie replied. "That's why I'm here. It looks like an accidental drug overdose or maybe a suicide, but anything to do with Satans Wrath makes me suspicions. Someone called 9-1-1 about midnight but didn't say anything. When the members arrived to check it out, his apartment door was ajar and they went in. We put the time of death in the early evening."

"Who was it?" Jack asked. In the pit of his stomach he already knew.

"Mack Cockerill. Half-full bottle of fentanyl beside him and most of a bottle of whiskey gone."

Damn it. Jack glanced at Laura, who closed her eyes and pinched the bridge of her nose.

"Receipt we found in a liquor bag shows that the whiskey was purchased yesterday. Only his prints on the bottle and the one glass. Haven't got the tox results back yet, so I'm only making a presumption."

Jack nodded silently. "You find his cellphone?"

"No, it was gone."

"Likely tossed so you wouldn't pull any phone tolls. Don't take that as being suspicious. Simply a precaution Satans Wrath would make so as not to give you any intel on their club."

"Okay … so you going to tell me what's going on?" Connie asked. "I saw the look you gave each other."

Jack hesitated as he tried to decide what to say.

"Okay, that's it! Where were you last night, Jack?"

He made a placating gesture with his hands. "It was Natasha's birthday. I was home around six and we all went out for pizza. If you want a more detailed alibi I can give it to you, but in my opinion, Cockerill's death was a suicide."

"Anything to back that up as opposed to being accidental?"

"Cockerill was in trouble with the club for taking drugs and getting drunk. I think he was on the verge of getting kicked out. They were the only family he had. No other friends."

"Goddamn it!" Connie exclaimed. "Why do I do this to myself? Why did I even think for a moment that I might get a straight answer from you?"

"What're you talking about?" Jack said. "I've been straight with you!"

Connie studied his face. "Look, neither of you were happy when I told you what happened." Her voice was firm and matter-of-fact. "Which is odd, because I'd expect that hearing about one of those guys dying would have both of you leaping up and doing a line dance."

Jack exchanged a bland look with Laura.

"So I know there's something you're holding back," Connie stated. "I think he was either your informant or someone you were about to bust. If he was your informant it raises a red flag, because if he was, is it possible someone found out and murdered him?"

"You're good, Connie, I'll give you that." Jack eyed her for a moment, then said, "I'm willing to give you the whole story, but I must warn you, in doing so, it'll leave you with a decision to make."

"Not again," she said bitterly. "A tough one, no doubt."

"Not tough in my mind. Frustrating perhaps."

"Was he tied in to your … delicate matter two weeks ago at the farmhouse?"

"If he was … and I were to give you all the details, what would you do?"

"What do you mean? I'd pass it on to the investigators. If he was your informant, we don't need to worry about protecting him."

"The investigators would then scoop the others up for interrogation."

"Yes."

"These guys have all been through that many times in their lives."

"So you're saying they wouldn't talk and would demand lawyers?"

"Yes, and if the investigators don't have any forensic evidence strong enough to convict them, then …"

"I know they don't," Connie said grimly. "Meaning, they'd be cut loose."

"Exactly. Then the Gypsy Devils would know it wasn't one of their guys who talked. How do you think they'd respond? Knowing Satans Wrath made them torture and murder three people when it was Satans Wrath with the leak?"

"With extreme violence, I presume." Connie's voice was sullen and she shifted uncomfortably in her chair.

"Yes, and in my opinion, the Gypsy Devils wouldn't care if innocent people got in the way. There could be a loss of civilian life. How would you feel about that? Knowing that your actions did nothing to solidify the murder investigation and then contributed to the murder of innocent people?"

Connie stared at Jack, but didn't speak.

"I know you're angry over what happened in the farmhouse. This is a continuation of that same delicate matter. Do you want me to tell you whether or not Cockerill was our informant and if so, supply you with all the details?"

Connie sighed. "I'd like to know. If he *was* your informant, I'll keep the information to myself. I came here to find out whether Cockerill's death should be classified as murder. To do that, in my mind, I need to know if he was your informant."

"Then I'll tell you." Jack waited a beat. "I wish you *could* classify it as murder. The perpetrator would be Assistant Commissioner Mortimer."

Chapter Nineteen

Early Friday afternoon Rose signed off on the operation plan. She then delivered it personally to Mortimer's secretary before going to see Jack and Laura in their office. On entering, she gave them a thumbs-up.

"It's done?" Jack asked.

Rose smiled. "It's done. Great job, you two. I know you've been working day and night these past couple of weeks, but even so, I'm amazed with what you accomplished."

Jack nodded. "Usually I'd suggest we go for a drink after work, but I feel so burned out, all I want to do is go home and introduce myself to my family."

"Likewise," replied Laura. "My husband's taken to protesting by growing a beard again. He won't shave until I spend a whole night with him."

Rose grinned. "Then the both of you … go home. Take the weekend off and get some rest. I suspect things are about to get busy."

Neither Jack nor Laura needed any further convincing.

***

Jack was finishing breakfast Sunday morning when he answered a call. He'd checked the call display but the number was blocked.

"Corporal Taggart, this is Jacob Isaac calling."

"Who?" Jack asked in confusion.

"Your former assistant commissioner."

"Oh, of course. Yes, uh, sir?"

"I'd like to meet with you on a matter of some urgency. In confidence. I'm hoping you can come to my place. If you can, my wife, Sarah, will go to church without me this morning and I'll put on a pot of fresh coffee for us."

"A matter of urgency?" Jack repeated.

Isaac's voice was grim. "Tomorrow I'm going to ask you to perform what may be the toughest undercover assignment you've ever had. I'd like to prepare you for it."

One hour later, Jack arrived at Isaac's home and was ushered into the living room, where he was served coffee. Jack saw Isaac eyeing him as he took his first sip. *What the hell is going on?*

"I won't keep you waiting," Isaac said. "I realize that inviting you to my house is highly unusual."

Unusual? More like unheard of. "Yes, sir," he acknowledged.

"Let me start by stating something I suspect you already know. The toughest part of catching criminals is often due to decisions made by our own administration."

Jack nodded. *The enemy from within.*

"There was a retirement dinner for me last night that Sarah and I attended."

"Sorry I wasn't there," Jack said, offering up a little humour.

Isaac gave a slight smile. "I wish you had been there, too, but it was for commissioned rank only."

"I hope you had a good time," Jack said. "Now that you're officially retired, I can say this without sounding like a brown-noser. You're highly respected by those of us who are not in the commissioned rank."

"Thank you. I was enjoying myself last night until I'd occasion to speak with your new assistant commissioner." Isaac paused and met Jack's gaze levelly. "Your name came up."

"Not in a good way, I presume."

"No, not in a good way." Isaac shook his head. "I must confess I was so disgusted that Sarah and I left shortly after."

Oh, crap. Mortimer. You son-of-a-bitch. You're not approving the op plan.

Isaac seemed to read Jack's thoughts. "He's not going to give it the attention it deserves. I reminded him about the previous conversation we'd had. The one where he agreed a task force was needed and promised to give your operational plan the urgency it deserved. His remarks last night made it clear he didn't consider the matter urgent and told me that other units, such as CFSEU, were too busy for now." Isaac paused, then added, "I doubt he'll ever submit your plan to Ottawa."

Jack momentarily recalled Natasha's birthday and the fear on his kids' faces when they heard their mailbox rattle. *Yes, nothing urgent about living under those conditions — or allowing Pure E to get away with torture and murder ...* He subconsciously clenched his fist. *Christ, I don't know whether to cry in frustration or scream in rage....*

"He told me that he's going to call you and Staff Sergeant Wood in tomorrow to notify you of his decision. I want you to be prepared and not act like you are now."

What do you mean? I haven't said a word.

"Making a fist and scowling will not go over well. He'd view it as insubordination, if not a direct threat to his person."

Jack hadn't realized he was doing either and quickly relaxed his fist and took a deep breath. *This is unbelievable. Working day and night — and for what? To have my family live in fear? If Mortimer wasn't going to authorize it, he could have said so weeks ago.*

Isaac cleared this throat. "In my experience, people like Assistant Commissioner Mortimer tend to have someone else deliver such messages, or send their response back on paper. Calling the both of you in concerns me."

"I submitted the op plan, but Rose signed off on it. I'd expect him to call her."

"Yes, and if it was only her, perhaps the alarm bells wouldn't have gone off in my head as loud as they did." Isaac looked dismayed. "I believe he's looking for an excuse to have you transferred. Perhaps hoping you'll react in a way to justify his intention."

"He said he accepted my apology before," Jack offered lamely.

"Yes, but you need to understand that people like him hate and fear people like you. Your output requires operational decisions that could result in criticism later."

"Sometimes tough decisions need to be made if we're to get the job done," Jack argued. "I do what I think is right."

"I also do what I think is right." Isaac studied Jack's

face. "There were times when I questioned your investigative methods — but we did share a common goal. That was to ensure criminals were brought to task. People like Mortimer are different."

Good, you dropped the rank in front of his name. You hate the bastard, too.

"People like him go by the theory that the furtherance of their careers outweighs anything they once swore to uphold. To them, it's not about catching criminals, but maintaining a perception of doing the job while being careful not to make waves."

"I should've seen this coming," Jack lamented. "He called me in last Monday and spoke to me about informants. The one I had that he knew about —"

"The one caught exposing himself?"

"Yes, Mack Cockerill. I was ordered to turn him over to CFSEU. I told Mortimer that Cockerill's motive wasn't financial and that he was turning to me because he needed a friend. Mortimer said I wasn't competent enough to handle informants and that my methods of recruitment were subverting justice. Under orders, I called Cockerill to terminate our relationship. Two days later he died of a drug and alcohol overdose. I believe it was suicide."

Isaac briefly closed his eyes. When he opened them his face looked cold and hard. "We can't let him win," he said forcefully.

"Who?" Jack asked callously. "Mortimer or Pure E?"

"Either," Isaac said bluntly. "There's more." He paused, seemingly upset by what he was about to say. "You'll also be told to cease any undercover activities."

"He said that?" Jack replied in surprise.

"He mentioned your long hair and beard. Said it would no longer be tolerated."

No undercover? He's shutting me down completely.

"I know how you feel," Isaac said. "but bear in mind that people like him don't usually stay in the field for long. He'll be clamouring to get back to Ottawa to curry favour with either the commissioner or whatever politician holds the power to pull strings. I bet he's gone in two years."

"I've thought of that, sir. The problem is that Pure E's made this personal for me and my family. I was counting on having a task force to give an appropriate response. Now I'm told there'll be no task force, no informants, and no undercover. He's not allowing me to do my job."

Isaac looked Jack in the eye and said, "Suck it up, Buttercup. Sounding like a crybaby won't accomplish what needs to be done. I told you on the phone that tomorrow could be your toughest undercover assignment ever. That assignment will be to clean yourself up and go in and woo Mortimer."

Woo Mortimer? Somehow I don't think a thousand red roses would do it.

"If I didn't think you were up to the task, I wouldn't have bothered to call you."

"But even if I were to convince Mortimer I shouldn't be transferred, he's still putting a stop to any plan to go after Pure E."

"Yes, I'm curious myself as to how you'll get around that."

Curious as to how I'll get around that? What're you talking about? It'll be bloody impossible.

Isaac leaned forward to ensure direct eye contact. "The thing is … I know you will. I've complete confidence in you."

Jack swallowed.

"There's one piece of good news that I'll pass on. Prior to leaving, I lobbied to have the intelligence unit increased in size. Come next April, I expect there'll be two more constables and a new sergeant's position opening up. I'd like you to do what it takes, wear a muzzle if need be, to ensure you're still a candidate to receive your third stripe. I believe you'd be a valuable asset in that position."

"Thank you, sir."

"I want you to keep that under your hat for now. I would also suggest you be careful about our little talk today. If Mortimer were to find out, it'd do little to enhance your future chance of success."

"If I change my appearance and demeanour, won't he suspect I was tipped off?"

"I doubt it," Isaac replied. "The idea of me assisting someone in the non-commissioned ranks wouldn't be anything he could fathom. In his mind, you don't do anything unless it's to better your own career."

Jack bit his lip. *Isaac has confidence in me, but how the hell can I do it? No undercover, no surveillance teams, no wiretaps …*

"You're a smart cop, Jack. Find a way around him. Pure E needs to be stopped. If he's allowed to get away with threatening your family, it'll encourage him to go further next time. If not your family, then someone else's."

"You mentioned you believed Mortimer would be gone in two years," Jack said. "Would you allow your family to be threatened for that long?"

Isaac took a deep breath and slowly exhaled. "No, I wouldn't, so I expect you to take action soon."

Jack nodded silently.

Isaac frowned. "A response to Pure E is necessary. I appreciate that most of the tools you need to do the job have been removed."

Most? More like all.

"You still have your ability to think outside the parameters and come up with a viable solution. I'm positive you're the man for the job."

"Positive?" *How can you be positive? I'm not.*

"Look at it this way. I'm a lot smarter than Mortimer, yet you still managed to do end runs around me all these years."

"Sir, you were always in charge and I respected —"

"In charge?" Isaac scoffed. "I may have been calling the shots on paper, but you and I both know who was pulling the strings." He paused and his voice became grave. "Don't give up, Jack. Not with Mortimer at the helm. Not when you're needed the most."

Chapter Twenty

Jack returned home and sat with Natasha on the sofa to tell her what he'd learned.

"You're saying they're going to let the bikers get away with threatening us and our children?" Natasha's tone was angry. "I *know* you!" She tapped his chest for emphasis. "You're not going to back off! What am I supposed to do? Take Mike and Steve out of school, quit my job, and live in the Arctic while you go on a one-man crusade down here? If Mortimer isn't going to approve —"

"I'm not by myself," Jack replied. "I've got Laura. Plus other UC operators who volunteered to help as soon as they heard about the bikers coming to our house."

"Okay ... and in the meantime? What about our family! What can you do that won't cause us to suffer a backlash?"

Jack leaned over to cup her face with his hands. Then he looked her deeply in the eyes. "Don't ask. There's lots I can do ... and soon. We have a new informant. Highly placed. Satans Wrath is going to be getting nailed left, right, and centre. Pure E won't know what hit him, let alone who."

"But what about us?"

"Don't worry. You know I'd never do anything to jeopardize you or our boys."

He dropped his hands while she appeared to reflect on what he said. The anger left her face, but now she looked tired and worn out. *I've put her through so much over the years.* "I'm sorry," he said softly. "I love you so much."

"What did Laura have to say about it?"

You're supposed to say you love me, too. "I didn't see the need to spoil the rest of her weekend. Rose's, either, for that matter. I'll tell them tomorrow. The assistant commissioner has weekly meetings with the section commanders every Monday at 9:00 a.m. I expect he'll call Rose and me in after lunch."

Natasha's expression was unreadable. "Trust me," he said. "I'll deal with it."

At last she murmured, "Okay."

Thank you for trusting me. Jack smiled. "I'm also going to do something that I know will cheer you up." He ran his fingers through his beard. "This is coming off, along with the moustache. Then tomorrow on my way to work I'll get a decent haircut."

"Won't work," Natasha said.

"What do you mean?"

"I'm still upset. If you think getting rid of your hair will fix everything, you're wrong."

"Okay. How about I cook dinner tonight? Chicken cordon bleu with a bottle of Pinot Grigio?"

"That might help," she conceded.

***

At 9:00 a.m. Monday, Jack, wearing a navy-blue suit and tie, greeted the hairstylist. He'd called Laura the day before and told her he had some personal running around to do and wouldn't be in to work until ten or ten-thirty.

At 10:00 a.m., when Jack put on his coat, he discovered he'd received a voice message from Rose, telling him not to be late as Mortimer had called a meeting for ten-thirty. He tried to return her call as he hustled to his car, but it went to voice mail. At ten-thirty he rushed into his office and saw Laura. "Where's Rose?" he asked, flinging off his coat.

"What the heck did you do to yourself?" Laura exclaimed. "Have you got court?"

"No, I'll explain later."

"Rose left a moment ago to meet with Mortimer. You're supposed to be there."

Jack ran down the hall and brushed past the secretary. Mortimer was seated behind his desk and Rose sat before him.

"Sorry if I'm late," Jack said, noting Rose's astonishment when she looked at him.

"Who are you?" Mortimer demanded.

"Corporal Taggart, sir."

"Yes? Where is he?"

"No, sir … I'm Corporal Taggart."

Mortimer looked taken back. "You've changed your appearance. Why?"

"I was told my photo has been posted in the biker's clubhouses," Jack replied as he sat down. "I thought it prudent to change my appearance. I realize it will negate allowing me to perform certain undercover operations, but I think it's for the best."

"It's more than for the best!" Mortimer snapped. "One reason I called you in is to order you to cease any further undercover activities."

"Thank you, sir," Jack replied, sounding relieved. He then smiled nonchalantly.

"You don't mind?" Mortimer's eyebrows shot up.

"Certainly not. I've been doing it for years. Working nights and often away from home. It takes a toll on one's family. Perhaps now I won't need to deal directly with criminals."

"Which in your unit is what I expect," Mortimer replied. "You should be above that sort of thing."

Rose sat slack-jawed, then turned to Jack. "What do you plan on doing?"

Jack met her gaze. "I was thinking now that the operational plan has been completed, I'd liaise with the Canada Border Services Agency." He scratched the side of his face to hide the wink he gave her. "Maybe I could identify drug-smuggling methods and report on them."

Rose's outrage didn't allow her to register the wink. "Report on it?" Her eyebrows knit. "You mean regurgitate it back to CBSA? Give them their own information and make it sound like we discovered it?"

Jack winked again, this time slower. "Working day shifts will also give me time to take night classes in French to further my career." Rose's face became expressionless, but a slight shift of her eyes toward Mortimer and back said she'd clued in that he was up to something.

"I must say, I'm pleased," Mortimer said. "Progressive

thinking's exactly what's needed — which brings us to another matter." He picked up the operation plan and waved it in their faces.

"A problem, sir?" Rose questioned.

"I'm not going to approve it," Mortimer said bluntly, then studied their faces for a reaction.

Jack shrugged indifferently and glanced at his watch, giving the impression that he couldn't care less.

"Why aren't you approving it?" Rose asked. "Is there something you'd like amended — perhaps more justification for one of the targets?"

"No, the report appears to be thorough in that regard."

Rose's voice sounded calm, but Jack saw her knuckles turn white as she gripped the arms of her chair. "Then I don't understand, sir."

"These types of criminals should be handled by the police," Mortimer stated. He glanced at Jack and added, "Municipal police, I mean."

"The Combined Forces Special Enforcement Unit is made up of many officers from outside agencies," Rose said.

"You don't need to address me on that issue," Mortimer said frostily. "I'm fully aware of CFSEU and that it comes under our area of responsibility."

Therefore decision-making.

"I expect your unit to provide information on systemic issues or perhaps report on criminals of a higher calibre associated with white-collar crime."

Like embezzlers who don't carry guns. Gotcha.

"Forwarding something like this to Ottawa would be an embarrassment. They're busy enough as it is."

"Sir," Rose said in a tone that revealed a conscious effort

to control her emotions, "Corporal Taggart's report outlines Satans Wrath's three-three team. It's a team of professional cold-blooded killers. They are high-calibre criminals. Surveillance of them coupled with wiretap could be a way to gain evidence on Purvis Evans."

"You appear to have a problem thinking outside your own small world," Mortimer replied. "Granted, these individuals may have been involved in criminal activity at one time or another, but at the moment I-HIT is busy with active cases. Who knows when or even if these individuals will commit another murder? It could be years from now, perhaps never. I'm not approving a colossal waste of manpower for what in reality would be a fishing trip."

Mortimer's gaze switched back and forth between them. He then made a face as if he'd tasted something rancid and said, "You're both dismissed."

Jack smiled cordially as he stood. *You think it could be years before they commit another murder? Not if I've anything to do with it.*

Chapter Twenty-One

Once outside in the hallway, Rose grabbed Jack by the arm and faced him. "Damn you, Jack! What the hell is going on? What were you doing in there?"

"Let's get back to the office and I'll clue you in," Jack replied. "Laura needs to hear it, too."

Rose fell in step with Jack, but felt the need to vent. "I thought you'd have decked him in there," she seethed. "Instead, you acted like you couldn't care less."

"Decked him?" Jack gave a lopsided grin. "Come on Rose, violence is no way to solve an issue."

"Cut the crap! You arrive looking like you stepped out of *GQ* magazine and show no concern that your op plan is turned down." She looked at him accusingly. "You knew ahead of time!"

"Of course I knew. I hardly slept last night, I was in such a rage. Mortimer was hoping to get a reaction out of me to justify having me transferred." He glanced back and shook his head in disgust. "The last time I had to act that hard was when I was undercover buying child pornography. The urge to punch that guy was about the same."

"How'd you know and why didn't you warn me?" Rose replied crossly.

"I found out yesterday and thought there was no use ruining your weekend, as well. I was going to tell you when I came in. I figured Mortimer would be in his Monday-morning section-heads meeting. I didn't expect he'd call us in so soon."

"He's cancelled the section-heads meetings," Rose said.

"Likely afraid someone would say something that'd force him to make a decision," Jack suggested.

"So how'd you find out?" Rose asked.

"How about I explain in your office? It's sensitive."

"Fine." After a few more steps she said, "You did better than me at keeping your cool in there. I think he actually fell for it."

"I hope so."

"You'd never have gotten away with that with Isaac," she said.

"With Isaac I wouldn't have had to."

Minutes later, with both Jack and Laura present, Rose closed the door to her office. She took a seat, then took a deep breath and slowly exhaled. At last she looked at Jack. "Okay, let's have it."

Jack told them of his meeting with Isaac, who'd told him that Mortimer wasn't going to approve the op plan and was also looking for a reason to have Taggart transferred. He wrapped up by saying, "Isaac still believes that somehow Pure E can be made accountable."

"We can't do it on our own," Laura protested. "These guys aren't amateurs. We'll need large surveillance teams, wiretaps, informants, and no doubt undercover —"

"Suck it up Buttercup," Jack said. When Laura frowned at him, he added, "That's what Isaac said to me when I cried about the same thing. He told me I sounded like a baby."

"But what I said is true," Laura argued. She looked at Rose for confirmation.

Rose gave Jack a hard look. "What's your plan?"

"Plan?"

"Don't tell me you don't have one. You made a promise last month not to go behind my back. You said you were angry yesterday. You'd still be angry unless you had a way around this — so what is it?"

"Mortimer doesn't know who we have."

"Your new informant," Rose said.

"Yes, and I think our new informant views Pure E about the same way we view Mortimer. He'd be happy to rid the club of him, but at the same time he's still loyal to the club. Despite that, I believe we've got enough leverage that we'll be able to use him to make lots of arrests. He's already told us about three hundred kilos of weed coming in around the end of the month."

"Plus cocaine," Laura added. "He said —"

"— that there's a possibility of a little cocaine coming, too," Jack finished. He gave Laura a quelling look. She got the message and quit talking.

"Details of which you'll pass on to Crime Stoppers," Rose said.

"Exactly. In time Satans Wrath will realize they're receiving extra police attention. It won't take much to suggest that Pure E's actions are to blame."

Rose nodded. "With your informant, you'll have a better chance of monitoring the three-three. Who knows, maybe you'll even locate Damien's body."

"That'd be nice. I'm still hoping to catch Pure E on a wire."

"Really?" Rose sounded doubtful.

"I know, we won't get the opportunity to run wire ourselves, but if we find the body and I tip off Crime Stoppers, they'd pass it on to I-HIT. If I provide the right info, I-HIT might get a wire."

Rose took a moment to massage her temple with her fingertips, then said, "As much as I hate to admit it, Mortimer did raise a valid point. Nobody knows how long it'll be before the three-three do another hit."

"It's not like we have to watch them all the time," Jack replied. "Our informant will let us know. I don't think it'll be long. Pure E wants to make a name for himself."

"You're right about that," Laura agreed. "He took over less than a month ago and there've been four murders. So I'm with Jack. It won't be long."

Jack nodded. *Especially with a little incentive.*

Chapter Twenty-Two

Immediately upon returning to their office, Laura rounded on Jack. "Why don't you want Rose to know about the cocaine coming in? Our friend said it was one hundred and twenty kilos. That's huge, yet you told Rose that there was a possibility of 'a little coke' coming in." Before Jack could respond, she added accusingly, "You promised not to go behind her back."

"That was before my family was threatened," Jack said brusquely. "I tried to do it right. What am I supposed to do? This time it was only a threat. Next time …"

Laura fell silent, then sighed audibly. "Obviously there's more to your plan than you told Rose."

Jack grimaced. "It wasn't *your* family who was threatened." He waited a beat. "I know you said you'd stay with me until it was over, but maybe you should ask for a transfer. Things could get ugly around here."

"Are you kidding?" Laura looked taken aback. "In case you don't know it, I consider you family. Them paying you a visit was like paying me a visit. I told you I'll be with you until this is over." She glared at him, then said, "Spit it out. What's the deal on the coke?"

"It might come in handy to use as bait."

"Bait?"

Jack mulled over what he intended to do. "You absolutely sure you want in? We've worked in the grey zone before, but this is inky black."

"We're not going to let him get away with threatening us," Laura declared bitterly. "Mortimer's taken away the tools we need to do the job. I don't see any other choice." She paused, then punched him in the arm. "Bow out? No way. It's like I'm in the middle of a movie and being told to leave the theatre. I'm staying to the end. I'll even buy the popcorn."

Jack sat at his desk and when Laura did likewise he eyed her for a moment. "Okay. I do have a plan. In my mind we have three priority targets. Pure E being number one."

"Goes without saying."

"The thing is, if he suspects that either you or I are going after him, he'll come after our families."

"We should shove him in front of a bus," Laura suggested.

"If anything like that was to occur and the club felt we were responsible, it'd jeopardize our families, as well."

"I wasn't being serious."

"I know, but we do have to be careful. Then there's my number-two target — Vicki."

"Vicki? I thought it would be Buck or perhaps the three-three."

"Guys like Buck and the three-three will always be around. They're like soldiers and would be replaced. As far as Vicki goes, I feel I owe it to Damien to get her. She set him up after he risked his life to save her and Buck." Jack paused, then said, "That bitch deserves what I want to use her for."

"Which is?"

"I'm thinking we could follow her to find Damien's body."

"She won't know where it is," Laura replied, "let alone go to it."

"I know."

"Then how? If she doesn't — oh, man." Laura's eyes searched his. "She won't be alive when we're following her."

"Right. Pure E had Buck murder his dad. Maybe he'd have him murder his mom, too, if the situation called for it. If not him, then someone in the three-three would."

"If the situation called for it?"

"The trick is to pass info on to Pure E and gain his confidence without him suspecting it came from us. Info that will give him reason to order a hit and then we'll be there to watch. The problem is it might be tough to follow them without a proper surveillance team. Maybe our friend can help, though."

Laura took a deep breath and slowly blew the air out, making her lips vibrate. "Gain his confidence? I'm almost afraid to ask."

"It's all part of the plan I have." Jack paused. "I think we should discuss that and the rest of my plan someplace other than here."

"Why?"

"Because it needs to be kept secret and you'll probably freak out and start yelling at me."

"It's that bad of a plan?"

"I'd like to think it's that good."

Laura made a face. "Can you at least tell me who the third target is?"

"Someone far worse than Pure E," he said bitterly.

"Worse?" Laura gave an unladylike snort. "I don't think such a person exists."

"Pure E is only one criminal. How about the man who wants to stop us from catching Pure E or others like him?"

Laura's face paled. "Mortimer?" she breathed.

"Forget the popcorn." Jack's voice was harsh. "Let's go for a drink and I'll tell you about my plan."

Chapter Twenty-Three

The following day Jack was in the office when he received a call he'd been anxiously awaiting.

"The three hundred keys of weed will arrive tomorrow morning," Lance said bluntly. "I don't know from where 'cause that ain't my concern. Could even be from more than one grow-op."

"You have the details?" Jack asked.

"Enough for you to do your thing. A truck's delivering it to some mall near Abbotsford at 10:00 a.m. A prospect from Whiskey Jake's chapter by the name of Daryl Voggel is looking after it and will oversee the exchange. It'll be split in half and two guys will mule it from there."

"What two guys?"

"Dunno their names. One's from Calgary and he's taking it back with him. He's friends with Voggel and will be staying with him while he's here. The other guy's from Prince George. Got no info on him."

"Abbotsford's about an hour's drive from here," Jack noted. "There are a few malls there. No thoughts as to which one?"

"No, but probably close to the Trans-Canada so it's easier to get in and out of. Lance paused. "I suppose you already got Voggel's address? All I know is he lives in Port Coquitlam."

"Yup, he does."

"Remind me to call you at Christmas if I need to update my mailing list."

Jack smiled.

"Voggel will meet the guy from Prince George tonight. I can't get any more info without drawin' heat. Especially if you bust them at the mall."

"I'll let the one hundred and fifty keys to Prince George go, but bust the Calgary shipment and throw the heat back that way."

"Fine by me."

"Does the cash change hands when they pick up?"

"Not on the Calgary end. That's taken care of by our club there. They're going to send us some meth later on to pay for it. Prince George is different. That guy'll pay when he picks up."

"What about the one hundred and twenty keys of blow you'd said your prospect, Buster Linquist, was handling?"

"It's due to arrive a week today. Probably late afternoon."

"Tuesday, October 28," Jack noted. "Is Shane McRooney still the mule?"

"Yup. I'll be getting delivery updates so I'll give you a heads-up the day before he arrives." Lance paused. "You gonna bust him on the highway before he arrives?"

"No, I'll seize the coke after it arrives."

"That's smarter. What with the phony paperwork, it'd fool a judge or jury into thinking he didn't know what he was haulin'. It'd be better to wait until you see Buster comin' and goin' so that you'll know the trunks've been opened."

"I don't plan on arresting anyone for the coke. I'll also direct the heat to Montreal."

"Not arrest anyone? You're gonna try and turn McRooney? He can't help you. All he could give you is Buster and if you wait and nail Buster, there's nobody he could give you except people under him. That's if he'd even co-operate, which ain't likely."

"Seizing the coke without making any arrests is part of a bigger picture. I won't try to turn or bust either one of them. My goal is to build trust."

"Trust? With who?"

"Pure E."

"Pure E? What the fuck?"

"It's part of a bigger picture. I won't get into that with you yet. How long before you expect Buster to be into the stash?"

"The storage locker closes at six for the night and it may be almost that before McRooney gets here and unloads. I expect the action'll start the next day."

"Good. I'll tell you this much about the bigger picture. You're going to hear there's a dirty cop. Don't worry about it. It'll be me."

That night Jack and Laura saw a car parked at Voggel's address that was registered to a Martin Rondel with a Calgary address. Another car arrived later and was registered to a Thomas Bailey with a Prince George address.

At 9:45 a.m. the following day, Jack and Laura, each in a separate vehicle, followed Voggel, Rondel, and Bailey, who all drove to the High Street Shopping Centre located alongside the Trans-Canada Highway in Abbotsford. The three men parked and then went into a coffee shop.

At 10:30 a.m. they saw their three targets, along with a fourth man, exit the coffee shop. The stranger went to a van and drove it over to where Rondel and Bailey's cars were parked. Meanwhile Voggel watched from his vehicle.

Moments later several duffle bags were transferred from the van to the trunks of both cars. The van left and Rondel and Bailey drove away soon after, but Voggel remained parked, speaking on his phone. He also appeared to be looking around, and Jack drummed his fingers on the steering wheel as they waited.

Laura lowered her binoculars. "Couldn't see the plate on the van," she relayed into the phone. "How about you?"

"Negative. Don't worry about it. Sit tight. Voggel is watching the lot. "

"Would've been nice to have a proper surveillance team. Might've even have seen Voggel collect the money inside the coffee shop."

"Doesn't matter," Jack said. "We're not going to court regardless."

"Only because of Mortimer. Instead of getting four guys, we have to settle for one. You going to call Crime Stoppers?"

Jack had no time to answer. "Voggel's leaving," he said. "Let's get out on the highway and make sure Rondel's on his way first."

Voggel took the ramp heading west on the Trans-Canada toward Vancouver while Jack and Laura headed east. They soon caught up to Rondel and Bailey, who were both travelling within the speed limit.

"Perfect," Jack said. "In about an hour they'll be at Hope. Bailey will take the exit to head north while Rondel heads east to Calgary. I'm hanging up to call the tip line."

"Love it when a plan comes together," Laura said.

Jack made his anonymous call to Crime Stoppers. He told them that Martin Rondel would be on the highway leaving Hope in about an hour on his way to Calgary and that he had one hundred and fifty kilos of marijuana in his trunk. After describing Rondel's car, he mentioned he'd have more information for Crime Stoppers in the future and was assigned an identity number for future reference.

An hour later Laura saw a marked patrol car pull Rondel's car over east of Hope. Seconds later Jack also passed the patrol car and noted a second patrol car arriving. He felt pleased and called Laura. "Okay, time for me to call Whiskey Jake."

Whiskey Jake entered the office at the Satan's Girls Entertainment Agency and nodded at the secretary. She pushed her takeout order of Chinese food aside. "Hey, Jake. Got somethin' for you." She then handed him a padded manila envelope. "It's a phone. Someone shoved it through the mail slot in the door last night."

"A phone?"

"I heard it ring at about 9:00 a.m., then again an hour later."

Whiskey Jake examined the envelope. A typed sticker read PRIVATE: ONLY TO BE OPENED BY WJ. He frowned as he carried the envelope back to his office.

Using disposable phones was the norm for club members, but they weren't usually delivered in this manner. He opened the envelope and took out the phone and looked for a note. There wasn't one, so he set it down. Moments later it rang. The display said the number was blocked. He answered it.

"You alone?" a man asked.

"Yeah, who's this?"

"I'll tell you in a sec, but not if you're inside a building. Go outside so I know there's nobody listening on your end ... if you get my drift."

A moment later Whiskey Jake stepped out onto the sidewalk. "Okay, I'm clear. Who's this? I don't recognize your voice."

"I'm a cop."

"Yeah, right. Pretty funny. No ... who is this?"

"I'm an RCMP officer. I work out of 'E' Division Headquarters."

"What the fuck?"

"I got some information to pass on to you. All you gotta do is listen. I'll call you again in a day or two. At that time if you decide what I'm about to tell you is worth something, I'll continue to pass stuff on to you. If not, you'll never hear from me again."

"I don't understand. I'm an honest businessman. I'm not involved in —"

"Shut up and listen. You're not incriminating yourself if you keep quiet."

Whiskey Jake paused. "Okay ... talk."

"The heat is really being turned up on you guys. This morning the narcs watched a weed deal go down in Abbotsford. It involved one of your guys. Someone by the name of Voggel. Also a guy from Calgary by the name of Martin Rondel. They said he came out to pick up one hundred and fifty keys of weed." Jack waited a beat. "You listening to me?"

"I'm listening, but I'm not saying anything and don't know anything about it."

"You don't need to say anything. The investigation started in Calgary, but they want you guys to think uniform stumbled on it. They're going to have Highway Patrol bust Rondel on his way back. Probably near Hope. I tried calling you earlier, but you didn't answer. Might be too late to save Rondel, but there's that other guy."

"What other guy?"

"Surveillance said they spotted another guy picking up at the same time as Rondel. From what I heard he's from Prince George. They plan on following him when he arrives in Prince George in the hope of busting more people to build a conspiracy. There's nobody following now because it's about an eight-hour drive. They just called ahead to have a team waiting when he arrives."

"You a narc?" Whiskey Jake asked.

"Nope. I'm in a more valuable position than that. My job is being a bum-boy for the brass. Sending out snot-o-grams to members over policy errors or briefing the brass on things going on they should know about. Pretty much anything of importance is funnelled through me or a couple of others. I never leave the office, but I know pretty much everything. When I call again, I expect to get paid what you think it's worth."

"You trying to get me for bribing a police officer?" Whiskey Jake asked suspiciously.

"Are you kidding? I don't even want to *meet* you. That being said, should someone leave a fat envelope that I find someplace, it'd make me happy. We can talk about that another time. This isn't a one-time thing. We got a new boss. Assistant Commissioner Mortimer. He's got a bee up his ass because of those stunts you pulled on Taggart in the intelligence unit."

"Dunno know what you're talking about."

Jack chuckled. "Yeah, sure you don't. It worked on Taggart. He doesn't want anything to do with you guys. He's cleaned up his appearance and looks like a Jehovah's Witness — but Mortimer's another story. He's top brass and has organized a Canada-wide investigation against your club. It's already picking up steam and will be going international. Money and resources from other investigations will be reassigned to work on you guys. I'm telling you, *I am in a position to help you*" — Jake emphasized every word — "providing you make it worth my while."

"The cops are always working on us," Whiskey Jake said disdainfully.

"Never like this. You'll need me. Treat me good and I'll treat you good."

"You, uh, think my office is bugged?"

"Not by the RCMP. At least, not yet, but I don't generally have access to what Vancouver city cops are doing. One more thing. If even the slightest rumour spreads about me feeding you info, I'll never call again. Same thing goes if you ever try to find out my name. Your club doesn't have any rats that I know about, but I'm not taking any chances. Don't tell anyone about me! You got it?"

"I hear what you're …"

But his caller had hung up.

"He go for it?" Laura asked, tamping down her excitement as soon as Jack called her back.

"I think I sold it."

"How'd he respond when you mentioned Mortimer?"

"He didn't comment and I didn't expect him to. I was only laying the groundwork. Once I toss Mortimer's name out a few more times, we may get a response."

"A response such as Mortimer getting a home visit like you did," Laura replied.

"I'd love it if they drove their hogs across his lawn or something."

"So would I." Laura felt a lump in her throat. *It's the "or something" that bothers me.*

"Maybe it'd convince Mortimer to reconsider the op plan," Jack continued.

"More likely he'd pee himself … then crawl to them on his hands and knees and beg them to leave him alone."

Jack was silent for a moment. "You're right. Rut marks on his lawn won't be enough."

Oh, man …

Chapter Twenty-Four

Lance Morgan arrived in Stanley Park at the same time as Pure E. Moments later they bought coffee from the concession stand and joined Whiskey Jake, who was waiting at a nearby picnic table.

Whiskey Jake waited until Pure E took a sip of coffee, then smiled. "Got some interesting news."

"I presume you didn't call me to talk about the weather," Pure E replied.

"Nope. I got a call from a cop a couple hours ago."

"Who? Taggart?" Pure E asked.

"No, but from what I heard, we don't need to worry about him anymore."

Lance's face remained passive. *Not worry about Taggart? Fuck, are* you *stupid.*

"What do you mean?" Pure E frowned.

"This guy wouldn't give me his name," Whiskey Jake continued, "but is looking to make some cash. He let me know that the narcs were watching one of our weed deals go down this morning. It involved a guy our boys sent from Calgary and a dealer from Prince George. His info was right on. He also told me that Taggart has cleaned himself up and doesn't want anything to do with us. That I might not've believed, but the weed deal was real, so that part is probably true, too."

Lance's brain spun as Whiskey Jake went into detail about the phone he was given and the call he'd received. *Jack, what the hell are you up to? Trying to make it look like you're no longer involved so that later when someone gets whacked we won't point the finger at you?* He eyed Pure E. *Someone? Guess I know who that's gonna be.*

"So, sounds like we got a rat cop." Pure E looked smug. "That's good. Fine if he doesn't give us his name. We'll call him Rat Cop." He eyed Whiskey Jake. "Were you able to warn the runners in time?"

"Not for Calgary. The cops grabbed him outside of Hope."

"Fuck," Pure E muttered.

"We were able to get word to the Prince George guy in time. He turned around and came back. The weed'll be passed off to someone else until we figure out what to do."

Pure E eyed Whiskey Jake. "And he said the heat came from Calgary?"

"Yeah, but, uh, yeah, that's what he said," Whiskey Jake replied.

Pure E glared at Whiskey Jake. "But, uh, what?"

Whiskey Jake hesitated, then said, "He said some head cop by the name of Mortimer is coming after us because of what we did to Taggart. He said the guy is ordering an investigation against us right across Canada and probably beyond."

Pure E's lips curled back as he appeared to think about it. "Who is this fuckhead?"

"A new boss is all he said," Whiskey Jake replied. "I never heard his name before."

Lance's face remained impassive when Pure E briefly locked eyes with his. It wasn't necessary to say *I told you so*.

"Fuck!" Pure E backhanded his coffee cup off the table and sent it flying. "I don't trust any cop, rat or otherwise!" He paused a moment before continuing, "He said the heat came from Calgary, but we can't be sure. Maybe the cops wanted to let the Prince George guy escape. Maybe that's where the heat's coming from."

"Rat Cop did try to call me a few times in the morning, but I didn't get the phone until noon," Whiskey Jake said. "By then it was too late to save the Calgary end. I did give Basil a call. He's going to look after the case."

"We should still warn Calgary," Lance noted.

Pure E nodded. "You take care of that. Let 'em know they might have heat, but don't do any further business with the guy from Prince George until we figure things out."

"Do I let Calgary know about Rat Cop?" Lance questioned.

"No. If they do have a leak, I don't want to jeopardize him in case he's who he says he is. I'll talk to Basil. Tell Calgary that Basil thinks the investigation started there because of something the cops said."

"When Rat Cop calls, what do I tell 'im?" Whiskey Jake questioned. "Do I keep packin' this extra phone around or not? If so, are we gonna pay 'im or grab 'im and see who he is?"

"Fuck, if he's bein' straight, he's worth a lot," Pure E said. "He's obviously paranoid. If we make a move on 'im he's liable to shut down, so keep the phone close and pay him fifteen hundred bucks. Tell him it would've been double if he'd told us in time to save the other half."

At 4:45 p.m. the following day Whiskey Jake received his next call from Rat Cop.

"You got something for me?" Rat Cop asked.

"Yup. Got fifteen c's."

"Fifteen hundred bucks? Is that all? I was expecting a little more," Rat Cop grumbled.

"Would've been double if you'd connected with me earlier yesterday. Right now we don't trust you. If you're being straight with us, things will improve."

Rat Cop hesitated. "Yeah … okay, but trust goes both ways. I don't want to meet you in person."

"I'm fine with that. How do you want to do it? I'm free at the moment."

"I just got off work. Gotta whip back to my apartment and change out of uniform. You know where the Home Depot store is in Coquitlam?"

"I can find it."

"You driving that white Lexus of yours?"

"Uh, yeah."

"Come alone and be there in an hour."

An hour later Whiskey Jake arrived at the store and parked. In no time he received another call. "I'm watching you. Drive a block east of where you're at. There's a Starbucks there. Leave the envelope for me on your right rear tire and go in and have a coffee. If all goes well, I'll be calling you again soon."

Whiskey Jake did as instructed. After buying a coffee he sat looking out the window. Soon a guy in jeans and a dark hoodie, face concealed, walked quickly up to his Lexus, retrieved the envelope, and then disappeared behind a row of cars.

Whiskey Jake returned to his Lexus and pulled out of the lot, but caught a glimpse of the guy in the hoodie walking into a commercial complex in the next block. He smiled to himself when he saw there was a casino in the complex. *You got a gambling problem, Rat Cop? Fucking perfect.*

"Anything?" Jack asked as soon as Laura answered his call from the casino.

"Nope, he eyed you as you headed toward the casino, then drove off in the opposite direction. I'm pretty sure he came alone."

"Good, but to be extra cautious, I'll hit the men's room and put my hoodie on under my jacket and pull track pants over my jeans. Pick me up outside."

Moments later Laura picked Jack up and drove out of the lot. She saw him smile when he counted out fifteen 100-dollar bills from the envelope.

"Not bad pay considering we seized half their weed," he noted. "Imagine the looks on their faces if they knew."

"I worry about the look on Rose's face if she knew," Laura replied.

Jack shrugged. "She was okay yesterday when we told her we had one hundred and fifty kilos of weed seized."

"I thought she seemed a little grumpy."

"Only because we had to use Crime Stoppers. Can't say as I blame her." He stared at Laura longer than normal and she sensed he was worried about her. "Today's Thursday," he said. "The coke shipment is supposed to arrive next Tuesday. Let's take tomorrow off and not work until Monday. I've a feeling we're going to be putting in long days next week."

"Three days off in a row?" *Wonderful!* "Yes, I'd like that."

"I thought that might cheer you up." He looked at the money in his hand. "We'll use some of this to cover investigational expenses. The rest can go to charity."

"What? You're not taking me shopping?"

Jack grinned. "I don't think Rose would approve."

The mention of Rose not approving made her feel depressed about Jack's plan. *Bet she wouldn't approve of murder, either.*

Chapter Twenty-Five

Rose felt antsy Monday morning as she waited for Jack and Laura to arrive at work. Jack had left her a note Thursday night saying they were taking Friday off, but over the weekend she'd thought about it and suspected they were up to something.

As soon as they arrived, she waved them into her office. When they sat down, she saw Jack look at her with a raised eyebrow. "You tell me if something is up," she stated.

"What do you mean?" he asked.

"You took Friday off."

"We did," Jack replied, then exchanged a puzzled look with Laura.

"I'm not begrudging you that. I know the two of you put in a lot of voluntary hours preparing that op plan."

"So what is it?" Laura asked. "Why would you think something's up?"

"Because I sense that there is." Rose spoke firmly.

Laura screwed up her face and looked at Jack questioningly.

She's hiding something. "Don't give me that crap. Not after all the two of you have put me through over the years. By now ... well, you should know we're on the same team."

"If I didn't feel we were, I wouldn't have told you that I tipped off Crime Stoppers," Jack said.

Rose nodded. *That sounded lame. Whatever they're up to is more than tipping off Crime Stoppers.*

"I know you care about us," Jack said. "No doubt you've lost more than a few hours' worth of sleep over the years, with the things we've been involved in."

"More like a few years' worth," Rose shot back.

"I feel bad about that, but you have to admit that the action we took during those times was appropriate under the circumstances."

Yes, on paper it seemed that way, but who are you trying to kid, Jack? You're trying to read my mind — if I sound accusatory you'll clam up. "Yes, the action you take always seems appropriate, but what do you consider appropriate now?"

"What do you mean?"

What do I mean? Damn you, you're stalling for time to think. "What I mean is your family's been threatened. You have a high-level source that, handled properly, could do significant damage to Satans Wrath, as well as an assistant commissioner who ... well, what can I say?"

"The word 'asshole' comes to mind," Jack said.

"So what're you doing about it?"

"We discussed this before," Jack replied. "The source gave us one hundred and fifty kilos of weed last week. I tipped off Crime Stoppers and the arrest was made. We plan to continue along the same lines."

"I thought you were in agreement with us doing that," Laura said.

"I was, but I don't see the two of you being satisfied with maintaining the status quo for long. If your op plan had been approved, we'd have caught more than one weed runner."

"You're absolutely right, but what choice do we have?" Jack asked.

That's just it — we don't. We're stuck with who we've got. Am I wrong to be suspicious? She sighed. "I guess we don't."

"Not as long as Mortimer's in charge," Jack said, glancing at Laura.

That subtle change in Laura's face when Jack looked at her … anxiety? About what? The mention of Mortimer? Or is it fear? Rose saw that Jack's face had hardened, and she felt her own fear grow. Fear that they had something planned, and she wouldn't know about it until it was too late. *But too late for what?*

Monday evening Lance called Jack to let him know that the McRooney's moving truck was on schedule and due to arrive in Vancouver with the one hundred and twenty kilos of cocaine the following afternoon.

By late Tuesday morning Jack and Laura, each in their own surveillance vehicle, parked at a rest stop alongside the Trans-Canada Highway two hours east of Vancouver. At 2:30 p.m. they spotted the moving truck and followed.

At 4:15 p.m. Jack watched the truck enter the Pacific Self-Storage compound located on the outskirts of Vancouver. The yard was surrounded by a high chain-link fence with rolls of razor wire laced along the top. Entry was through a gate beside the office. Beyond that were rows of storage units divided by laneways.

Jack smiled as he phoned Laura. A tall sign jutting above the compound had identified the storage facility, so she'd stayed a block behind so as not to attract attention to her vehicle. "Bingo. He's checking into the office."

"Peaks and valleys," Laura said. "We're on a peak. You able to keep the eye?"

"I should be able to. There's a commercial complex across the street with lots of cars for cover. It's safe for you to drive in and join me."

Moments later Laura got into Jack's SUV. They then watched as McRooney backed his truck up to one of the storage units. They weren't able to see what he unloaded, but at 5:00 p.m. he drove away.

"So who are we going to be?" Laura asked Jack.

"I've got some fake ID to rent a locker under the name of Roberts. If the place is being live-monitored by camera, I'll park near McRooney's locker and pretend we've got a flat tire. Shouldn't take me long to pick the padlock. If that doesn't work, then I'll stay overnight in whichever locker we rent and do it after dark. You could pick me up tomorrow morning when they open. I'll also need you outside to throw a little heat on any bikers who show up. That and take care of the dog."

"What dog?"

Jack passed the binoculars. "Look at the sign on the front gate."

Laura peered through the binoculars. "Oh, man. Guard dog on duty," she said. "What am I supposed to do with it?"

"Go to the far corner of the compound and keep the mutt busy while I steal the dope."

"How?"

"I don't know. Tease him and stick your fingers through the fence."

Laura faked a glare. "I get awful bad vibes about you, Mr. Roberts."

"You're not the only one. Rose is suspicious, too. She suspects something's up."

"Isn't there always?" She gestured with her thumb at several cardboard boxes in the back of his SUV. "Anything in 'em?"

"Mostly empty. They're for show in case whoever runs the place noses around. Got some candy bars and water in case I spend the night." He then gave a nod toward the facility. "We need to hustle. It closes at 6:00 p.m. and doesn't open again till 6:00 a.m."

Moments later Jack rented a storage locker. He was pleased to see that it was only three units down from McRooney's. Spending the night inside would not be necessary. In conversation with the manager, Jack learned that the facility had closed-circuit cameras, but they were only for backup in the event of theft; they weren't live-monitored.

He then drove to his assigned locker, but strategically parked his SUV so as to block the vision of anyone who might glance at the CCTV cameras.

Laura busied herself on the pretence of unloading cardboard boxes and placing them in the laneway to provide further cover for Jack as he picked the padlock on McRooney's locker.

Eureka! The lock sprang open. Jack then lifted the overhead door enough to duck inside. It didn't take long to find three locked trunks. Five minutes later those same trunks were stashed in the locker he'd rented.

"Well?" Laura gestured at the trunks.

Jack used his lock picks again and opened one trunk. It was packed with cocaine. "Beautiful," he said, then smiled at Laura.

They quickly counted what turned out to be forty kilos of cocaine. Jack glanced at his watch. "Closing time. We need to leave. I think we can assume that the other two hold forty keys, as well."

"You going to make the call?" Laura asked.

"As soon as we're back across the street."

Whiskey Jake was on his way to pick up Pure E and go to dinner and then clubbing when his rat phone rang. He smiled to himself as he answered. *Yup, Rat Cop, you're next to the Mounties' top man and you work for me.* "Yeah?" he answered.

Whiskey Jake's feeling of elation was short-lived.

Chapter Twenty-Six

Pure E's face became a mottled red. "What the fuck? How'd they find out?" he spluttered.

Whiskey Jake waited as an elderly couple walked past them outside Pure E's condo. "Rat Cop said the heat came from Montreal. He said one of our guys had approached the cops months ago sayin' he'd rat if they paid him. At the time the cops told him he was askin' for too much. Apparently this fuckin' Mortimer dude turned around and authorized it."

"Who the fuck was it?" Pure E fumed.

"Rat Cop says he doesn't know. He didn't find out about it until he was about to go home. Then some narcs from Montreal showed up, along with some from here, and they had a meeting. The fuckin' narcs are replacing the blow with flour, except for the top layer. He said their tech guys rented another locker and stashed their van in it. They're gonna put trackers in some of the keys and then put the trunks back. He said they'll also install cameras."

"Hopin' to do a bunch of us on conspiracy," Pure E stated. "Yup."

"Is the dope already gone?"

"Yeah, except for a few keys at the top of each trunk. He said the narcs were laughin' about maybe the tech guys gettin' their asses chewed by the guard dog, but said a couple of cops are waitin' outside the compound to distract it when need be."

"Fuckin' hell. This ain't no small change."

"No shit. We paid twenty-four a key. Times one hundred and twenty means we're out about three mil."

Pure E slammed his fist into the palm of his hand and swore again.

"At least the cops won't have anyone to arrest," Whiskey Jake said. "At least not on our end. Dunno know about Montreal."

"You send anyone over to look?"

"You mean to the storage locker?"

"No, I'm talkin' about the fuckin' vault the cops keep it in." He gave Whiskey Jake a look of disgust. "Yeah, the goddamn storage locker."

"Not yet, but all the details are right on."

"Check it out, anyway."

Whiskey Jake nodded. "What about Rat Cop? He'll wanna be paid."

"Obviously he's being straight with us. There's no way the cops would seize all this dope without arresting anyone. Keep him on the hook. Pay 'im three g's, but tell 'im that if he'd called us in time to save the dope we would've paid him ten times that much. Also get hold of Lance. Tell him to send that French guy he has in his chapter down to Montreal to let 'em know. Make sure to tell him that only their exec level is to know how we found out. I don't want word getting out about Rat Cop."

At 7:30 p.m. Buster Linquist parked his car two blocks away from Pacific Self-Storage. He zipped up his jacket to protect himself from the light rain and put a leash on his pit bull before walking the remaining distance.

It was an industrial area and the commercial properties were closed for the night, but he reasoned that if he was spotted he'd simply look like some guy out walking his dog. It didn't take long for him to spot a car backed into a parking stall across the street and facing the storage facility. The car lights were off, but the engine was running and he could make out two figures in the front seat.

Buster swore under his breath. *Yup, we got heat.*

At 9:00 p.m. Lance phoned Jack. "You know what they're calling you?"

"No," Jack replied.

"Rat Cop."

"I've been called worse. The point is, do they trust me yet?"

"Yes."

"Were McRooney and Buster told about me? I mean Rat Cop?"

"No, Pure E is protecting you. McRooney and Buster were told that word from Montreal was that the load was compromised. I sent Buster out and he spotted the surveillance to confirm everything. McRooney is going to let the rent expire, and if any heat comes his way, he'll blame it on whatever name is on the bogus moving invoice."

"Good."

"I'm also sending my VP out to Montreal to warn them they got a rat."

"André Gagnon still your vice-president?"

"Yeah. Also, you might like to know that Whiskey Jake has been told to send three grand your way."

"Perfect. I'd say that's a good indication they trust me."

"Yeah, so tell me, is this big picture of yours a plan to supplement your retirement?"

Jack grunted his disdain. "It would take more than three grand for that."

"It's the one hundred and twenty keys I'm talking about. We get ours at volume price, so the club is out about three million, but you could easily sell it quick for four mil."

"I'm not a dope dealer," Jack said.

"Yeah, I know. A lot of other things maybe." Lance paused, then asked, "Am I ever gonna get to see this big picture of yours?"

"You saw the opening feature. I wanted Pure E to trust Rat Cop."

"I'd say you got that — but what's next?"

"Next is to find out what the three-three did with Damien's body."

"How you gonna do that?" Lance asked. "Even I don't know."

"The story the club members have been fed is that Damien skipped the country to avoid his money-laundering charges."

"Yeah."

Jack's voice was cold. "I think it's time his wife joined him."

Chapter Twenty-Seven

It was suppertime Thursday when Whiskey Jake parked his car outside a coffee shop as instructed by Rat Cop. Although a different location than before, Whiskey Jake felt it was no coincidence that Hastings Racecourse was only two blocks away. *So Rat Cop, you like to bet on the horses, too.*

As before, he placed an envelope on his rear tire, entered the coffee shop, and seconds later, saw the man with the hoodie over his face retrieve it. Minutes later, Rat Cop called.

"Three grand," he whined. "Is that all I get for saving you guys from going to jail?"

Greedy prick. "Would've been thirty grand if you'd saved the dope."

"Yeah, well, I did the best I could. The narcs know they've been burned. Said they spotted one of your guys with a dog checking the place out. They removed all the electronic stuff and shut down their surveillance.

Now they're wondering how they got burned. Three grand ain't much. I really went out on a limb to save your guys."

"Get one thing clear. You didn't save any of our guys. Maybe a prospect, but nobody important. As far as the narcs go, they were bound to clue in when nobody went to the stash. I had a hard time convincin' someone to pay you what I did."

"Would the person who needed convincing be Purvis Evans?"

"Yeah, but if you're thinking of talking to him, forget it," Whiskey Jake said adamantly.

"What would he pay if I saved him from going to jail … along with all of your three-threes and Buck Zabat?"

"What the fuck you talkin' about?" Whiskey Jake's words drew the gazes of other customers. "Gimme a sec," he said, then walked outside.

"Thought that might catch your attention," Rat Cop said.

"What've you heard?" Whiskey Jake asked.

"There's a woman — Vicki Zabat."

"What about her?"

"She's making a deal with I-HIT and is going to testify."

"About what?"

"To start with, she was the one who set Damien up by calling Basil Westmount and pretending to be from her own lawyer's office."

I know, Buck told me. "I'm not sure what you're talking about."

"The hell you aren't. Anyway, she broke under interrogation. For immunity against what she did, she's going to testify that she was home when Buck spoke to Damien. She said Buck later told her he was wearing a wire so that the three-three could listen."

He told her about the wire? Fuckin' idiot didn't tell us that!

"Vicki said Damien told Buck that he ratted about the boatload of cocaine in France and right after that Buck brought in four guys from the three-three and she watched as they took him away."

"You're saying she knows the three-three?" Whiskey Jake was surprised.

"Don't know if she knew them or not, but she picked four guys out of the mugshots. They were Floyd Hackman, Vic Trapp, Pasquale Bazzoli, and Nick Crowe."

Shit!

"I'm told the case is circumstantial because they can't find Damien's body, but with Vicki's testimony there's a good chance of conviction. She'll testify that Buck told her he shot his dad under Purvis Evans's order. Coupled with Purvis Evans taunting Taggart on Damien's phone and the message left on the wall of the triple murder at the farmhouse — imagine what a jury will think. Gangsterism charges will be laid, too."

That fucking whore! She's dead!

"So what do you think?" Rat Cop prodded.

"I'll need to get back to you," Whiskey Jake replied.

"What I told you has gotta be worth a lot. I'm really sticking my neck out."

"Any idea when the arrests will take place?"

"At the moment the prosecution is drawing up some documents for whatever lawyer Vicki has to guarantee her immunity. I heard the lawyers are supposed to meet a week from tomorrow to finalize the deal. That'd be Friday, November 7. I'm guessing the arrests will happen shortly after."

"November 7," Whiskey Jake repeated.

"Yeah. Mortimer also suggested that I-HIT could offer immunity and entry into Witness Protection for someone in the three-three if need be, but it doesn't sound like the prosecution will need it."

"Is Vicki being protected?"

"Not at the moment. She will be after the documentation is agreed on and signed."

"I gotta go," Whiskey Jake said. "Call me later."

"Later? When?"

"You'll know when."

"How much will I get paid for —"

"I dunno. We'll talk … after."

Jack ended the call and looked at Laura, who repositioned herself in the passenger seat. She solemnly stared out the window. "You okay?" he asked quietly.

Her face snapped toward him. "I told you before that I'd go along with it!"

"Then why are you angry with me?"

Laura made a face. "It's not you per se. It's life. It's Mortimer. It's Vicki for killing the man who loved her. It's Pure E for having the audacity to threaten our families."

"My family," Jack corrected.

"Your family is my family," Laura retorted. "We're cops. We're all family."

Jack nodded.

"We shouldn't have to work like this. It's not how things are supposed to be. You and I being judge and jury … it's not right."

"I agree, but what choice do we have, other than giving Satans Wrath free rein to do whatever they like?"

"And that's why I'm angry! I feel like we've been backed into a corner with no way out and I hate it."

"Me, I've found a way out. If you don't want to take the route I'm taking, walk away. I sure as hell wouldn't blame you. In fact, I'd probably respect you more for making an intelligent decision."

Laura scowled. "You know I'd never do that. We're partners."

"I know. I was trying to manipulate your thoughts by sounding like I was giving you a choice. That way you wouldn't be angry with me."

Laura folded her arms across her chest and stared straight ahead. "You're an asshole."

Jack snorted. "Talk about stating the obvious." He saw a fleeting smile, then she frowned, perhaps because she'd smiled when she didn't want to.

When Laura continued, her tone was calmer and more matter-of-fact. "What's obvious is that Vicki is going to get whacked. Are you sure it won't be tonight?"

"I'm sure. We'll know more once our friend calls, but Satans Wrath isn't stupid enough to act on it without careful planning. I've given them a week. I think they'll use all the time they have before making their move."

Laura nodded. "So what do we do now?"

"The hardest part of the job. We wait and try to avoid the ants."

"Ants?" Laura questioned.

"Automatic negative thoughts."

"Where your brain torments you with every imaginable thing that can go wrong."

Jack nodded. *Yeah ... and when it comes to murder, there are a lot of ants.*

Chapter Twenty-Eight

Jack was watching the nightly news on the television with Natasha when he received a call from Lance.

"You sure know how to stir up a hornet's nest," Lance said as soon as Jack answered.

"Thought it might catch Pure E's attention," Jack replied. "When, where, and how?"

"I'll tell you about when. Pure E's concerned it could be a trap."

"So he doesn't trust Rat Cop completely."

"Maybe. Or maybe he's only being cautious. He ordered surveillance on Vicki for the next several days to see if she's being protected. He also wants the boys to check her car and look for any trackers."

"They won't find any," Jack stated. "Floyd Hackman and Buck Zabat are both three-three and in your chapter. I presume you'll be the one passing on orders to them?"

"No. Before I got to the meeting, Whiskey Jake and Pure E were already there. The other guys in the three-three

— Crowe, Trapp, and Bazzoli — are in Whiskey Jake's chapter. He'd already volunteered to oversee it."

"Damn it."

"No choice for me on that. WJ's head's too far up Pure E's ass. That decision was made before I arrived. However, because Buck's in my crew, I should be able to find out some details right after it's done. I'll tell Hackman to report to me to see how he handled it."

"After" is not what I wanted to hear. "Okay, tell me what else you know."

"Whiskey Jake will meet all of the three-three and debrief them. Usually he'd only pass the order on to Trapp, but this is heavy. There can't be any mistakes."

"At Stanley Park? Near that concession stand you told me about?"

"Yup, likely in the next two days. Probably late morning or afternoon. Whiskey Jake likes his nights free to hang out with Pure E and isn't one for getting up early."

"He might not pass the order on for two days? I gave them a deadline of a week tomorrow. That's not a lot of time to waste by sitting —"

"Some action is being taken right away," Lance interrupted. "Pure E said to put our surveillance team on Vicki to check for heat before bringing in the three-three. That'll include checking her vehicle for any trackers, as well as scanning the sky to check for aircraft surveillance. Pure E wants to ensure it isn't some kind of trap."

"There won't be any heat on her."

"If they don't spot any heat, then Whiskey Jake will meet with the three-three at the park to give them their orders. The three-three will then get involved with the surveillance and do periodic counter-surveillance with each other to ensure they're clean, as well. If you try to follow any of them with a regular four- or five-car team, you'll be spotted."

Four- or five-car team? We'd need forty. Instead I've only got Laura.

"When it comes to the day of the hit, the three-three will meet at the park again. At that time they'll go over their plan with Whiskey Jake. If he approves it, then they'll head out and do their thing."

"What about Vicki? Will she be watched the whole time?"

"Yup. The surveillance team will monitor her from the beginning. Once Whiskey Jake authorizes the plan, the three-three will tell the surveillance team to break off and they'll take over."

"Pure E put out the bullshit story that Damien skipped the country to avoid his charges. Won't the surveillance team clue in when Vicki disappears? Especially knowing that the three-three's involved?"

"No, the three-three is sort of like our Black Ops. They do more than hits."

"Such as?"

"Things like helping hide guys who are wanted in other countries."

"I see."

"The regular surveillance team will be told their job is to ensure Vicki isn't being watched so she can be smuggled out of the country. They'll also be told she isn't to know about it in case she gets the urge to tell her sister or someone."

"I doubt she'll be checking her rear-view mirror. No reason to."

"Even if she does, our guys know their stuff. They've had a lot of practice following our competition. On the day of the hit, the three-three will all have new vehicles that they know are clean from any bugs or trackers. At that time they'll meet at the park to go over the final details with Whiskey Jake. When they do, there'll be prospects guarding the parking lot. Then when they leave, they'll drive through areas with busy commercial airline flight paths to get rid of any possible air surveillance."

"Their phones?" Jack asked, more for confirmation than anything else, for the reply was what he expected.

"All their regular phones will be shut off so they can't be traced through GPS. They'll use disposable phones to communicate with each other. Once the hit is done those are tossed, too."

"They're thorough," Jack commented.

"That's their job."

"And you've got no idea what they do with the body?"

"No, that info is known only to them."

"I presume Pure E will get Buck to do the hit?"

"That didn't come up in conversation, but he capped his old man without regret, so I doubt it'll bother him. Pure E is also pissed off at him for telling his mom he was wearing a wire when he talked to Damien. Guess it's possible he could be ordered to do it."

"Only possible?"

"Buck's kind of proved himself already, so I'm not sure if Pure E will get him to do Vicki. I suspect that decision will be left up to Buck and the rest of the three-three."

"Okay. Anything else?"

"Yeah, your fee. Pure E told Whiskey Jake that if you're being straight and nobody is watching Vicki, then you're to be paid ten grand."

"Glad I'm appreciated," Jack said.

"You gonna pay down your mortgage?"

"I'll give it to charity."

"Yeah, like maybe a home for unwed fathers."

"Glad to hear you're not gender-biased," Jack said, then hung up.

Jack called Laura. "Sorry, did I wake you up?"

"No, I'm in bed, but awake. You hear from our friend?"

"Yes." Jack gave her the details of Lance's call.

"So what comes next?" she asked.

"I think Stanley Park is the weakest link when it comes to the three-three," Jack replied. I want to set up surveillance there and verify what we've been told. On the day of the hit, we'll need to see what vehicles they're using."

"From what you said, we'd never be able to follow them," Laura noted.

"Not in Vancouver, but what about out on the highway?"

"Highway?"

"They were out on Sumas Mountain when I called Damien to warn him."

"And Pure E answered," Laura said.

"Exactly. I don't see them taking Damien all the way out there, killing him, then bringing his body back into the city to dispose of."

"I-HIT searched Sumas Mountain. At least, as best they could."

"All along Taggart Road, but there are other roads up there."

"Maybe it's not even up there."

"Maybe, but even if we get an inkling where it is, it might help. I want to identify the vehicles the three-three will be using the day of the hit, then head out on the Trans-Canada ahead of them and wait."

"While they're doing all their heat checks in Vancouver," Laura said musingly. "They'll think they're already clean before they get to us."

"Hopefully. Let's set up in Stanley Park by 9:00 a.m. tomorrow. It'll be good to see how they operate and what they're driving. If they switch vehicles later we'll know they're about to do the hit."

"These guys have been around. Even if we do spot them on the highway, they're going to be difficult to follow. We should have individual surveillance teams on every one of them."

"I know, but there's no way to do that without Mortimer finding out. Not to mention, this isn't the sort of thing you'd want anyone else involved in."

"You mean conspiracy to commit murder?"

"Gee, do you really think they'll hurt her? I was thinking they'd only give her a severe reprimand."

"Save that one for our judge or jury," Laura said dryly.

"Which is why we can't involve anyone else," Jack said.

Laura's sigh was audible over the phone.

Yeah, I'm not happy about it, either. "The bikers usually park in a lot north of the concession stand. I'll pick you up at 7:15 a.m. I want you in and out of the office before anyone comes in. You grab a surveillance van and I'll meet you at the park. I'll dress as a homeless guy and tuck myself into the bush near the concession stand while you set up on the parking lot. If they park elsewhere I'll see them when they arrive at the concession stand. Between us, we should be able to see what they're driving when they leave."

"You going to arrive pushing a shopping cart and drinking from a brown paper bag?"

Jack chuckled. "No wine. With these guys, we'll need to be on our toes."

Laura was silent for a moment, then said, "Okay, whatever."

By her tone Jack knew she was troubled. "Something wrong?"

She didn't answer.

"Are you there?"

At last Laura said, "Burning Vicki reminds me of how we burned the Barlows. For them it turned out to be more than a figure of speech. Vicki is evil, but I still hope she doesn't die like that. I don't think I could handle it."

Jack's mind flashed back to the grotesque scene at the farmhouse. He could still smell the burned flesh. He swallowed, then replied, "Me neither — which is why Pure E needs to go."

"He needs to go to hell," Laura stated. "Hope you and I don't meet him there." With that, she hung up.

Chapter Twenty-Nine

"It's only 6:00 a.m.," Natasha complained.

"Sorry, hon, didn't mean to wake you." Jack was digging through a dresser drawer in search of the green woollen skullcap he'd once purchased at a military-surplus store. He was already wearing three shirts and the shabby jeans he kept for doing yardwork.

Natasha sat up in bed. "Not shaving all week, especially after being so clean-shaven, made you look kind of sexy — but this? Can I only hope you're dressing as a hobo today because it's Halloween?"

"Actually I'm going dressed as a wino — and sorry, I may look like this for the next week."

"Humph," Natasha grunted, then lay back down.

"If it'll make you feel better, I expect to be home for dinner."

"With a cheap bottle of wine, no doubt."

"Possibly, depending on how well the begging goes," Jack replied.

"I wish you luck. Looking like that, you can beg all you want when you come home, but you'll still be sleeping in the basement. A cheap bottle of wine might be the only comfort you get."

A light rain was falling when Jack, the woollen skullcap pulled down over his ears, walked into a wooded area close to the concession stand. He'd brought a sheet of plastic, which he laid on the ground, along with an old sleeping bag. Beside that he put a garbage bag partially filled with empty cans and bottles to give the appearance he was earning money through recycling.

Once settled, he took off one of the gardening gloves he was wearing and phoned Laura. "You comfy?" he asked.

"Yes, nice and dry. Better off than you, I bet."

"It's not bad. I'm warm and dry. I also brought a thermos of coffee and some snack bars. It's more than most of the homeless have, but this still gives me an appreciation of how some people live."

"Except at the end of the day you've got a warm bed to go home to," Laura noted.

"You're right about that. Mind you, I was told this morning that I'd be sleeping in the basement."

Laura snickered. "It's Halloween tonight. Mike and Steve going out?"

"Yes. Mike's going as a mad scientist and Steve is going as a banana."

"Cute."

"Hope nobody comes to our house dressed as a biker. Natasha will shoot 'em."

"She still skittish over the phone they left in your mailbox?"

"She's not the only one," Jack replied.

"You're not skittish. You're angry."

Jack decided to change the subject. "How're you fixed for cover vehicles?"

"Not bad. Some dedicated morning joggers are also parked in the lot. I don't think the van'll stand out."

"Good. I parked in the lot that's to the south of you. Chat with you later."

The morning dragged on. Finally, at 10:30 a.m. a man approached the concession stand. Jack, using a monocular, guessed he was in his mid-fifties. He appeared to be South Asian and dragged one foot as he walked. The man took keys out of his pocket and entered the stand through a side door. Twenty minutes later a young woman entered and at 11:00 a.m. the stand opened for business.

There were few people in the park and after the lunch hour, the South Asian emerged from the small building with a small paper bag in his hand and began making his way toward Jack, his one foot dragging with every step. When he reached him, he pulled a takeout cup of coffee from the bag and handed it to Jack. "This is on the house," he said, slurring the words slightly. "Cold and damp this time of year."

Jack played the role he'd set for himself and quietly accepted.

"My name's Tom," the man said. "I'm the cook," he added, with a nod toward the concession.

"I'm Jay," Jack replied, then took a sip. "Thanks." He saw Tom eyeing him curiously. *Does he suspect something?* "Have you worked here long?"

"About six months," Tom said. "When I moved my family from India sixteen years ago, I drove a taxi, but last spring I had a stroke."

Driving a taxi for that long means he can probably read people. Jack cleared his throat. "Happier to be here rather than India?"

Tom seemed to contemplate the question. "Yes and no. My wife and I have a son and a daughter. In India I think they were actually happier."

"Missing their friends," Jack suggested.

"No, not that. In our little village in India my children were content with having less. Since coming here they've seen what the world has to offer and always want more. They've become greedy and are not as happy as they were back in India. My daughter became an accountant, but my son … well, he's not done well."

The woman from inside the concession stand leaned out and yelled to attract Tom's attention, then gestured to a young couple outside the stand.

"Gotta get back to work," Tom said.

"Thanks for the coffee."

At 3:30 p.m. Laura called Jack. "Got two guys who pulled up in a wreck of a car and got out. I don't recognize them, but they both look like FPSers."

"FPSers" was a term commonly used by the police to denote criminals. It came from having their prints on file with the Fingerprint Section in Ottawa. "Description," Jack said.

"Both look to be in their late thirties. One's wearing a red-and-black-checkered woollen lumber jacket … brown hair short enough to see his scalp … tat of something on the back of his right hand, and a cross earring in his right ear. His buddy's wearing a grimy green nylon jacket, black hair in a ponytail, and a goatee. Both are husky. They look like they spend a lot of time pumping iron."

"Steroid monkeys?"

"Could be. I've taken some good pics. Their car is an old Chevy Impala. It's red, rusted, lots of dents. The rear passenger window is all cockeyed and half-open. Okay … they're both heading your way."

"Are you able to run the plate?"

"Running it now."

Minutes later, Jack saw the two men. Ponytail was talking on a phone, then nudged his buddy and gestured at Tom, who'd appeared from the side entrance of the concession stand.

Tom, what the hell are you doing with two guys like that? He zoomed in with his phone and took a few pictures, before using his monocular for a better look. He realized that Tom had an envelope in his hand while talking to Ponytail. Then Ponytail stepped in the way and Jack was unable to see what was taking place.

Laura called him. "The car is registered to a Lorraine Dole. Minor convictions for theft and several drug-possession convictions. No outstanding warrants."

Jack saw the two thugs head back in the direction

they'd come. Tom cast a worried look Jack's way, then went back into the building.

"Did you see them?" Laura asked.

"Yes, they were here. I've never seen them before. They met a guy by the name of Tom who works as a cook at the concession stand. I saw an envelope in his hand, but don't know if they gave it to him or if it was the other way around. The two goons are heading back your way. I'm feeling nervous. Tom brought me a coffee this morning and I think he was suspicious."

"Think you've been burned?"

"I don't know. Hope not. Do a loose tail on the two when they leave. I'm gonna call our friend."

Seconds later Jack had Lance on the phone and asked, "You guys have any contacts or someone to act as a lookout for you in Stanley Park?"

"I'm busy," Lance replied. Before Jack could respond he added, "The keys are in my office in a tin box in my desk drawer ... right side."

"You can't talk," Jack said.

"Give me a sec." Then to someone Lance said, "I won't be long."

Jack heard a murmur of voices over the phone, which soon become distant. "Okay," Lance said, "you want to know if we've any contacts at the park?"

"Yes. Specifically at the concession stand."

"I don't think so. We don't want anyone to know we go there."

"You don't *think* so?"

"That place is supposed to be ultra secret, but like I said, the three-three are thorough. I guess it's possible they pay someone to keep an eye open for them, but my gut says otherwise."

"Good."

"I'm talking to Whiskey Jake about some legit club business, but he did say he'll be meeting the three-three tomorrow in the park."

"Thanks for the info. Gotta go." Jack called Laura.

"The two FPSers are getting into their car," she reported.

"I spoke with our friend," Jack said. "He doesn't think they have a contact at the park but isn't sure. He also told me WJ is meeting the three-three here tomorrow."

"So we've wasted our day," Laura replied.

"Maybe, but I'd still like to make sure the two FPSers aren't connected. I'll grab my wheels and catch up to you shortly."

"Better hustle — we'll be in rush hour. The passenger, who's the guy with the ponytail, has just taken a piece of paper from the sun visor, written something, and put it back. Okay, they're backing up."

Jack tucked his stuff deeper into the woods, then hurried to his SUV. He caught up to Laura as she exited the park with the Impala in front of her. The direction they were taking led into the heart of Vancouver.

Ten minutes later their quarry drove into a car parkade on East Hastings, and Jack parked nearby on the street. He then saw the two FPSers walk out of the parkade and cross the street to the Black Water Hotel.

For Jack the Black Water brought back chilling memories. His thoughts were distracted when Laura double-parked beside him. He lowered his window.

"The Black Water," Laura said musingly. "Sounds familiar. Didn't you have something to do with that place?"

"I spent several months undercover in there before you came on the section. Do you remember the bad guy you did the UC on who went by the nickname Spider?"

"How could I forget? We spent two weeks in court on him. He's the guy who murdered the pensioner after seeing him withdraw money at an ATM."

"I introduced you to him in a coffee shop, but his usual hangout was the Black Water. A lot of real badasses used to hang out in there."

"How about bikers?"

Jack frowned. "At one time dealers for Satans Wrath used to supply speed to the lower-level dealers in there, but from what I've heard, the clientele has degenerated so much that I'm not sure they could come up with the money to make it worthwhile for the bikers to bother with the place."

"So you're not sure. Maybe Tom was being paid for ratting you out."

"Maybe. Tom glanced nervously in my direction after meeting with the two FPSers, but they never looked my way. You'd think they would if he was talking about me."

"So what do you want to do?"

"I'm dressed like a homeless person, so I should fit in. I'll go in and take a look, but while I'm doing that, check out the car in the parkade. You mentioned a piece of paper the guy stuck in the sun visor. I'd like to see what he wrote on it, if it's still there."

Moments later Jack walked into the bar. It had changed in the years since he'd last been there. The stage where strippers had once slithered around a pole was gone, replaced by more tables and chairs. The pool tables once located at the rear were also gone.

Much of the clientele looked more desperate than before. Clusters of gaunt-faced addicts, some of them women, peered out with sallow eyes.

He saw Ponytail and Checkered Jacket sitting with a woman with long greasy black hair and dressed in a red miniskirt and yellow tank top. Blackened tracks on her arms said she'd been using drugs for years. Doubtless a prostitute. He guessed she was in her early twenties.

He felt his phone vibrate. It wouldn't suit his image to be seen talking on a cellphone, so he ambled into the men's room and checked that he was alone. He'd missed a call from Laura, but she'd sent him a photo of a list of twelve names.

Most of the names were identified only by initials or a first name and a brief description of a business, such as a corner store, travel agent, insurance-company receptionist, and so on. Other names and initials had various street corners and times beside them. The first six names had check marks beside them, and the last of these was *SP — Tom*. Jack guessed that SP stood for Stanley Park, and Tom was the man from the concession stand. None of the names that followed had been ticked off.

"So what do you think?" Laura asked as soon as Jack called her.

"I don't know what it's about, but it's got nothing to do with us. Our two FPSers are sitting with a hooker and drinking beer."

"Maybe Lorraine Dole, the car owner."

"Could be. Either way, I feel my cover at the park is safe. Let's call it a day."

"Sounds good. I'll wait till you're out of there."

Jack hung up and glanced at the wall beside the urin-
als. A memory surfaced of the time some junkies had
shoved him against it when they'd become suspicious and
decided to search him. They'd threatened to jam a needle
into his arm and overdose him if they found anything. At
the time he hadn't been wearing a wire or carrying any
identification, and came out of it unscathed.

Back then he'd soon forgotten the incident. Now that
he was older and had a family, such memories affected
him more. He felt a chill and zipped up his jacket. *Who
am I kidding? It's not the cold that's making me shiver.*

Chapter Thirty

On Saturday morning the rain had quit, but the sky was grey and there was a cool ocean breeze. Jack parked in the lot south of the concession stand while Laura continued past in a surveillance van to the lot in the north.

Minutes later Jack set up his fake homeless camp and called Laura.

"You in position?" she asked.

"Yes. How's it look where you are?"

"Nothing for cover at the moment," she replied. "Want me to park in the lot in the south and go out on foot? There are lots of trees for cover."

"Yeah, for now. Play it by ear. If it's busier later you can use the van."

The morning passed and was uneventful. At 11:00 a.m. the concession stand opened, and a short time later Tom brought Jack a free cup of coffee again. Their conversation was short, with no mention of the two thugs Jack had seen the day before.

At noon Jack ambled down to the concession stand. Three young men Jack guessed to be in their late teens or early twenties waited their turn behind him. Their language was vulgar and Jack sized them up. One, in a red ball cap, looked to be in physically good shape. His two friends weren't. One was skinny and the other pudgy with bad acne.

"May I take your order?" the young woman behind the counter asked Jack.

"One jumbo hot dog please," Jack replied, then stepped aside to make room for the next customer.

Ball Cap stepped forward and waggled his tongue suggestively at the woman, then said, "So, you got jumbo hot dogs — you like goin' down on jumbo hot dogs, sweet lips?"

Pudgy and Slim both laughed, but abruptly stopped when Ball Cap reacted to Jack's scowl.

"What the fuck you looking at?" he said.

Three assholes … but this isn't the time. Jack maintained his scowl and his silence.

"Is there something you'd like to order?" the young woman interjected coldly.

Ball Cap directed his attention back to the woman. "Hey, what the fuck's with the attitude? I'm just fuckin' with you, babe. Where's your sense of humour?"

"Are you placing an order?" she asked again.

"Yeah, I'll have a cheeseburger."

Jack waited silently as Pudgy and Slim placed their orders without incident.

Tom had spied Jack placing his order, and when the food was ready, he delivered it to the front counter. "This one's on me."

"Thanks ... but no," Jack replied, reaching for the crumpled five-dollar bill he'd kept in his pocket. "I'm no charity case," he added. "I got my pride."

"Hey, fuck!" Ball Cap exclaimed. "If you're givin' it away, I want mine for free, too!"

"Yeah, us, too," Pudgy and Slim said.

"No, s-sorry," Tom stuttered. He nodded at Jack. "This is a friend of mine," he added in his slurred speech.

Ball Cap sneered. "You sound funny."

"I ... I had a stroke," Tom replied.

"Yeah? Well, figures." He turned to Pudgy and Slim. "The only friend the gimp can get is a bum." He then elbowed Jack aside and handed the woman twenty dollars. "I'll pay for my two buddies."

Okay, assholes, take your food and get the hell out of here. Once Ball Cap received his change, Jack stepped forward to pay.

Ball Cap nudged Slim with his elbow, then grabbed a plastic ketchup bottle from the counter. "Hey, how does this thing work?" he asked, intentionally squirting ketchup in Tom's face and down his shirt. "Oh, I see how it —"

Jack rammed the heel of his hand into Ball Cap's shoulder, sending him reeling backward.

"What the fuck? You got a problem?" Ball Cap roared, tossing the ketchup bottle aside as he faced off with Jack.

Jack stared him down in response, then caught the subtle nod Ball Cap made to Pudgy.

"Yeah, you got a problem?" Pudgy asked belligerently, stepping forward.

Jack shifted his gaze to Pudgy, but could see Ball Cap in his peripheral vision. He suspected the distraction Pudgy offered was to allow Ball Cap to deliver a sucker punch. His suspicion was confirmed. Ball Cap aimed his fist for Jack's temple … but it never landed. Jack used his forearm to direct the blow harmlessly away while delivering a knuckle-twisting blow to the base of Ball Cap's nose.

Blood sprayed across the young man's face as he staggered backward and fell to the ground.

Jack looked at Pudgy and Slim, who stood with their mouths agape. "Naw, I don't have a problem," he said. "How about you two? Do you have a problem?"

The pair looked at Ball Cap on the ground holding his hands to his face and moaning.

"No, no problem," Slim said.

"Me … me, neither," Pudgy said.

"You will if you ever come back here again. I suggest you take your dumbass friend to a hospital."

Pudgy and Slim exchanged a glance.

"Go before I lose my temper and become angry," Jack said. Then, as if talking to himself, he mumbled, "The doctor said I shouldn't get angry. Don't get angry." He patted his pockets. "Where're my pills? I know I shouldn't quit taking them …"

Pudgy and Slim helped Ball Cap to his feet and each held an arm to steady him as they left.

Jack saw the young woman staring at him. She was trembling. "It's okay," he said, "they won't be back." She nodded, but then he realized she was afraid of *him*. Tom was also staring at him, but more in curiosity.

Tom then reached for some paper napkins to clean himself. "You really on medication?" he asked.

Jack grinned. "That was for their benefit. I figured if his two friends thought I was crazy they'd be more inclined to leave."

"Sort of what I thought," Tom replied. "You deliver quite a punch. You've had training," he said matter-of-factly.

"I used to be a soldier." *Time to change the subject.* "To give you a tip, try not to act nervous around punks like that. Be firm, exude self-confidence … and look them in the eye. If they persist, call the cops. That's what you pay your taxes for."

"I know, I know," Tom replied. "It just isn't my nature. I've always tried to avoid conflict. Since my stroke, I even find it hard to go out in public. I feel like everyone is staring at me."

"They might be," Jack replied. "I bet most are admiring you for having the strength and determination to carry on."

Tom didn't answer and Jack realized he was distracted.

Jack turned around and saw two uniformed police officers, accompanied by a park ranger, approaching. *Crap, not now, guys. That's all I need, for the three-three to show up and see you …*

"Turn and place your hands on the counter. We're not going to hurt you," one officer said.

Jack saw that their name tags identified them as McDonald and Baker.

"We heard that you may have forgotten to take your medication or perhaps lost it," Baker continued. "I'm simply going to pat you down. Perhaps I'll find it."

Okay, guess the charade is over. "You won't find any medication," Jack said as he placed his hands on the counter and spread his legs. "What you'll find is my badge in my front pocket. I also have a pistol holstered in my waistband over my right hip."

A minute later Baker handed Jack his pistol and badge back. "We received a call that the three guys you had a run-in with were hassling people in the park." He smirked. "Looks like they hassled the wrong guy."

"One of them squirted ketchup on me," Tom said.

"So I see." Baker nodded.

Tom gestured to Jack. "When he pushed him away to make him stop, the guy tried to punch him."

McDonald looked amused. "We spoke to them and they said they'd been attacked by a wino and were on their way to the hospital. Also said you were a mental patient and that you were looking for your pills." He eyed Jack's clothing, then looked at his partner and sadly shook his head. "I heard they weren't payin' these Mounties enough," he said in a stage whisper. "Probably explains why he went crazy."

Jack returned their grins.

"Want him charged?" Baker asked. "We've ID'd them and can round them up."

"No, but thanks, anyway. What I gave him is far more than he'd ever get in court. Let him think he was thumped out by a wino. Might deflate his ego a little."

Baker chuckled, then his face became serious. "Looking at how you're dressed, I suspect you don't want a couple of uniforms hanging around."

"You're right about that," Jack replied.

As the officers left Tom looked at Jack. "Thank you for coming to my rescue."

"Yes, thank you," the young woman echoed.

"No problem. Sorry I lied about who I really am."

"That's okay," Tom said. "I suspected you were a police officer when I first met you."

Jack raised an eyebrow.

"Not many homeless people are on a dental plan. You also stayed put the whole time. Didn't scrounge for empty bottles or butts."

Jack nodded. "I'd appreciate it if the both of you kept my presence secret."

Both Tom and the young woman assured him they would, then Jack paid for his hot dog and headed back to his sleeping bag. He was halfway there when Tom caught up to him. "So you're not here because of … you know … yesterday?" he asked.

Jack paused to finish chewing the bite he'd just taken of his hot dog. "Those two guys you met around the side? Involving the envelope?"

Tom nodded.

"No, it's nothing to do with that, although I'm a little curious."

Tom's face revealed his grief. "My son was sent to jail a couple months ago. It's the second time he's been caught selling crack. He's addicted to it."

"Sorry to hear that."

Tom hung his head. "Yesterday I paid those two men money for my son."

"I understand that it must be difficult, but if you continue to pay for his mistakes — especially over drugs —

he'll never learn to stand on his own two feet."

"I know, I know." He sighed audibly, then said, "I'm so ashamed. I know it's wrong." His tone became desperate. "He's my son. I worry. It was only five hundred dollars."

"Which for you is a lot of money."

"Yes, it is," he admitted.

"Of course you worry. You love him and want to protect him."

"Yes, I want to protect him. I'm his father." He looked at Jack. "You think it's wrong?"

"It's not wrong to love your son, but there comes a time when he has to be responsible for what he does."

Tom appeared to think about it, then said, "Maybe you're right."

"You mentioned your daughter is an accountant?"

"Yes, she works hard. She's made my wife and me very happy."

"She must be smart. I'm sure your son is, too. Perhaps he'll change his ways."

"Yes, I pray that he will." Tom eyed Jack carefully. "So you're really not here because of me or those two men from yesterday?"

"Definitely not. The men I'm interested in meet here on occasion to discuss and plan serious crimes. I hope to follow them when they leave to see what they're up to."

Tom's face brightened. "I could help you. I'm here almost every day. If you have any pictures or could describe them, I'd be happy to let you know if they show up."

"Actually that'd be appreciated. I hope to be here myself, but if they ever show up and I'm not around, I'd like to know."

Jack brought out his phone and slowly scrolled down through the appropriate photographs while Tom studied the pictures. He then handed Tom his business card. "They're dangerous," he warned. "All I'd like is a phone call. Don't talk to them or ever try to follow them."

Tom rolled his eyes. "Don't worry. Phoning you will be as brave as I get."

"Thank you," Jack said. "Now I'd better get back to my position."

"Two of the pictures look like those guys," Tom said.

Jack turned and saw two members of the three-three walking toward the concession stand. "It is them," he said anxiously. "I need to go."

He moved off. Seconds later he called Laura. "Where are you?" he asked. "Floyd Hackman and Vic Trapp are standing at the concession stand."

"I'm back in the van and in the lot to the north. They must've parked elsewhere. Do you have a problem?"

"That's funny. Two guys asked me a short time ago if I had a problem. Why does everyone think I have a problem?"

"I take it you don't have a — uh-oh. Hang tough." Laura's tone became tense. "Two cars just arrived in the north lot. One's a white Lexus."

"Whiskey Jake," Jack said.

Laura was quiet for a moment. "Confirmed it's WJ. Three just got out of the second car. Pasquale Bazzoli … Nick Crowe … Buck Zabat."

"Perfect," Jack said. "I don't have any problem at all. It's showtime."

Chapter Thirty-One

Jack watched the bikers congregate at a picnic table. A couple of minutes later Buck Zabat stood up and stomped off a few paces, then returned and waved his hands in what appeared to be anger at Whiskey Jake.

Gee, Buck, the idea of murdering your mom not to your liking? Then Jack watched as Buck thumped his own chest with his finger. *Guess I'm wrong about that.*

After a moment Whiskey Jake and the three-three got to their feet, and Trapp patted Buck on his back. There was no doubt in Jack's mind who'd volunteered to do the murder.

The bikers left, with Hackman and Trapp heading to the south parking lot while the others went to the north lot. Once they drove off, Jack met with Laura and told her what he'd seen.

"It makes me feel sick," Laura said. "Murdering his dad is bad enough. Now he wants to do his own mother."

"Satans Wrath is his family," Jack reminded her. "He's disowned both his parents. In his mind they've completely gone against everything he was taught to believe."

"That Satans Wrath comes before all else." Laura looked disgusted. "So now what?"

"Stick to our plan. Continue surveillance here at the park until they meet again before the hit. Then it's a simple matter of identifying what they're driving and wait for them out on the Trans-Canada."

"It's not that simple," Laura replied tersely. "What happens if they don't go that direction, or if they do, but we lose them? We'll have had Vicki killed for no reason."

"There's plenty of reason to see that bitch in the ground," Jack said bitterly.

Four days later Jack and Laura's surveillance came to fruition. For fear of using the surveillance van a second time and having it noticed, Laura drove her own car to the parking lot south of the concession stand, parked it, and then posed as a jogger. She used a trail to traverse the short distance to the point where she could see the parking lot to the north.

It was 8:50 a.m. and Jack had barely crawled into his sleeping bag when he received a call from Laura.

"Heads up, two guys arrived in the north lot in a silver Nissan Altima. I can't see the plate, but I recognize the driver. It's a prospect for the Westside chapter — John Appleton." Laura paused. "This is happening. They wouldn't have prospects guarding the lot otherwise."

Laura sounded tense and Jack understood why. *Today is going to be the day Vicki dies. Playing a role in that isn't something she relishes.* "Who's the other guy?" he asked.

"I don't know. I've got my monocular on him now. Short brown hair, clean-shaven, early twenties."

"Maybe a new prospect. What're they doing?"

"Parked in the lot and sitting in the car."

Jack felt tense, as well, but for him it was fear of what could go wrong. "What's your position?"

"Sitting on the seawall, but now that they're here I better move."

"Head back to your car. Once the real players arrive I'll let you know, then you can drive past the lot and record all the plates and vehicle descriptions."

"Will do."

By 9:20 a.m. four of the three-three had arrived and met at a picnic table. None of them arrived together, which indicated they had probably come in separate vehicles. The only one who didn't show up was Buck Zabat. *Perhaps they decided that killing your own mother was too much, even if you were willing to do it.*

Ten minutes later Whiskey Jake arrived and joined the group. Jack then called Laura to have her drive past the parking lot and obtain the vehicle info.

The meeting didn't last long. Nick Crowe appeared to do most of the talking while Floyd Hackman, Vic Trapp, and Pasquale Bazzoli just listened. When Crowe was finished, Whiskey Jake spoke.

Jack felt a familiar anger — not at the bikers, but at Mortimer. If it hadn't been for the assistant commissioner, he'd have had listening devices planted to pick up the actual conversation. That and separate surveillance teams assigned to every one of the participants.

Minutes later he watched as Whiskey Jake gave a

thumbs-up to the others, and they all climbed to their feet and departed. Jack called Laura to tell her.

"I've recorded the info," she said. "Besides the prospects' and Whiskey Jake's Lexus, there are six other vehicles. One's a rental van and the others are registered to names I've never heard of."

"Two must belong to citizens," Jack said as he gathered his belongings and hurried back to his SUV. "But the rest ..."

"I found a spot to watch when they leave," Laura said. "I'll let you know what they're driving then."

"Sounds good. As soon as they're gone, we'll head out on the Trans-Canada and wait. From what our friend told us, I expect they'll be doing heat checks in the city for an hour before heading out on the highway. Still, let's hustle to make sure we're there ahead of them."

"How far out should we go?"

"I think it'll be around Abbotsford."

"Okay, about an hour out. Where do you want me to set up?"

"We'll start about three-quarters of the way. You set up at the Number 10 overpass and I'll continue east and set up on Number 13."

"Sure would like to know how they plan on grabbing Vicki."

"Me, too. I bet they do it when she goes to visit her dad for lunch." Jack paused. "Hopefully my theory that they dispose of bodies out that way is correct."

"And hopefully by then they'll have completed all their heat checks," Laura added.

That, too. Jack again reflected upon the situation they were in. *Mortimer, you asshole ...*

Minutes later Laura reported on the vehicles being driven by the three-three. Trapp drove a white rental van, Hackman a red Camaro, Crowe a blue Ford Fusion sedan, and Bazzolia was in a black Dodge Ram pickup truck.

At 10:30 a.m. Laura took the exit ramp off the Trans-Canada Highway and parked where she could see the eastbound traffic, but at the same time do some surveillance on her own if the three-three took the same exit.

Fifteen minutes later Jack did likewise at the next exit. He turned on the radio as he waited, but the music did little to ease the tension he felt. *What if they don't come out this far? What if they shoot Vicki and don't try to hide her body? What if they do come this way but spot us?* He cursed under his breath. *Damned ants.*

At noon Jack's fingers fumbled for his phone when Laura called.

"You nailed this one!" she said. "They're eastbound past my exit."

Jack felt his adrenalin surge, but made an effort to be calm. "You sound like you had doubts."

"Like you didn't."

He chuckled.

"Hackman's in the lead, followed by Trapp, Crowe, and Bazzoli in the pickup. They appear to be driving consistent with the rest of the traffic. I'll fall in behind."

Soon the entourage continued past where Jack was waiting. He drove back onto the Trans-Canada and maintained a distance. Laura was barely visible in front of him. She was doing likewise with Bazzoli's pickup.

"They've passed the Mount Lehman exit and are still eastbound," Laura reported.

"Good. I've got your back," Jack replied.

Minutes later Laura said, "Okay, they've taken the exit at Clearbrook Road."

"Into Abbotsford," Jack commented. "Good."

Suddenly Laura yelled, "Hang back! Hang back!"

Jack hit the brakes and pulled over onto the shoulder of the highway. "What's up?"

"Bazzoli stopped on the exit ramp and I had to drive past. He's got a video camera and is pointing it at every car that passes him."

Jack cursed. Laura's vehicle was effectively burned once their targets left the main route they were on. "You still got the eye on the other three?"

"Yes, they're heading north on Clearbrook Road. Still have lots of other cars for cover. "What do you want me to do?"

As Jack reached for a map he said, "Stay with them and I'll sit tight. If the traffic thins or they go off the main routes you better break off."

Moments later Laura spoke again. "They've turned east off of Clearbrook onto Hillcrest Avenue. It's a busy road. Two lanes each way and they're a block ahead of me."

"Okay, stay with them. I'm following you on a map. Call out the occasional street as you pass by."

"Will do." Seconds later, Laura said, "Passing Minter … passing Lynden … Adelaide … coming up to a red light. Indicators on to turn right … Okay, they're now southbound, but I'm too far back to see a sign."

"It's Lilac Street," Jack replied.

"I'm pulling up to the intersection now. It's all residential. They'll burn me if I follow."

"It's not that long a street. A few other streets branch off, but those have easier access roads than Hillcrest. We can check who owns or rents what houses later. Is there anyplace to sit and watch for them when they come out?"

"Yes, kitty-corner at the intersection there's a grocery store. Ample parking."

"Good. Hopefully Bazzoli will show up soon. If he does, I'll join you."

A moment later, Laura grumbled, "Bad news. Hackman and Trapp continued on, but Crowe pulled over. I think they're still doing heat checks."

Jack cursed again and punched the dash. The pain in his knuckles didn't take his mind off the problem. "Keep watching from the grocery lot. There's nothing else we can do."

"I've got the binos on Crowe now. I can see that he's videoing passing cars as well."

"These guys shouldn't be called the three-three," Jack muttered. "The 'paranoid squad' would be more apt."

Another five minutes passed, then Laura said, "Okay, Bazzoli showed up and parked facing northbound across the street from Crowe."

"I'm on my way," Jack replied.

"Crowe is out and joining Bazzoli in the pickup," Laura said. "He has his camera in his hand. No doubt they'll be comparing images."

Ten minutes later Jack arrived in the lot where Laura was waiting and she got in with him. "No change," she said, gesturing down the street. "They're both sitting in the pickup with their heads down, no doubt comparing the plates they each recorded. I'm surprised it's taking them so long."

"They probably recorded in Vancouver, too. It might take them a while."

Laura nodded, then gestured when a truck parked nearby, partially blocking her view. "I can't see past the intersection."

"Don't worry, I can." Jack reached for binoculars. "Maybe their comparing videos is a good sign," he suggested. "It might indicate they're close to their destination."

"I'm surprised it's in an urban area," Laura said. "I figured they'd lead us to a farm or some acreage."

"Me, too."

"I wonder if Vicki's dead yet."

Jack was silent for a moment. "Me, too."

The next several minutes passed in silence, with Jack peering through binoculars, then he said, "We've got action. A white Honda Civic has arrived … double-parked … and the driver's leaning out and talking to Bazzoli and Crowe. Long hair … beard … can't see the face well enough for an ID and the plate is too dirty to see. Honda's moving … okay, whoever it is has now parked facing northbound behind Bazzoli. Crowe's hurrying back to his car … he's mobile … no, only turning it around to face north, too."

"Want me to go back to my wheels?" Laura asked.

"No, I don't want to chance them seeing your car again."

Laura nodded. "What do you think they're up to? More heat checks?"

"I'd say they're waiting for something." He lowered the binoculars and rubbed his eyes with his fingertips. A vehicle stopping for the red light at the intersection caused his pulse to quicken. He jammed the binoculars back to his eye sockets.

"There's a white Cadillac Escalade waiting for the east-bound light on Hillcrest," Laura announced excitedly.

"I see it." Jack adjusted the dial on the binoculars. "It's Vicki."

"She alone?"

"Appears to be." Jack tossed the binoculars to Laura, then drove to the lot exit, half a block north of the inter-section. They were in time to see Vicki continuing east-bound on Hillcrest through the intersection. Bazzoli and Crowe pulled out to follow while the third biker waited at the light with his indicator on to head west.

"Our friend was right," Jack said. "They had a surveil-lance team on Vicki independent from the three-three."

"And the three-three have now taken over." Laura breathed out noisily. "Oh, man."

Jack remained at the exit, watching the Honda Civic and the traffic lights at the intersection. Every second counted, if he was to succeed in catching up to Bazzoli, Crowe, and Vicki. "Duck down. My appearance has changed but no use letting the guy in the Civic see you."

Laura did as instructed while Jack drove out onto the street toward the intersection. He was able to time his arrival to proceed through an amber light and head east seconds after the Civic had gone west.

"You're clear," Jack said, stepping on the gas. Laura sat upright as the SUV sprang to life. Moments later they spotted their three target vehicles and Jack tapped the brake to slow down.

"They're driving slow," Laura noted and grabbed the map. "I wonder if Vicki is doing heat checks or simply doesn't know the area."

Jack nodded. *The woman definitely doesn't know what she's getting into.*

Seconds later Vicki turned right down a residential street. Neither Crowe nor Bazzoli followed, opting instead to go left into a mall parking lot across the street.

"Vicki turned down Tulip Crescent," Laura noted. "Now what?"

"We can't follow her."

Jack opted for the same mall lot. There were few vehicles to provide him cover from being seen, but Crowe and Bazzoli had turned right after entering the lot, then parked side by side so they could talk, apparently. Jack drove in the opposite direction and parked far enough away that Laura needed binoculars to see clearly.

Five minutes later both Crowe and Bazzoli drove out of the lot, crossed Hillcrest and headed down Tulip Crescent.

Laura lowered the binoculars and looked at Jack.

"We wait," he said tersely.

Chapter Thirty-Two

Vicki studied the house as she parked in the driveway. Buck had described it as a basic three-bedroom bungalow with an attached garage. *A far cry from the mansion he grew up in, but you gotta start somewhere.* She glanced at her watch: *2:00 p.m. on the dot.*

She felt anxious as she went to the front door. Her last face-to-face meeting with her son a month ago hadn't gone well. When he'd found out she was responsible for setting up his father to be murdered, their conversation had disintegrated rapidly. He'd sworn at her and she'd slapped his face.

She had feared that she'd never see him again, but this morning's unexpected and apologetic phone call from him said otherwise. He had said he was thinking of leaving the club. That brought new hope. It was what she'd wanted all along.

Buck opened the door before she rang the buzzer.

"Oh, sweetie, I'm so glad you called," Vicki said tearfully.

"Mom," Buck uttered. "I …"

Vicki hugged him. "It's okay, it's okay," she said, patting him affectionately on the back. "So we had a fight. Who doesn't? The important thing is that we're talking."

He swallowed, then gently broke free of her embrace. "So is it true? Are you really thinking about leaving the club?"

"We'll talk about it. I've got coffee on," he replied, closing the door.

She kicked off her shoes and he hung up her coat. She followed him through the living room. "So you bought a house," she said, glancing around. "It looks nice. The next thing I know you'll be making a grandmother out of me." She smiled at the thought as they arrived in the kitchen.

Buck turned and faced her. His expression was grim.

"You okay?" she asked.

He gave a slight nod, but it was directed beyond her. She turned and gasped when she saw two men. She knew they belonged to the three-three.

Buck's voice seethed with anger. "You bitch! You really thought you'd get away with ratting on us?"

Vicki opened her mouth to scream, but one man drove his fist into her stomach. She emitted a gurgling sound and doubled over. It was easy for him to grab her by the hair and deliver another blow to the base of her skull, rendering her momentarily unconscious.

Seconds later she found herself sprawled on her back. Her attacker sat on her chest, using his knees to pin her arms to the floor while holding her by the throat. Her body convulsed as her lungs demanded air.

"Hurry up," he said. "She's coming around."

She gasped and arched her head back and saw Buck rooting through her purse. She managed to choke out his name, but he ignored her as he found her keys and walked away.

Vicki tried to call again to Buck, but the other man was covering her face in plastic wrap and she could only mouth his name. Her vision blurred and she frantically twisted and turned her head. It didn't help, and the man continued to wind the plastic wrap around her head.

She fought for air while writhing and kicking out, but the plastic stuck to her lips. Every time she tried to inhale, a small concave piece of plastic would pass her lips into her mouth. Her head jerked as she fought in vain to bite it. Eventually her body stilled.

Chapter Thirty-Three

Jack and Laura had continued watching the intersection of the street Vicki had driven down. They sat in silence, both lost in their own thoughts. Twenty minutes passed, then Vicki's vehicle exited Tulip Crescent and moved west on Hillcrest.

"It's not Vicki driving," Laura said gravely. "It's Buck."

Jack felt his hand give an involuntary twitch. It was as if his body was pushing away his thoughts. Buck had murdered his father, but being involved in the murder of his own mother seemed worse.

"What do you think they're up to?" Laura asked.

"I think Buck sucked his mother into coming out and is driving her car back to Vancouver."

Laura's face was grim. "That's what I figured. Nice son to have."

Neither spoke for fifteen minutes, then the red Camaro driven by Hackman exited Tulip Crescent and went westbound on Hillcrest. Trapp followed in the white van, Crowe in the blue Ford Fusion sedan, and Bazzoli in the pickup truck.

Jack waited until the procession passed, then pulled out to follow.

"Vicki's probably in the van," Laura stated.

Probably stuffed in a garbage bag. He glanced at Laura. "Yeah, probably. Bet the Camaro is being used to scout ahead."

Minutes later the procession arrived at the entrance to the Trans-Canada Highway, where all of their four targets headed east. Trapp, Hackman, and Crowe drove at a speed consistent with the traffic, but Bazzoli drove more slowly and Jack was forced to lag behind.

"Damn it!"

"What do we do?" Laura asked. "Pass Bazzoli and risk that he's still collecting plate numbers, or hang back and risk losing the other three?"

"I'll maintain my speed and pass Bazzoli … once," Jack replied.

Laura ducked down in the seat until Jack had passed. When he caught up to Trapp, Hackman, and Crowe, he eased off the gas and followed from a distance.

On nearing Exit 95 leading to Sumas Mountain, the procession slowed considerably. Jack glanced in his side mirror. "We've got Bazzoli coming up fast. After passing him once, if he spots me going slow at this point he'll burn us for sure."

"What're you going to do?"

Jack sped up. "We'll take Exit 95 to Sumas Mountain ahead of them. Let's hope they do the same."

"Lot of wilderness up there," Laura said. "As someone in I-HIT told me when they were looking for Damien's body, it was like looking for the proverbial needle in the haystack."

A few minutes later Jack took the exit, then swore aloud when the procession continued east on the Trans-Canada. He waited a moment for them to gain some distance and once more pulled out to follow.

"At least we know they're not disposing of bodies on Sumas Mountain," Laura offered lamely.

"Use the binos. If Bazzoli pulls over again I'll have to do likewise and hope he's far enough ahead not to see us."

Laura did as instructed. Using binoculars in a moving vehicle was not easy. "Okay, I've got an eye on Bazzoli's pickup. He's driving slow. I'd say he's doing about twenty under the limit."

Jack adjusted his speed accordingly. "See any of the others?"

"Possibly Crowe, but no sign of the van or Camaro."

"Shit."

"Ditto," Laura replied.

Twenty minutes later Laura reported, "Okay, Bazzoli has sped up and is taking the Vedder Road exit into Chilliwack. I think Crowe's in front of him."

"Let's chance they don't stop. I'm going to follow."

Not long afterward Laura said, "They're signalling to go north on the overpass. Visual contact broken."

Jack took the exit and their eyes frantically searched for their targets. Then Jack let out another anguished curse and punched the dash. Bazzoli and Crowe had simply crossed over the overpass and were now on the westbound ramp heading back toward Vancouver. No sign of Trapp or Hackman.

"It's over … we lost." Laura's words were bitter. "Trapp and Hackman could've turned off anywhere." She gestured with her thumb toward the westbound lane of the Trans-Canada Highway. "You still going to try and follow them?"

"No point," Jack replied. "We need to find out where Trapp and Hackman went."

"Maybe they're on their way back, too."

"Maybe."

"They could've dumped Vicki down a well," Laura said. "It wouldn't take long."

"Yeah, but the smell might give it away. I'm thinking they bury their bodies. Someplace deep where they'll never be found. That would take longer."

"So what do you want to do?"

"Two choices. One is to feed them another victim and start our surveillance from where we lost them this time. Maybe give them the guy who delivered the coke from Montreal."

Laura made a face. "What's your second choice?"

"There are four main exits leading off the Trans-Canada between here and where we first lost sight of Trapp and Hackman. The closest one this side of Sumas Mountain is the Number 3 Road, followed by Yale, Lickman, and Evans. How about I whip you back to grab your car, then we can space out and watch to see if we spot them returning to the Trans-Canada?"

"That'd narrow it down, but there's still a lot of ground to cover even if we do see which exit they appear on."

"I know, but most is rural or industrial. We could check with land titles to find out who owns what."

"Or rents what."

"Might take us a month or two. So," he glanced at her, "choice number one might be faster."

Laura eyed Jack. "I still vote for choice number two."

"Thought you would. My guess is the spot we're looking for is closer to the middle. You take the Yale Road exit and I'll watch from Lickman."

Three hours later it was dark. Four times during that period Jack had felt his pulse quicken when a white van appeared on the overpass he was monitoring, but each time his hopes were dashed. He heard his stomach growl and decided to call Laura. "You hungry?" he asked.

"I'm okay. How long do you want to stay out? Oh, hang on. Got another white van." The seconds ticked past. "Nope, wrong model."

"I think we're flogging a dead horse and it's been a long day. Want to pack it in?"

"Okay, but I don't like the idea of making another human sacrifice."

"I know. I'm tired and more than a little frustrated. Maybe another opportunity will arise without us encouraging it."

"I'd prefer that," she said.

"Do you want to stop by my house for a drink?"

"Thanks, but no. I don't drink when I'm feeling depressed."

Jack sighed. "I hear you."

"What time do you want to start work tomorrow?"

Jack didn't answer, just grabbed his binoculars. *Bingo!* "Guess who's taking the westbound exit off the Lickman Road exit onto the TC right at this moment."

He heard Laura gasp.

"I'll give you a hint," he said. "One's driving a red Camaro and the other a white van."

Chapter Thirty-Four

Jack and Laura were following Trapp and Hackman back toward Vancouver when Lance called Jack. "I heard from Hackman. He said that loose end had been dealt with and that they were all going for drinks. They plan to see how Buck's doing after he's got a few drinks in 'im."

"Will you be able to get some details as to how it went down?"

"Yeah. Hackman will pop by my place about 6:00 a.m. tomorrow to talk about how Buck handled it. I'll get more details then."

"Do you know where they're going for drinks?" Jack asked.

"Crowe's place in Burnaby. Why?"

"They used a rented van."

"You followed them?"

"No. We spotted it at the park. I'd like to get a look in it."

"It'll be clean. Like I told you, these guys are pros."

"You're probably right, but I still want to check. Call me as soon as you meet with Hackman."

***

Jack and Laura drove past Crowe's house several minutes after Hackman and Trapp had arrived. Jack parked a block to the north and shut off the ignition so that the exhaust from the SUV's engine wouldn't give him away. Then he slouched in his seat and used binoculars to watch. Laura, parked one block to the south, did the same. They knew they were in for a long night. After what their targets had done, there would be a lot of drinking.

At 5:30 a.m. the next morning Trapp, Hackman, Bazzoli, and Buck left the house. Buck was staggering.

Jack phoned Laura. "Looks like they succeeded in getting him drunk," he said.

"I see that," Laura replied. "I wonder how his assessment went."

"Must not have gone too bad. He's still alive."

Buck then got in Bazzoli's truck and the two men left together. Jack saw Trapp kneel near a tire on the van, then rise and leave in the Camaro with Hackman.

"You see that?" Laura asked.

"Yes … and the lights went off in the house. My guess is he left the keys on the tire for some prospect to come by tonight sometime and return it without waking Crowe. This'll be easy if I don't need to pick the lock."

"Easy, providing the prospect doesn't show up while we're in it."

"Guess there's that. I'll give Crowe a few minutes to fall asleep. Stay where you are and call if you see anyone coming."

Half an hour later, Jack had finished his search of the van — his guess that the keys had been left on the tire had proven correct. Lance's assumption that Jack wouldn't find anything was also correct. He returned to the SUV and started the engine.

"Your offer for a drink still open?" Laura asked. "I could use a beer and then talk about what we're going to do next." She paused. "If you're not up to it, then —"

"Not up to it?" He pretended puzzlement. "Let me see, I've got two voices talking to me in my head. One is telling me to have a beer."

"And the other —"

"Is saying, 'Weren't you listening? Do what he says, have a beer!'"

At 6:45 a.m. Jack slid a glass of beer across his kitchen table to Laura and sat down. They clinked glasses in silence and each took a swallow. Jack would've found the taste more pleasant if Laura's eyes hadn't remained on him … waiting. "Okay, it was still a pretty good day," he said.

"Tell that to Vicki."

Her voice was croaky and he wondered if it was from being up for twenty-four hours or from stress. *Probably both.* He returned her gaze. "Vicki was a calculated move. She may not have led us to the spot where they're hiding bodies, but I'm sure we'll find out where that is soon. We've got more info now to help us narrow it down."

Laura grimaced. "The Lickman Road exit covers a lot of territory."

"I saw their headlights before I realized it was them. They came from the north side, off a road called Industrial Way. I had a chance to check it out on the map while we were watching Crowe's place. There are pockets of residential areas that you can get to off Industrial, but most of the property in that area is farmland or for industrial use."

Laura's face brightened. "You're thinking we can find it without making another human sacrifice?"

"Yes, without another human sacrifice." *Good, that cheered her up.*

"Great breakfast conversation, you two!" Natasha said, entering the kitchen in her bathrobe. She leaned over and kissed Jack, said hello to Laura, then gave Jack a disapproving look.

"Human sacrifice is more interesting than talking about the weather," he said, hoping to lighten the moment.

"Not that," Natasha replied. "The boys will be down soon to go to school. How do I explain to them that you're drinking beer at this time of the morning?"

"Beer?" Jack raised his glass. "Tell them I made wheat smoothies."

Natasha smiled. "You've always got an answer for everything." She glanced at Laura. "I bet he never thought to offer you a coffee, right?"

"Actually the beer — uh, wheat smoothies were my idea," she confessed. "As far as coffee goes, thanks, but no. I plan on getting to sleep soon."

Jack yawned. "Good plan. We need more than a few hours. Today's Thursday. Let's take tomorrow and the weekend off and start up again on Monday. Then we'll begin by collecting names and doing a grid search, working our way out from where Trapp and Hackman got on the TC."

Laura nodded. "No argument from me on that idea."

"Me neither," Natasha said, opening a cupboard to start packing lunches for the boys. "It'd be nice to get reacquainted with you, Jack. Maybe introduce you to your children."

Jack ignored the jibe and turned his attention back to Laura. "Something else that might help us would be to see the key rings of two members of the three-three."

"See if they each have a common key," Laura responded. "If they do, it could be for wherever they hide the bodies."

"Exactly. It would narrow down what brand of lock we're searching for, let alone if it's a house key or something else."

"How do you propose to get your hands on their keys? I doubt even our friend could ask for those without a good explanation."

"Could get uniform to help. Bikers are checked often enough that it wouldn't arouse suspicion. Maybe detain them briefly and claim there's an unpaid parking ticket or something. It would be a chance to photograph their keys." He felt his phone vibrate and looked at the display. "Speaking of our friend," he said, then answered.

"I went for a walk with Hackman," Lance said. "Buck seems to be handling things okay. If anything, the guys say it kind of made them feel that Buck really was one of them. That he had a right to belong to the three-three."

"Did you learn any details?" Jack asked, meeting Laura's gaze.

"Yup. Buck called Vicki to say he'd bought a house in Abbotsford and that he was thinking of getting out of the club. Told her to keep it secret and invited her out to see his house so they could talk first."

"*Does* he have a house out there?"

"Naw, it belongs to a prospect. Darren Jenkins."

"Never heard of him."

"He's with the Eastside chapter. He's only been prospecting about three weeks."

"Then I take it that Jenkins wasn't home when it happened, because he wouldn't be trusted yet?"

"You're right. The three-three said they needed to borrow it for a meeting."

"Guess you could call it a meeting. How did it go down?" Jack asked.

"Buck let her into the house and Hackman and Trapp were hiding inside."

"What about Bazzoli and Crowe?"

"They covered off the street from outside."

"Go on."

"Hackman and Trapp did the dirty work. Once they started in on her, Buck left to drive her wheels back to Vancouver. He's also going to tell the sister that Vicki slipped out of the country to join Damien."

"Do you know how they did it?" Jack asked.

"Hackman gave her one to the gut to drop her and then sat on her while Trapp used plastic wrap to finish her off." Lance paused, but when Jack didn't respond he added, "Got no idea what they did with the body after that."

"Stay in touch," Jack said tersely, then hung up. He saw that Laura's gaze was still on him. When he spoke, his voice was quiet. Not to hide what he was saying from Natasha, but out of a sombre feeling for what had taken place. "Asphyxiation." He glanced at Natasha, who was using plastic wrap to cover the boy's sandwiches, then turned back to Laura and added, "Plastic wrap."

Laura pushed her half-full glass of beer away. "I've had enough. I'm going home."

Jack understood. He rose to his feet and dumped both their beers down the sink.

Chapter Thirty-Five

On Monday Jack and Laura started gathering information to identify the names of people connected to properties in the areas they were interested in. Some names were gathered through company records and property-tax records. As the week progressed, other names were gathered by driving through areas they'd outlined on a grid map and collecting licence-plate numbers.

Their initial search focused on areas close to the road where Jack had first seen them. When none of the names they obtained could be connected with the bikers, they expanded their search area and kept looking.

Late Friday morning Jack received a call from Lance. The biker sounded all business as usual. "Wanted to let you know that Pure E is going to be gone for a few weeks. He's flying to Montreal tomorrow to chat with the boys."

"About anything in particular?"

"Wants to see if they're making any headway figuring out who blabbed about the 120 keys of coke you took two weeks ago. Also wants to stop in at his old stomping grounds to visit some buddies and take care of some personal business."

"Winnipeg?"

"Yup. He's scheduled to return first of December."

Jack saw Rose in the doorway waiting to speak to him. "I have to go. Let me know when he's back."

"Yeah. I figure you want to keep track of him for that big picture of yours."

More like he is the big picture. Jack hung up and looked at Rose.

"Mortimer wants to see you and me at four this afternoon," she stated.

"What am I? Chopped liver?" Laura grumbled.

"At least it gives me time to put on my suit and tie," Jack said. He'd shaved since last week's homeless persona.

"Any idea what it's about?" Laura asked.

"I was hoping you two could tell me."

"No idea," Jack said.

"What exactly have you been up to?" Rose asked.

Jack waved Rose over and gestured at the documentation on their desks. "Trying to find out what they did with Damien's body. I-HIT searched the area around Sumas Mountain without results, so Laura and I decided to search elsewhere. See if we could find some other biker connection out in that vicinity."

"Where do you start? There's a lot of biker connections out there. Satans Wrath have got their puppet club in Port Coquitlam, they've got —"

"Satans Wrath wouldn't trust the Gypsy Devils for something like this," Jack said. "They even lied to their own club about his murder."

"They made the Gypsy Devils torture and murder one of their own, along with his brother and sister-in-law," Rose noted.

"Yes, but they wanted those bodies to be found. They even set the barn on fire to make sure we did. Killing their own is different. That's not something they'd want others to know about."

"I see." Rose examined a couple of the documents on their desks. "You've gone to a lot of work. Why'd you pick this area?"

"It's not too far past Sumas Mountain and is mostly rural. I thought it'd be a good place to start."

Rose appeared to ponder his reply, then said, "Mortimer, 4:00 p.m. Don't forget."

Assistant Commissioner Mortimer gestured for Rose and Jack to take seats in front of his desk. He then stared at them long enough to make them feel uncomfortable, before smiling and rubbing his hands together. "Do you recall when we first met?"

"About a month and half ago," Rose replied, sounding puzzled.

"Second of October, to be precise," Jack said. "I attended the site of a triple murder that morning, then at noon an informant of mine was murdered."

"Yes, you thought he was murdered." Mortimer looked snidely amused. "And what did I tell you in that regard?"

"You expressed your doubt," Jack replied.

"Yes … and you were so adamant I was wrong." Mortimer paused. "I brought you both in to let you know that I wasn't wrong." He sat back and folded his arms across his chest.

"Sir?" Rose eventually asked.

Mortimer leaned forward, placing his palms on the outer reaches of his desk while focusing on Jack. His snide look had been replaced by a cold stare.

Okay, jerk-off, you look like a fat toad getting ready to hop. Get on with it.

"I was given a report from the Combined Forces Special Enforcement Unit this morning. They picked up a wiretap conversation in a car last weekend between a drug dealer and some biker from Satans Wrath."

"Did CFSEU tell you which biker?" Jack asked.

Mortimer appeared irritated at the question. "They mentioned Black Bird."

"I'm not sure, but I think that belongs to a biker by the name of Nick Crowe," Jack said. He glanced at Rose who glared at him. *What's that for?*

"His name doesn't matter," Mortimer said with a hint of exasperation. "What matters is what was said." He paused, perhaps waiting to be prodded for the information. When he was greeted by silence, he continued, "The biker told the dealer that they snuck Vicki Damien out of the country last week." Mortimer stared at Jack, apparently waiting for the message to sink in. He then clasped his hands together and sat back. "You obviously know what that means."

Sure, it means the bikers knew the car was bugged.

"Vicki went to join her husband," Mortimer stated matter-of-factly. "They wouldn't have bothered to smuggle her out unless he'd requested it." He then pointed his finger at Jack for effect. "You wasted I don't know how much manpower and taxpayer dollars by sending I-HIT off on a wild goose chase."

"I'm sorry," Jack said. "I obviously made a huge mistake."

"There was also some mention that she had to double-cross the police to stall for time."

Rose gave Jack a sideways glance. "Double-cross the police?" she questioned.

"No doubt that was referring to when she told Corporal Taggart about some of her husband's money laundering," Mortimer said smugly. He looked at Jack. "Obviously there were way more accounts you didn't discover." After a moment he added, "This is exactly the reason I warned you not to come off half-cocked and jumping to conclusions."

Jack hung his head. "Sir, you've no idea how embarrassed I feel." *That you're in command, that is.* "I truly don't know what to say."

"Well, the important thing is that the truth has been established." Mortimer gave a consoling smile. "We all make mistakes."

"Thank you, sir."

"Let's look at it as water under the bridge. I trust you've moved on to more important issues."

"Sir?"

"For instance," Mortimer elaborated, "have you enrolled in French lessons yet?"

"I was too late to sign up for adult courses this fall, but plan to start in the winter classes."

Mortimer's smile seemed genuine. "Excellent. Where will you be taking classes?"

"Simon Fraser."

"I've a daughter living at home who's going to SFU. She's taking criminology." Mortimer smiled, perhaps thinking about his daughter, then his face became serious as he refocused on Jack. "I'm glad you've accepted my guidance. I believe you have the potential to make a fine police officer someday."

"Thank you, sir."

"You both may leave."

I'll find Vicki's body and when I do, how will you respond if I bring her in, face still wrapped in plastic, and lay her on your desk? Ah, probably a bad idea …

"It's my fault. I should've spoken…." Rose hissed as they headed down the hallway.

"Pardon?" Jack answered. *Damn it, here it comes. She clued in about our search.*

"Vicki's dead! Don't deny it!"

"Of course she is. I never said she wasn't."

"Nick Crowe is with the three-three."

"Yes."

"You made it sound like you hardly knew him. You were trying to deceive me!"

"I said that for Mortimer's benefit so he wouldn't think I was still involved with bikers. No full-patch member of Satans Wrath would be dumb enough to mouth off to someone outside the club about smuggling Vicki out of the country — but it would've been fruitless to tell Mortimer that."

Rose still didn't appear to be satisfied. "The bikers obviously knew the car was bugged, so I think she did disappear last week because it would match the story."

"Probably."

"When exactly did you and Laura start searching the area you're looking at to find Damien's body?"

"This Monday." Jack frowned. "What're you getting at?"

"You know damn well what I'm getting at! It's a hell of a coincidence that Vicki disappears at the same time you decide to search a certain area."

Jack took a deep breath and slowly exhaled. "Okay, it was no coincidence."

"I didn't think so!"

"You know I had to take action." Jack's tone echoed his bitterness. "Pure E threatened my family. He needs to be stopped … without risk to my family."

"Yes, but we're talking about Vicki."

"She was a secondary target. She set Damien up to be murdered."

"Yes, but it was mentioned that she double-crossed the police. I don't believe that was in regards to Damien's money-laundering. Too much money was involved for that. You did something."

"Yes, I did. I leaked word to the bikers that she was going to testify against them."

"Christ," Rose muttered.

"I did it hoping to find out where they hide bodies." Jack saw Rose staring at him. *Okay, part of it was to avenge what she did.*

"That was something I should've been informed about," Rose stated firmly.

"I am informing you."

"Only after the fact and because you know I clued in."

"Okay, but either way, she deserved what she got. She shouldn't have ratted out Damien. You play with the bull, you get the horns."

"You should've talked to me about it first."

"What would that have accomplished, other than risking your neck on the chopping block if we were found out?"

"Or risking that I wouldn't have approved."

"Yes, that, too," Jack admitted.

"Except I know you'd have done it regardless, which leads me to conclude the real reason is that you really were trying to protect me." When Jack didn't respond she continued, "Don't! I'm a big girl. I can handle the heat."

"Not the heat Mortimer would generate. You're worth protecting. I don't want to risk all of us getting tossed out on our asses." Jack waited a beat. "I think you have the potential to make a fine police officer someday. Let's not ruin that."

Rose wasn't amused. "That asshole. I couldn't believe he said that. I almost lost it in there."

"Don't. His days are numbered. He won't last long."

"You're thinking he'll either screw up and Ottawa will notice or that the stress will get to him." Rose shook her head in doubt. "The problem is he's insulated himself enough not to take the blame for his screw-ups. As far as stress goes, I doubt he cares enough about anything to feel stress."

"Stress" will be an understatement once I'm done with him.

"So about Vicki … do you know the details? Have you talked to your informant?"

"Yes. Crowe and Hackman from the three-three killed her last Thursday afternoon at a prospect's home in Abbotsford. They held her down and used plastic wrap to asphyxiate her."

Rose winced.

"Laura and I tried to do surveillance to see where they'd take her body, but lost them."

"In the area you're searching," Rose concluded.

"Yes."

"If you do find it, I suggest you use Crime Stoppers to alert I-HIT."

"I don't know," Jack replied. "I'd love to rub Mortimer's face in it myself."

Rose looked startled. "Forget that! In the past you skidded by on things that could've been a coincidence. With Mortimer you can't even pretend to be doing real police work."

"I was only joking, but thanks for trying to protect me."

"I'm your boss. It's my job to protect you. Not the other way around."

They'd arrived at the door to his office. Jack looked at Rose and said, "Right, you're going to protect me. Got it."

Rose eyed him suspiciously, then continued down the hall to her own office.

Sorry, Rose, but nobody could protect me from what I'm about to do.

Chapter Thirty-Six

It was approaching supper hour on Monday when Whiskey Jake left Satan's Girls Entertainment Agency and headed for his car. His exclusive phone rang and he reached for it. *Rat Cop. I wondered how long it would be before you wanted your money.* "It's me," he answered.

"Where are you?" Rat Cop asked.

"Out on the street. It's safe."

"Jesus fucking Christ," Rat Cop grumbled.

Whiskey Jake smiled. *So you know we aced her. What the fuck did you think we were gonna do?* "What's up?"

"What's up? You know what's up. I met with Mortimer."

"Yeah, him. What'd he have to say?"

"Vicki never showed up for her meeting on Friday with the prosecutor. Her lawyer said he didn't know where she was. Everyone's freaked out."

"Yeah, so what did Mortimer say?"

"He said there's something on a wire about her double-crossing the police to stall for time so that you guys could sneak her out of the country."

"Interesting. Does he believe it?"

"He doesn't know what to believe … but I do. You guys better come through for me on —"

"Relax. I've been waiting for you to call. I got somethin' for ya."

"It better be good. The shit's really hit the fan. I stuck my neck out big time."

"You'll be happy. Ten large."

Rat Cop paused. "Okay, that's fair."

An hour later Jack retrieved ten thousand dollars delivered to a drop site by Whiskey Jake. This time the money, all in hundreds, was stashed inside a Chinese takeout box and placed under a Dumpster. After retrieving it, Jack was picked up by Laura. He gestured to the box and said, "It went smoothly."

Laura nodded silently.

"You okay?" Jack asked.

"I'm okay, just tired. It's been a long day."

"We're off tomorrow. It's Remembrance Day."

"I wish it was Forgetting Day," Laura replied. "I can't stop remembering."

"The farmhouse?"

"Yes, the farmhouse, Vicki, Pure E, everything."

Jack thought how haggard Laura had been looking lately and felt a twinge of guilt. "We'll get him, Laura. Pure E will pay for what he did. That's a promise."

"And Mortimer?"

Jack tensed at the thought of Mortimer. *Ease up. She's stressed enough.* "The plan will work. Don't worry about him."

"Right … don't worry."

***

Over the next week, Jack and Laura continued to gather information on people and businesses in the area they were searching. When titles and ownership documents within the next grid section failed to reveal anything, they drove to the area and collected licence-plate numbers.

The following Monday they were driving along a country road and saw a dairy farm situated well back from the road with a car parked in the yard. "I'm going to drive in and scoop the plate," Jack said as he turned into the driveway.

Laura looked at a map of land titles. "Says the owner is a David McGregor. I already ran him for a record. There's nothing." She looked at a large square section on the map and added, "He owns a big chunk of land."

Jack shrugged. "Let's get the plate number regardless. The three-three could be renting to keep their names off the land titles."

When Jack drove into the yard a middle-aged woman came out of the house, so he rolled down his window and smiled.

"Hi! Can I help you?" she asked.

"Friends of ours moved out to this area recently and are renting a house," Jack said. "We accidentally left their address and phone number behind, but I think this is the area."

"*You* left the number and address behind," Laura piped up. "There's no *we* about it."

The woman grinned. "We don't have any renters. What's their name?"

"Ray and Susan Wilky," Jack said.

"Wilky … no, I don't know them." She looked apologetic. "We've lived here for over thirty years, but lately there've been so many farms gobbled up and subdivided that there are lots of people in the area we don't know. Sorry I couldn't help."

"No problem. We'll keep looking. Sorry to have bothered you."

"Good luck," the woman said, then waved as they drove out of the yard.

By the time they reached the main road Laura had confirmed that the car in the yard was registered to David McGregor.

Jack drove for a couple of minutes past some open fields, then slammed on the brakes.

"What's up?" Laura asked.

"That," Jack replied, pointing to a sign posted on a tree behind a barbed-wire gate; it warned that trespassers would be charged. Tire ruts in the soil led through the clump of trees beyond.

"What of it?" Laura asked.

"Let me see the map."

Laura handed Jack the map. "This is still McGregor's property," she said. As Jack studied the map, she added, "She seemed like a pretty nice woman to me."

"Me, too," Jack said. "Friendly and open. I also didn't see any other signs to warn of trespassing." He pointed to the map. "The rest of their land is cleared for pasture, but this small area on the corner is cut off by a ravine. Likely not big enough or worth the effort to put to use."

"So why post a No Trespassing sign?"

"Exactly. We're not even in sight of their house. If someone did trespass, I doubt it'd be noticed."

Jack undid the gate and drove through. Moments later they came upon a compound surrounded with a chain-link fence with a double strand of barbed wire on top. A padlocked steel gate was the only entry point. Inside the compound was a shipping container. A sign inside the gate said:

INFECTIOUS WASTE
MANAGEMENT SITE
DO NOT ENTER

A couple of magnetic signs were stuck to the side of the container. One was the international symbol that indicated a biological hazard. The other warned that the area was under 24-hour monitoring and said that trespassers would be prosecuted. Closed-circuit television cameras were clearly visible inside the compound and were directed at the gate and the container.

Laura raised an eyebrow. "What do you think?"

Jack shut the engine off. "I think the cameras are for show. I don't even see any power lines." He studied the yard again. "I'm going in for a look."

Laura gestured to the sign. "Infectious waste? If it is, we should be wearing hazmat suits."

"You can wait if you want."

"You're a jerk," Laura replied, opening the door.

Seconds later Jack was picking the lock on the gate when his eyes drifted to a small pile of moss-covered stones alongside the fence. The moss on one stone didn't line up properly, indicating it'd been moved. Laura saw what he was looking at and went to take a look.

"Forget the picks," she said, holding up a plastic baggie containing two keys.

"Excellent."

"If the McGregors were running this, they'd likely have the keys at their house," she noted.

Pure E, you bastard, your days are numbered.

Laura stared at him. "Hey, you're scaring me," she said.

Jack realized his face had revealed the rage and revenge he was keeping bottled inside. "Sorry, I'm okay. Get over here. Let's check it out."

Laura took the keys out of the baggie. "My guess is the three-three don't want any evidence on their person to connect them to this place … if it *is* the place, that is."

"Yes, so much for my idea of trying to match keys on their persons." He looked at Laura. "Go ahead. Do the honours."

Laura used one key to open the gate and seconds later stuck the second key inside a padlock hanging from the rear doors to the container. The lock popped open. She swallowed, then looked at Jack. "Be my guest."

Jack slipped the padlock out of the clasp. He took a deep breath to calm himself, then opened the door. There was a smell he recognized. The same smell as in the farmhouse kitchen where two charred corpses had been tied to chairs. He then knew he'd never find any bodies. He also knew he'd found what they'd been looking for.

"Is that what I think it is?" Laura asked, pointing at the metal apparatus inside.

Jack nodded, then entered and lifted a lid on a container that was the size of a chest freezer. Attached to the compartment was a tall rectangular metal box. "It's an animal incinerator," he said, staring into the loading chamber. "Meant for livestock."

"Oh."

He expected more comment from Laura, but then he glanced at her face and saw her swallow. *Yeah, words aren't adequate to describe what's been happening here.* His gaze shifted back to the loading chamber and he thought of Damien. *Glad he was already dead.*

"What now?" Laura's face was grim.

Jack let the lid fall with a bang. "Go back to the office and see what we can find out about everyone in the McGregor family."

"She doesn't seem like the type."

"I agree, but who knows what the rest of her family is like? Maybe a son or daughter is connected."

"Then what do we do after that?"

Jack's voice was harsh. "We wait until Pure E returns from the east, then take him for a ride."

Laura stared at the incinerator for a moment, then nodded.

Chapter Thirty-Seven

Over the next few days Jack and Laura took an in-depth look at the McGregor family to see if they could come up with a connection, either direct or indirect, to the three-three or anyone with even a trace of criminal affiliation.

The McGregors had two sons and two daughters. All were university-educated, married, and had professional careers. None had any involvement with the law other than minor traffic infractions.

Late Friday afternoon Jack looked across his desk at Laura. "I don't think they're connected in any way. My guess is someone from the three-three is paying them to use the property and the McGregors think it's for a legit business."

"I agree," Laura replied.

Jack scowled. "That puts a wrench in our plan. There's no way I can call Crime Stoppers. I-HIT would install hidden cameras and then be forced to bring in the McGregors as witnesses to who rented the property."

"And the trial would drag on for a year or two and the witnesses would be killed unless they were put in Witness Protection."

"Yes."

"Even if Pure E was, you know, no longer in charge."

"I wouldn't chance it even if he wasn't around. We don't know who'd replace him. We saw what happened to the Barlows."

"So what do we do? Let the three-three continue on their merry way? Killing and torturing?"

"No. We'll disband the three-three and make it so none of them go near the incinerator again."

"How?"

"Simple. When Pure E disappears, Rat Cop will burn the three-three."

Laura made a face. "Wish you wouldn't use that expression."

"Sorry. What I mean is Rat Cop will say someone in the three-three is talking, but he doesn't know who. Satans Wrath wouldn't risk using any of them after that."

"That might work."

"It will."

Laura appeared to mull it over, then said, "Part of the plan you told me about the day you took me out of the office, because you figured I'd yell at you, was to turn the one hundred and twenty kilos of coke into three tonnes. Have you talked to Natasha about what we'll be doing in your garage?"

"I will tonight. Friday's our date night and we have dinner without the boys. I already reserved a stretch limo identical to the one that Mouse from the Gypsy Devils has." He paused. "Don't worry about Natasha. She'll go along with it."

"Even sitting in a car with a psychopath?"

"She's intelligent, intuitive, and being married to me proves she can handle stress. Think of what she and I have been through over the years. What she has endured. What my children have endured. They're strong."

"They've had to be."

"I know. So I'm confident she'll be able to handle him. Otherwise I'd never put her in that position. No worries. I'll train her on what to say and she'll have backup. She won't be with him for all that long." He paused. "It's not like there's anyone else I know who speaks Russian and whom I can trust to never talk about it. Once I explain it to her, I'm certain she'll agree."

"You talked *me* into going along with it. I'm sure she will."

Jack refilled Natasha's glass of Cabernet Sauvignon as she cut into a barbecued steak. "How'd you like to help me out on an undercover assignment?"

"I thought you weren't allowed to work undercover anymore," Natasha responded.

"Mortimer won't know about it."

She eyed him warily. "So what do you want me to do? Go out dressed as a hooker, your date, or both?"

Jack smiled. "None of those. I want you to wear a gown with lots of jewellery. Dress like you're going to the opera."

"We never go to the opera."

"You won't be this time, either — but you'll be in a fancy limo."

"Doing what?"

"I want you to offer a guy three tonnes of coke. He'll be searched before being put in the limo, so safety won't be an issue."

Natasha appeared to think about it, then her face brightened. "It sounds like fun." She raised her glass. "Did you say three tonnes?"

"The target will be made to think we have that much. There's a scenario I'll get you to act out. Part of it will be making some phone calls in Russian."

Natasha took a sip, then moved the wine around in her mouth before swallowing. "You'll be with me, I presume?"

"I'm afraid not. There'll be two bad guys. I'll be doing a UC on one while you're in the limo with the other. Laura will drive the limo and Sammy Crofton will be in the back with you for protection. Benny Saunders will be with me."

"Who am I calling who speaks Russian?"

"The calls will be bogus. They'll be to me."

"You? You only know a handful of Russian words and half of them are just mushy stuff."

"I know, but what I do know will allow me to fake an accent. The bad guys don't speak Russian. It doesn't matter what I actually say."

"I take it I'm needed because I speak Russian?"

"Yes."

Natasha stared quietly at Jack for a moment. "Does it have something to do with the bikers who came to our house?"

"Yes. The target who'll be in the limo with you is Purvis Evans. National president of Satans Wrath."

Natasha abruptly put her glass down. "He's the one who ordered the guys to do it. The one you call Pure E."

Jack nodded.

Natasha's face darkened. "That bastard. Sure, I'll do it." She paused, then looked alarmed. "Won't he recognize me?"

"I don't know if he's seen your picture, but to be safe, I'll get you to buy a red wig and wear a gala masquerade mask to hide your upper face. You'll be dressed like you're going to a fancy event and will be sitting in the shadows. He won't know who you really are."

"I see." She raised her glass and swirled the wine around, but put it down without taking a sip and looked at him curiously.

"You okay?" he asked. "We'll role-play the scenario over and over to cover different responses or questions he may have. I know you'd be good at it, otherwise I wouldn't have asked."

"It's not that. Why did you specify a red wig? Is it to satisfy some fetish of yours?"

"Maybe after," Jack said, trying to sound sexy.

"Yeah, I thought as much." Natasha smiled briefly, then her face became serious. "When do I do it?"

"In two weeks. He's away at the moment, but due back the first of December, which is a Monday. I think we'll get the opportunity the following Friday or Saturday. He tends to go out clubbing on weekends with one of his guys by the name of Whiskey Jake. He's the one I'll be dealing with."

"Okay, so I'll arrange a babysitter for both those days. Whichever day it isn't, we'll still have a babysitter. Perhaps we could go out for dinner?"

"Uh, there's something I didn't mention. I plan on bringing Whiskey Jake to our garage while you're in the limo. I think it best if Mike and Stevie are farmed out for the night."

Natasha looked incredulous. "You're bringing him to our house?"

"The garage. That's where the supposed three tonnes of coke will be."

Her eyes flashed anger. "You're not bringing him to our —"

"He'll be blindfolded and his hands tied. Don't worry. He won't know where he is. When we're done, Pure E will never bother us again."

Natasha gave Jack a hard look. "Never?"

"Never."

She took a sip of wine, then another. "Okay." She gave a wry smile. "Knowing he's the one who threatened my children, maybe you should search me before I get in the limo. Make sure I don't put a bullet in his head."

Jack glanced toward the living room where Mike and Steve were playing a video game. When he answered, his words were cold. "He's not getting off that easy."

Chapter Thirty-Eight

The following week, although uneventful, was tense for Jack and Laura as they waited for Pure E to return. Rose thought they were still trying to find out where Satans Wrath were disposing of bodies. Jack had decided not to tell her they'd already found it. She was receptive to a lot of things he did while working in what he called the grey zone, but his plan went well beyond that.

Friday arrived and Jack was driving Laura home after work. She'd been unusually quiet all day, and when he stopped at a light, all she did was stare out the window in silence. "You okay?" he asked.

"I want this to be over." Her tone revealed her anxiety.

"Our friend told me that Pure E is still flying back Monday. If he follows his usual pattern, he and Whiskey Jake will go out clubbing by the weekend. It'll be over soon."

Laura nodded. "We also have one hundred and twenty kilos of coke sitting in the locker. Monday is December 1. Are you going to pay the storage fees for another month?"

"No, I'm going to pack it in my garage tomorrow."

"Do you need help?"

"No, I can handle it. Then on Monday we'll take the coke and make it look like — hang on, phone." The call display said the number was blocked. "Hello?"

"Hello, Jack. Stuart Wilson calling."

"Hey, Stuart." He looked at Laura and said softly, "It's the Vancouver Police Department's top detective homicide investigator."

"Hey, compared to you Mounties, we're all top detectives over here," Wilson said.

"You didn't hear me right. I said 'defective,' not 'detective.'"

Wilson chuckled.

"Don't you know it's Friday? Laura and I are on our way home."

"For olive soup, no doubt," Wilson said.

"Might do that if you're calling to tell me some bad guy is dead."

Wilson's tone became serious. "It's Tamas Dubashi. He's dead. Early this afternoon someone bashed him repeatedly in the temple with a blunt object, possibly the butt of a handgun."

"Tamas Dubashi?" Jack exchanged a puzzled look with Laura. "Sorry, neither Laura nor I knows him."

"You don't?" Wilson sounded surprised. "He was calling you on the phone when he was murdered."

"I didn't get any calls."

"That's because he only managed to enter the first eight numbers. He was killed before entering the last two."

"Maybe a coincidence."

"No, there's more." Wilson paused. "You do trust me enough that you'd tell me if he was your confidential informant or something, wouldn't you?"

"Yes, you know I trust you. He's not my CI. Where'd it take place? You said there was more."

"His body was found behind a concession stand in Stanley Park and —"

"Stanley Park!"

"Yes … and your business card was shoved down his throat."

Chapter Thirty-Nine

Jack and Laura sat around Wilson's desk as Jack explained that he'd dressed as a homeless person to conduct surveillance and that Tamas Dubashi had given him coffee.

"And you knew him only as Tom," Wilson noted.

Jack nodded. "He seemed like a really good guy. When he found out who I really was, he offered to keep an eye open and let me know if our targets showed up. That's when I gave him my business card."

"You said on the phone you might have a lead."

"On Friday, October 31, I saw two guys meet with him. Both looked like FPSers. One of them phoned as they approached the concession stand and Tom met him outside and gave them money."

"You saw that?" Wilson asked.

"I saw an envelope and spoke to Tom about it the next day. He told me his son recently went to jail for selling cocaine and that the two goons collected five hundred dollars from him for his son."

"A drug debt his son owed before going to jail perhaps," Wilson said.

Jack sighed. "At the time I thought that, but not now. Why would anyone kill Tom because of his son's drug debt? The son's in jail. It's unlikely he'd be in a position to pay off the debt regardless."

"If not for a drug debt, then what?"

"Christ, I should've talked to him about it more," Jack lamented. "I even gave him a lecture."

"A lecture?" Wilson questioned.

"I told him his son needed to learn to stand on his own two feet and that there comes a time when a person has to be responsible for what they do."

"What did he say to that?"

"Just said he was worried about his son, but I didn't delve into the matter. Our targets showed up and I forgot all about it." Jack clenched his fist in frustration. "Son-of-a-bitch, I should've spoken to him again."

"Would you be able to identify the two men again?" Wilson asked.

"We can do even better. At first I was concerned that Tom was tipping off the people we were working on, so we followed them. Laura's got some good pictures of them and has the plate number of the car they were driving."

"Right here," said, Laura, thumbing through her cellphone. "Got a photo of the car, too. It's registered to a Lorraine Dole. Record for theft and multiple convictions for drug possession. I'll forward them to you."

Wilson received the photos and studied them briefly.

"Next is another photo you'll be interested in," Laura said. "It's of a list of twelve names they had tucked in the sun visor. It looks like Tom was sixth on the list."

Wilson looked at the photo. "Abbreviated ... initials ... check marks." He eyed Jack. "What do you make of it?"

"My guess is they're running a protection racket. I bet if you identify the other names on the list you'll find they have relatives or partners in jail."

Wilson nodded, then wrote down some information before gesturing to a colleague seated at the next desk. "Van Dusen, run this name ASAP. If she has any known associates, get me photos."

To comply with the request, Van Dusen had to leave the room. Wilson said, "Should only take him ten minutes. Hope you don't mind waiting."

"Are you kidding? We'll wait as long as you want." *Sons-of-bitches shoved my business card down his throat. Christ!* He stared at Wilson. "Like I said, Tom was a good guy. He didn't deserve this."

As they waited, Wilson cleared his throat. "I, uh, heard that the bikers left a message for you at that triple murder last month. Wrote it on the wall in blood."

Jack nodded.

"Any chance this is another personal message for you?"

"It's personal to me."

"Could Satans Wrath be behind it?" Wilson prodded. "Maybe found out Tom was trying to help you?"

"No, I'm positive Satans Wrath wasn't behind it." He glanced at Laura. "We've a good source. We'd know if that was the case."

Wilson nodded, then took a moment to make some notes before looking up again. "You said you followed the two guys," he prompted.

"After getting the money from Tom, they went to the Black Water Hotel bar. I saw them meet a hooker. Probably Lorraine Dole."

"The Black Water." Wilson paused. "Man, what a hole that place is. You're right, even the bikers don't go in there anymore."

"The place did make my skin crawl," Jack replied.

"Literally, I bet," Wilson replied.

"Fortunately I didn't stay inside long enough to pick up any little hitchhikers. Once Laura sent me the list of names, I figured they had nothing to do with what we were working on and left."

"And the next day you returned to the park, which is when Tom told you about the money?"

"Yes, it was the last time I spoke with him. Our targets showed up when he and I were chatting, so I left. Haven't been back since." Jack waited until Wilson finished writing. "You think the butt of a pistol was used to kill him?"

"Looks like it. Whoever did it probably didn't want to attract attention with the noise of a gunshot."

"I think the culprits are those two guys," Jack said, "but there was another incident. It involved three punks. I don't think they'd be capable of this, but I'll tell you about it."

"Okay, shoot." Wilson picked up his pen.

Jack then told him about the three punks who'd tormented Tom by squirting ketchup on him and the altercation that followed.

"I'll check that out, as well," Wilson said, "but from what you say, I tend to agree. If any of the three punks had had a gun, I suspect they'd have threatened you with it after you punched the one guy in the face."

"I've got something," Van Dusen announced as he approached. "Dole's frequently been seen in the company of a Lester Burnside. A real badass with a long violent record. Got photos and records on him and Dole, as well as another associate of Burnside's."

Jack and Laura crowded around Wilson's desk to view the photos.

"That's him," Jack and Laura said in unison, both pointing to Burnside's photo.

"Yeah, that's the one in your pictures who was driving the car and wearing the checkered jacket," Wilson agreed.

"The other guy I don't recognize," Jack said.

"Nope," Laura agreed. "The other guy definitely isn't the guy with the ponytail."

Jack pointed to Dole's photo. "She's the woman they met in the Black Water."

Wilson glanced at Van Dusen. "Good going." He stabbed at Burnside's photo with his finger. "This could be our murderer or possibly an accomplice. Go back and keep checking. Get what you can on anyone ever associated with him."

When Van Dusen left, Jack, Laura, and Wilson looked at Burnside's criminal record. It included numerous assaults, an armed robbery, break-and-enters, and stolen-property offences. He'd been on parole for the last six months after serving time in Kent Federal Prison, a maximum-security prison about an hour-and-a-half's drive from Vancouver.

"The asshole's been around," Wilson said. "I'll scoop him up, but you can bet he won't talk. Unless we get DNA or something." He shook his head.

Jack picked up a calendar. "The murder happened this afternoon," he stated, "which is the last Friday of the month."

"Yeah," Wilson concurred.

"The day I saw Tom turn over the envelope was the last Friday of last month."

"Right."

"After which Burnside and Ponytail went to the Black Water — but there were other names on the list that weren't checked off. My guess is the people who are on the second half of the list are collected from the next day."

"Meaning tomorrow these two assholes could show up to collect from the other names," Wilson said. He checked the list. "And the next person in line is identified as 'Wong — E. Cordova/Main 10:00 a.m.'"

"East Cordova and Main Street," Jack repeated. "Looks like someone doesn't want the bad guys coming to their home or business."

"Either that, or the bad guys don't want to be seen," Laura suggested.

"I'll set up there tomorrow," Wilson said. "If they show up I'll grab them."

"Which, as you mentioned, may not get you the results you want," Jack said.

Wilson raised an eyebrow. "You have another idea?"

"These guys made this personal for me. I'd like to reciprocate. How about I try a quick undercover scenario to see if I can get an admission?"

"How the hell could you walk up to two guys one day after a murder without scaring them off?"

"If I scare them off, it's not like you'd lose anything. You plan to pick them up for interrogation regardless."

"Uh, Jack," Laura cautioned, "are you forgetting about Mortimer?"

"Mortimer?" Wilson questioned.

"That asshole," Jack said. "I'll need to keep this secret." He then told Wilson how he'd been ordered not to work undercover, have any informants, or do any police work involving direct contact with criminals.

Wilson frowned. "Jack, I don't want to get you into trouble."

"Trouble? I never get into trouble. Besides, I won't tell if you don't."

Wilson looked more concerned than amused. "You sure?"

"I'm sure."

"Okay, but then I've another issue. Will you be packing and wearing a wire?"

"Not for the first meeting. Like you said, with a cold approach they're going to be nervous. I don't want to risk being armed or wired in case they pat me down."

Wilson's eyebrows knit together into a solid line. "The Black Water is only a couple blocks away. What if they take you back there? That place is a hellhole."

"I don't see them chatting to me on a street corner for long. If it goes well, I expect that's where we'll go."

"I don't know, Jack." Wilson sounded apologetic. "I don't have anyone who either isn't known or could go into that dump to provide you protection without being spotted."

"No worries, Laura will provide cover for me. If she's wired, she could relay to your team outside."

"No worries?" Wilson repeated, looking at Laura. "I wouldn't sit in there unless I was inside a tank."

"I'll be okay," Laura replied. She looked at Jack. "Mind you, talking about the place making your skin crawl doesn't exactly make me happy."

"Don't worry, I'll buy you a flea collar," Jack said.

"Only if it has diamonds on it," Laura replied.

Jack smiled, then glanced at Wilson. "So? What do you think?"

Wilson sighed, then said, "Okay, but there's still Mortimer. If you do obtain an admission, in a year or two it will likely go to court. I can't promise to keep your name out of the papers then."

"Don't worry about Mortimer," Jack said coldly. "He'll be gone before then."

Chapter Forty

Early the next morning Jack and Laura returned to Wilson's office. Laura was wearing a woollen cap and a grubby three-quarter-length blue nylon raincoat. Her jeans were tattered and one of her running shoes had a broken lace that was retied partway up. "What're you? Homeless or a junkie?" Wilson asked.

"A little of both," she replied.

Wilson nodded his approval. "If you do end up in the Black Water, you'll look right at home."

"Yup, nothing I like more than having beer for break-fast," Laura responded. She glanced at Jack. "Or wheat smoothies, as you call them."

Wilson gestured to some photos on his desk. "Take a look. We found a match for the guy who was with Burnside when you photographed them."

Jack and Laura each confirmed it was the man with the ponytail.

"His name is Archie Richards," Wilson said. "He was

in Kent Prison and his time overlapped with Burnside's. He got out a couple months earlier and his record is even worse than Burnside's."

"Hopefully the two of them will show up to collect from Wong this morning," Jack said.

"Yeah, about that." Wilson shook his head. "I still don't know how you plan on running this. I've got three guys coming in to assist. They'll be in cars and parked within the vicinity. I'll have the visual on you from a surveillance van and call the shots from there."

"That'll do," Jack replied. "Laura can hop in with you when I'm on the street. She knows how I work, so she can read the situation better. As far as how I'll go about it, cold approaches tend to be fluid. Sometimes they work, sometimes they don't. We'll have to play it by ear."

Wilson nodded. "What about the person they're collecting from?"

"Identify Wong for later if you can, but don't pick anyone up until I'm done. There has to be someone feeding Burnside and Richards information from inside the prison. Tom's son has only been in a couple of months, and Burnside and Richards were released before he got there. Even if I succeed this morning, it could still take time to identify all the players."

"Understood." Wilson eyed Jack. "So?"

"So?"

"How do you do it?" Wilson asked. "First approach them, I mean?" He then jokingly added, "After Wong pays, are you going to walk up and say something like, 'Hey, guys, nice day. By the way, didn't I see the two of you murder some guy in the park yesterday?'"

Jack pretended to think about it. "Yeah, that might work."

"You asshole," Wilson muttered.

An hour later Jack walked past the surveillance van parked near the intersection of East Cordova and Main Street. He was early, but was hoping Burnside and Richards might be early, too. If things went wrong, he preferred not to have this guy Wong caught in the middle. A light rain was falling so he opted for shelter in the doorway of a coffee shop on the corner.

At 10:00 a.m. an older Chinese man arrived and waited on the corner across from him. *Okay, as I told Wilson, sometimes these plans are fluid.*

Jack hustled across the street and approached. "You got the money?" he asked.

The man reached in his pocket, handed Jack a wad of money, then walked away. *What the hell? Why would you just give it to me, no questions asked? Don't you at least want to know what happened to Burnside and Richards?*

Jack retreated back to the coffee shop entranceway and counted the money. Five hundred dollars. Twenty minutes later he spotted two men standing at the intersection and looking around. Neither was Burnside or Richards, but by their hardened faces, he figured they were no strangers to the inside of a prison.

One was tall and skinny with bushy hair that had been dyed orange. *Looks like something someone used to clean their ears.* The other man was husky, with a week's worth of stubble on his face. *Where are Burnside and Richards? Still washing the blood off themselves? Guess this is it. Showtime.*

"Hey, you guys here for the five c's?" Jack said as he approached.

The man with the stubble looked perplexed. "Wong send ya?"

Jack didn't answer, opting instead to pull the wad of money from his pocket. When Stubble reached for it, Jack shoved it back in his pocket."

"What the fuck? We ain't got time to play games. Give it to me."

"I'm keepin' it," Jack replied.

"Whaddaya mean?" Stubble's lips curled and he stepped closer in an obvious act of intimidation. "Fork it over, mother, or Wong Junior will end up being chop suey."

"Like I'd give a shit," Jack said, moving his face closer and locking eyes with Stubble. "I collected this from Wong twenty minutes ago. You guys are late."

"What the hell?" Stubble glanced at Bushy Hair and stepped back. "Did Wes call ya? We ain't that late. Who're you?"

"I'm the competition," Jack said.

"Whaddaya mean, competition?" Bushy Hair asked.

"I don't know Wes, but I guess me and him got the same idea," Jack replied. "I've been coming up with chumps willing to pay me for protection, but I didn't know someone else was already doing it. That is, until last month when someone told me they were already paying. At first I didn't believe it, so I waited and watched. Sure enough, I see these two dudes collecting, too."

Stubble and Bushy Hair exchanged open-mouthed glances.

"Take a look." Jack showed the pair the photos he'd taken of Burnside and Richards on his cellphone.

"That's Les and Archie," the Bushy Hair said.

"Is that their names?" Jack asked. "They ain't too bright. I followed them and they left the chump list in their car. I got a picture of it, too."

Stubble glanced at the photo. Jack saw his jaw clench and his hands curl into fists.

"The thing is," Jack hurried to say, "you guys only got a dozen names. I've got a hundred."

"A hundred!" Stubble stared at him. "Bullshit. We got Kent sewn up. If you were dippin' in we'd know."

"Kent, hell, I've got names from all the jails," Jack replied. "The only problem is I don't have the muscle or the knowledge to really convince people." He paused to look at their faces. "You guys look like you've done time. Me, I never have. I know I can't walk the walk and talk the talk. I'd like to partner up with you." He paused to let them digest his words. "I could supply you with almost ten times as many names." He waited a beat. "For a percentage of course."

"If you ain't been on the inside, how the fuck did you come up with the names?" Stubble asked.

Jack glanced around on the pretext of ensuring nobody was within earshot, then lowered his voice. "It's my girlfriend. She works with a support group for women who have husbands and boyfriends in jail. She knows which women are scared shitless and gullible enough to pay. So far, my girl has been bullshitting them by saying she has connections with different gangs on the inside that she can pay to keep their guys safe, but it'd be nice if we actually did have some muscle."

Stubble glanced at his buddy. "I'm gonna make some calls. You wait with him."

When Stubble left, Jack gave Bushy Hair a friendly smile. "So ... my name's Bruce. What's yours?"

He sneered, then replied, "John Fucking Doe."

"That's quite a mouthful. Mind if I call you JFD for short?"

An uneasy silence ensued until Stubble returned. When he did, he cast a suspicious look at every car and pedestrian passing by, then turned to Jack. "You're coming with us. Got some people who wanna meet you."

"Where?" Jack demanded.

"Not far. The Black Water. We can walk."

"I'm a janitor. I gotta be at work by two this afternoon."

"You'll be done by then," Stubble replied.

Be done by then ... as in wrapped up in a body bag? Oh, yeah, this'll be fun. A few drinks, a few laughs ... what could possibly go wrong?

Inside the surveillance van, Laura saw Jack glance in her direction and scratch his neck. "Get me out of here," she said to Wilson. "I need to grab my car. They're going to the Black Water."

"How do you know?"

"He indicated I need a flea collar."

Chapter Forty-One

Twenty minutes later Jack found himself sitting with Stubble and JFD at a table in the centre of the Black Water bar. Natural instinct told him to sit with his back to the wall, but exhibiting such paranoia was something a cop would do. He'd also have preferred to sit closer to an exit in the event he had to fight his way out. Then again, if given a choice, he wouldn't be there at all.

The bar had already been open for a few hours. The cheap drinks sought by those who had an early morning taste for alcohol or a fix to start their day attracted a clientele not particularly choosy when it came to the victuals. For Jack it was the sort of place that caused him to wash his hands as soon as he entered the men's room and again before he left it.

Some customers, whose body odour and bloodshot eyes denoted their alcoholism, stared despondently at the drinks in front of them. Others, addicted to stronger substances, were in various states of mental alertness.

Some addicts sat in clusters, giving off a nervous frantic energy as their bodies told them they needed to score again. Others were on the nod — eyes closing and heads briefly dropping to their chests, then jerking up again. One such person sitting a few tables away was an imposter. *Good job, Laura, you fit right in.*

Stubble and JFD each ordered a bottle of Pilsner beer; Jack ordered a glass of draft. The glass made a better weapon. It could easily be broken on the table leg, providing a jagged edge to slash someone's jugular.

After they'd each paid for the drinks, Jack leaned into his two companions. "So, who we waitin' for?"

"You'll see," Stubble said, then turned his gaze elsewhere in an obvious indication he didn't want to talk.

Jack saw that JFD was sizing him up, but considering how their conversation had gone before, he decided to ignore him and quietly busied himself by using his thumbnail to scrape remnants of lipstick off the rim of his glass.

Minutes later Jack saw Stubble give JFD a nod. He looked toward the entrance to see Burnside and Richards approaching. Richards was wearing the same green nylon jacket he'd worn previously, but today Burnside wore a brown V-neck sweater. *Where's your red-and-black lumber jacket, asshole? Too bloody?*

When they arrived at the table, Burnside stood glaring at Jack. "This him?" he asked.

"Yeah," Stubble replied.

Jack glanced at Burnside, then turned his back and took a sip of beer.

At last Burnside and Richards took a seat on each side of him. By their build and the size of their necks, Jack believed that his original assessment that they were on steroids was correct. He then realized that all eyes were on Burnside. *So you're the cock of the walk.* Jack faced him, as well. "So, your buddy tell you what's going on?"

Burnside glanced at Stubble. "He told me."

"Good. I'm looking to partner up with —"

"Show me the pictures … now!" Burnside ordered.

"Sure, no problem." Jack held his cellphone and Burnside and Richards leaned in.

"It wasn't yesterday," Richards said, looking relieved.

"I told you he said last month," Stubble stated.

Burnside fidgeted with the cross dangling from his earlobe while staring at the pictures. Then he leaned back and looked at Jack. "When exactly did you take 'em? How long were you following us?"

"I took them at the end of October," Jack replied. "Then I followed you. That's when you left your list in the car and I got to thinking we should partner up. I was going to talk to you then, but decided I should chat with my girlfriend first and get as many names as I could."

The conversation stopped when the waitress approached. Burnside and Richards each ordered a bottle of Pilsner. As soon as she left, Richards looked at Jack. "So you ain't seen us or been following us in the last month?"

Jack shrugged. "No need. I got your list. Yesterday I had to work, so I figured I'd reach out to you this morning. I only guessed that your two buddies were involved when I saw them waitin' at the intersection."

"After you took our money," Burnside said.

"Yeah, but hey, what's five hundred bucks? That's nothing compared to what we could make if we partner up."

"How'd you know we were collecting five hundred?" JFD asked.

"I didn't. I asked Wong if he had the money and that's what he gave me."

"And your old lady ... she some kind of shrink or somethin'?" Richards asked.

"Somethin' like that," Jack replied. "She's taken psychology courses."

"And you really got a hundred names?" Burnside asked.

"More or less. Guys are always gettin' released, but new ones appear."

Burnside paid for the drinks when the waitress returned, then turned to Jack. "Show me your list."

"I'm not that stupid," Jack said. "I'm not bringing it with me until I know I can trust you guys. That's somethin' we still need to work out."

Burnside glanced at his colleagues. "I think he's all right. He took these pictures a month ago. With what happened yesterday ... there ain't no way anyone could've predicted that."

"What happened yesterday?" Jack asked.

"None of your fuckin' business," JFD said.

Jack wrinkled his brow. "Sounds like it could be if we're gonna partner up."

"It ain't got nothin' to do with you, so forget it," JFD said.

"Fine, but that brings me back to the issue of trust. I got something in mind that you could do to alleviate that."

"Which is?" Suddenly Burnside shifted his gaze across the bar and said, "What are you doing in here?"

Jack glanced back and saw Lorraine Dole approaching.

"No Johns out there now," she replied. "Me and some of

the girls just came in to warm up."

"Yeah?" Burnside replied. He gave a wave of his hand to where two other women were about to sit down. "Go sit with them, then. I'm busy."

Jack then turned back to Burnside. "You collect on the last Friday and Saturday of the month, right?"

Burnside nodded.

"Okay, I work Saturday afternoons, so that day isn't good for me, but how about, as a show of faith, next month you let me collect from the Friday people? There's only six on the list, so it wouldn't cost you much. Do that, then I'll give you the hundred names I got. Then we can work out some sort of percentage deal."

"You want us to give you three grand?" JFD sounded incredulous.

"What? You're whining about three g's?" Jack scoffed. "That's chump change. With me on board the pot will be about fifty g's a month. By my math, that's a lot better than the six you're collectin' now."

"By my math, it's a fuck of a lot better," Burnside said.

Jack eyed him. "Good, so you wanna partner up?"

Burnside twiddled his earring, then at last said, "Yeah. I think that'd be good."

"Great," Jack said, raising his glass to toast.

Burnside didn't respond. "The thing is, there's another guy I gotta talk to first."

"Oh?"

"Yeah. Our guy on the inside. He'll be here soon."

Time to bruise an ego … something a guy like him won't appreciate. "So that guy is the boss? He tells you when to jump and you do it?"

Burnside scowled. "I don't jump for nobody! We need Wes 'cause he gets us the names, but I run the fucking show." He looked defiantly at his colleagues. There were no challengers.

"Sounds like we got a deal then." Jack stared at Burnside a moment. "Right?"

Burnside looked at his colleagues again. Richards and Stubble nodded, but JFD made a point of looking away. Burnside issued a snort of disgust, then turned to Jack. "Yeah, sounds good, but I still gotta talk to Wes. At least make him feel like he's in the loop."

"I understand," Jack said. "It's better to keep everyone happy."

Burnside nodded, then clinked his bottle on Jack's glass.

"Good," Jack said, before taking a swallow. The others at the table did likewise, except for JFD, who looked displeased. Jack tapped Burnside on the arm. "If John Fucking Doe is going to sulk about it, I'll buy the next round to cheer him up."

"John Fucking Doe?" Burnside questioned.

"That's what he told me his name was."

Burnside gave another snort. "His name is John, but John Fucking the Dog would be better."

"Fuck you," John said.

"Personally, I think JFD has a nice ring to it." Jack grinned.

Burnside grinned back. "Yeah, me, too." He glanced across the table at John. "Whaddaya think? JFD?"

"I don't give a shit," he replied sullenly.

"JFD it is then." Burnside nudged Jack. "I'm Les. Beside you is Archie and that's Derrick across from you."

Jack introduced himself as Bruce, then motioned to the waitress to bring another round. After paying for the drinks, he turned to Burnside. "Listen, about me collectin' from those six people next month, any chance of you making an intro today? They might not all be as easy as Wong was, and I still have time before I gotta get to work."

"Yeah, uh, about that," Burnside replied. "Don't go back to that guy in the park."

"Why not?"

"Yesterday Archie and me had a problem with 'im."

"A problem?"

"A problem I took care of." Burnside then spoke to his colleagues. "It's already on the news. He's gonna piece it together sooner or later."

"Piece what together?"

Burnside was blunt. "He's dead. Stay away from there."

"Dead? What the fuck — you killed him? Why?"

"Had no choice. The fucker tried to call some cop on us. I couldn't believe it. He looked me right in the eye. Cocky as shit, then took out a cop's business card and was tappin' in the number." Burnside shrugged. "So I thumped him."

Jack recalled the advice he'd given Tom over the adolescent punks. *Exude self-confidence and look them in the eye. If they persist, call the cops.*

"What's with you?" Burnside said. "I had no choice."

Jack realized his face had given away how horrible he felt. *I intended it for adolescent punks — not hardened criminals.* He tried to look nonchalant. "Thumped him? What with, a rock?"

"No, the butt of a piece." Burnside eyed him suspiciously. "You looked upset."

"What if he wasn't dead? He could've said something later. Maybe in the ambulance."

"Oh, so that's what's buggin' ya." Burnside smirked. "No worries. I made sure he was dead. I even shoved the cop's fuckin' business card down his throat."

"Good." Jack took a sip of beer and wiped his mouth with the back of his hand. "See, that's the sort of shit I was talking about earlier. You guys know how to handle yourselves. Me trying to convince people to fork over money ... well, I don't have that muscle you guys got."

"Yeah, but don't worry. You got smarts," Burnside replied. "Anyone can see that. You supply the names and we get the cash. We'll make a good team."

"That's what I'm hopin' for." Jack glanced around. "So where's Wes? I don't have much time. I still need my job."

"I'll call him." Moments later Burnside ended his call and said, "He's pulling into the parkade right now."

"Great."

Burnside looked past Jack. "Fuck, hang on a sec. My ol' lady is wavin' for me to come over. I'll be right back."

Jack watched Burnside saunter over and sit next to Dole. Then Burnside and Dole, along with the two other women at the table, leaned in to whisper. When they did, Burnside turned to look briefly at Jack, then around the room.

Jack glanced at Laura and she gave him a hard look. *Yeah, I don't like that, either.* He thought about what he'd learned. *I've got Burnside for the murder, providing my testimony of what he told me holds up in court — should I bail out now? Then again, the inside man is about to walk in.*

An image of Tom handing him a cup of coffee flashed through his mind. *You were a good guy, Tom. You deserve justice.*

Chapter Forty-Two

Burnside listened to what Dole was saying. The initial fear he felt changed to rage. "You sure?" he asked.

"Yeah, she's sure. Tell 'im, Alice." She leaned closer to the woman across the table, who also leaned in. So did her friend.

"It's him," Alice replied. "Doesn't look quite the same, but I'm sure. I sat listening in court for a week when they put my brother away, so I saw a lot of him."

"Yeah, and Spider's still not out yet," Dole said. "And that was like, maybe seven or eight years ago." She gave Burnside a hard look. "Hope the fuck you didn't say anything to 'im."

Burnside grimaced, then looked at Alice. "You're absolutely fucking positive?"

"Yeah, I'm positive. There was a lady cop who testified, too. I'm not sure, but that could be her sitting over there. The one with the woollen cap an' looks like she's on the nod."

Burnside tried to look casual as he glanced around. "She don't look like a cop."

"Maybe she isn't," Alice replied. "I'm not certain about her, but I am about him. His name's Jack Taggart."

"Jack Taggart! Yesterday, that was … that card. Fuck!"

A stocky clean-cut man entered the bar and Jack knew then who their inside man was. He looked too out of place to be anything else. *Wes is a prison guard! You're going down, you bloody turncoat.* It was no surprise when Burnside waved Wes over to join him.

Jack tried to appear nonchalant while discreetly casting glances at the table. Wes had taken a seat beside Dole and by the concern on his face and head-shaking, it was evident he wasn't pleased. *Come on, you bastard. Get over here and talk to me. Say something I can hang you with.*

Moments later Burnside returned to where Jack sat. "Got a slight problem," he said, sitting down.

"That being?" Jack asked.

"Wes is a little freaked out. He's worried you could be a rat or a cop."

"I thought you were the boss? Tell him to quit acting paranoid and come over so we can talk business. Either that, or maybe I should go over and talk to him."

"He won't talk to you until I search you. Wants to make sure you're not wearin' a wire. You got any objection to that?"

"Fuck no. If that'll make him happy, then do what you gotta do."

"Good. I'll tell him you ain't got a problem. Go to the can — I'll be there in a sec." He looked at JFD and added, "Go with him and wait'll I get there."

Burnside stalled until Jack entered the men's room, then whispered to Richards and Derrick, "Stay calm and don't gawk around. I got somethin' to tell ya."

"What's up?" Richards asked.

"Fuckin' Bruce is an undercover cop."

Richards gasped. "No fuckin' way!"

"Alice recognized him. Don't look, but four tables behind you is a broad wearing a woollen cap. Could be his partner, but we ain't sure. With him there's no doubt."

Derrick wasn't convinced. "Alice's zoned out a lot. Maybe —"

"No, he's the guy who put her brother away. She said his name is Jack Taggart. That was the name was on the business card I shoved down the guy's throat yesterday."

"Mother of Christ," Derrick said. "We already told him everything."

"Yeah, well, the thing is, if he was wearin' a wire, there's no way he'd've gone in there to let us search him."

"So what we gonna do?" Richards asked.

"The same thing I did to the guy yesterday."

"Fuck, you plan on killin' a cop?"

"Ain't like we'd get any more time for it if we were caught. You still have your shiv in your boot?"

"Yeah, I got it," Richards replied, tapping the handle of a steak knife protruding from the top of his boot under his jeans.

"We'll have to wing it. Knifin' him could get noisy if he screams. The fuckin' guy from yesterday didn't make a sound when I clubbed him with my piece. I think that'll be the way to go. When it's done, we'll shove him in a shitter stall. If there ain't no noise, we could leave before anyone knows what happened. If he does yell, I'll shoot him. Same for that broad if she moves from her chair."

Richard and Derrick nodded silently.

"Once we go in, I'll tell JFD to cover the door and make sure nobody comes in. Derrick, you'll search him." He looked at Richards. "When that's done, you say somethin' to distract him, then I'll cave his fuckin' skull in."

"What about Wes?" Richards asked. "He okay with it?"

Burnside frowned. "No, he ain't, so I told him we were only going to search for a wire, then leave."

"He believe ya?"

"I dunno. I gave him some bullshit that if we don't find no wire, then it'd only be the cop's word against ours in court. Dunno if he thinks I'm dumb enough to risk that or not. The thing is, once it's done, Wes couldn't say anything. He'd be in shit, too."

"What if he tries to stop us?" Richards asked.

"If he tries to do that, I'll waste him." Burnside scoffed. "No way I'm going back inside. Not without a fight."

Jack entered the men's room with JFD and glanced around. "We're alone. It's a good time to get this over with." He held his jacket open.

"We were told to wait," JFD said. The hostility in his voice indicated it wasn't negotiable.

Moments later Burnside entered, along with Richards and Derrick.

This isn't good. It doesn't take all of them to pat me down.

Burnside directed an order at JFD. "Stand by the door. Make sure nobody comes in!"

As JFD moved toward the door, Burnside must've seen the look of concern on Jack's face. "It's okay," he said reassuringly. "Don't want somebody walkin' in on us and thinkin' we're a bunch of queers."

"It's not that. Why the audience? You could have patted me down yourself."

Burnside gave what looked like an apologetic smile. "Yeah, I know. To be honest, I don't even wanna do this."

"Then why bother?"

"I trust you, but Wes is fuckin' paranoid. I went along with it to keep him happy. He said if you're wearin' a wire, I'm to make sure you don't walk out. That's why I brought the boys along. It's for show."

"I see."

Burnside smirked. "You're not wearin' one, are ya?"

"Nope. See for yourself," he said, opening his jacket again.

A small commotion at the door caused everyone to turn.

"I'm coming in," Wes said, shoving JFD aside as he approached.

Jack saw a flash of anger on Burnside's face, then he calmed and said, "Hey, you're just in time. We're about to get started."

Wes didn't reply, just looked concerned as he stood beside Burnside.

Derrick searched Jack and was thorough.

Been searched a few times yourself, Derrick?

When he was done, Derrick stepped back. "He's clean." He then made eye contact with Richards.

Richards promptly pointed to behind Jack. "Man, look at the size of that fuckin' rat!"

Oh shit, you're acting on cue. Jack moved his head and torso slightly as if turning to look, then spun back — ready to grapple with whatever was coming his way.

Simultaneously Wes yelled, "No! Stop!"

Jack caught a glimpse of the butt of a pistol in Burnside's right hand coming down in a vicious arc toward his temple. His training told him to use his forearm to block Burnside's arm — but that training didn't include a third person stepping between him and his assailant.

Wes, who'd intervened from Burnside's left side, had tried to make a grab for the gun. He didn't succeed, but when Burnside blocked Wes across the chest with his left arm, he was momentarily distracted.

Derrick then lunged and grabbed Jack around the throat with both hands, shoving him back against the counter while choking him.

"What the fuck?" JFD yelled from his position near the door.

"He's a cop!" Richards yelled back.

Burnside hammered Wes on the bridge of his nose with the butt of the pistol. The noise sounded like the crunch of celery as blood spurted out. Dazed, Wes wobbled on his feet and Burnside delivered a second blow. This time to the temple and Wes fell in a heap on the floor.

Jack had put his left arm across the top of Derrick's arms so he couldn't raise them to protect himself, then delivered his right fist to the base of his nose and upper jaw. Derrick stumbled back, holding his hands over his face as blood gushed out from between his fingers.

As Burnside was turning away from Wes, Jack made a grab for the gun and managed to wrap his hand around the barrel and keep it pointed toward the ceiling.

Burnside tried to yank the pistol free while stepping back. But despite stumbling over Wes's body, Jack clung on. Briefly their eyes locked and they embraced in a life-and-death struggle. Burnside then opted to try to gouge out Jack's eyes, but Jack twisted and turned his head away while punching Burnside in the stomach.

Then Richards stepped in and pummelled Jack on the side of the head and rib cage. For Jack, fear and adrenalin had kicked in and the blows had little effect.

"Shank 'im! Shank 'im!" Burnside yelled, wrapping his arm around Jack's neck and pulling him close.

Damn it, Laura! Get in here! You must've heard the noise! "Help!" he screamed and looked back over his shoulder at Richards. *Fuck! He's pulling a knife out of his boot!*

Richards straightened, then positioned himself to ram the knife under Jack's rib cage and up into his liver.

Burnside twisted his body sideways to prevent Jack from kneeing him in the groin. As he did, Jack used the momentum to carry the spin further and they fell through the door of a cubicle.

Jack's goal was to wedge himself with his back on the floor between the toilet and the wall while holding Burnside in his own headlock as a shield to protect himself from Richards. He succeeded — sort of. In falling to the floor, he bashed his rib cage against the side of the toilet, knocking the wind out of him. Gasping, he still clutched the gun barrel, but his and Burnside's arms were pinned between their bodies so that despite their struggles, the pistol remained pointed at the wall behind their heads.

Jack glimpsed Richards's face above and kicked out with his feet to try to stop him from using his knife. For a moment he thought it had worked, until a hand reached from underneath the wall of the cubicle beside him and grabbed him by the hair.

He tried to resist, but was unable to stop his head from being yanked through the opening into the next stall. He heard Laura screaming from the bar area and knew she was fighting her own battle as he tried to twist his head and break the grip on his hair.

Richards was staring down at him now, and Jack saw the determination in his face — then saw the knife coming down to his throat. He jerked his head again in an unsuccessful attempt to break free. *I'm going to die.*

A second later blood splattered across his face and sprayed up the sides of the cubicle as Richards raised the knife for a second time.

Chapter Forty-Three

Laura had seen Burnside speak to Jack after returning to their table. She then saw Jack glance in her direction before heading into the men's room with the man with bushy orange hair.

Anyone watching would have thought it was only a glance, but for Jack and Laura it conveyed a message. Years of undercover together had honed their skills. If Jack's face looked intense, it translated as danger. A swallow meant a strong fear for his life. Fingertips slightly raised as he walked indicated he was being forced by someone with a weapon. No indications, which was the case now, meant he wanted her to stay put and wasn't concerned enough to request help. *As unconcerned as you can be when you're with murderers.*

Burnside, Richards, and the third man then entered the men's room. *Okay, is this one of those situations where they simply went in to light up a joint?*

Seconds later she saw the clean-cut man, a guy she figured for a prison guard, heading to the men's room as well. He paused at the door as if trying to decide whether to enter. *He looks scared … like something's going on. He's going in. Oh, man....*

There was a guy drinking by himself at a table close to the men's room. He was dressed shabbily and had a dirty white beard. She went over. "Hey, you wouldn't happen to know the time would ya? I've been waiting for my friend to show and thought she'd be here by now."

"Yeah, I know the time. It's time for another beer!" He gave a toothless grin that broadened when Laura smiled back. "Sorry, I don't have a watch," he added.

"Mind if I join you? I hate sitting by myself. I'll buy ya a beer."

His nicotine-stained fingers fondled his near-empty glass. "Yeah, that'd be nice."

Laura took a seat and listened for any sounds coming from the men's room. She hadn't had time to place her order before she heard one man yell at another to stop.

"Jack's in trouble! Men's room!" Laura said loudly when she clicked the transmitter button hidden in her sleeve. As she started to rise, she lifted the bottom of her sweatshirt to reach for her pistol holstered over the front of her hip. She was about to grasp the handle when a blow to the back of her head sent her sprawling across the table.

"You ain't goin' nowhere, you fuckin' cunt!" her assailant, a woman, screamed.

Laura rolled over in time to deflect a second blow with her forearm, then tried to stand, but the woman flung the weapon — a beer bottle — aside and lunged, using her body to pin Laura to the table while yanking her hair and clawing at her face.

Laura reacted by grabbing her around the waist and rolling off the table. She was hoping to land on top — but didn't. The woman ended up sitting on her chest, which meant Laura was unable to grab her pistol.

"You put my brother in jail. Now it's payback time, bitch." Laura's assailant sneered down at her, then pressed her thumbs hard into Laura's windpipe.

Laura had been in that same circumstance many times. At the academy they'd trained for it. She clasped the woman's wrist with one hand and struck her solidly on the elbow with the heel of her other hand, knocking her face first onto the floor, while still holding on to her wrist.

Laura's training would've made it easy to wrench her assailant's arm behind her back to gain control and then handcuff her. A scream for help from Jack told her she didn't have the time.

Forget the niceties. Laura twisted the woman's wrist further — locking her elbow. She then bent over and stomped on the elbow with her foot. The crunch and scream of pain that followed said she was no longer a threat. It was then that someone else jumped on her back, putting her in a headlock while wrestling her to the floor.

For a moment Laura felt fear clog her throat and had to fight to keep the tears from clouding her vision. The fear she felt wasn't for her. It was for Jack. She'd never heard him yell like that. The panic in his voice said the situation was dire — and it was her job to protect him. A job, it appeared, that she'd failed.

She put both hands behind her head, using her fingers to clasp the back of her attacker's head while simultaneously shoving her thumbs into the eye sockets. The attacker emitted a sickening gurgle of a scream — then was off her. Laura saw that it was Lorraine Dole.

Two of Wilson's men arrived, and one grabbed Dole by the hair and flung her to the floor. One of Dole's eyeballs dangled from its socket like a wayward grape. His partner looked momentarily stunned at the sight of the two injured women.

Laura didn't care. She glimpsed Wilson and Van Dusen entering the bar with guns drawn. "Follow me!" she yelled, then kicked the men's room door open and burst inside with gun in hand.

Two of the bad guys stood at the open doors of two cubicles, but stepped back when she rushed in. The clean-cut man was sprawled on the floor. *Good, Jack, you got one of them.* She heard the command from the officers behind her, yelling for the two men to raise their hands. She ignored them. Her focus was on the fight taking place inside the cubicles.

She first saw Richards on his knees, holding Jack's bloody head by his hair. *Oh, God, no!* In his other hand Richards held a knife raised high. Her finger started to squeeze the trigger, then she hesitated. *The knife handle is above his fist? He's holding the knife by the blade!*

"Shoot 'im!" Jack screamed, flailing his head like a madman trying to break free.

"Drop it!" she yelled.

The order was likely unnecessary. Richards had the dumbfounded look of a person in shock. He slowly loosened his grip and the knife fell to the floor. The tendons in his hand had been severed and the blood continued to flow. He let go of Jack's head and held his hand.

Laura realized what had happened. Richards had tried to stab Jack but missed and hit the tiled floor. The sudden jar caused his hand to slide over the sharp edges of the steak knife, slicing it open.

"For Christ's sake, shoot him!" Jack yelled again, still flailing his head.

Laura picked up the knife. "It's okay, I've got it," she gasped, still panting from her fight in the bar.

"Not him! Burnside! He's got a gun!"

Laura turned in panic, but Wilson rushed past and entered the stall ahead of her. He stuck the muzzle of his pistol in Burnside's ear. It had the desired effect. Burnside let go of the gun and slowly put his hands up. Wilson then grabbed him by the back of the collar and flung him face down on the floor outside the cubicle.

Richards was being handcuffed by Van Dusen, so Laura turned her attention back to Jack. He was lying on the floor wedged between the toilet and the wall. His face and throat were mottled with blood and one of his eyes was so swollen that only a slit remained.

"Oh, man! You okay?" she asked.

He gazed up at her. "I don't know," he mumbled. He gingerly felt his ribs, then his face. "Do I look okay?"

"No … you don't. Your face …"

He put a hand up to his swollen eye. "Shit, Natasha's going to be so pissed off."

"What happened?"

"I took a few punches." He pulled his shirt up, raised his head, and looked at his torso. "Guess I wasn't knifed. I was pounded so much I wasn't sure." He then grabbed the rim of the toilet and wriggled his way out.

"Jack, maybe you should get checked out," Laura suggested as he slowly got to his feet.

"I'll be okay. Maybe some bruised ribs. I've got some notes I need to make."

"Can't that wait?"

"No. I've got some important stuff I need to quote word for word. First, though, I want to check on one of the guys out there," he said, gesturing to the outside of the cubicle.

The clean-cut man was sitting on the floor with his back to the wall. Blood dripped off his chin from an open wound on the bridge of his nose. More blood coagulating in his hair indicated he had another head wound. One of Wilson's men was putting handcuffs on him.

"Hey, Wes, you okay?" Jack asked him.

"I'll live."

Jack's voice was solemn. "Thanks for trying to save my life."

"Yeah, well … if I wasn't cuffed, I'd shake your hand and thank you."

"For what?" Jack asked, glancing up at several uniformed officers entering the men's room. "You're going to jail."

Wes gave a wry smile. "Won't be much different from where I work now, except I'll be lookin' at the bars from the other side." His face grew serious. "No, I mean it. I've been wanting out for a long time … but couldn't see a way. I wish I'd never gotten into doing what I was doing."

"Then why did you?" Jack asked.

Wes swallowed. "Over time … I got more and more scared of these guys." When Jack made no response, he continued, "After I got married and had kids, I got really scared. It started off with me slipping them the odd joint or gram of hash. In my mind, I hoped they'd never hurt me if things went sideways." He swallowed again. "It kind of progressed from there." He shook his head, perhaps in self-recrimination. "They had me by the balls." He glanced at the other prisoners. "Now I can say I'm finally out. I got you to thank for that."

"Might be a couple of years before you can *really* say you're out," Jack pointed out. "I'll be testifying against you — but I'll also tell how you tried to save me."

"Won't be a trial," Wes replied. "I'll cop to it first chance I get. I'm guilty. Nobody knows that better than me."

Jack nodded, patted him on the shoulder, then stood up and approached Wilson.

"Okay, that was interesting," Wilson said. "Mind telling me what the hell happened?"

"To start with," Jack replied, "it went really well. I sat and had a beer with Burnside, Richards, and those two." He pointed to the two men handcuffed on the floor. "The one with the orange hair I know as John Fucking Doe."

Laura shook her head in wonder. *Jack still has his sense of humour. Doesn't what happened affect him? I'm still shaking. He's like a bloody rock — literally.*

"The other one goes by Derrick," Jack went on. "Burnside told me how he killed Tom yesterday when he refused to pay protection money and tried to call me. Richards was there, but Burnside did the actual murder. Then the four of them talked about being in the protection racket. After that Burnside went over to talk to Dole and a couple of her friends."

"That's when we were burned," Laura said. "One of those women was Spider's sister."

"Spider?" Wilson asked.

"An old case," Laura explained. "Years ago we did a UC sting and put Spider away for murder. I suspect his sister saw us at the trial."

"So *that's* what happened," Jack said. "I thought enough years had passed. The sister must be the kind to hold a grudge, and all the drugs she's no doubt used don't seem to have affected her memory."

Wilson eyed Jack. "Apparently not. Perhaps hatred hones the memory."

Jack continued, "When Burnside was talking to the hookers, Wes arrived and joined them. Right after that, Burnside came back to our table and told me he wanted to search me for a wire."

"After he'd already confessed to you?" Wilson questioned.

"Yup. He told me Wes was their inside man and that he was paranoid and wanted the search done. So I went to the men's room with John Fucking Doe, who didn't know what was going on until the fracas started."

Fracas? Jack, a bunch of guys tried to kill you. That's more than a fracas.

"Burnside, Richards, and Derrick came in about a minute later," Jack said. "Derrick searched me, then Richards tried to distract me so Burnside could clobber me over the head with his gun. Wes tried to stop him and got clobbered himself."

"So Wes only wanted you searched for a wire?" Wilson asked.

"I don't know if he even wanted that. I'm sure he'll tell you once you interview him."

"Then what happened?" Wilson asked.

Jack shared all the details, then finished by looking at Laura and saying, "You saved my life."

"So what else is new?" she replied in an attempt at humour.

Jack turned back to Wilson. "After that, you saved my ass from Burnside. I was exhausted. I wouldn't have lasted much longer."

Laura saw Jack swallow nervously. *So you do get scared. Good, after what you put me through, I'm glad.*

"Yeah, well, that's typical," Wilson said. He, too, made a half-hearted attempt at humour. "We're always being called in to save you Mounties over one thing or another."

"After we solve the case for you," Jack retorted.

"No denying that," Wilson said. "Without any fatalities, either. I'm impressed."

Jack ignored the sarcasm. "So that's it in a nutshell. You can get the finer details later. I need to get back to your office and make notes on this ASAP. You might want to read them before doing interviews."

Wilson nodded. "Thanks, you two," he said seriously. "I owe you one."

"Just keep the press away from us and make sure Mortimer doesn't find out," Jack said. "At least not any time soon."

"No worries," Wilson said assuredly.

Laura was still holding Richard's knife in her fingertips. "You'll want this."

"Yeah, thanks," Wilson replied. "Laura, better make a note of the time and date you gave it to me for court. As we're doing that, I wouldn't mind hearing what happened in the bar after you called for help."

Laura dug out her notebook, then said, "Spider's sister and then Dole jumped me once I did."

"I wondered what was taking you so long," Jack put in. "I thought maybe you were doing your nails or something."

"Maybe next time I will be." Laura waited a beat. "As far as today goes, it took me a moment to teach them that you shouldn't obstruct justice."

A uniformed officer cleared his throat. "The two you taught … one has a broken arm."

"It wasn't broken when she whacked me on the back of my head with a beer bottle," Laura replied. She glanced at Jack. "Spider's sister," she explained.

The officer continued, "The other one who's got her eyeball hanging out of the socket —"

"That's Dole. She jumped on my back."

"Guess you weren't doing your nails," Jack muttered.

"Some people might think your methods are a little harsh," the officer noted.

"Some people weren't there," Laura said. *Or if they were there, wouldn't understand how a split second can mean the difference between life and death.*

Laura then wrote down the time and date of when she'd given Wilson the knife. When done, she saw Jack staring at the cubicles. *Thinking about how lucky you are to be alive, Jack? I hope so. Hope you think about it long and hard, because quite frankly, I've had enough.*

Chapter Forty-Four

Jack walked out of the men's room with Laura and saw the paramedics arriving to assist Lorraine Dole, who lay on the floor holding her eyeball to its socket with her fingertips.

"Over here!" Alice wailed at the paramedics from a nearby chair. "My arm's broken. I need something. Got any Oxy?"

Jack paused to view the situation and saw a uniformed officer glance at Laura, then give her a thumbs-up.

"Looks like some people agree with your methods of teaching," Jack said, while eyeing an old man approaching them.

"Like I said, you had to be —"

The old man tapped Laura on her shoulder and she spun around with her fists cocked. It was apparent she thought she was in mortal danger.

"Sorry to scare you, ma'am," the man said, stepping back. "This is yours." He was holding out the woollen cap she'd been wearing earlier.

"Uh … thanks." Laura took the cap, then said, "Sorry, I never did get around to buying you a beer."

"That's okay. I could see you were busy." As he strolled away he looked back and added, "Maybe next time, sweetie."

Normally Jack would have found the incident amusing, but Laura was acting hypervigilant — a common sign of post-traumatic stress disorder. *I've put her through so much shit over the years. Then this. What if it'd been worse? She could've been knifed in the back.* He glanced around at the faces in the bar. Not many were as friendly as the old man's. *I really screwed up.*

"Hey, he thinks I'm a sweetie," Laura said as they headed toward the exit.

Jack saw her smile, but could tell it was fake. *She's embarrassed for overreacting.*

"I better warn my hubby," she continued. "He might have competition."

Who the hell wouldn't react that way after what she'd been through? No wonder she wants a transfer.

"What? Not even a smile?" Laura asked.

Somewhere in his conscious mind he'd heard Laura, but it didn't really register.

"Jack, what's wrong? Are you okay?"

"No, I'm not," he admitted. "I screwed up." He paused as he looked at her. "You could've been killed. I should never have put you in here alone."

"I wasn't alone. You were in here, too."

"Yeah … right. A lot of good I did. I wasn't there when you needed help."

Laura looked disgusted. "You really mean it, don't you?"

"Of course I mean it. You could've been knifed."

"I could have been knifed," Laura repeated, as if contemplating the possibility for the first time.

Jack found her attitude irritating. "Don't pretend you didn't already think about it. I saw how you overreacted to that old guy."

"Who wouldn't be nervous?" she snapped. "This place is a —"

"I'm not criticizing. I'm just worried about you."

"You're worried about me?" Laura shoved the door open and stepped out onto the sidewalk, then turned to face him.

Uh-oh. She's got her hands on her hips. She's really pissed off.

"You jerk!"

Yup, she's pissed off.

"After what you put me through in there you have the nerve to say you worry about me? *I* handled it! You're the one who needed rescuing!"

"Oh … that. I'm not saying I don't appreciate what you went through in there."

"You mean what I'm always going through with you."

"Yes, exactly. Which is why I worry. It's bound to affect you. It would anyone."

"Maybe you should spend more time worrying about yourself," she shot back.

"I do. I'd be dead if you hadn't been there."

"Exactly! Thanks a lot," she replied crossly.

"What do you mean?"

She shook her head. "Nothing. Forget it."

"I've been married long enough to know that when a woman says 'nothing' it always means something. What is it?"

He saw Laura clench her jaw.

He reached for her shoulder to give her a friendly squeeze in the hope of getting her to open up, but she brushed his arm aside and strode away. *Okay, I'll wait until you cool down.*

When they reached the car, Jack got in the passenger seat. He stared at the hotel as Laura drove past and his brain replayed the image of the death grip he'd had on the pistol — and his futile attempt to wrestle it out of Burnside's hand.

"Neither of us had to be in there," Laura said flatly. "We should've left it for the Vancouver police to investigate."

"Are you forgetting that Tom befriended me?" Jack replied. "Not to mention, it was my business card that was shoved down his throat."

The anger on Laura's face melted away and she looked glum. "Yeah, I know," she eventually replied.

"I also told him to stand up for himself and call the police. My advice got him killed. Would you have let that go?"

Laura sighed. "No, I guess not."

A few blocks later Laura stopped for a red light and he saw her staring at him. "What?" he asked.

"Come Monday you can't go into our office looking like that. You've already got a shiner and by the looks of your eye, it'll take a few days for the swelling to go down. If Mortimer saw you it'd be hard to convince him you were beat up in French class."

Jack nodded. "Right," he mumbled. He was glad when the light changed and Laura focused her attention back on the road. Her comment about his face made him feel agitated. Perhaps because it brought another image to mind.

That of being pinned to the bathroom floor with Richard's determined face leering down at him — and the knife flashing toward his throat. His hand gave an involuntary jerk as he relived the panic he'd felt. *I almost died.*

"I think I could use a few days to recover, as well," Laura said next.

How would Natasha and the boys get along if I were dead? Guess they wouldn't have to worry about bad guys photographing them. Damn it, my hands are shaking. Make fists. Try to stop it before she sees.

Laura glanced at him. "Jack, you're shaking … all over."

This is embarrassing. "Yeah, bloody cold today." He reached to turn on the heat, but his fingers fumbled with the controls.

Laura nudged his hand aside and did it for him. "It isn't that cold," she said. "You're going into shock."

"Me? Don't be silly. I'm okay. It's nothing." *Time to change the subject.* "We'll take a couple of days off so I can avoid the office. I'll leave a message for Rose. Then … then I'll tell her we'll be out doing surveillance or something. This is Saturday. Maybe not work until Wednesday."

The car slowed and pulled over to the curb. He looked at her. "Why're you stopping?"

Laura reached for his forearm. "Okay, tough guy, listen to me. You're going into shock. You're talking really fast and your voice sounds like your shorts are too tight."

"No, really, I'm okay."

"Listen to me! No, you're not!" She stared intently at his face. When he didn't respond she continued, "This is me you're talking to. I've been there. Last time I got the shakes was at the farmhouse. They went away after a bit, but a few hours later they came back. I ended up bawling my eyes out in the women's washroom." She paused to give a reassuring smile. "That's not a choice for you. After what happened today, I don't trust you to stay out of trouble in a washroom."

Jack knew her attempt at humour was to calm him, but he wasn't ready to admit she was right. "The bathroom floor was cold." He folded his arms over his chest and squeezed to try to stop the trembling. "I was stuck between the toilet and —"

"Quit lying to me," Laura said. "It's disrespectful."

Jack was silent for a moment. "Yeah, okay. Guess it did shake me up a bit."

"Shake you up a bit?" Laura questioned. "You were scared for your life!" Her words sounded like an accusation.

"Okay … I was scared."

"And you told me you'd be dead if I hadn't come in to save you." She sounded bitter and angry.

"Uh, yeah."

"So how the hell do you think that'll make me feel?"

"Feel?"

"When this is over and I transfer out?"

"What are you talking about?"

"When I leave and you get killed!"

"You mean, if I was to get killed," Jack replied.

Laura literally spit the words out. "No, I mean *when*, not *if*! You'll never be happy doing anything else! You're not going to stop!"

Jack stared back. Her eyes had welled and a fleck of spittle clung to her chin. *She seems angry, frustrated, and scared all at the same time. What the hell do I say?*

Laura's eyes searched his. "Who else knows you as well as I do in these situations? Who would you trust if I wasn't there? Someone else would probably act prematurely and blow an investigation." She glared. "Of course, you'd already know that, which means you'd start working alone! It's only a matter of time till …"

I prefer not to think about that. "I appreciate your concern, I really do." He reached for her hand, half expecting her to pull back. He was surprised she didn't and gave it a squeeze, then held it. "Nobody knows what the future will bring, but whatever happens to me won't be your fault. You have your own life to live." He released his grip, but she held on.

"Don't you see?" she said. "Your life is my life. I love you. I can't walk away."

"You love me?" Jack swallowed. "But I love Natasha."

Laura threw his hand away. "You asshole. Not like that. More like you're my kid."

Now I really feel stupid. He realized his concern for Laura had caused his body to stop trembling. *At least for the moment.*

He'd experienced tremors before. When you're busy you don't have time to think about yourself and question the what-ifs. It was usually the quiet times, when you should be relaxed or sleeping, that your mind played havoc with your nerves.

"Nothing to say?" Laura prodded.

Jack took a deep breath and slowly exhaled. "You don't have any kids. If you're going to think of me like that, I'd prefer you think of me as your bigger older brother."

"Me, too, but a big brother would look after me — not the other way around."

"Then let me look after you. Take a transfer. I'll be okay."

"It's like you didn't even listen to me." Laura shook her head.

"I've been listening. I'm telling you I care for you a lot. That won't change if you transfer out."

"That's not the issue." She met his gaze. "Looks like your nerves have settled."

Jack realized she wanted to change the subject — and so did he. "Yes. Better get going. Both of us need to make our notes."

Laura pulled away from the curb. "So … after we're done with Wilson we'll take the next three days off?"

"Yes, I think we need it." Jack waited a beat. "At least *I* do."

"Then on Wednesday we'll start work in your garage? Turn one hundred and twenty kilos into three tonnes?"

"That's the plan."

"Good. Then it's a simple matter of waiting for the right moment to kidnap Whiskey Jake and Pure E."

A simple matter of kidnapping. Jack gave Laura a sideways glance and grimaced. *She's right. Who the hell else could I ever trust to work with me? A simple matter, my ass.*

Chapter Forty-Five

Jack picked Laura up from her home Wednesday morning in his SUV. As he drove he was aware of her watching him. "What?" he asked.

Laura was blunt. "You get over the shakes?"

Jack felt apprehensive as he held his hand out. He was pleased when he saw he was able to hold it steady. "See? No worries. Like a rock."

"You weren't like a rock Saturday."

Jack nodded. "You'd think by now, after everything you and I've been through, that nothing would affect me."

"Maybe you're getting wiser," Laura said dryly, "and realizing you're not invincible."

"Maybe. It's given me a better appreciation for being alive, that's for sure. Dying seems scarier than it used to. I also worry how Natasha and the boys would handle it."

"Your eye's still swollen. What did Natasha have to say about it?"

Jack grinned. "She said it looked like I'd been talking when I should've been listening. I told her I was in a bar fight. She's a doctor. For her a black eye isn't worthy of any sympathy."

"Have you ever considered that it might be time to slow down?"

"You mean doing things like monitoring smuggling methods, plagiarizing someone else's work, and putting in reports? Perhaps filling in my evenings by learning French?" Jack snorted. "Oh, yeah, I'm giving it serious consideration."

Laura frowned.

"Hey, I did confirm a new job for you, though."

"You what? What did you do?" Laura demanded.

"Got you a job as a limo chauffeur for Friday. Booked Saturday, too, in case Friday doesn't work out."

"Oh." Laura appeared to relax. "When did you set that up?"

"I met with the owner of the limo service Monday morning."

"Jack, you were supposed to take time off and chill."

"I'm fine. It only took an hour or so. The owner is as straight as they come. I flashed my badge, then told him we'd use our own person to act as a chauffeur because it was a dangerous undercover situation. He was more than willing to oblige. He'll even supply you with a hat and jacket."

"I'm sure I'll look smashing," Laura said lamely.

"I told him it may involve a dirty cop, so he'll keep his mouth shut in the event he's ever questioned."

"Good."

"I also confirmed with Sammy and Benny that they're available."

Laura appeared to think about it. "You never told me how you sucked them into this."

"I didn't suck them in. UC operators are like family. They phoned as soon as they heard about Satans Wrath showing up at my house and volunteered to do whatever was necessary. Got the same call from a retired operator, as well, but I think Sammy and Benny will be enough."

Laura made a face. He caught it in his peripheral vision. "What is it?"

"I'm just thinking that it's quite the family we belong to."

Jack shrugged. "Most of the professional bad guys know it. It's what keeps us and our families alive. Their fear of what will happen to them if they cross that line."

"Unfortunately Pure E hasn't learned that lesson yet," Laura said.

"He soon will."

Laura nodded. "So … Friday. It doesn't give us a lot of time to turn one hundred and twenty keys of coke into three tonnes."

"We've got time. I told Rose we gave up on trying to find out where the three-three hide their bodies and are doing surveillance on some dealers who work for Satans Wrath. She's not expecting to see us in the office. Once we pick up what we need this morning, it'll only be a matter of slapping it together."

"If this goes wrong, it's you I'll be slapping."

Jack gave her a sideways glance. *She sounds serious.*

At noon Jack and Laura arrived back at Jack's garage and unloaded the supplies.

Laura looked at the lumber, Styrofoam sheets, duct tape, and cellophane wrap. "So we're to turn this into three tonnes of coke? I've never even swung a hammer."

"No worries. Cutting the Styrofoam into rectangular bricks and building the framework is easy. The big job will be wrapping the bricks to look like kilos of coke."

"How many do you think we'll need? If it was real, we'd need three thousand."

"I'll build the framework so that someone sitting on the floor and viewing it from a corner will think the pile is ten kilos square and thirty kilos high."

"And not realize they're looking at an empty shell."

"Exactly. The one hundred and twenty real kilos will go on top, but they'll need to be rewrapped so that the cellophane matches. We'll also need to make them appear to be interlocked to keep them from falling over, but I'll run strips of double-sided tape to hold them in place. Still, we'll need a double layer so there's no chance of the wood frame showing."

"So to answer my question?"

"Counting the one hundred and twenty to be rewrapped, we'll need about twelve hundred. Maybe even a few more to put on top."

"That's a lot of wrapping."

"Between the two of us, I figure we can wrap forty or fifty an hour. Thirty hours should do it. Maybe even less once Natasha comes home from work and pitches in."

"And Mike and Steve? What will they think if they see it?"

"I trust them not to say anything, but still, I thought it wise to tell them the garage is temporarily off limits. They know enough not to ask questions."

"They're your sons. I'm sure you're right." After a moment she added, "They probably think you've got a body stashed in here."

Jack shrugged. "Probably," he replied.

Chapter Forty-Six

The weather in Vancouver was normal for the first week of December — wet. It was dark when Whiskey Jake wheeled his white Lexus into a stall on the third level of a parkade located within a block of the nightclub he and Pure E intended to visit.

Jack parked the van he was driving alongside the door to an alcove on the parkade's second level. He grabbed his umbrella, then along with Sammy Crofton and Benny Saunders quickly bailed out. He wasn't worried that he was parked illegally. He knew he'd be back shortly — with an unwilling passenger.

On entering the alcove, Jack phoned Laura. "We're ready," he whispered. "You got an eye on the ground-level stairwell and elevator?"

Laura had parked the stretch limo she was driving on the street below. "Yes, it's clear."

Jack pressed the elevator button, then nodded at Sammy and Benny. The men donned masks and Jack opened the door to the stairwell so they could listen. Seconds later they heard their targets descending the stairs. "Forget the elevator," Jack whispered. He then left Sammy and Benny where they were and hustled down the stairs.

Pure E decided to voice his annoyance when he saw someone with an open umbrella tilted toward them heading up the stairs from the first floor. Briefly he wondered if the person realized they were there, so he paused at a landing with Whiskey Jake to avoid a collision. "Hey you fuckin' idiot. It's not raining in here —"

The umbrella tilted back. "*Da* — hand on wall!"

Pure E gasped. The man, wearing a white plastic anarchist mask, pointed a pistol at them.

"Hand on wall," the man repeated. "Quickly and we no kill you!"

We? Pure E glanced up the stairwell behind him. Two more men, both wearing anarchist masks, also pointed pistols at them. *This isn't a hit or we'd already be dead. The accent … Russian? Fuck, are we in conflict with them? I don't even know any Russians.*

"You think you can rob us?" Whiskey Jake snarled. "You got any idea who —"

"Shut the fuck up," Pure E interjected. "Do as he says."

"*Da*, do what I say," Umbrella Man said. "We no rob you. Only take you for talk with boss."

His boss? So, the Russian mob is in Vancouver.

Umbrella Man used the pistol barrel to motion toward the wall. "We search you. Hand on wall. Quick, quick!"

Seconds later Pure E stood spread-eagled against the wall alongside Whiskey Jake. They were both searched and relieved of their cellphones. Pure E felt relief when he saw them zip-tie Whiskey Jake's hands behind his back and put a band of duct tape over his mouth. It helped confirm that they weren't being killed.

Pure E felt the nudge of the pistol in his ribs, so he put his hands behind his back, expecting to receive similar treatment.

"No. Take jacket off," Umbrella Man ordered. "Tie in front."

Moments later Pure E had his hands zip-tied in front of him and his jacket was placed over his hands to hide the zip-tie from view. He listened as Umbrella Man made a phone call in Russian. When he was done, he looked at his two colleagues. "*Khorosho. Nikto vokrug.*" He then looked at Pure E. "I say good. Nobody outside. We take you for meet boss in car."

Pure E held his temper when Umbrella Man grabbed him roughly by the arm and steered him toward the stairs. He saw that Whiskey Jake was being kept behind. "Isn't he coming?"

"Only you meet boss," Umbrella Man replied.

When they got to the street exit, Umbrella Man opened the door and pointed. A chauffeur with an open umbrella waited alongside a stretch limo with the rear door open. *What the fuck! Who are these people?*

"You go with him," Umbrella Man said, indicating his accomplice. "You yell … you die," he added.

Pure E found himself propelled toward the limo and pushed inside. His captor did not release his arm until he'd been shoved face down on a sofa in the midsection of the limo. His captor then sat on his back and zip-tied his ankles together before retreating to a seat in the rear.

"Hello, Mr. Evans," a female voice said as the limo sped off. "You may sit up. Please ... try to relax and make yourself comfortable."

Pure E wriggled into a sitting position. The woman who spoke to him was sitting in the shadows near the front of the limo. Her Russian accent was thick, but her English was good. "Who are you?" he demanded.

"Who I am is not important. Look at me as a translator. My associate apologizes that he couldn't be here to greet you. Unfortunately he was called to an unscheduled meeting. We're on our way to meet him. Hopefully he won't be long."

Pure E leaned forward, hoping to see her better. The limo's overhead lights were off, but there was enough ambient light that he could make out an attractive woman wearing a full-length gown. A fancy mask covered her upper face and she had shoulder-length red hair. "What does your associate want with me?" he asked.

"*Da* ... yes, what do we want with you? I will tell you."

Pure E then noticed that she was holding a shot glass. She finished her drink in one gulp, then opened a bar and took out an additional glass and a bottle. He watched in silence as she filled both glasses, spilling a little as she did so. She then passed him a glass, which he had to accept with both hands.

"My associate wishes to offer you a business proposal. From what I know, it will be lucrative. Whether you accept his proposal or not ... it will not affect, uh, your well-being. Either way you'll be returned, so don't worry." She eyed him for a moment, then said, *"Na zdorovie!"* and shot the drink back. She then stared at him. "To your health! Drink!"

Pure E gulped the vodka back, after which she replenished it. Upon leaning back in her seat she said, "While you meet my associate, your friend, Mr. Jake Yevdokymenko, will be shown something in regards to the proposal. He will be allowed to call you later."

"What? Whiskey Jake ... what're you showing him?"

"I think that information is best relayed to you by Mr. Yevdokymenko. Or do you prefer I call him Whiskey Jake?"

"It doesn't matter," Pure E mumbled. "Whiskey Jake, Lefty, Yevdoky ... whatever." *They must've followed me from where I live to grab us in the parkade — and they know Whiskey Jake's real name.* He felt the bile rising in his throat and knew it wasn't from the vodka.

"Ah, we're here," the woman announced, looking up at an office tower as the limo pulled to the curb. "I'll call to let him know."

Pure E made a mental note of where they had stopped. *409 Granville Street.* He listened as the woman spoke Russian on her phone. Her voice sounded upset. She then looked over at him and said something in Russian. He stared at her blankly. "I don't speak —"

"What about our reception with the Chinese ambassador?" she said, ignoring him as she spoke into her phone. I'm already dressed ... oy ..." The rest of her conversation continued in Russian, then she hung up.

Chinese ambassador? What the fuck? Who are these people? He saw the woman staring at him. "I'm sorry," he said. "You got mixed up and spoke to me in Russian. I don't know what you said."

"What I said was ... we have a problem."

Chapter Forty-Seven

Whiskey Jake felt both fear and outrage when the man with the umbrella returned and grabbed his arm, then manhandled him up the stairwell to the second level of the parkade. Once there, the other man stepped outside the alcove and opened the side door to a van before returning and latching on to his other arm.

"You go inside van," Umbrella Man said. "We take you and show you something."

Whiskey Jake tried to voice his objection, but the tape prevented that. He was then hustled out of the alcove, but froze when he reached the outside of the van, instinctively reacting to the fear of where he was being taken … and what would happen to him.

His hesitation was short-lived. Umbrella Man grabbed him by the back of the collar and kicked the back of his knee. His body automatically sagged and he was shoved face down onto the floor of the van. He tried to squirm but the man sat on his back. The other man shoved his legs inside and slid the door shut.

As the van drove away, a cloth bag was pulled over his head, then duct-taped around his neck. Any hope he had of escaping or being able to see was gone.

"I sit on you, but we no go far," Umbrella Man said.

There was no more talking and Whiskey Jake figured they'd been driving for about forty minutes before the van came to a stop. He'd long since given up trying to remember the turns and traffic stops the van had made since his abduction. This time, however, he heard the sound of a garage door opening and the van pulled inside.

The man sitting on him said something in Russian and he heard the driver acknowledge with *"Da."*

After the garage door closed, he was rolled onto his back. "Do not make trouble or you die." As added incentive, he felt the muzzle of the pistol through the cloth bag on the tip of his nose.

He was then hauled out of the van and forced to sit on the floor. The tape was cut from around his neck and the bag removed from his head. He blinked several times to adjust to the light while Umbrella Man checked his hands, which were still zip-tied behind his back.

He was sitting on the floor of a two-car garage. The van was to his back and in front of him was what he thought was another car covered in a tarp. There was little else in the garage, so he focused on the two men wearing anarchist masks standing over him. The man who'd previously carried the umbrella was holding a hunting knife and slapping the blade against his hand as he stared down at him. *Oh, fuck.*

"Okay. We show you," the man said, then shoved the knife in his belt.

He used it to cut the tape from around my neck — thank Christ. Okay, don't act like a pussy and let the club down. I'm a president for fuck's sake.

The man then tore the strip of tape off his mouth.

Whiskey Jake did his best to sound defiant. "So? What the fuck do you wanna show me?"

"*Da,* don't move." The man nodded to his partner, then they took latex gloves from their pockets and put them on.

Latex gloves? That's what the three-three do before killin' someone. His fear subsided when he watched them pull the tarp back — then his mouth fell open. *Mother of God! That ain't no car! Fuck, I don't believe it! How many keys do they have?* He counted rows and then did the math. *Ten square … thirty high … fuck … that's three thousand keys!*

The man withdrew the hunting knife from his belt, then picked up a kilo brick from the top of the pile and knelt down beside him. He then shoved the tip of the blade into the kilo and withdrew a small amount of sparkling white powder. "Cocaine is pure. You want try?" he asked, holding the knife tip under Whiskey Jake's nose.

"I don't do that shit," Whiskey Jake replied, turning his face away. "It's for idiots."

The man shrugged to show his indifference, then returned the kilo to the top of the pile before facing him. "Now we wait."

"Wait for what?" Whiskey Jake asked.

"To see if your boss is smart man."

Chapter Forty-Eight

Pure E stared at the woman. "We have a problem?" he said, repeating her words. "What're you talking about? What problem?"

She ignored him and used the intercom to connect with the driver. "Take us for a scenic drive. Go over the Lion's Gate Bridge to start with." As the limo pulled away she turned her attention back to him. "My associate will be unable to meet with you tonight."

"All this for nothing?" Pure E replied.

"No, I've been instructed to outline part of the business agreement." She stared at him. "I know in the biker culture women are considered property and not worthy of discussing business at the corporate level. It's the same in Russia, but I trust you'll make an exception in this instance. "

"What business are you talking about?"

The woman hesitated. "This car has been swept for any electronic listening devices. We can talk freely. That being said, I'm not sure how much my associate wants you to know." She hesitated again, appearing to decide what to say next. "Ah, it may not be necessary. I suspect you are intelligent enough to read between the lines." She snickered. "Lines … that's funny, considering what the product is."

"Product?"

"Yes, it was intended to be a gift to an organization in a foreign country to provide them money to purchase … well, that's not important. She gestured with her hand as if in frustration. "Typical of politics, agreements are struck, but friends become foes and foes become friends. To make a long story short, the people who were to get it fell out of favour during the shipping process. The product can't be returned and is being temporarily stored in Vancouver. My associate is tasked with disposing of it."

"The product … what is it?"

"I thought that would be clear to you, but I will say it. The product is cocaine. Three tonnes."

Pure E felt stunned. "Three tonnes! You're joking, right?"

"No. Your colleague, Whiskey Jake, is viewing it now. Perhaps even partaking … that I don't know."

"You're letting Whiskey Jake see it … and sample it?"

"Yes. The price will be cheap. Fifteen a kilo."

"Fifteen thou?" *It can't be that cheap. Is she serious?*

"With that price, obviously there's no room for you to negotiate."

"Three tonnes … three thousand kilos … multiplied by fifteen … that's … that's a lot of money."

"Forty-five million. Yes, it's a considerable amount."

Is this some sort of set-up? Maybe trying to rip us off? "If I, uh, even knew anyone in that business, they wouldn't have that much money."

"Come, Mr. Evans. Even with the volume discount you are used to, fifteen is only half the price you've ever paid in the past. I told you, there's no negotiation. If you're not interested, then I suspect some of the local Chinese triads will be. If they accept our conditions and in turn lower their retail prices, the result may well put your people out of business."

You bitch! Pure E cleared his throat. "I wasn't trying to negotiate, simply trying to be honest."

"I see. If full payment is a problem, then we're willing to front five hundred kilo lots to you at a time. The price for that amount would be seven-point-five mil. Following each front, I expect my associate will demand payment within a month."

They're willing to front five hundred keys? If this is true, that would preclude them from being able to rip us off. But to front us that much? Holy fuck!

"Is that a problem?" she asked.

"No, uh, I was only thinking of distribution. I'm definitely interested, but I'll need time to talk it over with some people. It would involve travelling to other provinces."

"That's understandable. Unfortunately my associate and I do not live in Vancouver. His business only brings him here on occasion. So with that in mind, he'd like partial payment for the first front before we leave, which would be before Christmas."

"That's almost three weeks away. If your associate fronts me five hundred keys, I'm sure I could come up with the complete seven-point-five mil within two weeks. All I need is a few days to talk to my people and get the ball rolling."

"Full payment would be nice." She paused, then raised her shot glass again. "Okay! You get started on that, then my associate and I will meet you after to discuss delivery and payment schedules."

Pure E nodded. "How do I contact you?"

"Yes, about that … one moment." She rummaged in a compartment and handed him a cellphone. "I'll call you in a few days to check your progress. Next time we meet you'll be given a location for Whiskey Jake to drop you off. Nobody else is to know about the meeting until it's over. If you lie to us … behave like an amateur … or try to have anyone follow us, we'll know. Not only will we know, but rest assured it will be the last ride you ever take … in any vehicle."

You bitch, do you know who you're threatening? Pure kept his temper in check and spoke firmly. "We've been around a long time. Our club is in over forty countries. Obviously we're not amateurs and you'd be well advised not to threaten me. As far as being straight goes, if you're being straight with me, I'll be straight with you."

Her tone took on an edge of contempt. "I should tell you that CSIS, the RCMP, we consider them amateurs — but even they're far above your calibre." She pointed her finger at his face and said, "So no games!"

Pure E paused to reflect on what he'd been told. "I understand what you're saying, but it's not necessary. It's the product that interests me, not you."

She settled back in her seat. "There's something else I will tell you. Our intelligence indicates that you, person-ally, have already caught the eye of the RCMP. That made us hesitant to deal with you, so be warned, any slip-ups or lies on your part will result in termination."

"You know that the RCMP are after me personally?"

"Yes, of course we know."

"How?"

"How?" She smiled. "Simpler than you might imagine. Intelligence gathering in this day and age against terrorism is a priority for all governments and includes some collaboration. We've seen correspondence from one of the top-ranking RCMP officers in Vancouver — Assistant Commissioner Mortimer, who is dragging his heels at providing more services to counter terrorism because he considers you a priority."

Pure E paused when the man sitting in the rear had a sudden coughing fit. When he was finished, Pure E said, "Mortimer ... yes, I'm familiar with his name."

"His name?" Her tone became sarcastic. "He's your enemy! I'd hope you're more than familiar with just his name." She paused and her tone became matter-of-fact. "My associate will not deal with amateurs. I'd presumed you at least knew the basics about him. Where he lives, what he drives ... photographs."

"We, uh, we're working on it. What you've mentioned is something we do on a routine basis. Recently we did surveillance and took photos of someone in the RCMP Intelligence Unit, along with his family. If you doubt me, I could bring you proof. As far as Mortimer goes, he's new and only came to our attention recently."

"I see." She paused as if contemplating what he'd said. "Good — I believe you. Proof won't be necessary. An element of trust will be needed if we're to conduct business."

"Particularly if your associate is willing to front five hundred keys."

The woman smiled. "His trust in you relies on the fact that you're not suicidal."

"Suicidal?"

"That you'll fulfill your end of the bargain. As you must be aware, we've done our homework. There's no place in the world you could hide if you try to rob us."

At fifteen a kilo, we're already robbing you.

"You should know that Mortimer's interest made us question whether to contact you. Our other option is a local Chinese triad, as I've said. Fortunately for us, and perhaps you, the triad also assists their own government's intelligence agency. As a result, between the Chinese — who are extremely busy doing corporate spying, coupled with ongoing terrorist threats — CSIS has basically had to ignore us. That leaves only the RCMP to worry about. Although they declared you a priority target, they're still short-staffed due to terrorist threats. Given the choice, we decided to approach you first rather than risk dealing with the Chinese, who are hounded by both CSIS and the RCMP."

"I see."

She glanced at her watch. "I've another engagement tonight I must attend. I'll take you back. First, though, I need to make a call. I was instructed to give you a gift to make up for my associate being absent and for any inconvenience we may have caused."

"A gift?"

"How does twenty-five kilos at no charge sound? That'd be worth about three-quarters of a million at normal wholesale prices."

"I, uh, don't know what to say."

"I believe 'thank you' is the correct response."

Chapter Forty-Nine

Whiskey Jake waited in the alcove on the third level of the parkade. Soon he saw Pure E racing up the stairwell. "Jesus shit, am I glad to see you," Whiskey Jake said. "Who the fuck were those guys?"

Pure E paused to catch his breath. "Russians."

"Yeah, that I figured, but I haven't heard any word on the street about 'em. Glad you're okay. You won't believe what the fuck I saw and what just happened."

"I might."

"They let me go a few minutes ago, but first let me tell you what's in the trunk of my car. Right now I'm afraid to go near it."

"Twenty-five kilos of white?" Pure E replied.

"You already know? They told you?"

"They want to do business with us. The twenty-five is a gift."

"A gift? Like … free?"

"Yes."

Whiskey Jake shook his head in disbelief. "I guess they can afford it. You wouldn't believe how much they have. I saw it myself."

"Three tonnes?"

"Fuck, they told you. I counted it. Three fucking tonnes!"

"Where'd they take you?"

"They put me in a van and threw a bag over my head. I have no idea where we went. We drove for about forty minutes and ended up in a garage. They then showed me the stash and offered to let me sample it. Later I heard the guy speakin' Russian on the phone, then he and the other dude took twenty-five off the pile and put it in a duffle bag. Then they retied my hands in front and made me hang on to it. After that they bagged my head again, brought me back, then released me and told me to put the duffle bag in my trunk. Next the guy said you were being dropped off in five minutes and they left."

"Man … unbelievable," Pure E muttered. "At first I thought we were dead."

"Me, too, then I thought it was a robbery." Whiskey Jake took a deep breath and slowly exhaled to calm himself. "Okay, so what the fuck happened to you? Where'd they take ya?"

"Hang on, I want to google a commercial building they took me to on Granville before I forget." Pure E took out his phone. "Shit, no signal. Come on, let's go for a walk and I'll tell you what happened."

"What about the stuff in the trunk?" Whiskey Jake asked, gesturing with his thumb.

"Call one of the guys, then lend him your keys, and have him look after it. There's a Starbucks in the 200 block. He can meet us there."

Whiskey Jake placed the call, then listened in awe as Pure E told him what had transpired during his ride in the limo. When he was finished Whiskey Jake said, "Man, whoever these people are, if they're serious, we'll be fuckin' rich beyond anything I've ever imagined."

"I don't see someone giving us twenty-five keys if they're not serious." He took out his phone again. "I've got a signal. I'm going to google that address and put the word 'Russia' in and see what I get."

Whiskey Jake watched Pure E's face as he entered the address, then saw the look of jubilation. "What did you find?"

Pure E passed his phone to Whiskey Jake. "Take a look at the first thing that popped up. The Russian Consulate is on the tenth floor."

Whiskey Jake let out a low whistle.

Pure E grabbed him by the arm. His gaze was intense. "We're dealing with spies! There's no doubt about it." He paused and his face broke into a smile. "Betcha I'm the first national prez to ever do that." He then gave a thumbs up and added, "Fucking aye!"

An hour later Jack arrived with Benny at Sammy's house. As they took their shoes off in the foyer, Jack could hear Natasha, Laura, and Sammy's wife, Karen, talking in the living room. "How did she do … really?" he whispered to Sammy.

"Like I told you on the phone, she did great," Sammy replied. "A little nervous at first — she slopped some vodka while pouring a drink — but her voice was strong and confident."

"The spill was staged," Jack replied. "I wanted Pure E to think she might've been a little tipsy to justify her mistake of talking English on the phone about meeting the Chinese ambassador."

"Then she did a fantastic job." Sammy glanced at Benny. "Go into the kitchen and pour yourself a drink. I want to talk to Jack about something. We'll be right behind you."

When Benny was out of earshot, Jack looked at Sammy and raised an eyebrow.

"I know neither Benny nor I asked any questions when you wanted us to help you," Sammy whispered.

"I appreciate that," Jack replied. "This plan of mine … it's better if you only knew what you needed to know to do your part."

"That I understand. Not knowing everything will help protect us and give us some deniability in case the shit hits the fan."

"Good." Jack waited a beat. "So is there a problem?"

"Benny and I believed it was about Pure E. We're both willing to do pretty much anything when it comes to that sack of shit."

"It is about Pure E."

"Then why'd Natasha drop Mortimer's name into the mix? I damn near shit." Sammy glared at Jack. "You're setting the bikers up to waste him."

"No, I'm not. Are you kidding? Mentioning Mortimer was nothing. Satans Wrath were already aware that he's the new assistant commissioner."

"Then why bring his name up?"

"I wanted Natasha to make him think the Russian intel was up-to-date."

"But she mentioned surveillance, knowing where he lived, what cars he —"

"Routine stuff Natasha would say if she really did come from the background she pretended to." Jack paused. "I appreciate your concerns. Laura and I do have a well-placed source in the club. It's not my intention to have them kill Mortimer."

Sammy stared at Jack a moment. "I got your word on that?"

"You do." *It's not my intention, but hey, shit happens.*

Chapter Fifty

On Saturday morning Jack was dismantling the fake display in his garage when Lance called.

"You'll never believe what happened last night," Lance said excitedly.

"Hope it's good," Jack responded. "Did Pure E step in front of a bus?"

"No, he's very much alive. Him and Whiskey Jake met me an hour ago." Lance paused, perhaps to consider how or what to tell him. "I don't want you to freak out. Hear me through first while I tell you what happened."

Jack made an appropriate amount of astonished noises as Lance told him about Pure E being taken for a ride in a limo while Whiskey Jake was taken to view three tonnes of cocaine. "This is unbelievable," he expounded, after Lance told him about the twenty-five kilo gift of cocaine. "I know there's some badass Russians here, but they're low class. This is way above that."

"Way above … as in government agents," Lance said.

"They might be agents, but I doubt the Russian government would sanction something like this in Canada. Some banana republic sure, but not here. If it is a government agent, I bet he's trying to make some money without his bosses knowing. Probably the coke is supposed to be dumped in the ocean or something."

"Pure E was thinking the same thing. He said it sounded like a one-time opportunity."

"Three tonnes. If I could grab Pure E with his hands on that, he'd be going down for a long time."

"That won't happen. There won't be any colour-wearing members going near it. Pure E will meet with the Russkies to arrange things, but someone else will handle the actual distribution."

"Can you find out who the Russians are?"

"Doubt I can. Pure E said they'd only deal with him and would kill him him if he tried to have them followed."

"Will you know when he's meeting them next?"

Lance chuckled. "So that you can be there and make sure the Russkies know they're being followed?"

"Gee, that idea never crossed my mind."

"Yeah, I bet." Lance chuckled. "Doesn't matter. Pure E said nobody except for Whiskey Jake is to know about the next meeting until it's over. That won't be for at least a week or more. Pure E is flying out this afternoon to meet with the Halifax chapter, then will meet with the other chapters on his way back."

"When do you think he'll be back?"

"Next Friday, but listen, I'm not done. This is where I don't want you to freak out. The Russians spoke to him about your guy Mortimer."

"How the hell do the Russians know about him?"

"Something to do with working jointly on terrorism projects and sharing information. They said Mortimer has been holding back people for that because he considers Pure E more of a priority."

"I see."

"Pure E said he'd heard of Mortimer, but then he got razzed about it. He was basically accused of being an amateur. To prove otherwise, starting Monday, he's ordered surveillance and photos of Mortimer to be taken over the next week."

Perfect. Love it when a plan comes together.

"Along with his family, too," Lance continued. "That's if he has any."

Yeah, he's married and has a daughter living at home. I wonder if he has an alarm system. He sure as hell wasn't going to approve one for me.

"You got nothing to say about that?" Lance sounded surprised.

"I was thinking that it's the same as happened to me," Jack replied.

"Yeah, except this time the three-three —"

"The three-three? Why them and not your regular surveillance team?"

"Pure E didn't say."

Guess he really did take it to heart when Natasha told him that Mortimer was his enemy. "Using the three-three makes it pretty obvious to me."

"Yeah, I figured it would freak you out, but relax. He's adamant that Mortimer doesn't find out about it. He thinks if he did, it would make us look like a pack of amateurs. The three-three are the best, that's all. It's not a hit. At least not yet."

"Not yet?"

"If that changes, I'll likely know about it and will give you a call. For now, they're only doing surveillance and taking pictures. Mortimer won't know they're there, let alone see or hear anything."

As in not hearing the sound of the shot that kills you. "Okay, I'll trust you to keep me informed if anything changes. If I warn Mortimer, then he'd have your guys busted and I'd be afraid it would scare the Russians off. I'm sure Pure E is feeling the stress over this, too."

"You're right about that. Buying three tonnes of white … I doubt he could get any more stressed."

"Wanna bet? Do you know where Whiskey Jake is at the moment?"

"Yeah, he's with Pure E and will be taking him to the airport later. Why?"

"As soon as I'm done talking with you, Rat Cop is going to pass something on. With what's going on, if I turn the stress level up on Pure E even further, maybe he'll make a mistake and do something stupid — in regard to handling the coke, I mean, not Mortimer."

"Dare I ask what you plan on passing on?"

"I expect you'll be hearing from them right after, but I'm going to tell Whiskey Jake something that is not only true, but will make Pure E look stupid." Jack paused for breath. "Neal Barlow wasn't an informant."

"For real?"

"Yes, for real. Pure E's order that he be tortured to death, along with his brother and sister-in-law, was totally uncalled for."

"Fuck," Lance murmured.

"I wonder what the rest of your guys will think when they hear about it. Their new national president may not be as wonderful as they thought."

"They might not believe it. I do, but they might not."

"If Whiskey Jake doubts me, I have details. Things such as it was Pasquale Bazzoli from the three-three who handed out cans of lighter fluid to the Gypsy Devils. They in turn burned Roxanne to death and made Robert and Neal watch. After that they killed Robert and then gutted Neal last. It was Norman Thorsen from the Gypsy Devils, or Thor as you know him, who took a knife to Neal. That's when Bazzoli dipped a broom in the blood and left me a message on the wall."

"Yeah, knowing those details oughtta convince them." Lance paused, then said, "Christ, I figured Neal wasn't your rat because of things you've done to protect me. You're smarter than that, but I sure as hell couldn't tell them that." He paused a moment. "Pure E really screwed up. And leavin' the message for you on the wall …"

4 U JT — yeah that caught my attention.

"You not worried it'll heat up your real informant? And I don't mean me. Obviously it had to be one of the other GDs. Even I didn't know all those details."

"It wasn't a Gypsy Devil."

"What?" Lance exclaimed. "No! Besides Bazzoli, the only other guy there from our club was —"

"Mack Cockerill."

"Shit!" Lance was quiet for a moment. "That's why you're not worried. He died of a drug overdose weeks ago."

"That's right."

Lance paused, apparently thinking about it, then said, "I know you want to make Pure E look bad, but it may not go any further than Whiskey Jake and Pure E."

"I'm also going to say that the Gypsy Devils will find out after Christmas who the real informant is when it comes out in court. Now that he's dead, his identify doesn't need to be kept secret."

"That'll let the cat out of the bag," Lance said.

"No kidding."

"The GDs will go nuts. They'll want revenge."

"Maybe." Jack thought for a moment. "It's bound to make them sick — killing one of their own like that. Do you really think they'd try to take on your club? It'd be suicide. I could see them simply disbanding and going their separate ways."

"I doubt Pure E would risk it."

Of course he won't risk it. That's what I'm counting on.

"He'll want them taken out to be on the safe side — which I guess for you is one less club to worry about."

"Having the three-three kill Damien and Vicki, then keep it mum is one thing. I could see the three-three understanding that it was for the better overall morale of the club. Killing six guys to cover the previous murder of three others is something else. Sooner or later word of Pure E's stupidity will get out. His leadership will be questioned and he'll be less respected."

"A lot of death just to cause someone to lose respect."

"If you fly with the crows, expect to get shot."

Whiskey Jake was pleased when Rat Cop called him. He wasn't pleased when he heard what Rat Cop had to say. Neither was Pure E.

Chapter Fifty-One

It was dark Saturday evening when Jack parked his SUV at Deas Island Park. The location he'd picked was alongside the Fraser River and across from a marina. Laura used her own car and parked nearby. It was her job to distract anyone who happened by. Nobody did and it didn't take Jack long to unload five garbage bags and hide them at the water's edge.

Jack and Laura then drove to the other side of the river and parked near the marina, where Laura got in the SUV with Jack. He pulled out his phone.

Crime Stoppers were pleased with the tip. The exact location was given of where ninety-five kilos of cocaine belonging to Satans Wrath were hidden. The tipster said that the drugs were about to be picked up any moment by someone in a boat. Although the tipster's identity was never revealed, a number assigned to the tipster revealed that he'd provided a tip six weeks earlier that had led to an arrest and the seizure of one hundred and fifty kilos of marijuana destined for Calgary.

One hour later the tipster's credibility was enhanced when the cocaine was located. A flurry of activity ensued where most of the cocaine was substituted with bags of flour. Several officers then hid nearby to nab whoever came to pick up the drugs.

From across the river Jack and Laura had taken turns watching through binoculars. "No point having them sit out in the rain any longer," Jack said once the officers were in position.

Crime Stoppers then received another call advising that the police had been spotted getting into position and that the bikers were abandoning the stash. The tipster said that the bikers were concerned about their cocaine source finding out about the seizure because it might put an end to future deals with him. If that were to happen the bikers would go elsewhere and the tipster would not be in a position to assist. The tipster was assured that no press release would be made.

"So now what?" Laura asked.

"We go home."

"No, I mean in regards to the plan."

"My swelling and bruising, courtesy of the Black Water clientele, has almost gone. I think we should spend some time in the office before Rose becomes suspicious. Also we need to lay some groundwork with her about the Russians."

"You mean the *pretend* Russians."

"Natasha is real." Jack glanced at his watch and frowned. "I thought our friend would've called back to tell us when they plan on killing the Gypsy Devils."

"Me, too. Oh, man."

"What's wrong?"

"What's wrong? What if they're already doing it?"

"Pure E won't jeopardize losing three tonnes of coke by bringing attention to himself by murdering them now. That's why I said that the Gypsy Devils wouldn't find out until after Christmas."

"But you plan to tip the GDs off much sooner than that."

"Yes, but that'll depend on when Satans Wrath want to do it. We'll have to play it by ear."

"Yeah … play it by ear. I've heard that before."

"Relax. We'll have a couple of weeks to get our ducks in a row."

"A couple of weeks. That isn't long. Not for what needs to be done. Something could go wrong."

"Such as?"

"I don't know," she said, sounding irritated. "Dope deals never go down on time. There're always delays. In the meantime we could be starting a war."

"We *will* be starting a war," Jack stated. "The trick will be to limit the body count to who we want." He felt his phone vibrate and glanced at the call display. "Speaking of our friend, maybe your worries will be answered." He leaned over in the seat so Laura could hear.

"You sure put a bee up Pure E's ass," Lance said.

"Thought I might," Jack replied. He winked at Laura, but could tell by her face that she didn't share his glee. He turned his attention back to Lance. "Did it change his travel plans?"

"No, I met them at noon. He still flew out to Halifax."

"What took you so long to get back to me?"

"I was with Whiskey Jake. We called all the three-three in for a chat and set a date for uh, you know, it to happen."

"To lower the census by six."

"Yeah. Pure E doesn't want to stir things up until the thing with the Russians has gone ahead."

Jack gave Laura a thumbs-up. It felt good to see the relief on her face.

"As far as the GDs go," Lance continued, "it's set for Friday, December 19."

"Do you know how and where?"

"The three-three want to use the same prospect's house out in Abbotsford that they used for Vicki. I'm going to send one of my guys over to tell the GDs we want 'em to hang a licking on some dealers who live out that way."

"I presume the message will be passed on to Carl Shepherd, their president?

"Yup. He'll be told to have all his guys meet at the prospect's house for a debriefing. All the three-threes will be there. The GDs won't be expecting anything. Our guys will use silencers. Maybe take half of 'em out to the garage or maybe do 'em all at once. Whatever. That's up to the three-three."

"When are you going to tell Carl?"

"This week. I want to give plenty of notice so there's no excuse for any of 'em not to be there. Why?"

"Laura and I want to surveil him when he's told and see who he contacts afterward. Find out if there are any new prospects or GDs we don't know about. Monday and Tuesday we're not available, but we're clear after that."

"Okay, how about Wednesday? He works as a mechanic out of his garage at home, but if I send someone there around 4:00 p.m. he'll knock off work soon after. Then you won't be wastin' your time sittin' around."

"Much appreciated. Maybe there'll be more than six."

Lance let out a snort. "Yeah, well, either way, soon there won't be any."

Jack hung up and stared quietly out the window for a moment to collect his thoughts.

"So you were right," Laura said. "They're not doing it immediately."

"You less stressed now?"

"Oh, for sure," Laura replied sarcastically. "What have I got to be stressed about other than six guys have been targeted for murder and we'll be doing another kidnapping?"

"Kidnapping? Naw, I look at it as securing a dangerous criminal so he doesn't become violent while taking him on a trip of enlightenment."

Chapter Fifty-Two

Laura followed Jack into Rose's office and placed her coffee mug on the corner of the desk as she sat beside Jack. She saw Rose eyeing them from over the top of her reading glasses.

Pleasantries were exchanged, then Rose looked serious. "Okay, so what've you two been up to? I didn't see either one of you all last week."

"Doing a lot of surveillance," Jack said.

"What happened to your eye?" Rose asked. "Looks puffy."

You should've seen him last week.

"It's okay," Jack replied. "I've got a sty. I've been soaking it with warm compresses. It's starting to go away."

"I see. So … what's with all the surveillance?"

"We've got something big," Jack responded. "Our informant said that Pure E has met with some Russians who are offering to sell him three tonnes of cocaine."

Rose looked startled and sat back in her chair. "You're not putting me on?"

Yeah, we are.

"That's what our informant said," Jack replied. "He's never lied to us in the past, but that doesn't mean it's not bullshit. Maybe someone is trying to impress Pure E."

"Do we know who these Russians are?"

Yes, it's Mrs. Taggart.

"Our informant doesn't have a clue. He said that only Pure E is allowed to deal with them. At the moment Pure E is meeting with other chapters across Canada to arrange disbursement for when they get it. He's expected back Friday."

"Then obviously Pure E believes its real," Rose stated. "Goddamn Mortimer. We should be throwing everything we have at this. Drug Section, Integrated Proceeds of Crime, surveillance teams, wiretaps."

Laura heard Jack take a deep breath, then sigh. *Good one. It sounded real.*

"I know," Jack lamented. "Still, all this is in the preliminary stages. Maybe once Pure E returns we'll be able to identify who he meets. Our informant should be able to help out. If we're lucky, I'll be able to call Crime Stoppers."

Rose inhaled, then slowly let her breath out in an apparent attempt to calm herself. "Okay, so what're you up to until Pure E returns?"

"Oh, you know, just the usual."

Yeah … the usual kidnapping and murder.

At 9:00 a.m. Wednesday Laura slowly drove their SUV past Carl Shepherd's house. The windshield wipers sounded dismal, but she knew it wasn't the weather that had her depressed. It'd been another night of worry and no sleep.

"Good, the garage door is open and his crew cab's parked in the driveway," Jack said. "No sign of his wife's car."

He sounded cheery. Irritatingly so.

"Park down the block and I'll go in on foot. I'll be able to use an umbrella to hide my mask until I get there."

Laura did as instructed, then glanced at Jack's waist as he rummaged for his umbrella. He had a pillow to shove in his shirt to make him look fat, hoping to match the physique of Whiskey Jake. Once he found his umbrella, he stopped moving and stared at her face.

"What is it?"

"Your lipstick."

He's noticing my lipstick at a time like this? "It's called Electric Pink. Don't you like it?"

"I love it. Do you have it with you? I want to borrow it."

Laura eyed him suspiciously. "I've heard rumors that you sometimes wear lipstick."

"I don't anymore," he said, straight-faced. "That was a long time ago — back when I was young and really needed the money."

Laura reached for her purse. "Okay, smartass, what do you really want it for?"

"Hang on. Phone … it's Wilson." He gestured for her to lean in.

"Probably can't read your notes from last week," Laura said.

"Jack, I'm sorry," were the first words Wilson uttered. "I really screwed up. I never should've used you and Laura for that UC. Not after you told me about Mortimer."

"What happened?" Jack asked.

"One of our asshole inspectors took it upon himself to send Mortimer a letter, commending you and Laura for your work and expressing his gratitude. I only found out about it this morning when I got a copy. The original was mailed out yesterday afternoon."

Oh, man. Not now, not this. Laura looked at Jack and saw him bite his lip.

"I'm sorry," Wilson repeated.

"Not your fault," Jack said. "I would've been more upset if you hadn't let me help. It was my business card shoved down Tom's throat. I needed to be there. Don't worry about it. Maybe Mortimer will understand."

Mortimer understand? NFL.

A moment later Jack terminated the call, then looked at her and grimaced.

"Mortimer understand?" she said.

"Yeah, I know. Not fucking likely." He reached for his phone. "The letter will hit Mortimer's desk either today or tomorrow. I better give Rose a heads-up."

Laura listened in as Jack told Rose about Tom's murder in Stanley Park and their subsequent role in assisting with the investigation.

"You're finished, Jack," Rose stated. "Maybe I can save Laura, but you were directly ordered not to work UC. There's no way I'll be able to help you out of this one. He'll call you in and have you off the section immediately."

"Rose, I need you to hold Mortimer off until Monday." Jack sounded desperate. "We need these next few days. Tell Mortimer I'm home sick in bed. If he wants a doctor's note I'll have Natasha make one up."

"Why?" Rose demanded.

"I expect Pure E to meet the Russians as soon as he gets back. The cocaine could be transferred over to the bikers this weekend. My informant might get the details."

"This weekend? Since when does a drug deal ever go down on time? Especially one this big. There's no way you'll be able to wrap it up by then."

"At least let me have a shot at it. If I'm going out, let me go out with some pizazz. Three tonnes of coke would do that."

Rose hesitated. "Okay … but even if you succeed in taking down such a huge shipment, you'll be gone. There's no way he'll let you stay."

"I know, but three tonnes — what a way to go." He ended the call abruptly.

Laura blinked to banish the tears that had formed in her eyes. She'd seen the muscles along Jack's jaw tighten — he wasn't sad, just angry. "Jack, I —"

"Mortimer, that self-centred, ignorant prick! He's going down," Jack said. "Him and Pure E both."

Laura was appalled. "Jack, we can't kill Mortimer. It wouldn't be right."

"Wouldn't it?" he replied, then reached for his ski mask and pillow.

Chapter Fifty-Three

Carl Shepherd was bent over tightening a spark plug when he heard someone approach from behind. It wasn't unusual. People often walked into his garage from off the street. He was a good mechanic and his rates were low, providing the customer paid cash. Word of mouth brought in a steady income, which nicely supplemented the income from less honest sources.

"With you in a minute," he said, not bothering to turn around. The sound of his overhead garage door closing caught his immediate attention and he spun around. "Hey! What the —"

"I ain't here to kill you," said the man. Big and fat, he wore a ski mask and was pointing a pistol at Carl's face. "All I wanna do is pass on some info. Info that'll save your sorry ass from gettin' killed."

"Then why the fuckin' mask and gun?" Carl was more incensed than he was fearful. He'd enough experience to know that if this was a hit, he'd already be slumped over the engine with a bullet in the back of his head.

"Because if word leaks out I did this, it'll be *me* Pasquale sprinkles with lighter fluid."

Fuck, he's a Satans Wrath — nobody else knows that stuff.

"Anyone in the house?" the intruder asked. "Your old lady?"

"Nobody's home. My ol' lady dropped our kid off at daycare and she's at work."

"If you're lyin' to me, you get wasted first."

"I ain't lyin'. She works as a receptionist at a construction company. We only got the one kid. Nobody else lives with us."

"Good. Turn around and get down on your knees. I'm gonna zip-tie your hands behind your back."

"You that afraid of me? You already got a piece."

"What I'm gonna tell you will really piss you off. Then I'm takin' you for a drive to show you somethin'."

"Show me what?"

"Turn around and do as I say. I don't want you tryin' to do somethin' stupid."

Carl begrudgingly did as instructed. Once his hands were tied behind his back, his captor came around to face him. "Okay, you can get to your feet or sit on your ass. Whatever makes ya comfortable."

"I prefer to stand."

His captor waited for him to rise, then said, "What I came to tell you is we found out it wasn't Neal who ratted to the cops. It was one of our guys. You killed your own for no reason."

"What the fuck?" Carl felt enraged. He wanted to grab the man by the throat. "You're lyin'!"

"'Fraid not." The man waited a moment. "Told you it'd piss you off."

"You made us torch our own guy! Him, Bob, and Roxie.... What the fuck, man?"

"It wasn't my idea. Pure E ordered it. He wouldn't wait until we were sure who the rat was. The fucker just wouldn't listen."

"Then who was the rat?"

The man uttered the name like it was poison. "Mack Cockerill."

"Your fuckin' go-between you used with us? I heard he died of an overdose weeks ago."

"Yeah, we're not sure when he started rattin'. Probably a couple months before that. He'd started drinkin' heavy and poppin' pills. We were on the verge of takin' away his patch when he croaked."

Carl realized the stress was making him hyperventi-late, so he made a conscious effort to breathe evenly and keep his voice steady. "You're right about pissin' me off."

"Pure E figures you guys might find out about it next month if it comes out in court down in the States."

"Over that grass seizure the cops did in Dallas?"

"Yeah."

"So it wasn't Neal who ratted that one out. It was Mack."

"Yup, but if you're pissed off now, let me finish. Pure E put in an order to have all six of you guys whacked."

Carl took another deep breath and released it. "He fig-ures we'll come after him."

"Wouldn't you?"

"Some of the guys would. They'd know you'd get us all eventually, but someone like Thor ... he wouldn't care."

"Which is why Pure E decided not to take any chances. Late this afternoon you're gonna get a visit from one of our guys. It'll be a bullshit message to suck you all out to Abbotsford on the nineteenth of this month. Once there, you'll be wasted."

"So why're you tellin' me?"

"That fuckin' Pure E — what a world-class prick," the man responded, almost as if he was talking to himself. Then he said, "He's poison for the club. We got word that the cops are formin' a special task force to come after us because of the shit he's pulled."

"The message left at Neal's place."

"Yeah, that was only one of his fuckin' brilliant ideas." The man shook his head in disgust. "Me and a couple other long-time members been talkin'. We'd be better off without Pure E, but the thing is, he got voted in. Lots of our younger guys think he's a fuckin' hero. The truth is, he ain't got no class. The fucker rides me about my weight right in front of broads. A buddy of mine is exec level and Pure E calls him grandpa. The guy's got no respect for nobody."

"Yeah, so? I still don't get why you're tellin' me this."

"I'm thinkin' maybe we can help each other out."

"How?"

"To explain how, I gotta show you somethin'."

"Show me what?"

"Somethin' you need to see with your own eyes. Then we'll talk some more. We need to take a drive. I'm gonna blindfold you because I'm not drivin' around wearin' a ski mask. Some cop'll think we're out to rob a bank. I don't trust you to drive in case you try to jump or somethin'.

So … two choices. Choice number one is you can lend me your wheels to get there while you lie in the back seat. When we get there I'll put my mask back on. When we're done, I got a buddy who'll pick me up and you can drive back on your own. Choice number two is we can go in my car and you can do the round trip in the trunk."

"My keys are in my pocket."

"Good. Turn around and get down on your knees. I got a rag I'm gonna tape over your eyes."

Minutes later Carl lay on the back seat of his crew cab as his captor drove. He thought it strange that he was being given a play-by-play description of what streets they took, including the announcement that they had entered the eastbound lane of the Trans-Canada Highway. Later he was told they'd passed Abbotsford and were going north-bound from the Lickman Road exit to Industrial Way.

His captor eventually told him he was stopping to open a barbed-wire gate. Then he felt his truck bounce along a bumpy road and finally come to a stop, at which point he was pulled upright and his blindfold removed.

Carl blinked. They were parked in a forest clearing and in front of his truck was a chain-link fence surrounding a compound with a shipping container.

His captor had put the ski mask back on. "This is it," he said. "Time to get out." He opened the rear door of the cab.

His hands still zip-tied behind his back, Carl wriggled out of the truck, easing his feet to the ground. He watched as his captor crossed to a pile of rocks and lifted one, then held up a baggie containing two keys. He used one key to enter the compound and the second to unlock the shipping container, which they entered.

Carl focused on the apparatus in front of him. *What the hell is that?*

As if reading his mind, his captor said, "It's an animal incinerator. At least, that's what it's intended for. It can do a man in about three hours. Easy to operate, too," he said, flipping open a metal lid. "The body goes in here."

Fuck! Is he going to kill me here? Suckering me into thinking he was gonna let me live?

"This is where our three-three dispose of bodies. It's so secret that only they're supposed to know about it. I only found out by slappin' a tracker on one of their cars. Even that wasn't easy 'cause it's rare for any of 'em to come out here."

"Wh-why'd you bring me here?" Carl couldn't quite keep the fear out of his voice.

"To show you where you and your guys will all end up if Pure E has his way."

Carl just stared at the incinerator.

"By the way, did I tell you that Pure E is dealin' with some badass Russians at the moment? That's why he's waitin' till the nineteenth to waste you guys. He doesn't want to cause any heat that might scare the Russians off. The thing is, it's only him that's dealin' with 'em, which kinda worries us 'cause we don't know who they really are. They pick him up in a black stretch limo to talk to 'im, but aren't the type to shake hands and do intros, if you know what I mean."

Why's he blabbin' about that stuff?

"Come to think of it, the limo they picked him up in is identical to the limo one of your guys owns. What's his name?"

"Mouse."

"Yeah, him."

"What're you gettin' at?"

"I'm just sayin' we're kinda worried about Pure E dealin' with these Russians. I sure hope nothin' happens to him. He's gonna meet them again Saturday mornin'. The limo just pauses on the street and he hops in. Knowin' Pure E, he'll probably get there early."

Is he tellin' me what I think he's tellin' me?

The masked man eyed him for a moment. "Then again, I suppose if somethin' did happen to him, it wouldn't hurt your feelings. If he disappeared without a trace and you guys hung up your colours, I bet our club would be so busy lookin' for them Russians we'd forget all about you."

His captor took what appeared to be a tube of lipstick from his pocket. Carl watched his subsequent actions in silence, then nodded.

Chapter Fifty-Four

Laura had parked to watch the Lickman Road overpass and the ramp leading onto the Trans-Canada Highway. Once she confirmed that Carl was on his way back to the city, she called Jack and drove to pick him up.

"I think it went well," Jack said on getting into the SUV. "Guess time will tell, though."

"Time we don't have," Laura replied.

"We should get an indication when he gets a visit this afternoon. Our friend will let us know how that went."

"You don't think Carl will say anything about this morning?"

"I don't think he's that stupid ... or reckless. He has a wife and child to think about. Before he left, he told me he might not even tell some of his guys what's going on."

Laura nodded. "Handpick who he needs."

"Quite likely. Thor'll be picked. The guy's built like a gorilla. He'd be enough by himself. Carl also said he might drop a hint that some of his guys are thinking of leaving his club, so that way it won't cause any suspicion later when they disband."

"Basic club constitutions say they need a minimum of six to form a club or chapter. If only one quits and there isn't a replacement, they'd be finished as a club, anyway."

"Exactly. He also gave me his number to let him know exactly when and where to do their thing. I told him Saturday morning, but didn't want to sound like I knew all the details yet."

Laura looked solemn. "So what now? Do you really want to watch Carl this afternoon?"

"No, we can't risk being spotted. Let's call it a day. I want to pick you up at six tomorrow morning and go for a drive."

"A drive where?"

"Mortimer's house."

At 7:00 a.m. the following day Jack drove down a residential street in Edgemont Village in North Vancouver. "We're only a couple of blocks away. Time for me to be a little old man." He reached for the backpack he'd stuffed with various disguises. "You better duck down below the window."

Laura did as instructed and watched Jack slouch low in his seat. He put on a pair of thick black plastic glasses — without any lenses — followed by a fedora, which he pulled tight over his ears. When done, he rested both hands high on the steering wheel. Anyone glancing at him through the rain-swept windshield would think he was an old man.

"Mortimer's got a nice house," Jack reported as he drove slowly past. Three-car garage … Bingo!"

"What do you see?"

"Two houses down there's a van parked on the street that looks like the one parked near my house on the day our pictures were taken."

"Abe's Furnace Repair?" Laura asked.

"Give me a sec … coming up to it. Same type of magnetic sign on the door, but this one reads *Wayne's Carpet and Flooring*. Must be Abe's brother." He paused. "The plate's too dirty to read, but that's okay. Stay down. I'm going to widen the search and see if there's a mobile surveillance team, as well."

Ten minutes later Jack reported that he'd found what he was looking for. Three cars were parked side by side, all facing out, in a lot near a coffee shop two blocks away. Each one had someone behind the wheel. "Okay, got Floyd Hackman in one … Vic Trapp next … and Pasquale Bazzoli. Bet Nick Crowe and Buck Zabat are in the van."

"You get the plates and vehicle descriptions, Mr. Magoo? Or does dementia prevent you remembering?"

Jack chuckled. "Grab your notebook. Hackman's in a blue Toyota Camry. Backed in with no front plate. Same for Bazzoli, sitting in a black Nissan Rogue. Trapp's front plate was on. He's in a silver Ford pickup, licence —"

"Okay, okay, wait," Laura interrupted, digging in her purse from her cramped position on the floor.

"Sorry. I keep forgetting you're not as young and spry as you used to be. Am I speaking loud enough for you?"

"Jerk."

"Wow, you seem really sensitive this morning. Glad I didn't mention your weight."

"I'll have you know I weigh the same now as the day I left basic training."

Jack snickered. "Hurry up and start writing before I do forget. Then we'll go to my place. Natasha has to leave for work at eleven. I want to go over the call with her again."

Oh, yeah, that. Natasha's about to deliver a kill order. Laura thought about the professional killers clustered around Mortimer's house. *Timing will be crucial — but what if Pure E sets his own agenda? Oh, man …*

"Ready to copy?" Jack asked.

Laura stared at the pen in her hand. "I'm ready."

Chapter Fifty-Five

Jack saw the tension on Natasha's face. She sat beside him at their kitchen table, her eyes on the cellphone he was holding … and his finger poised to punch in the number. He glanced at Laura across from them. Her face was ashen, without expression. Between them lay a pen and a pad of paper.

Natasha's eyes slowly lifted and met his. "Okay … I'm ready."

I love you so much. Jack swallowed, then said, "Remember, hold the phone so I can listen. If you're unsure of anything, or I tap your arm, say something in Russian and have him wait while I write out what you need to say."

Natasha nodded and seconds later, Jack handed her the phone. "It's ringing."

"Hello?" Pure E answered.

"Yes, Mr. Evans." Natasha's voice was crisp and clear.

Jack grabbed the pad and quickly scribbled.

"Yes," Pure E replied.

Natasha saw Jack point to the pad. *Russian accent!* She nodded, then continued, "We shared a drink the other night. *Da?*"

"Yes, I know who you are," Pure E said. "Nobody else has the number to this phone."

"Good. Then it's still safe to talk. How are you making out with your business partners?"

"Really well. I'm in Calgary at the moment. I'll be home tomorrow."

"You've been telling people lots of people about our potential arrangement." Her tone was accusatory.

"No, of course not. I've only asked a select few how much product they can handle and how soon they could pay for the, uh, loan. Why would you even ask that? I told you, I'm not some amateur."

Natasha paused. "Perhaps it's a coincidence."

"Coincidence?"

"Remember the police officer we spoke about? Mortimer?"

"Yes."

"In the last few days he's stepped up his quest to go after you. A surveillance team currently assigned to terrorism has been seconded to start working on you, effective Monday, December 22. It's caused my associate to seriously reconsider our options."

Pure E responded with a string of profanity.

"Please, Mr. Evans. I don't wish to increase my knowledge of vulgar English words. It will not help."

"I'm sorry."

Jack drew a happy face on the pad.

Natasha swallowed nervously, then continued, "In my country we'd take care of a problem like that. In Mexico they call it *plata o plomo* — silver or lead."

"This isn't Mexico ... or Russia," Pure E stated. "The cops here are paid more. They're not so easy to bribe."

"So if he can't be bribed, are you willing to do what needs to be done?"

Pure E was silent for a moment. "That guy has become a real pain in the ass. Sure, if it'll make you happy, I'll deal with it. However, won't that bring more heat?"

Jack saw Laura staring at him so he gave her a thumbs-up. It didn't help her ashen appearance.

Natasha cleared her throat. "Not if they think someone else is responsible. It would result in less scrutiny as far as you're concerned because it would redirect their attention. My associate would be in a position to pass on intelligence to point the finger at the Chinese."

"He could do that?"

"He suggested it earlier, but one moment, please." Natasha turned to Jack and spoke rapidly in Russian.

"*Da, da,*" was all Jack could think to say.

Natasha turned back to the phone. "Yes, very easily."

"Then consider it done."

"Not yet, Mr. Evans." Natasha's voice sharpened. "Listen closely. This is of the utmost importance. My associate and I wish to meet you face to face prior to any action being taken. Is that understood?"

Jack felt his phone vibrate. He glanced at the display and decided to ignore the call. *Bad timing, Rose.*

"Yeah, but I could order what you want done right now and —"

"No! You're not to do that! Not now!" Natasha's tone revealed her panic.

Jack grabbed her arm and pointed to the pad of paper. *Russian accent!*

Natasha took two deep breaths, then said, "*Nyet, nyet, nyet!* I mean, no, no, no! You didn't listen to me. No action is to be taken until you meet with us in person. For my associate to transfer the blame, he has to schedule a meeting with a certain contact to make his claim seem authentic. Timing is crucial."

"I see. So when do you want it done?"

"Possibly about the time we meet, but he won't be able to confirm that until then."

"Which is when and where?"

"Two days from now — 10:00 a.m. Saturday. Our limo will pick you up in front of the car parkade on Seymour where it approaches West Georgia. One moment, please." Natasha spoke quietly in Russian before turning her attention back to Pure E. "My associate is always concerned about surveillance. Seymour is one way and there's no parking on the street ... so we won't wait long. Get in as soon as we pull up."

"I understand. So, 10:00 a.m. Saturday. I'll be there."

As Natasha ended the call, Jack received a text from Rose. It simply read *911*. The emergency text for him to contact her immediately.

Natasha touched his arm. "I'm sorry. The accent bit. I —"

Jack kissed, then hugged her. He was elated. "Are you kidding? You did great. If you weren't going to work I'd make you one of my wheat smoothies."

Her face broke into a smile.

"He's going for it?" Laura asked.

"Hook, line, and sinker," Jack replied.

"From what I heard he was anxious to do it," Laura said.

Jack shrugged. "He was a little eager. No worries. He'll wait."

"Yeah, no worries," Laura repeated.

Jack took out his phone. "Rose called me. Emergency," he explained, tapping in her number.

"Jack, where are you?" Rose immediately asked.

"At home. Relaxing and having a coffee with Natasha and Laura."

"Mortimer got the letter. He called me in and is absolutely livid. He demanded you see him in his office immediately."

"No doubt wants to commend me, as recommended in the letter," Jack said mildly.

"Are you nuts? What're you *really* drinking? He was literally frothing at the mouth."

"Sounds like rabies. Someone should shoot him."

"Damn it, Jack, this isn't funny."

Funny? I was serious. "You tell him I'm sick?"

"He didn't care. He wants to see you *now*."

"Sorry, no can do. Doctor's orders. I'll get Natasha to write a note if you like."

Natasha drew a sad face on the pad. "Will that do?" she whispered.

"Do you really think waiting until Monday will make a difference?" Rose asked.

"Word is, the deal may go down on Saturday. Laura and I hope to be watching when it does. Once confirmed, I'll call Crime Stoppers."

"Three tonnes," Rose murmured. "Oh, I hope so," she added wistfully. "It'd be some consolation. Something I could rub Mortimer's nose in long after you're gone."

"So you'll let him know I'm refusing to come in until Monday?"

"I'll tell him. It's not like he could make things worse for you than he already plans to."

"Exactly."

"Any chance Pure E will be around the coke when you call Crime Stoppers?"

"Normally he'd never be that close to the action, but three tonnes is a lot. He may want to see it with his own eyes."

"I'll be home Saturday. If you get a chance, stop by and let me know how it's going. Provided you're not too sick, of course."

Rose's tone was grave. It didn't match her attempt at humour, but Jack appreciated that she was trying to make the best of things. "I'll be okay by Saturday. I'll take two aspirin and go to bed with a doctor."

Rose was quiet for a moment and he heard her blow her nose. When she spoke, her voice was shaky. "I'm going to miss you, Jack."

"Thanks, Rose, I'll be —" He quit talking when he realized she'd hung up.

Chapter Fifty-Six

It was drizzling rain at 9:00 a.m. Saturday when Jack and Laura sought refuge in a coffee shop located not far from the parkade on Seymour Street near West Georgia. Thirty minutes later Whiskey Jake drove past in his white Lexus with Pure E beside him.

Laura went to the door to peer down the street, then returned. "They went into the parkade just like you thought they would," she reported.

Jack glanced at his watch. "Half an hour early. He's anxious."

Another twenty minutes passed before a black stretch limo drove slowly past. Jack grabbed his umbrella and stepped outside with Laura. They saw that the limo had stopped partway down the block. Seconds later Pure E dashed out of the parkade. The rear door of the limo opened as he neared and he quickly got in.

Laura's voice was a whisper. "That's it. He's done."

Jack wasn't sure if she was talking to herself or him. *He's done all right. Like a cooked turkey.* He reached for his phone. "Now it's Mortimer's turn."

At 10:40 a.m. Rose answered her door and motioned Jack and Laura inside. "Any news?" she asked anxiously.

"I was going to ask you the same thing," Jack replied. "Did anyone call you?"

"No. Did you get the coke?"

"I'm afraid that's not going to happen."

"Oh." Rose looked glum. "I'm sorry. Come in. I'll put on some coffee." As Jack and Laura took off their shoes and jackets, she asked, "Why'd you think I might've had a phone call?"

Jack took a deep breath and slowly exhaled. "I'm here because I promised to let you know what I've been up to."

Rose no longer looked glum. She looked upset. "What you've been up to?"

"Uh —"

"The idea was to tell me *before* you did something."

"Oh, was that the promise?" Jack feigned surprise.

"What've you done?"

Jack paused, feeling both elated and excited, but knowing Rose wouldn't feel the same. *Well, maybe she'll get excited, just not in the right way.* When he spoke, his voice was matter-of-fact. "Something to ensure that Mortimer doesn't show up for work on Monday."

"What?" Rose looked at Laura, who nodded. She turned back to Jack. "How?"

"We found out from our informant that the three-three have been set up on Mortimer's house for the past few days. They plan to kill him to impress the Russians they're dealing with."

"Christ! Are you serious? Have you called him?"

Jack felt smug, but tried not to let it show. "Two months ago he ordered me not to deal with informants. I didn't want to upset him, so no, I haven't called him."

"You didn't want to upset him?" Rose looked dumbfounded. "We need to warn him!"

Okay, time to nip this in the bud. "I did, through Crime Stoppers. That was about an hour ago. I'm sure the appropriate measures have been taken by now."

"Oh," was all Rose uttered. She then gave Jack a hard look. "Why would they target Mortimer? The man's one of the biggest assets they have."

"All the informant said was that Pure E wants to impress the Russians with what a tough guy he is."

"How'd Satans Wrath even know about Mortimer?"

"Finding out who the top guy is isn't hard. They gather their own intel. They could've obtained that information through a simple phone call. After what the bikers pulled on me, they expected some sort of backlash. When none came, it gave them reason to think they could get away with doing whatever they wanted."

Rose shook her head. "I'm at a loss about what to do. Maybe I better call him and make sure he's okay."

"Then he'd wonder how you knew. Why not put the coffee on and —"

Rose's phone rang and she answered. "Inspector Dyck," she said, giving Jack a concerned look.

I-HIT? That can't be good. Jack's concern was alleviated once it was revealed that I-HIT had been called in as a support unit to interrogate several men suspected of planning a murder. *Good. Love it when a plan comes together.*

Rose looked at Jack and Laura as she spoke into the phone. "Yes, Jack is likely still the most knowledgeable about the club. I'll speak to him and Laura, as well." She then repeated Mortimer's address as she wrote it down and ended the call by saying, "The three of us will be there within the hour."

Crap! That's not in the plan.

Rose sounded stern. "Mortimer and his family are okay. All five members of the three-three were arrested near his house by our tactical units. They've been separated and hauled in for interrogation."

"They won't say anything," Jack said, "other than to demand their lawyer."

"We've been requested to meet at Mortimer's and help analyze the situation and assist with whatever action is deemed necessary," Rose stated.

Okay, maybe that's a good thing. I'll be in a better position to control what's said and what happens.

"There's something else you may find interesting," Rose added, giving Jack another hard look. "Inspector Dyck said he managed to find out some background information on the tipster."

He what? That's supposed to be confidential!

"Which he particularly wants to talk to you about."

Okay, this is a bad thing.

Chapter Fifty-Seven

Jack and Laura, followed by Rose, parked behind a row of both marked and unmarked police cars in front of Mortimer's house. Although the bikers had been arrested and taken back to the office, several black-clad members of the emergency response team, carrying Heckler & Koch MP5 submachine guns, had remained and set up a security perimeter.

"What do you think?" Laura said. "Maybe they're here to keep you and me away."

Normally Jack would have added his own witticism, but his mind was consumed with what Dyck might know. He gave a lopsided grin in response and climbed out of the SUV.

Moments later Jack, Laura, and Rose were greeted at the door by a uniformed officer and ushered into the living room. Inspector Dyck was seated on a sofa alongside two other members of I-HIT — corporals Connie Crane and George Hobbs. Also present was Sergeant Dale

Patterson, a supervisor with Protective Policing Service, a unit that usually provided security for foreign dignitaries and politicians. *Gee, is the prime minister showing up?*

A large stuffed leather chair sat empty and everyone knew not to sit in it. Jack made eye contact with Dyck, who nodded cordially, but looked grave.

Suddenly Mortimer burst into the room. "Okay, they're still packing their suitcases." He glanced at the latest arrivals, who were bringing chairs in from the kitchen. "Good, you're here. We may need your help."

He looked at me as if there was nothing wrong between us. What an asshole.

Mortimer then sat in the oversize leather chair and directed his next comment at Dyck. "Didn't you call CFSEU?"

Oh, yeah, all hands on deck when your *family is threatened.*

"Yes, sir. Sergeant Roger Morris. He's on his way."

"I don't have time to wait!" Mortimer snapped. "Give a rundown on what's happened to bring everyone up to speed. I want to accompany my wife and daughter when they're escorted out."

Dyck nodded. "Crime Stoppers received a tip this morning that a hit squad from Satans Wrath was about to kill Assistant Commissioner Mortimer and said that they were currently awaiting opportunity outside his house."

"Stop!" Mortimer yelled. He pointed to a uniformed officer standing in the foyer. "Close the living-room drapes immediately!"

Wonder if I should say I think I see a sniper on the roof across the street. Probably not a good idea.

Dyck continued as the curtains were being shut. "Our units were called in and five members of Satans Wrath were located and arrested. Two were in a van parked down the street and three others were located in vehicles parked about two blocks away. A sniper's rifle equipped with a silencer was recovered from the van, along with two handguns and several bulletproof vests. Camera equipment was also seized."

"Were they wearing the vests?" Rose asked.

"No, I'm told they were simply stored in the back of the van, along with the guns."

"What about the vehicles parked nearby?" Jack asked.

"They were clean," Dyck replied, "but a camera taken from the van showed that several surveillance photos had been taken during the past week. They included Assistant Commissioner Mortimer pulling into his garage, photos of his wife loading groceries into her car, and some of his daughter exiting her car from where she parked to attend university."

"I wonder why all the photos?" Hobbs said.

"Somebody better find out what was going on!" Mortimer spluttered. "This is about me! My family! It's outrageous!"

"Yes, I know exactly how you feel, sir," Jack said.

Mortimer breathed heavily for a moment, then his anger dissipated, only to be replaced by fear. His voice trembled, along with his jowls. "I … I don't understand why. If this'd happened to Assistant Commissioner Isaac it would make sense, but I've done everything I can to ensure they're left alone. It doesn't make sense. Why would —"

"Sir," Dyck interjected, "I may have an answer for that. I've obtained some information about the tipster." He leaned forward on the sofa and looked at Jack. "Corporal Crane has spoken to me about you."

Oh, shit. Jack glanced at Connie, who gazed back without expression. *Damn it, Connie. What the hell did you say behind my back?*

Dyck cleared his throat. "She said you're the most knowledgeable about Satans Wrath and have been involved in numerous murders associated with them over the years."

"What does that have to do with the tipster?" Jack asked.

"I'd like your opinion on whether or not the tipster really knows what he's talking about."

Is that all? Connie, is that a smirk? You knew I was nervous! Jack refocused on Dyck. "What do you know about the tipster?"

"It's my belief he's a member of Satans Wrath. If I'm right, it would lend more credence to what he said."

Jack resisted the urge to look at Rose, mostly out of fear that if she saw the innocence he was trying to portray on his face, she'd explode. He kept his gaze on Dyck's face. "What makes you think that, sir?"

"I found out that this particular tipster has supplied information twice before."

Jack risked a glance at Rose.

"Twice?" Rose said, looking at Jack.

"Yes, twice," Dyck confirmed. "Like today, the information supplied before was not only accurate, but involved Satans Wrath. The first tip resulted in the seizure of one hundred and fifty kilos of marijuana destined for Calgary about a month and a half ago."

Jack saw Rose nod. *Yeah, that's the one I told you about.* He turned back to Dyck.

"The second time was last Sunday," Dyck continued. "The tipster gave a stash location for what turned out to be ninety-five kilos of cocaine. Unfortunately, unbeknownst to our members, the bikers spotted them setting up on the stash. The tipster alerted Crime Stoppers again. Although no arrests were made, all the cocaine was seized."

Jack felt dryness in his throat and swallowed as he forced himself to remain focused on Dyck.

"This morning when the tipster called, he said that Mortimer was being targeted because the top guy in Satans Wrath was —"

Jack interrupted to say to Mortimer, "That'd be Purvis Evans, alias Pure Evil, alias Pure E. You may recall that his name came up a couple of months ago?"

Mortimer appeared irked. "Yes, I remember."

"Uh, anyway," Dyck went on, "the tipster said that Pure E is arranging to purchase three tonnes of cocaine from some Russians."

"Three tonnes," Mortimer repeated. "That sounds like a lot. Is it a lot?"

"Yes, sir, it's a lot," Jack replied.

"To let me finish," Dyck said, "Crime Stoppers was told that Pure E is looking to impress the Russians with his power by murdering you. Apparently it's his belief that you're weak and —"

"Weak?" Mortimer exclaimed. "Don't they realize I'm a commissioned officer?" He looked bewildered. "If they think I'm weak, what must they think about the rest of you?"

A silence fell on the room, then Dyck resumed. "The tipster indicated that they viewed you as someone who was afraid to come after them. They concluded that due to your high rank, you were representative of our leadership. Apparently they felt that they could assassinate you without any serious repercussions — yet still impress the Russians by murdering a high-ranking official."

Mortimer's mouth open and closed a couple of times, but nothing came out.

"Jack, this is where I'd like your opinion," Dyck said. "Knowing how accurate the tipster has been about the inner workings of Satans Wrath, do you think he could actually be one of their members?"

"Wouldn't surprise me," Jack replied. "It could well be someone in their executive level who hopes to take over by making Pure E look bad to the others."

"Any idea who in the club might do that?" Dyck asked.

"Damn it, forget about what biker wants to take over the club," Mortimer said. "We need to focus on what's happening today. My situation." He looked at Dyck and then Rose. "Did something like this ever happen to Assistant Commissioner Isaac when he was in charge? If so, what did he do?"

"I don't believe he ever faced a situation like this," Jack responded, "but perhaps you should call him. He's read lots of reports about Satans Wrath over the years submitted by numerous law-enforcement agencies."

"Not a bad idea," Mortimer said. "I'll do that now." He retrieved a cellphone from his pocket and called Isaac. After explaining what had happened, he then named who was in the room with him. After a pause he looked at Jack. "He wants to speak to you and suggested I put you on speaker."

Isaac's voice boomed into the room. "Corporal Taggart?"

"Yes, sir, I'm listening."

"You had an informant connected to Satans Wrath. The one you referred to as Weenie Wagger. Hasn't he heard anything?"

Jack smiled to himself. He'd told Isaac about Cockerill's death when Isaac warned him that Mortimer wasn't going to authorize his operational plan. *Okay, I'll play along.* "Uh, no, sir. Assistant Commissioner Mortimer doesn't believe I'm experienced enough to handle informants. I was told to turn the one I had over to CFSEU. I did, and then he either committed suicide or died of an accidental drug overdose. We're not sure which."

"I see, but surely with your ability as an undercover operative and the surveillance you do, you must have had some inkling that something was going on. It sounds to me that if Crime Stoppers hadn't been lucky enough to receive the information when they did, the consequences could've been disastrous."

"No, sir. Assistant Commissioner Mortimer ordered me not to work on Satans Wrath or do any undercover operations. We've taken a new direction since you left."

"A new direction? So what have you been doing?"

"Well, this winter during the evenings I intend to take classes to improve my French and my standing within the force, but for now I've been spending most of my time liaising with Canada Border Security to learn how they catch smugglers and correlate their information to see if there are certain trends."

"I see. That certainly is a new direction." Isaac paused, then addressed Mortimer. "Ralph, I wonder if you shouldn't reconsider your decision to leave the bikers alone. Perhaps you really should look into them."

"Me?" Mortimer exclaimed. "*I'm* not looking into them! It's me they're threatening … and my family! I need to be transferred forthwith."

Jack waved his hand to catch Mortimer's attention. "Sir, about taking a transfer, these guys have chapters right across Canada and in at least forty other countries."

Mortimer's eyes bugged. "Did you hear that?" he yelled. "These guys are everywhere!"

"I don't believe any of them are in the Arctic region, if that helps," Jack said.

Mortimer looked aghast. "I … I need protection!" he stammered.

Yeah, dicks like you need protection. Let me run out and buy you a condom.

"Perhaps a transfer to a northern location might be the right move," Isaac said. "Maybe then they'd forget about you. What do you think, Corporal Taggart?"

"They might forget and they might not," Jack said. "The problem is the arrest of Satans Wrath's three-three team today will be a big blow to their ego, as well as their standing in our society's criminal element. As long as Assistant Commissioner Mortimer is alive, he'll be a constant reminder of their failure. That won't sit well with them."

"Oh, God," Mortimer groaned.

Isaac was silent for a moment and Jack wondered if he'd gone too far. When Isaac did speak, his voice sounded grave. "Ralph, I believe you're fortunate to be alive — and I sincerely mean that."

Come on, sir. I wouldn't really have him killed.

"I recommend you assign Corporal Taggart back to his previous duties. If anyone can find out what future plans Satans Wrath have in regard to you, *he* can."

"Yes … yes of course," Mortimer replied. "Consider it done. Immediately." He looked at Jack, Laura, and Rose. "Go! Whatever it is you used to do — get out there and find out what's going on!"

Dyck jumped on the opportunity to leave. "Sir, I'd like to go with my investigators and see if anything develops in the interrogations of the suspects."

"Yes, of course. Go!"

Jack saw Rose glaring at him as they stood to leave. He knew he was already in trouble, but couldn't help himself. "*Au revoir, le commissaire-adjoint* Mortimer."

Mortimer appeared to be elsewhere in his thoughts, but he gave Jack an encouraging nod. "*Adieu, Caporal* Taggart."

Jack walked out with Connie while Rose was putting on her shoes. He then nudged her with his elbow and said, "Thanks for telling Dyck that you considered me the most knowledgeable about Satans Wrath. I take that as a compliment."

Connie gave him a sideways glance. "Yeah? I also told him you've been involved in numerous murders over the years. Sounded like he got his wires crossed and thought I meant Satans Wrath and not you."

"Oh."

Yeah … oh." Connie looked perplexed.

"What's wrong?"

"I wish I hadn't said that. You probably took it as a compliment, too."

"Maybe a little."

"You're an asshole."

"So I've been told."

Connie sighed. "Your work is different than mine. I don't like getting involved in what you call the big picture, but I guess someone has to do it. I respect that you're good at what you do."

"Thanks, Connie. Glad you're talking to me again. I've missed you."

"I sure as hell didn't miss you."

"Not even a little?"

"Yeah, maybe a little. Like a dog missing its fleas."

Jack smiled to himself. Connie left just as Laura and Rose joined him.

"Okay, tell me what the hell's really been going on," Rose demanded.

"Going on?"

"You never told me about the ninety-five kilos of cocaine! Was that part of the three tonnes?"

"Some of it might've been. My informant told me they'd received a sample of twenty-five kilos of cocaine from the Russians. Later we discovered the bikers were changing stash locations for their coke and called Crime Stoppers in time to intercept."

"Then why do I think you're still holding something back from me?"

"I'm doing my best," Jack replied, sounding like his feelings were hurt.

"Your best? Your best isn't telling me things after the fact! Your best is to sit down with me and discuss what you plan on doing before —"

"Hang on, I'm getting a text. Maybe it's my informant." Jack read the text and smiled to himself. *Gotta let Rose see this.* He glanced nervously at her and partially turned his body as if trying to hide what he read. She took the bait.

"Who's it from? Your informant? Show me!" Rose demanded.

Jack held his phone so Rose and Laura could both read the text. It was from Isaac.

DON'T KNOW HOW YOU DID IT & DON'T WANT TO KNOW
BUT IF YOU HAVE TIME TODAY I'D LIKE TO POUR YOU A SCOTCH.

Rose looked at Jack in surprise. "Isaac is inviting you to his house for a drink?"

"Nice of him, but Scotch … I don't know," Jack said. "I'd prefer a martini."

Rose grimaced.

"What's wrong? I'm only joking. Of course I'll go see him."

"*What's wrong?*" Rose seemed taken back. "I've always respected Isaac. He's one of the smartest men I've ever met."

"I agree. So?"

"He obviously believes you had a hand in what happened today, yet still thinks the world of you."

"Guess he has faith in me and trusts me to do what's right."

Rose turned on her heel and left.

Chapter Fifty-Eight

It had been two hours since Pure E approached the limo. His eyes hadn't adjusted to the darkness when he'd leaned inside the opened passenger door. That was when Thor had grabbed him by the neck and collar, literally jerking him off his feet. His throat made a gasping, gurgling sound as he was slammed to the floor of the limo and punched repeatedly in the stomach, leaving him gasping for air.

As the limo drove off, Thor maintained his grip, pinning him to the floor by his throat while Carl wrapped duct tape around his mouth. Seconds later his ankles were zip-tied together, followed by his wrists zip-tied through the zip-tie on his ankles, forcing him to remain in a fetal position.

Pure E was dazed and in shock. The men he saw in the back of the limo were Gypsy Devils — Carl Shepherd, Norman Thorsen, and David Greene. *They must know I put a hit out on them, but how'd they know about the Russians and when to pick me up?* His mind raced. *Whiskey*

Jake! That fucking bastard! He even brought me early so the Russians wouldn't show up at the same time.

Thor delivered a punch to his face, splattering his nose and leaving a taste in the back of his mouth like he'd been sucking on a copper pipe. *Christ, they're going to kill me!*

"Easy does it," Carl cautioned. "Don't want to get Mouse's limo all bloody. We'll have lots of time for that soon."

Thirty minutes later the limo pulled into a garage and the overhead door was shut. Mickey O'Bryan then opened the rear door to the limo and grabbed him by the hair and dragged him out onto the cement floor. *Oh, fuck ... no. I'm lying on a plastic sheet! This is it. This is where I'm gonna die.*

Pure E knew all too well what the plastic sheet was for. Bloody messes were much easier to clean up. His eyes betrayed the terror he felt when his clothes were taken from his body. A box cutter was used to slash away at them because the zip-ties made yanking them off impossible.

Over the next hour Pure E endured unfathomable pain, but he didn't die. He only wished he could. Thor had told him not to worry about all the bloody cuts on his body. He said he'd cauterize them for him ... and lit a propane torch.

Eventually Pure E lost consciousness. If he'd been lucky, he would've stayed unconscious. Instead, he came to as he was being hauled out of a van in a small clearing surrounded by a chain-link fence.

A shipping container! Maybe they're going to lock me in there! I might be found.

He was dragged into the container and Carl kicked him in the ribs to get his attention. "Hope you don't mind us using your incinerator, do ya?"

The other Gypsy Devils laughed, and then Carl opened the lid on the hopper.

Pure E frantically tried to twist away while trying in vain to beg for his life through the tape over his mouth. His muffled utterances seemed to bring only pleasure to the men looking down at him. They laughed.

Seconds later he was hoisted by the arms and lifted to the edge of the loading chamber.

"Take a look," Carl said. "One of your guys left a message for ya!"

Pure E's head was lowered, but someone grabbed him by the hair and jerked his face upward. The message scrawled in lipstick on the inside of the hopper lid read *4 U Pure E.*

Pure E knew then that Whiskey Jake wasn't to blame. The handwriting had not been made by a left-handed person, which Whiskey Jake was. His thoughts were interrupted when he was dumped into the chamber and the lid closed. As he lay waiting in the darkness, he pieced it together. *Taggart! He set this up!*

The instant roar of the flames sounded like a jet engine and the intensity of the heat was immediate. For a moment his body writhed in the eerie red glow.

Chapter Fifty-Nine

At 7:30 a.m. Monday Lance saw Whiskey Jake arrive at the Westside chapter clubhouse and went outside to meet him.

"Anything?" Whiskey Jake asked.

"No. Our guys have done round-the-clock surveillance downtown, but there's been nothing."

"Pure E mentioned that they only come to Canada on occasion."

"Bet they don't turn up downtown. They might even know we're watching."

Whiskey Jake let out a string of curses, then said, "It's all because of the three-three. They couldn't have got grabbed at a worse time. That's what freaked the Russians out."

"Yeah, it's not looking good, that's for sure."

"No shit," Whiskey Jake replied. "Hang on, my phone's vibrating. It's the one Rat Cop gave me!" He quickly answered and held the phone so Lance could hear.

"You've got a problem," Lance heard Jack say. "A big one."

"You heard? Whaddaya know? " Whiskey Jake replied.

"Of course I heard. Five of your guys being arrested outside of Mortimer's house is big news."

"Oh, that," Whiskey Jake said without enthusiasm. "Yeah, our lawyer says they'll all get out this morning."

"They were all separated and interrogated."

Whiskey Jake gave a snort. "That's no big surprise."

"This might be. One of them was offered one-point-five mil to become a rat."

"One-point-five?" Whiskey Jake exclaimed.

"Yeah, and he accepted."

"No way! You're bullshitting me! None of 'em would ever do that."

Lance frowned. *Jesus, Jack. What're you up to?*

"I'm not bullshitting," Jack said. "The guy who blabbed gave details about Damien's murder and how Vicki was suffocated with plastic wrap in some prospect's house out in Abbotsford. Even supplied a map to some animal incinerator they used to get rid of the bodies."

"No! Oh, fuck, no!" Whiskey Jake turned ashen.

"Believe me now?"

"Who blabbed? Who was it?"

"That's the bad news. I'm not privy to that. It's being kept secret."

"When will the arrests happen?"

"Guess that's the good news. They don't think his word would be accepted in court without a lot more corroboration. They want to wire up the incinerator and someplace out in Stanley Park where you and your buddies meet. They're hoping to catch Pure E on a wiretap giving orders."

"Oh, fuck. Is there any way you can find out who's talking?"

"No, and I have to go. Maybe I can call you later today."

Whiskey Jake turned to Lance when the call ended. "I feel like I got punched in the gut. Pure E's not around. What the fuck we gonna do?"

"What *can* we do? We can't go and kill five of our own guys for the sake of one. We need to sit tight and keep our noses clean until we figure out who the rat is."

Whiskey Jake looked stunned. "The thing is, now we can't use anyone from the three-three without putting ourselves in jeopardy."

Which is what Jack wanted. "Obviously."

"Which means we may never find out. We won't be able to use any of them again."

Lance pretended to ponder the situation. "Maybe that's not a bad thing."

"Whaddaya mean?"

"All this shit started when Pure E came to power. Up to then, it'd been years since we had to waste anyone. Damien never operated that way. Pure E's been too much of a loose cannon. We need to change. Torturing people, threatening cops … look what it's got us. Our younger guys need to be taught."

Whiskey Jake glanced back at the clubhouse. "Yeah, you're right." He shook his head. "I know you tried to warn him not to do what he did. If he does show up, we both better talk to him."

"It's been two days. He won't be showing up."

Whiskey Jake stared at Lance. "You certain he's dead?"

"I was certain his days were numbered when he ordered that message be left for Taggart in the farmhouse."

"Yeah, that guy. Guess the Russians did him a favour."

"Yeah, looks that way." *Then again, you don't know Taggart as well as I do.*

An hour later Jack arrived at work and Rose waved him into her office.

"How was your weekend?" Jack asked pleasantly.

"Don't even go there! My phone hasn't stopped ringing all weekend. Did you know that Mortimer ordered someone to come in yesterday and get the paperwork so he could submit his resignation? He's hoping if he quits it'll pacify the bikers."

"I didn't know. That's great news!" Jack caught her angry glare. "So why are you ticked off? Can you really sit there and tell me you're sorry to see him go?"

"No, not really, but your actions … what you did to him without my knowledge … well, it proves to me you can't be trusted."

"I *did* come to you."

"After the fact."

"Sort of during the fact."

"Don't play games. I know that Pure E is still your number-one target. Now that you've been given Mortimer's blessing, there's no doubt in my mind that you've concocted some sort of plan you haven't told me about."

"I don't have any plan in regards to Pure E."

"It doesn't matter if you do or not, because I'm going to be with you every step of the way."

I probably shouldn't tease her … but what the hell. "You've always been supportive," Jack replied.

"I don't mean that. I mean side by side. When you leave the office, if it has anything to do with Pure E — and I mean anything — you're not leaving without me."

"That's awfully nice of you to offer to help, but —"

"I'm not offering and I'm not being nice," Rose said tersely. "I'm ordering you."

Guess the time for levity is over. "Then I need to bring you up-to-date. My informant called me Saturday evening and again yesterday. He told me that Whiskey Jake dropped Pure E off Saturday morning to meet the Russians and that he hasn't been seen since. They think the Russians heard about the three-three being arrested and killed him to sever any ties."

Rose leaned forward in her chair. "What time was Pure E dropped off?" she wanted to know.

"Between nine-thirty and ten."

"The same time you called Crime Stoppers."

Guess I better not use the word "coincidence." "Uh, I suppose so."

"Does anyone have any idea who these Russians are?"

"Nope, not a clue."

Rose stared at Jack long enough to make him feel uncomfortable. When she spoke her tone was like ice. "Natasha is Russian — maybe someone should ask her."

Jack didn't blink. "I said hello to Isaac for you Saturday afternoon when we had a Scotch together. I told him you'd seen his text invite to me and that you'd said how much you respected him and admired his intellect."

"I wasn't referring to the bit where he said he didn't want to know how you did it," Rose said dryly.

"Weren't you?" Jack waited a beat. "I presumed part of

your respect for him was because he knew when to ask questions and when not to."

Rose bit her lower lip and appeared to mull over what he'd said. Then she took a deep breath and exhaled. "It's just not in my nature to be okay with not knowing."

He nodded in understanding. "Come to think of it, I'm the same way." He glanced at his watch. "It's noon in Ottawa. Have you heard anything about who might replace Mortimer? I bet the rumour mill is working overtime."

"I've already received a couple of calls. It looks like the top candidate in the running is Irene Lexton."

"Irene Lexton? She was in charge of I-HIT for several years."

"I'm told she wants to come back."

"If she hasn't been brainwashed or corrupted by politics in Ottawa, she'd be a good choice. She knows her stuff and from what I've heard is meticulous and hardworking."

"Her getting the job doesn't worry you?"

"No, why should it?"

"Like you said, she was in charge of I-HIT. She knows your reputation, too."

"You're right." Jack paused, then tried to be optimistic. "Maybe Isaac will invite her over for a Scotch to welcome her back."

Two months passed before Assistant Commissioner Irene Lexton arrived in Vancouver to fulfill her new position as Criminal Operations Officer in charge of the Pacific Region.

It was with interest that she read an intelligence report discussing the circumstances surrounding her predecessor's unexpected resignation. The report discussed the disappearance of Purvis Evans and noted a reliable and confidential informant as saying that Satans Wrath believed their leader had been killed by high-level Russian cocaine traffickers. The rest of the report was minor in nature, noting that the Gypsy Devils had dissolved as a club and gone their separate ways. The intelligence report was submitted by Corporal J.B. Taggart.

Lexton then retrieved an old operational plan that Mortimer had retained but not approved. Mortimer's handwritten scrawl on the back of the report noted a time and date when Corporal Taggart was ordered to turn over all informants and never work undercover again. *Six weeks later Mortimer has a hit team waiting outside his house. Yeah, Jack, hell of a coincidence.*

Lexton took a new file folder from her desk and labelled it *JT*. A moment later that file folder containing copies of both reports was locked in her office safe.